Praise for Edith Zeitlberger's Novel

"[T]his is an amazing read—with complex characters—set in a beautiful Vienna of the early 1900s. If you enjoy a great love story with plot and a range of emotions, then this is your book. Thanks, Edith, for a terrific first novel."
~CA Farlow, author of The Nexus Series and *The Paris Contagion*

"Cosy lesbian romance with many sympathetic characters you'd want to meet in real life. A perfect read for a rainy day."
~Karmen Špiljak, author of *A Perfect Flaw* and *Add Cyanide to Taste: A Collection of Dark Tales with Culinary Twists*

"*Fractures and Hinges* is a beautiful story of two noblewomen finding love after heartbreak."
~Jazzy Mitchell, author of *Leveling Up, You Matter,* and *Undertow*

"I pounced on this ebook and was thrilled to find it quite well written. I loved how the writer pulled me in, I could feel the emotions the protagonists were experiencing—and that is key to understand and care about them."
~Gun Bach

"The story of this novel, playing at the beginning of the 20th Century, pulled me in from the beginning. I enjoyed the multi-dimensional characters Sophie and Eleanor, and the way they met each other for the first time. The way the author describes their moods and feelings is very intense."
~Joseph Banks

Fractures

and

Hinges

By

Edith Zeitlberger

LAUNCHPOINT PRESS

2022

Portland, Oregon
www.LaunchPointPress.com

*To the Chattering Teacup,
who rightfully kicked me in
the butt when I needed it*

Acknowledgments

Thank you to all those who read and helped with the first edition of this book. Special appreciation goes to KJ, Jazzy Mitchell, Karmen, and J.E. for insightful commentary and support.

A very big thanks to Lori L. Lake for taking a chance with the manuscript and this writer for the second edition. Even though English isn't my first language, she always encouraged my efforts and supported me to make this a better book.

And most of all, to the Chattering Teacup for always letting me know it is quite alright!

Edith Zeitlberger
Vienna, Austria
April 2022

Author's Notes

Trigger Warning: Please note that in this book, there is discussion and repercussions from the rape of a secondary character. This event, which occurs prior to the opening of the story, is an important element to one of the subplots. Though the assault is not shown in a scene, some readers might find mention of it upsetting.

This novel is a complete work of fiction. Any inaccuracies regarding the historical facts are completely my own. (I might have taken a few liberties.)

"Mysteries of attraction could not always be explained through logic. Sometimes the fractures in two separate souls became the very hinges that held them together."

~Lisa Kleypas in *Devil in Winter*

Prologue

On the day of Eleanor's eighteenth birthday, she was happy. Well, she was as happy as she could be under the circumstances. Growing up as the daughter of a reserved mother and a very strict and choleric father who seemed to have no warmth or affection for his children did not make for a very happy childhood or youth. Eleanor's only source of heartfelt honest love was her maternal grandmother. She often wondered how it was possible for her own mother to be the daughter of such a warm woman and become such a cold person oneself.

The celebration of her birthday was that day, before the grand ball tomorrow when her parents would formally introduce her into society, which was, at least in Eleanor's opinion, a complete and utter waste of a pretty dress. She had known for a long time that her fate was already sealed, not that she minded. Her remote cousin, Henry Edgewood, was a rather suitable husband. Wealthy, handsome, and charming, his position convinced her parents to give their blessings when Henry asked for her hand in marriage. Eleanor loved him dearly, much the same as a brother, but love him she did.

Ever since they were children, Henry had been her best friend, confidant, and protector. Henry was the only one who knew her deepest secrets, and she had never told anyone of this fact, which was something binding them together more strongly.

Eleanor was sitting under the shade of a big oak tree in her parents' garden, enjoying the warmth of the early summer, when she saw Henry crossing the lawn. With his hands in his pockets and a smile on his handsome face, Henry neared the tree at a leisurely pace. Eleanor knew he'd always had a soft spot for her. Despite title and wealth, Eleanor's youth had been anything but full of roses. She had always been defiant, and possessing a stubborn streak inherited from her grandmother had not made it easier for her.

Henry's childhood had been worse. Scars on his back were testimony to his father's hatred of his younger son. Arthur Edgewood was known for his volatile and violent temper, especially after his oldest son Edward died in a pistol duel. Henry had often been the recipient of his father's foul moods because he could never measure up.

After Henry's brother's death, Arthur Edgewood flew into a rage unlike any other. If it hadn't been for one of the footmen, Henry would have been beaten to death by his own father. The footman lost an eye and his place for defying his lordship, but seventeen-year-old Henry kept his life. After the ordeal, his mother sent him to Darnsworth Castle to recuperate, and Eleanor grew much closer to him during that time.

Shielding her eyes against the sun, Eleanor laughed as Henry lowered himself to the grass next to her. "Henry!" She kissed his clean-shaven cheek in welcome. "I am so glad you're here."

"Hello, Eleanor." He reciprocated the gesture with gentle lips. "Your parents have gone out of their way to celebrate."

"Not so much because of my birthday," Eleanor said with a sad smile, "rather because of the announcement of our engagement."

"Ah, I suspect you have a point. Nonetheless, I propose we make the most of it. Is Charles coming?"

"No. Father did not find it necessary for him to neglect his studies for my birthday."

"I am sorry. I know how fond you are of your little brother and that the feeling is mutual. He will be missed." Henry took Eleanor's small hand in his larger one. "At least there is some good news. My cousin Cathleen will be here. You will adore her. She's a good sport, you'll see."

With a frown, Eleanor asked, "Is she the one who had to marry the older-than-God Lord Northcott?"

"The very same, my dear."

Together they returned to the house for lunch with Eleanor's parents which was, as usual, a strained affair despite Henry's best efforts to keep the conversation light and flowing.

Later in the evening, Eleanor stood in front of her body-length mirror in her dressing room putting on perfume, a gift from Henry, when she heard a faint knock on her bedroom door.

"Come in!" she called out with delight, knowing only one person who would seek her out to calm her nerves before she had to put on a pleasant face with a fake smile for the benefit of her parents' acquaintances.

Henry, dressed meticulously in tails and polished shoes, leaned against the doorframe with his hands casually in his trouser pockets and an expression of admiration on his face. "You are very beautiful, my dear."

"Thank you." Eleanor blushed at his honest words. "You're quite handsome yourself."

"We do make quite a good-looking couple, don't we?" Henry came into the room and stood behind Eleanor's left shoulder, gazing through the mirror into her eyes.

Her long blonde hair, now made up in a complicated bun with a few tendrils falling down, teased her pale neck. She had the most wonderful blue eyes, the colour of a clear summer sky. Her skin was pale and flawless, her lips the perfect shade of red, and although her nose was perhaps a bit too large, it gave her that aristocratic appearance fit for the future Duchess of Darnsworth. She wore a dark blue dress that contrasted with the lighter shade of her eyes.

"With the cut of your gown and your bare shoulders, without a doubt you'll be the belle of the ball."

She blushed and he pressed a chaste kiss to one shoulder and gave her an encouraging smile, then offered his arm. Together, they made their way downstairs to face the crowd.

Instead of a sit-down dinner, her mother had ordered the servants to prepare a buffet which made it easier to mingle, and after a proper amount of time, music started to play, and they enjoyed themselves on the dance floor. Henry was a wonderful dancer, and Eleanor was delighted to be in his arms dancing to her favourite music, forgetting everything else around her and living in the moment. Three dances later she had to stop for a break, slightly out of breath, but becomingly flushed from the exertion and the joy of it all. On Henry's arm, she strolled out into the brightly lit garden, each of them with a glass of champagne in hand.

Eleanor was sipping from her flute when she saw a vision stepping through the French windows. The woman's dark red hair flowed freely in the current fashion, and her perfect white skin was aglow in the light of the many torches. Eleanor thought her smile mesmerising, and when the woman came nearer, Eleanor gazed into the most beautiful green eyes she had ever seen. A dark green dress clung to her curves, and the low line of the front of the dress drew one's eyes to her perfect cleavage.

Eleanor gripped Henry's arm like a vice before she found her voice and whispered, "Henry, who is this?"

"Who?" he asked with confusion before he caught sight of the woman in question. A grin formed on his lips. "Cathleen, finally! I was worried you would not be able to make it after all."

"Henry, darling." Cathleen greeted him with a kiss on his cheek. "I'm sorry. It took us longer than I thought. Martin was completely exhausted after our journey, and I had to see him off to bed before I could leave."

"Eleanor," Henry turned to her, "please meet my cousin, Lady Cathleen Northcott. Cathleen, my fiancée, Eleanor Shaftsbury."

Cathleen smiled warmly. "It's such a pleasure to meet you. Congratulations are in order, I guess. An eighteenth birthday is something special, is it not?"

Eleanor blushed at the woman's genuine words. "Yes, thank you. After Henry told me you would join us for the weekend, I've been looking forward to meeting you."

"So was I. Your mother told me of your engagement. Congratulations for that as well."

"Thank you, Cathleen," Henry said.

Eleanor watched him regarding them fondly. He was right about inviting his cousin to meet her. She could already tell they'd get along famously. He winked her way. Oh, she knew how much he loved it when one of his schemes worked out. He excused himself and left them to their own devices while she forgot all about him and wandered arm in arm along the lit path talking and laughing as if she and Cathleen had known each other forever.

In the end, the rest of the evening was pleasant enough, perhaps a touch boring, but Eleanor supposed it could have been worse. After her father announced their engagement, they endured the long line of well-wishers, most of whom conveniently forgot, much to her chagrin, that it was also her birthday.

Chapter One

Lord Henry Edgewood, the ninth Earl of Houghton, leaned back into the cushions of his carriage. He was on the way from his gentlemen's club in Westminster to his London home in Mayfair at Number 6 Grosvenor Square and faced with plenty of time to think about his life. He wasn't quite sure what had caused his pondering about the last five years of his life. Maybe it was the constant complaining of his peers in the club which he had witnessed again and again. Or perhaps the first real scent of spring in the air after a long and cold winter. Either way, it caused a frown to appear on his otherwise smooth forehead.

Their home used to be a place full of laughter and life, but for the past three years it had been too silent for his liking. Up until this time he had never had reason to join his peers' string of discontented complaints regarding their wives' supposedly outrageous demands. But now he wasn't actually dissatisfied, he was worried.

His wife Eleanor, the Duchess of Darnsworth, used to be the centre of their lively home. It pained Henry to admit that for the last few years, everything had become more solemn, hushed, and serious. All inhabitants, both upstairs and downstairs in equal measures, were gloomier, less light-hearted. But worst of all, his wife, dear friend, and confidante had transformed from an openly affectionate woman into an aloof and distant person hardly recognisable to them any longer. Her Italian grandmother and their daughter Charlotte seemed to be the only ones who could reach Eleanor.

At the age of forty-five, Henry was in the prime of his life, and he was saddened that his family life was not what it used to be. Not that it had ever been conventional in any way, nothing could be further from the truth, but it used to be a place where he could be himself. Where he felt comfortable and didn't have to pretend. If his fellow club members knew the truth, they would never regard him the same way again, and he would be a societal pariah, something he wouldn't dare risk. But people only saw what they wanted to see, and they only believed what they wanted to.

Henry Edgewood was a man of average height with a lean body, a bald head, and warm dark eyes behind wire-framed glasses that added to his attractiveness. His fast wit, high intelligence and gentle nature made him a highly regarded and respected man. When attending a social function with his wife, they used to turn heads because Eleanor, slightly taller than her husband, was an admired beauty and she was seen as vibrant and appealing. Not only did they complement each other through their physical appearances, but Eleanor was just as sophisticated, educated, and charming as her husband. His lordship was the envy of many of his peers.

Henry was saddened that these days his wife seemed preoccupied only with a rigorous épée training regimen, riding her beloved horses into the ground, or sitting in one of London's many galleries for hours staring at dark and disturbing works of art. Nothing he could do or say would make her change her routine. Everybody walked on eggshells around her, and it was taking a toll on all of them, but there was not a single thing he could think of that would make it better, at least nothing she wanted to hear without ripping off his head.

The carriage stopped and his driver jumped down to hold open the door for Henry to climb out. Henry ducked out of the carriage.

"Thank you, Parker, this will be all."

The man tipped his hat in acknowledgement before mounting the carriage again to drive to the back of the house.

Lord Edgewood climbed the stairs of his home in Mayfair with lightness in his steps, and before he could announce his arrival, his trusted butler Benson opened the front door. Benson wore an immaculately groomed suit that matched the material of a black eyepatch over his left eye. His otherwise placid face was made to look ever-so-slightly sinister by the patch, and yet Benson managed always to remain dignified and proper, his silver hair perfectly cut, his shoes buffed to a shine, and his black cravat perfectly tucked and centred.

The butler bowed slightly at the waist while he held the door open for his lordship to enter. Henry nodded in greeting and took off his gloves to hand them over to Benson, with his hat, coat and walking cane.

On the small table in the hall, he found the afternoon mail waiting for him. Thumbing through the usual business correspondence that could be taken care of at a later time, Henry found a letter addressed to his wife from a Hungarian aristocrat.

"Where is my wife, Benson?" Lord Edgewood asked as he crossed the hall to his study.

"Her Grace is in the gymnasium, milord. She is exercising with Mister Carstairs," Benson informed his master dutifully.

"Of course, she is," Henry mumbled under his breath, changing his direction towards the back of the house where the gymnasium had been built a few years prior. "Thank you, Benson."

"Milord." The butler bowed before he returned to his other duties.

The familiar sound of épées crossing welcomed Henry when he entered the gymnasium. Both opponents were dressed in perfect-fitting fencing attire: white knee-length trousers, white vests, socks, shoes, and gloves. Their faces were protected by fencing masks. He observed their well-coordinated moves that almost resembled a dance, albeit a deadly dance.

Even if it were not for the distinct form of her female body, Henry would recognise his wife. Eleanor distinctly had the upper hand in this special *pas de deux*. She forced her opponent backwards through skill and determination, offering him not a single weakness to start a counter-attack.

With his back finally against the wall and the tip of the épée against his chest, Jonathan Carstairs called a stop to their practice session. Although he had been the one who initially taught the duchess how to use this weapon, the student had surpassed her teacher a long time ago, and it was not beyond him to acknowledge that he had found his master in her.

As soon as her tutor yielded, Eleanor lowered her épée and took off her mask and gloves. Shaking out her short white hair, she brushed a few strands from her sweaty forehead and regarded Jonathan with piercing blue eyes and a hint of triumph in them.

"Well fought, your Grace." Jonathan's compliment was sincere.

"As did you. Thank you for the exercise, it was most welcome."

"It was, as always, my pleasure," Jonathan answered with a slight bow.

Lord Edgewood announced his presence from the doorway by calling out, "Well done indeed, Eleanor."

"Henry!" Eleanor exclaimed at her husband's unexpected presence. "I thought you were still at your club."

"I have just returned, my dear." Henry approached his wife as she dried off the sweat from her neck. "And I found something very interesting in the post."

"Oh?"

Henry handed over the envelope and carefully watched his wife's facial expression for any sign of intrigue or interest. When he found none, he felt all his hopes dashed.

"I'm not interested," Eleanor stated curtly, and without a second glance at the two men, she left the gymnasium.

He had noticed a short flicker of pain in those blue eyes before she handed back the letter. This was not what he had hoped for. He thought maybe the invitation would elicit a different reaction. Noting that Jonathan sat respectfully off to the side, Henry sat close to him on one of the benches lining one wall of the gymnasium. He had to admit he was at his wits' end for how to deal with Eleanor's sorrow.

He ran his hand over his bald head and hung it in defeat. "Three years, three agonizingly long years. I thought one day she would overcome her grief and live again. I hoped this invitation would help but I was completely wrong. Goodness, what else can I do?"

"Nothing much," Jonathan said as he put a reassuring hand on his lover's shoulder. "She has to want it herself."

Eleanor ascended the stairs to the second floor, her lips tightly pressed together, keeping her tears firmly in check. Her hands wrung the towel, squeezing it sharply. She knew Henry meant well and had been nothing but patient with her, but no matter how hard she tried, she couldn't get past the pain. The invitation by Count Nikolaus von Radványi was flattering, and his request for a business partnership intriguing for he was known for possessing the best thoroughbred horses on the continent. The count had continued his father's work quite successfully, just as she had her grandmother's.

Eleanor's grandmother, the Duchess of Darnsworth, had inherited her own father's passion for horses and was well known in Scotland and England for breeding and owning the best hunting horses. Even the late Austrian Empress had visited her grandmother's stables during one of her visits to Scotland. Eleanor, who often spent most of the year at her grandmother's castle in Scotland, met the famous Elisabeth of Austria for the first time when she was fourteen years old during the empress' first visit.

Elisabeth's passion for hunting had sparked an interest in the special breed of horses used for this pastime, and Eleanor's grandmother was honoured to welcome her Royal Majesty at Darnsworth Castle. Elisabeth had been as beautiful as rumours used to say and was also an accomplished rider and horsewoman. Despite a difference in ages, Eleanor and Elisabeth found a common ground, and at the end of the visit, the duchess made the empress the gift of one of her best horses. After that, the monarch visited Scotland regularly during her travels abroad.

Eleanor not only inherited her grandmother's title, estate, and wealth, she also followed in her grandmother's footsteps as a successful horse breeder. Today's invitation by the count reminded her of happier times. Not only did she dearly miss her late grandmother, she also missed the passion for the horse business. She still kept a firm hand on the proceedings, but the spark was missing.

Upon entering her room, Eleanor went straight to her large four-poster bed and slowly lowered herself to the edge. With her hands resting on top of the bedding next to her thighs, she took deliberate breaths to ward off the onslaught of emotions she had barely been able to control for the last three years. People used to say that time heals everything, but she had her doubts. Why was it so hard?

A soft knock on the door stirred her from gloomy thoughts.

"Come in!" she ordered more harshly than she intended, knowing it had to be her lady's maid, Rose, who would want to prepare her bath.

A small blonde woman in her early twenties carefully opened the door and curtseyed at her mistress before she found the courage to ask what she had come for. "Shall I prepare your bath, your Grace?"

"Yes, please," Eleanor answered softly. She watched the maid disappear through the door leading into the en-suite bathroom before her eyes landed on a photograph on the bedside table. Reaching out to touch the smiling face in the silver frame, Eleanor stopped herself mid-motion, sighing at the memories the image brought to mind. After a moment she took the photograph in both hands and gazed upon it feeling a physical pain in her heart.

She vividly remembered the day the picture was taken, two years before her life changed in the most dramatic and heartfelt way. She and Cathleen spent the summer in Scotland at Eleanor's estate just like they always did. Their days were spent with taking care of the old castle, making sure everything on the surrounding land was running smoothly, and tending to the horses. Every now and then Eleanor's duty as a chieftain in her own right was called upon to settle various disputes between the members of the clan. She would sit in the Great Hall with her sash proudly worn over her left shoulder and Cathleen by her side where she would listen, for what felt like hours on end, to the grievances of her people. But as often as they could, they'd escape and go for a lengthy ride.

On a splendid summer's day, the sun was high up in the sky with only a few tiny clouds. Cathleen had donned her favourite green riding dress and another new top hat. Her wild red hair was tamed by a maid in a sensible bun at nape of her neck. Green riding breeches were tucked into shiny black boots and with white gloves, she held her crop. She waited for Eleanor in the entrance hall to leave for the stables.

Eleanor stood at the top of the stairs, hidden by a column and admired her lover from above. Cathleen looked beautiful in the green dress and Eleanor couldn't wait for her to lose another top hat and let her hair fly as she rode like the wind over the meadows.

Cathleen's impatient voice drifted up the stairs. "Eleanor, are you ready yet?"

"I'm right here, darling," Eleanor answered sheepishly as she descended the stairs.

"Where shall we go today? What do you think?"

Eleanor had thought about it with longing. "Let's go to our special place."

Cathleen threw her a surprised look but with a smile, she agreed. They collected their horses and set of in a leisurely trot away from the castle across the fields towards Loch Ruthven

After riding nearly an hour, they could see the sun reflecting off the dark blue water of the Loch. And just as Eleanor predicted, Cathleen certainly lost another top hat before they were even close to their destination. It wasn't that the wind was blowing that hard. Cathleen's wild streak emerged more strongly with every mile they galloped. At the age of thirty-seven, Cathleen's wild side was still as present as it had been at twenty-four, when Eleanor met her for the first time. Her fiery red hair was still held together in a semblance of a bun, but Eleanor was convinced even that would change as soon as they stopped.

"Come on, dearest!" Cathleen turned slightly in her saddle to look at Eleanor. "Don't hold back! We both know you are the better rider."

"We have been riding for quite a while now, after all. Maybe I want to take it slow for a change."

Cathleen snorted in an unladylike manner at the unlikely supposition. "Of course, you do."

With a laugh, she spurred her chestnut mare to pick up speed, followed by an equally laughing Eleanor on her steel grey stallion.

They raced each other to the shores of Loch Ruthven. Eleanor arrived first and got off her horse to wait for Cathleen to leap from her saddle right into her waiting arms. Cathleen slung her arms around Eleanor's neck and gazed deeply into her blue eyes, a happy smile on her slightly freckled face.

"So, what is the occasion?" Cathleen asked.

"Don't tell me you have forgotten?" Eleanor spoke gently, refraining from chastising her and knowing full well her lover had forgotten their anniversary. The past few weeks had been relentlessly busy, so she wasn't really cross with Cathleen for forgetting their special day.

Cathleen wrinkled her brow in concentration, and when she finally realised what Eleanor was talking about, her hand flew to her mouth in embarrassment.

"Oh, no. Eleanor, oh, my love, I'm so sorry. I completely forgot!"

"I know you forgot." Eleanor smiled indulgently.

She tried to free herself from Eleanor's arms, but Eleanor refused to let her go and instead tightened the embrace.

"But I'm a complete nitwit. This is awful."

"You are not, and it is not," Eleanor reassured her. "I love you and I wanted to spend the day with you. Just the two of us. And I think I fell even a little more in love with you today."

"Why? How?"

"Because no matter what, you enjoy life to the fullest. Because I love you in this riding habit, which brings out the colour of your eyes so perfectly. Because I love your exuberance and uncompromising joy. And I love you for losing another hat and all the pins in your hairdo and letting your gorgeous hair fly wild in the wind."

After Eleanor's passionate speech, Cathleen gazed a moment into her beloved's eyes before she leaned in and kissed her with the same passion she had for life itself.

They had no need to hurry, nobody was hassling them or disturbing their time together, and when they had to come up for air, they rested foreheads against each other. With unspoken agreement they held hands and walked along the beach of the Loch with their horses' bridles in their free hands, guiding them along.

Eleanor led the way to their little retreat, an old uninhabited cottage on a secluded hill where they spent the next few hours in blissful ecstasy, giving and receiving pleasure just like the intimate lovers they were.

Completely spent and utterly satisfied, they lay in one another's arms. Cathleen rested with her head on Eleanor's chest listening to the slowing of her racing heart. "Happy anniversary, my love," she whispered before pressing a soft kiss on her chest.

"Happy anniversary." Eleanor grinned. "Before we return home, I want to ask you something."

"Of course."

"I want a picture of you."

"You have pictures of me."

"No. Yes. What I mean is . . ." Eleanor exhaled and tried to gather her thoughts, which wasn't an easy task, since Cathleen's hands were doing such wonderful things to her body again. "What I mean is, I want a picture of you in this riding dress, with your hair loose and that special expression you share only with me."

"Oh, sure, why not. But we still have time here and now, don't we?"

"We certainly do!" Eleanor agreed breathlessly and pulled the sheet over their heads with joyful laughter.

"Your Grace?"

Eleanor jumped and nearly dropped the photo frame.

Rose spoke softly, but she still managed to startle Eleanor who felt self-conscious upon angling her tearstained face toward the voice. She knew her eyes were glazed and red from crying and was thankful her maid pretended not to notice.

"Your Grace," Rose offered kindly, "your bath is ready."

"Yes, of course." Eleanor acknowledged with slight embarrassment before she put the photograph back on the bedside table and got up. Wiping away tears, she turned her back to her maid, who immediately stepped forward to help her undress. Standing in undergarments, Eleanor dismissed Rose and went into the bathroom, stripped out of her remaining clothes, and lowered herself into the steaming, fragrant water. She lay back and closed her eyes, desperately trying to get rid of the haunting images of the past.

After his wife left the gymnasium, Lord Edgewood retired to his study. He sat behind his desk, another letter of invitation right in front of him, and pondered how he could convince Eleanor to accept and take a prolonged trip to Vienna, if only for the sake of a change of scenery. Henry was convinced it would do her good to spend some time away from the reminders of the past. The house was full of such mementos, and it often seemed to him Eleanor did everything she could not to have to let go. She behaved as if she thought she was still not ready—or almost as if the reminders were a punishment. For what, though, he had no idea.

Maybe Charlotte could help. Their daughter always had a way of getting through to her mother when others failed miserably. He would talk to her as soon as she returned from her ride with her cousin and her brother. Suddenly, his brow smoothed out at the prospect of a plan.

Chapter Two

The boisterous arrival of three young people didn't go unnoticed. Henry opened the door of his study to find his children talking and laughing in the hall, all the while thrusting their riding gear in the footman's waiting arms.

"Children!" Henry admonished them good-naturedly. "Let poor Cedric go! He can only take so much."

"Papa!" Charlotte exclaimed at the sight of her father. She greeted him with a light kiss on his cheek and received one in return.

"Hello, my dear. Did you have a nice ride?"

Philip, Henry's son and heir, said, "We did," and greeted his father with a grin.

"Sir." Martin nodded at the man, who had been a father to him as long as he could remember. At twenty-seven, Martin was the eldest of the threesome. He had lost his father at a young age, at which time he and his mother had moved to Number 6 Grosvenor Square

"I am glad to hear it." Lord Edgewood beamed at his children. While only two of them were of his flesh, certainly all three were children of his heart. Charlotte, at twenty-two, had been presented at court four years earlier, and she still did not have a special admirer. Neither had her brother set his eyes on a particular young woman, but he was a mere twenty years old and could not be expected to marry so young. The three were often in high spirits, and Henry was glad to have their youthful exuberance in the house.

"Charlotte," Henry said, "before you go to your room, would you join me in my study? It will only take a minute."

"Of course, Papa," the young woman readily agreed, wondering what was on her father's mind.

While Philip and Martin went upstairs to change for the afternoon tea, Charlotte followed her father into his study and sat on the comfortable settee in front of the fire, which she highly appreciated. Despite the sun, the first days of spring were still cool, and the fire helped eliminate the chill. With hands folded in her lap, she waited expectantly to find out what was troubling her father.

Henry collected an invitation from his desk and handed it over. She felt his eyes upon her, waiting for her reaction. She took a moment to peruse the invitation.

Impatient, he said, "Well? What do you think?"

"I think it would be wonderful. What does Mama say?"

"That is the problem you see." Henry took a seat next to his daughter. "She doesn't know about it. This is the second invitation to Vienna I found in the afternoon mail."

"Oh, I see." She understood without the need for her father to elaborate further. An opportunity to travel to the continent was not interesting to her mother now, perhaps not ever again. Chewing on her bottom lip, Charlotte wondered if he wanted her to talk to her mother.

He put his hand over his daughter's wrist. "She already cast aside the first one without a second thought, I'm afraid. "I know I shouldn't ask you this, but will you speak to her? You of all people in this house seem to be the only one your mother at least listens to."

Charlotte knew this was true, although she had no idea why. "All right, Papa. But you have to give it time. Right now, the timing would be completely wrong."

"Do what you think is best, my dear. All I want is for your mother to think it over. If she is not inclined to a lengthy stay, we could keep it short or let go of the idea completely."

"I may require a new dress to repay me for the favour you ask of me, Papa." Charlotte's eyes twinkled with mischief. "But now I must go and change into one of my old dowdy frocks. Tea will be served shortly, and you know Mama does not appreciate us being late."

"Certainly." Henry stood as his daughter rose, shaking his head at her antics as she slipped out of his study. With a heavy sigh he attended to his papers. There was a lot to do before he could so much as think of afternoon tea.

Charlotte's maid had a day off, so she summoned Rose, her mother's maid, to help with her change of clothes.

"Tell me, Rose," Charlotte asked while the maid was helping her out of her riding dress, "how was mother today?"

"Quite well, milady."

Rose spoke carefully, and Charlotte was aware that Rose knew it wasn't her place to comment on her mistress' demeanour. Still, Charlotte glanced over her shoulder, into the earnest face of the young maid, and implored, "Please, Rose, you can tell me the truth! How was she really?"

"Sad."

Her whisper let Charlotte know that this was all she would say.

"Thank you."

Rose finished undressing her in silence, readied the bath, and took her leave. Alone in her bathtub, Charlotte contemplated her father's request. How should she approach her mother on the subject? For she knew how unrelenting her mother could be if she made up her mind on a matter. Rose said she had been sad, which was, of course, not surprising. Her mother had been nothing else for the last few years, as if a part of her had died. She could charm everybody with her wit and humour if she wanted to, yet her smile never really reached her eyes anymore.

Society didn't approve of women such as her mother or men like her father and Jonathan. Theirs was a special family. Contrary to many other young people of their acquaintance, Charlotte and her brothers had always felt loved by their parents and their parents' paramours. It was as if they had two sets of parents. Her mother's wealth and title as well as her father's connections did help in shielding their family from prying eyes and from being shunned by their peers. Her parents had always maintained a discretion some would have wished others to uphold. But Charlotte knew their relationship, as loving and caring as it was, was also a lie. She often felt sorry her parents weren't allowed to live the lives they deserved.

Lately, whenever Charlotte studied her mother's eyes, she found a trace of bleakness in them. There was a time when those sky-blue eyes shone with happiness and laughter. But for the past few years none of them had been able to chase away Eleanor's sadness. Charlotte was truly afraid nothing ever would. More often than not, there was an emptiness in her mother's eyes and a distant expression so far from the woman she used to be.

When Cathleen died, a part of her mother died with her.

Although Charlotte had told her father to give it time before he expected her to approach her mother, Charlotte feared the right time to do so would never occur. Now was as good a time as any. The worst that could happen was her mother changing the subject, refusing to think or speak about it, as she had done so many times before.

Charlotte was determined to change her mother's mind about the invitation. She herself had always wanted to go to Vienna, and now that the family had a perfectly good reason to do so, she wouldn't let it slip through her fingers. And what was more, her father was right; it would do her mother good. With a last glance into the mirror, Charlotte left her room and went to her mother's study so they could go downstairs for tea together.

Eleanor sat behind her desk, deeply immersed in correspondence with the keeper of her stables in Scotland. A knock on the door interrupted her train of thoughts and she answered impatiently. "Yes? What is it?"

When the head of her daughter peeked around the door, Eleanor's irritation vanished. She put her reading glasses on her desk, smiling at the fresh and youthful face of her daughter.

"Hello, darling," Eleanor said warmly.

"Good afternoon, Mama. I thought I'd come and get you for afternoon tea. I didn't mean to disturb you."

With a wave of her hand, she said, "Nonsense. Did you have an enjoyable morning?"

"Quite so, yes. What about *your* morning?"

Eleanor frowned at the expression on her daughter's face. "Why do you ask?"

"What? Well . . ."

"Did your father send you by any chance?"

"No, of course not."

Eleanor knew Charlotte was lying, and not very convincingly. She met her daughter's reluctant gaze. "No point denying it. Let's hear the truth this time."

"All right, yes, he did. But only because he's worried." She took Eleanor's hand in her own, entwining their fingers.

Eleanor tightened the hold on her daughter's hand and breathed out heavily. "I know."

"I miss your happy laugh and so does Papa."

"I am sorry, my darling."

Charlotte got straight to the point. "Ever since Mummy died you've been nothing but sad. We know you miss her terribly, so do we."

"But?" Her mother's voice was hoarse.

"But you promised her you would find somebody," she reminded her mother softly.

Eleanor closed her eyes at the sudden onslaught of another memory.

A single tear stole its way down her cheek. She was barely able to stifle a sob when she felt her daughter gently brush away the tear. In her memory, as if transported back in time, she sat in a comfortable chair by the window in the bedroom she shared with Cathleen, watching the laboured breathing of the woman on the bed. It had been half an hour since the doctor's visit. He changed the bandages on Cathleen's chest and injected the highest dose of morphine so far.

Eleanor knew it wouldn't be long now. The cancer had spread all through her lover's body. Cathleen's organs were failing, and the doctor estimated a matter of two or three days before Cathleen Northcott would leave this mortal plane.

The frail woman on the bed slowly opened her eyes and blinked, disoriented, before her piercing green gaze met Eleanor's. She seemed to have to muster up strength to hold out her hand for Eleanor. In an instant, she rushed to her side. She sat on the edge of the bed, leaned close, and carefully took the outstretched hand in one of her own. She lifted it to her lips to gently kiss the tips of the fingers, closed her eyes, and cursed herself when her eyes started to water. She brushed the tears away angrily.

"Hush, don't cry, my love," Cathleen whispered, caressing Eleanor's cheek softly. "Open your eyes. Let me see those beautiful blue eyes of yours. Let me see the love in them."

Bravely, Eleanor did as Cathleen requested, gazing at the face that had

held her captive since the first time she laid eyes on it. Although her hair had lost its shine, her eyes were sunken in with dark circles underneath, and her cheeks were hollow, Cathleen was still the most beautiful woman Eleanor had ever seen, and she loved her with an intensity and passion that took her breath away.

Cathleen had been ill for two years. After the doctors detected cancer in one of her breasts, they removed the mass in the hope of getting rid of the cancer. But unfortunately, soon after, the second breast was affected, and she underwent another painful surgery only to learn the disease was already spreading through her body. The wound on her chest, painful and raw, was open and smelled bad, so for the last three months, the doctor came by at least twice a day to change the bandages. During all that time, Eleanor refused to leave her side or trust her care to somebody else. Eleanor knew her lover was slowly wasting away, but she still refused to let her go. Her heart ached to see her beloved wasting away. All those wonderful years they had spent together, Cathleen had been her most cherished treasure. She was intelligent, sophisticated, funny, loving, caring, and the gentlest lover Eleanor could have hoped for. Theirs had truly been a blessed life. Full of love and laughter.

"I want you to promise me something, darling," Cathleen requested. Despite her exhaustion, she tightened the grip on her lover's hand.

"No, please," Eleanor begged, knowing already what Cathleen was going to ask of her.

"Please, Eleanor," Cathleen insisted with sudden strength in her voice. "Promise me you'll find someone to make you happy again."

"I can't," Eleanor whispered brokenly.

"Yes, you can. You deserve to be happy. You have so much love to give and deserve to receive. You need to let me go, my love. Promise me to find love again!"

Eleanor finally relented. "I promise." How could she not—she could never deny anything to her lover.

That promise brought a satisfied smile to the sick woman's face, making it easier for her to close her eyes forever and leave the love of her life behind with the knowledge she would not stay alone for the rest of her life.

But Eleanor's world had stopped spinning. She stumbled through life in a dream-like state ever since. With Cathleen gone, Eleanor missed all the colours in the world, and nothing seemed to bring her joy, not even her beloved horses.

And with that heart-breaking memory in mind, Eleanor opened her eyes to gaze upon her daughter, knowing her lover had asked the impossible from her. She knew both Cathleen and Charlotte meant well, they all did. They didn't want her to be lonely in a house full of people.

"I tried, Charlotte, I really did," Eleanor said, "but you know it is more than difficult. I haven't met anyone who's touched my heart even remotely, and I doubt I ever will."

"Mama, have you ever regretted the way you've lived your life?" Charlotte asked the one question she had always avoided with any of her parents.

"What do you mean, darling?"

"I mean, have you ever regretted you had to marry Papa to be able to spend your life with Mummy?"

"No," Eleanor did not have to think about it, especially since Charlotte seemed so honestly interested. "Never. I love your father dearly, and I know for certain he feels exactly the same way. How could I ever regret having you and your brother? And I did have the opportunity to spend my life with the most wonderful woman. So, what is there to regret?"

"Nothing, Mama," Charlotte said, pleased. "I think we should go downstairs. I'm sure the others are already waiting for us."

"You are absolutely right. We never want to miss this cherished tradition."

Philip and Martin shot their sister a questioning look when she entered the drawing room. They guessed their father had had a serious conversation with her regarding their mother, and by the expression on their sister's face she wasn't content with the outcome.

Charlotte was not altogether disappointed, but she couldn't call their talk a success either. Every now and then during tea, she cast an unsuspecting glance at her mother only to find her deep in thought, a frown marring her forehead.

Martin, despite his engagement in the conversation, keenly observed his surrogate mother. For as long as he could remember, this woman had been as much a mother to him as his biological mother. She may not have given birth to him, but she loved him just the same. He counted himself the luckiest of all his friends. After his father's death and the loss of his inheritance to his father's so-called friends, Martin and his mother had found a new home with the ones he now proudly called Mama and Papa.

Although, he did miss his mother dearly, he knew Eleanor had been in sheer agony over her death. The most prominent evidence of how much it had affected her was the colour of her hair. Her once golden hair had turned snow white overnight, and then Eleanor cut it off in a fit of grief and mourning. Since then, she wore it short, which suited her. Her appearance was quite distinguished with her white hair, piercing blue eyes, patrician nose, flawless skin, and regal bearing befitting a woman of her social position.

But Martin knew most of her bearing was superficiality. Deep down she hadn't been able to let go of the woman with whom she'd spent most of her life. Maybe this invitation Henry had spoken about would do her good. The only thing standing in their way was Eleanor herself.

He would need to talk to his siblings; they surely would find a way to make it happen. Just like his brother and his sister, he wanted to see her laugh again. All of her joy had been gone since his mother died. The absence of her smile was a heartfelt loss because her sunny grin genuinely transformed her whole face. She was even more beautiful when she smiled. They would have to think of a way to make it happen again.

Much to Eleanor's displeasure Henry had insisted on taking her to the opera this evening. Only his heartfelt plea and sweet way of apologising for having pressured her finally made her consent.

At dinner, Eleanor had barely followed the lively conversation about politics, sports, and the theatre. She thought about the heart-to-heart she'd had with her daughter. Maybe her family was right, maybe it was time to move on, but hadn't she tried already and failed utterly? True, she had done so for Henry's sake mostly, but her efforts were a disappointment. Now the last thing she wanted to do was go out in public.

Rose helped Eleanor dress and put on her jewellery, then she wrapped a shawl around her shoulders. The maid opened the door and Eleanor took her fan and opera-glasses from her vanity and glided out of the door, pausing in the hall to say, "You do not have to wait up, Rose. I will undress myself. You can take care of my clothes tomorrow."

"As you wish, ma'am," Rose acknowledged with a curtsy.

"Good night, Rose."

"Good night, your Grace."

Henry was already waiting at the bottom of the steps, wearing a tail-coat, a white scarf around his neck, an overcoat over his arm, and a silk top-hat already on his head.

"You are magnificent, my dear," he said.

"Oh, please." Eleanor waved him off, "You have seen me in this gown before. So, stop gushing because we do not want to be late now, do we?"

"Certainly not, dear," Henry said.

He ordered Benson to tell Parker to bring the carriage to the front, then Benson helped Eleanor with her wrap and Henry with his overcoat. As they were about to leave, the door to the library opened and the whole family came to wish them a nice evening.

"Mama, you look wonderful," Martin and Philip announced at the same time, laughing at their synchronised exclamation.

"Why thank you, darlings." She felt a light blush steal over her cheeks and was touched that her sons thought so.

"You really do look gorgeous, Mama." Charlotte kissed her cheek and grinned at her.

Accepting her daughter's kiss, Eleanor cast a questioning glance at her husband's lover. Jonathan was watching her with a critical eye. In a rather arch voice, he said, "This gown can only enhance your natural beauty, Eleanor."

"Thank you, dear." Eleanor regarded Jonathan fondly. He was as dear to her as a brother. Slightly taller than Henry with dark hair and streaks of grey, compassionate grey eyes, and a well-groomed beard, he was quite dashing. Jonathan was, at least in her opinion, not only a wonderful partner to Henry, but also a congenial completion to their family.

"Well said, all of you." Henry ushered his wife towards the door. "Let's go. After all, you're the one who said we can't be late. Good night, everybody. Try not to rob poor Jonathan of his last shilling, you scoundrels."

"Who? We?" The three of them tried to sound as innocent as possible.

"Good night," Henry said, "you horrible offspring." He chuckled as Benson closed the door behind them. Parker held the door of the carriage while Henry helped his wife climb inside. When he had boarded, they set off towards Covent Garden.

They rode in companionable silence for a while until Henry felt the need to express his regret. "I apologize for trying to put pressure on you," he said ruefully. "If you are not inclined to go to Vienna, we won't."

Eleanor sighed. She knew he meant well, and she hadn't been reasonable in her initial responses but had taken her ire out on him. She put her gloved hand over the one in his lap, giving it a reassuring squeeze.

"You do not have to apologize, Henry. I know why you did it. And I do appreciate it." Leaning over, she lightly kissed his cheek.

"Just think about it. You still have plenty of time to decide one way or the other."

"I will, I promise."

They fell silent once more until Henry cleared his throat. She couldn't help but roll her eyes because she knew another difficult matter was on his mind.

"Yes?" Eleanor encouraged him softly.

"I was wondering," he started reluctantly, "if you have noticed something about Charlotte?"

She couldn't help but chuckle at her husband's carefully phrased words, already knowing where this would lead. She took pity on him and released him from his torture. "If by 'something' you mean her interest in the fairer sex, then yes, I have noticed. Quite a while ago, to be honest."

"Oh." Henry sounded surprised she had known for so long, when in all honesty, he shouldn't be. Eleanor had always known about their children's joys and worries.

"Like mother like daughter, isn't that what they say?" Eleanor said with a ring of sadness in her voice.

"Maybe so, but you are nothing like *your* mother."

"Nobody is like my mother." Eleanor snorted very unmannerly. "That woman is evil personified. Cold, harsh, self-righteous, and full of loathing for everybody who dares to disagree with her. Most of all, she does not even know how to spell the word love."

"Are you sure? I always thought she was quite enchanted with our children."

"Only so far as she could use them as pawns in her ambitious machinations." Eleanor shuddered at the thought of her mother meddling in their children's lives. "I am glad we put an end to it before she could think of it any further."

"Thank goodness."

"I just wish . . ." Eleanor wouldn't finish though.

"You wish what?" Henry asked curiously.

Eleanor sighed heavily before elaborating on her thought. "I wish it would be easier for Charlotte to live her life the way we were not allowed to, Henry. I've always hoped our children would not have to resort to such falsehoods as we had to. But now it seems they are going to have it more difficult than before."

"Don't worry, my dear." He patted his wife's hand. "We are here for her. She can count on us, and I am quite sure the same can be said for her brothers. Her life is easier than that of many others of our persuasion. On the one hand there is still a lot of pressure on our daughter due to her social standing, but her wealth is going to make up for a lot of it. If she decides to live her life to her heart's content, she has my fullest support."

"I wouldn't have expected anything less of you. Thank you, dear."

Inside the concert hall, after the first act, Henry offered his arm to Eleanor to step out for a glass of champagne. Handing one of the glasses to his wife, he saw by the gleam in her eyes that she had enjoyed the opera so far. Nearly congratulating himself for his decision to bring her here, he winced when he heard the unmistakeable voice of Lady Margaret Harrington.

"Well, well, if this isn't the prodigal daughter," Lady Margaret drawled, holding out her hand to Henry who dutifully kissed the back in greeting. Behind the well-known society lady, he glimpsed her latest conquest, a young man, his beauty equal to a Greek statue, with a divine body and a shock of black hair.

"Margaret." Eleanor greeted her frostily with a kiss to her cheek.

"Your Grace." Lady Margaret kept her lips against Eleanor's cheek longer than was fashionable. When she withdrew, she nearly laughed at Eleanor's expression of discomfort. "Meet the young Lord Pennhurst," Margaret said. "Daniel, darling, meet the Duchess of Darnsworth and her husband Lord Edgewood."

"Your Grace." The young man leaned over Eleanor's hand and kissed it carefully before he took Henry's offered hand in greeting. "Lord Edgewood."

Before she could prevent it, Margaret hooked her arm through Eleanor's, leading her towards her box and leaving the men to follow at a respectable distance. The duchess cursed the fates for this unexpected encounter. Eleanor abhorred this woman and felt she had good reason for it. In the past Margaret had tried to lure her into her web. On one of the few occasions when she had to accompany Henry to a weekend with one of his business associates, Cathleen hadn't felt well enough to go with them. The first signs of her illness occurred, which none of them had realised at the time.

As soon as Eleanor and Henry arrived at the weekend site, Lady Margaret, the sister of the host, tried to sink her claws in. At first, Eleanor had been amused at the woman's blatant flirtations, but after a while it became quite tiresome. It wasn't that Lady Margaret Harrington wasn't beautiful or fascinating to talk to; she was intelligent and witty. Under different circumstances Lady Margaret could have become a friend. But her constant need to conquer made her unattractive in a dangerous sort of way.

"My dear, Eleanor," Margaret said sweetly now, as she led her toward the box, "you shouldn't be such a stranger. Time to move on, life has so much to offer."

"Life has to offer *you*, you mean."

Margaret put her hand over her chest in mock hurt. "Still miffed, I see."

Eleanor stopped, gazing at her through lidded eyes with barely disguised contempt. "You do not interest me in the slightest. Never have and never will. I offered you friendship, but I came to believe you are incapable of such a feeling. You tried to take away what was dearest to me and for that I will never forgive you. So please, do not pretend we are something which we are not." She removed Lady Margaret's hand from her arm, gathered her gown, and stormed off towards their box.

Henry hastily bid his goodbyes and followed after his wife, whom he found breathing heavily in their box and trying desperately to fend off the tears streaming down her cheeks.

"Darling, are you all right?" Lord Edgewood asked worriedly.

"No, Henry, I am not all right, and I have not been, not for the last three years," Eleanor replied harshly. "My strength is gone. It seems as if all I can do is cry. One would think that after three long years I have run out of tears, don't you think? It's pathetic!"

Gently, Henry turned her around and pulled her against his chest, much the same as so many years before when they were their children's age, that fateful summer when Eleanor had met Cathleen and he had become engaged to the distraught woman in his arms. Ever since then, Cathleen had comforted Eleanor, but now it was him again, and she let him for the first time since her lover died. He knew his wife's tears were also tears of anger at herself for letting that scheming Lady Margaret get to her and for her own inability to cope with the sorrow which was her constant companion since Cathleen's death. How he hated to see her like this, knowing nothing he could do or say would ease her pain.

This was the reason he wanted them to go to Vienna over the summer. To be somewhere else, where Eleanor wasn't constantly reminded of her loss. London wasn't the place to be, but neither was Scotland. Cathleen and Eleanor had spent a lot of time at Darnsworth Castle, just the two of them or with the children, which provided them with the illusion that nothing existed but their love and the love for their children. He should have envied them but try as he might, he couldn't. Marrying Eleanor had granted him a life of his own, although he could only live it in the sanctuary of his home, but it was still more than other men of his type had. So how could he have begrudged her any piece of happiness for which she had fought so hard?

He led his wife to the chaise in their box where they sat next to each other, Eleanor still in his arms. She snuggled into his side, feeling tremendously better after this unpleasant encounter. Henry gently kissed the top of her head.

"I know she was responsible for that awful quarrel between yourself and Cathleen. But I never knew the whole story. Tell me, please!"

"In retrospect, it was completely ridiculous." Eleanor wiped her nose with a handkerchief before she continued. "Do you remember the weekend where we met Margaret for the first time?"

"Yes, I thought you got along quite well back then."

"We did," she admitted, "at least at first. She was refreshing to talk to amongst those other boring wives of your friends. First, I didn't realise what was going on because you know ever since I met Cathleen, I never looked twice at another woman."

"I know, dear." Henry chuckled at the memory of how his often-times-clueless wife had turned many heads of supposedly proper ladies—and still did, if the effect when they entered Covent Garden earlier were any indication.

"When I realised what was going on, I made it quite clear nothing more but friendship could ever be between us. I thought she would honour the boundary, but on the second night she came to my room, trying to seduce me. All I could do was throw her out as fast as possible, locking my door firmly behind her."

Eleanor sat up, drying her eyes, and wringing the soaked handkerchief in her hands, before Henry stilled her by covering her fluttering fingers with his own large, warm hand.

"When we came back, Henry, I wanted to tell Cathleen instantly, but with Philip's broken leg and Martin's sprained wrist after their riding accident, the whole affair slipped to the back of my mind. That was until a letter from Lady Margaret arrived for Cathleen."

"Goodness! It sounds like there was no limit to the lengths the woman would go to get what she wanted."

"Indeed." Eleanor stood and paced in front of the chaise, keeping the reins on her temper at the memory of the atrocity of this viper. "She brought her weapons in position, and I delivered the poison for the arrow she was shooting at my love. I still cannot believe how stupid I was."

She shook her head, clenching her hands into tight fists. "In her letter she bragged about our supposed night of passion. I am certain Cathleen wouldn't have believed a thing if she hadn't included the knowledge of a scar one could only know about if they had seen me nude."

At this piece of information Henry sat up straight. "If you hadn't shared this passionate night with her, how did she know about this delicate detail which I don't even know about?"

"Oh, please, don't look at me that way, Henry!" Eleanor chastised him with annoyance. "You know I'm not lying."

"Sorry, dear," Henry had the grace to appear reprimanded. Embarrassed, he brushed his hand over his bald head. "But how did she know?"

"It was utterly stupid," Eleanor said. "One evening after dinner, we ladies retired to the library for coffee and the conversation moved on to the latest fashions. You know, reform clothes and such. One of the ladies made an unexpected joke of how much easier and less hurtful it must be to clothe so daringly."

"There is some truth in it."

"Certainly. And I agreed whole-heartedly and told them of the scar on the small of my back caused by the hook of my corset. The ladies expressed their sympathy, and we laughed about the silly incident, but Margaret was present as well, and I'm certain this is the only reason she knew about it. Unfortunately, she used this knowledge in the worst possible way."

"I am sorry," Henry said softly.

Eleanor took her seat again and leaned her head against her husband's shoulder, inhaling his comforting scent. She closed her eyes before she continued. "Cathleen was so hurt. While she trusted me implicitly, she felt extremely vulnerable at the time. If I knew then what I know now, I wouldn't have reacted the way I did. She was hurt because of the implication of the letter, and I felt hurt and angry at the same time that she could at all think it possible."

"I remember the tension between you two at that time," he whispered.

"It was awful. We wasted so much time being angry at each other. And it nearly destroyed what we had. I still can't believe somebody would do such an awful thing merely to get a strange sort of revenge for not having been able to make a conquest."

With a gentle squeeze of his wife's shoulder Henry stood and offered his hand. Eleanor gratefully took it and rose as well. He took the handkerchief from her hand and got rid of the teary streaks on her alabaster cheeks.

"This evening did not at all turn out as I intended for which I am truly sorry, my dear," Henry said apologetically. "I meant to offer you a distraction and a welcome change."

"It is not your fault." Eleanor patted his chest. "Take me home, please. I am not particularly fond of another meeting with that woman."

"Of course." Henry let go of her hand to fetch their coats and ask one of the pages to fetch their carriage.

With their heads held high, they left the building, and soon enough Parker arrived. As before, Henry helped Eleanor inside before he followed after her.

"Home, Parker," his Lordship ordered. Their driver gave a short snap with his whip and the horses took off in a leisurely gait.

They stayed silent for the entire ride, both lost in their own thoughts. When they arrived at Grosvenor Square, the duchess retired to her room instantly, not without thanking her husband for the effort and a goodnight kiss to his cheek.

Henry watched her climb the stairs with great fatigue; he knew this emotional evening had exhausted her. He wished he could do something to bring back the lively spark to this usually passionate woman he had the good fortune to call his wife. But the death of her lover had left an empty shell behind, a shell he no longer recognised.

Shaking his head, he handed coat, scarf, gloves, and silk-hat to Benson. He really hoped Eleanor would do some needed soul-searching about how she wanted to go on with her life. He knew she didn't want to continue like this, but to interfere would only lead to her retreat. She had to come to a decision on her own, anything else simply wouldn't work.

He headed to the library where he was greeted by his surprised children and lover.

"Papa, you are awfully early," Philip exclaimed. "We didn't expect you and Mama before midnight."

"Do not worry, son," Henry said, while he went over to the table to pour himself a stiff whiskey. "I merely came to tell you we are back and to get myself a drink before I go upstairs with a good book. So, please, by all means, continue with your game."

Charlotte observed her father curiously before she left the table to join him at the window where he stood peering into the darkness and drinking his whiskey. She put her arm through her father's and leaned her head against his shoulder.

"It is about Mama, isn't it?" she asked knowingly.

"Yes."

"Do you want me to go upstairs?"

"No, darling, let's give her space. She has a lot on her mind after today and needs time to think about many things. I believe it would be best if we all took a step back. She might surprise us."

"All right," Charlotte agreed more cheerfully, then she kissed her father's cheek and took a seat at the table.

Soon enough their game of cards was in full swing again. The children barely registered when Henry left the library with a book in hand to retire for the night, though Jonathan gave him a nod and a smile as he shuffled the cards and called out, "Last hand now, you reprobates."

Chapter Three

"Mister Benson?" Rose said, all the while concentrating on her needlework. She was mending the seam of Lady Charlotte's riding dress. She would love to go to the continent and could no longer hold back about it, so she simply had to ask. "Do you think we are going to the continent this year?"

"Why would you ask, Rose?" Benson looked up from his newspaper and at the expectant faces all around the table. None of them could conceal their eagerness at the prospect of a journey to Vienna, he thought. Of course, they had heard about the invitation, not only the first one, but a second had later been received by mail. Not even Mrs. Chambers, the cook, could suppress the sparkle in her eyes at the thought of going someplace where none of them had ever been. Of course, the servants at the table had not thought of the possibility that if the family decided to go to Vienna over the summer, perhaps the staff would be left behind. The family could give them the time off and rely on servants provided by an agency in Vienna. No. That could not happen. Benson shook his head as the thought was too preposterous to entertain for a second.

"I ask because," Rose explained, "it seems his Lordship is as much taken by the idea as everybody else. She paused in her work to look sorrowfully at the butler. "Her Grace, though, she doesn't agree with the others."

Benson grumbled, "Unfortunately not. No."

He gazed at the others, and it was heart-warming to see them shake their heads sadly at the mention of the duchess. Benson was proud of the servants; their loyalty toward the family was complete and unshakeable. Her grace and His lordship employed a rather fascinating group of people, and not only did they treat them respectfully, they also paid more than was usual. The maids were perfectly safe from any unwanted advances and so were the footmen and stable hands. The duchess and his lordship were determined to make sure each and every one of their servants was treated with dignity and respect by the family as well as by their guests. One rather dim-witted baron once made the mistake of violating this iron rule. His fate was sealed when her grace caught him red-handed as he was trying to force himself on Rose on the floor in her grace's room. She had been outraged and before said baron knew it, he was tossed out on the street and in addition shunned from every important social circle in London.

"Why are you all so gloomy?" Mrs. Kavanaugh, the housekeeper, asked as she entered the parlour and saw crestfallen faces. She had just finished her bookkeeping and joined them for a cup of tea before any of them could call it a night.

James, one of the footmen, was bold enough to explain it to her. "We were talking about the family and if they are going to Vienna this year."

"Oh?"

"Yes, well." Benson cleared his throat when a discussion threatened to start. "I think we will have to wait and see, won't we? Now if there is nothing else . . ." He fixed his gaze on James and upon Cedric, the other footman. "Why don't you two go to the library and make sure everything is in order when they decide to call it a night and end their game of cards."

"Yes, Mister Benson," they chorused as they stood and left the table. Rose finished her work on the riding dress and bid good night along with the more seasoned members of the servants.

"Stop making such a big secret out of it, George," Mrs. Chambers said softly. Her admonishment of Benson was good-natured, and she was the only one among the servants able to get away with it. They had known each other long enough to allow for the occasional teasing.

Mrs. Kavanaugh covered her folded hands gently. "Now, Hetty," she said, "Mister Benson doesn't have to say anything at all."

The butler smiled indulgently at Mrs. Chambers and Mrs. Kavanaugh. He knew they would only stop pestering him for now. Tomorrow was another day, though, so he could get it over right now once and for all. It wasn't as if he knew anything for certain. He gazed down his nose at Mrs. Chambers.

"I really don't know, Hetty. But I do believe—no, I am *convinced*—that as soon as her Grace agrees to the journey and a rather prolonged stay in Vienna, we are definitely going. I am afraid she isn't very agreeable at the moment though. I hope she will change her mind."

"So do we, George, so do we."

As Henry had suggested, Eleanor spent a lot of time over the next few weeks in deep thought. She knew she couldn't mourn Cathleen forever. There was no avail, life went on and she had promised exactly that: to move on with her life and find a new companion and possible lover.

She exhaled heavily and took a seat behind her desk and opened the top drawer on her right-hand side. Under a sheet of paper she found, bound with a dark red ribbon, a bundle of letters. Eleanor took them out of the drawer, lifting them to her nose. She closed her eyes, certain she could still smell Cathleen's delicate perfume. She didn't dare open the ribbon and read because she knew they would bring back another onslaught of tears such as so many times over the past three years.

Eleanor was tired, tired of her life without her lover, tired of the constant grief, and tired of her inability to move on. So far, her loved ones had been more than patient with her, but she knew they couldn't bear it much longer. Neither could she, if she was completely honest with herself. Henry was right; the invitation to spend time with his relatives in Vienna was her chance to come to terms with her life again.

Determined to stand by her decision, she left her study to inform her husband of her change of heart. On the way to Henry's study, she ran into Benson who informed her with a disagreeable expression that the Viscountess of Langdon was waiting in the drawing room.

"Thank you, Benson." Eleanor sighed. "Would you please inform his Lordship?"

"Certainly, your Grace." Benson bowed and left in the direction of Henry's study.

Eleanor gathered her skirts, and with long strides she hurried to the drawing room. Before she opened the door, she took a deep breath, reminding herself to stay calm no matter what.

"Finally, Eleanor," the viscountess said bitingly. "I was beginning to wonder if Benson had neglected to inform you of my presence. I wouldn't put such a thing past him."

Eleanor decided to let the crochety comment go, instead greeting her mother with forced cheerfulness and a kiss to her cheek. Her mother had never really cared for or trusted their butler. It was probably due to the badge he wore over his left eye which gave him a rather scary-looking appearance when he was, in all reality, one of the most good-hearted persons Eleanor could think of.

"Hello, mother."

"What is going on? I haven't seen such colour on your cheeks for quite a while. And where is your husband?"

"Right here," Henry announced from the doorway. He closed the door to greet his mother-in-law.

The viscountess held her hand out gracefully before she turned towards her daughter, her expression haughty and cool, lacking all warmth or affection. Eleanor often wondered how such a woman could have given birth to her or her brother. Her mother was the most opinionated, self-righteous, and bigoted woman she had the unfortunate luck to know. Gazing at the older woman from the corner of her eyes, she realised, not for the first time, that her mother's face reflected her personality quite well. The lines around eyes and mouth could never be mistaken for anything else but signs of constant displeasure at other human beings.

Her skin was deeply wrinkled; her pinched face and thin lips did nothing to soften the impression of an unhappy woman. Her mother's hair, just as white as Eleanor's, was pulled into a tight bun at the back of her head, giving her a stricter and more unforgiving appearance. Compared to Eleanor's grandmother, this woman seemed older than her years.

Benson arrived with tea and sandwiches. Mrs. Chambers had obviously heard of the guest and sent up refreshments. Thankfully, their servants could be relied on, and their efficiency was unrivalled. Mrs. Chambers had probably wreaked havoc when she heard of the viscountess' arrival, and she would never allow for the Duchess' mother to have reason to say a single negative word about her household. The trust in their abilities and loyalty was well earned. Eleanor made a mental note to thank Mrs. Chambers personally for the effort after her mother had left. The thought alone brought an involuntary smile to her lips because the viscountess would view such a thing way beyond her station and completely out of line, but then again, theirs wasn't a conventional household. Eleanor slipped effortlessly into her role as hostess; her mother wouldn't expect anything less. She would do nothing to give the woman the satisfaction to criticise her.

"Thank you, Eleanor." She took a careful sip and rewarded her daughter with a holier-than-thou expression. The tea was just as she loved it.

"I hear you and Henry decided to make an appearance in society again," her mother said with a sniff. "It's about time."

"How . . ." Eleanor was surprised but stopped herself before she finished the sentence. Of course, her mother would know about the disastrous visit to the opera. This woman had her eyes and ears everywhere.

"Although Lady Burlington told me she saw you leave after the first act."

"Did she now, and pray tell, Mother," Eleanor asked sharply, "how is this any of her business?" Lady Emmeline Burlington was the worst busybody London had ever seen. The only reason the woman ever visited the opera or the theatre was to spy on her fellow peers so she could relay the latest gossip at her infamous dinner parties.

"You don't need to raise your voice," her mother chastised.

"I didn't feel well." Henry came to Eleanor's rescue. "It must have been something I ate at dinner."

If he hadn't interfered, he was convinced that his wife and his mother-in-law would have been at each other's throats in an instant. Henry preferred their false civility over a dispute any time because he knew his mother-in-law wouldn't fight fair, and he didn't want her to strike a vicious blow at his wife, especially when Eleanor seemed so much more content than she had for months.

"Really?" The viscountess obviously did not quite believe him.

"I am afraid so," he assured her with what he hoped was a pitiful expression.

She was still not entirely convinced but she apparently decided to let it go for now. "The reason for this visit is another, though," the viscountess offered non-nonchalantly.

"Indeed?"

"Yes. I was wondering if you would awfully mind if I went north this summer. I haven't been there for three years and would be partial to spend the hot season in a cooler climate."

"You would have to take your own servants," Eleanor answered with a frown.

"I am aware of this, Eleanor," her mother replied with an impatient roll of her eyes.

"Then of course you shall. I hope you enjoy your time."

"Thank you," the viscountess managed to press out through her thin lips.

Eleanor was well aware that the viscountess still couldn't believe her own mother had bequeathed her wealth and title to her *granddaughter*, passing over her own daughter. But the viscountess shouldn't have been surprised at all; her mother and her daughter were of the same cloth. They'd always had a certain understanding—and the same "unnatural" leanings. Her late mother's companion had been much more than a mere companion, just as Henry's cousin Cathleen had been more to Eleanor than a mere friend.

So, Eleanor was the rightful owner of the title and inheritance, she was married to a very respectable man, and had born two perfectly healthy children. Furthermore, Eleanor had always been very discreet but that didn't mean the viscountess had to agree with what Eleanor did nor had she ever approved of Lady Cathleen Northcott.

The viscountess took the last sip from the delicate cup before she put it on the table and rose. "Now that this is settled, I have to leave to be on time for Lady Burlington's dinner party."

"Please, by all means, don't let us keep you," Eleanor offered with a fake smile. The sooner her mother left the better.

"Goodbye, Eleanor. Henry." She straightened the skirt of her dove grey dress, which was delicately embroidered in a most intricate manner with ivy leaves in black silk. The bodice of her dress revealed a lean body. Her mother's pinched face perfectly fit her pinched body. Black gloves completed her evening dress. Eleanor could also detect her mother's favourite perfume for the occasion, and the smell of lily and jasmine followed her out of the room.

"I will accompany you to your carriage," Lord Edgewood chimed in, as he held the door for his mother-in-law.

After her mother and Henry had left, Eleanor sank back into the cushions with a sigh of relief. How she loathed these visits. Her mother had the uncanny talent of bringing out the worst in her. But this time there had been a rather pleasant twist to the unpleasantness. Her mother had been forced to ask a favour. Eleanor knew how much effort it must have cost her to ask if she could stay at Darnsworth Castle. The viscountess had never forgiven her mother—or her own daughter—that she hadn't inherited the money and title of Duchess of Darnsworth.

Eleanor got up to go to her room and get ready to leave. It was time to make a visit and ask for advice, or, rather, confirmation for her recently made decision.

When the duchess entered the house in Kensington she was overwhelmed by many happy memories. They brought a bittersweet smile to her lips as she followed the butler to the drawing room.

"The Duchess of Darnsworth, madam."

"Eleanor, sweetheart." Contessa Giulia Silvestri, an elegant woman in her mid-eighties, rose from her comfortable chair by the window. She put down a book on the side-table to welcome Eleanor warmly in her arms. Eleanor bent down slightly to fully return the embrace and inhale her grandmother's familiar scent.

"Hello, Nonna," Eleanor whispered with a choked voice. Calling the contessa Nonna—Grandmother—had always been the most natural thing to Eleanor since she could remember. This fragile-looking woman with her backbone of steel had been her late grandmother's lover for over forty years. It was nearly impossible to think of the one without the other. It had been hard for the contessa after her grandmother's death but somehow, she had managed.

The contessa ended the embrace and held Eleanor at arms' length to examine her. "You do look better than you have for quite a while, *Cara*," Giulia stated with a critical eye.

"I do feel better."

"Come, sit with me!"

She took hold of Eleanor's hand and led her to the sofa where they sat close to each other.

"Mother came by today," Eleanor explained with a groan. "She asked if she could stay at Darnsworth Castle over the summer."

"What did you say?"

"I told her she would have to take her own servants."

Giulia smirked at Eleanor's straightforwardness. "I can only imagine what it must have cost that woman to ask her own daughter's permission to make use of an estate she's always regarded as rightfully hers." She let out a hoot and with a small flicker of glee, the contessa inclined her head. "Well done, my dear."

"She hates me, Nonna," Eleanor said mournfully. "My own mother hates me."

The contessa sighted. "It is true. Your mother never held much love for either of her children. Especially for you who were always my Bridget's favourite."

Bridget McAllister, the late Duchess of Darnsworth, on the other hand, had held a special love for her granddaughter, and Eleanor was well aware of it.

"I am sorry, child," the contessa said ruefully, "that your mother never knew how to love. She has always been more her father's daughter than her mother's in this regard. Your grandmother was the most considerate, loving, and warm woman I have ever known, and she loved you dearly."

"I miss her, Nonna." Eleanor closed her eyes sorrowfully at her memory and laid her head into her nonna's lap, who without a second of hesitation let her hand sift through Eleanor's short silky white hair.

"I miss her too, *Cara*. Very much so."

They remained that way for quite some time, each lost in her own thoughts. Eleanor reminisced about her childhood days, when she spent every summer at her grandmother's vast estate in Scotland, riding and romping across the green hills of the Highlands. She remembered evenings in front of the hearth in her grandmother's room playing board games or listening to the duchess read from her favourite books. Her nonna, Giulia, would sit in a comfortable chair next to her grandmother, doing needlework or sketching, all the while indulgently smiling at them as they had their noses deep in another novel by Dickens.

Where the duchess had been tall and statuesque with hair the colour of ripe corn and eyes matching a summer afternoon, Nonna was the complete opposite, small in stature with thick dark hair and fiery dark eyes. People often underestimated the contessa's resoluteness but soon found out that the small, fragile-looking woman was made of steel. She was not somebody one would want as an enemy. Underneath her fierce temper though, lay a heart full of love for those close to her. Just like Eleanor's grandmother, her nonna was a very loving and gentle woman.

Eleanor startled the contessa from her own thoughts when she said, "Henry received an invitation from his cousin, who lives in Vienna. Her daughter is going to marry one of her father's business partners, and she asked us to celebrate with them." She looked into her nonna's eyes to gauge her reaction but couldn't read her.

"What do you think?"

Eleanor studied her hands, now neatly folded in her lap. "I came to the conclusion that it might not be such a bad idea. First, I felt pressured when Henry asked Charlotte to convince me. But after I have given it a lot of thought, I think I agree with him. Meeting new people and visiting a foreign country might not be so bad after all, and I might also catch a glimpse of the emperor's famous white horses."

"Your grandmother would have enjoyed that as well." Giulia smiled sadly. "For the last three years I've been as worried about you as the rest of the family. I'm glad you've come to this decision. How long will you stay?"

"I am not sure," Eleanor said sheepishly. "I haven't even told Henry yet. You are the first to know. I'm sure we'll be abroad at least for the whole summer. Henry and Jonathan will take care of the details as meticulously as they always do. I'm also quite certain the children will appreciate the change. They deserve it, we all deserve it. It was not very pleasant to be around me for quite a while, but recently I have been feeling more certain that I might be able to move on."

The contessa put her small hand against Eleanor's cheek before she answered with conviction. "I am happy to hear you say that, my darling girl. Now I will not worry so much about you."

Eleanor covered the warm hand with one of her own and swallowed the lump in her throat.

On her way home from Kensington, Eleanor was preoccupied with thoughts about the lengths she would have to go to mend fences with Mrs. Chambers. Henry's well-meant attempt to explain their sudden departure from the opera had put their cook and her talents on the spot. After the perfectly prepared tea she had sent to the drawing room for the viscountess, Eleanor had meant to give her gratitude to Mrs. Chambers. Instead, her mother was likely to pass on the comment to her staff, and it would get back to their cook.

Mrs. Chambers deserved better than the inadvertent criticism Henry had expressed. Poor Henry hadn't actually realised what he had done. If he had, he surely would have rushed to the kitchen soon after her mother had left and asked for Mrs. Chambers' forgiveness which was never beneath him. The last thing they needed right now, when they would soon travel to Vienna, was for their cook to quit.

As soon as Eleanor entered the hall, she handed her outer garments to Benson and asked him to send Mrs. Chambers and Mrs. Kavanaugh to the library.

"Both, your Grace?" Benson raised his eyebrow imperceptibly. He had a good inkling what this was all about. It didn't take a genius to realise that her grace was going to explain to Mrs. Chambers the unfortunate comment by his lordship about his upset stomach the other evening. Of all the people in the world, it had to be the Viscountess of Langdon to whom he had said something so humiliating. It was no secret at all that the cook despised the duchess' mother with a passion nobody would have ever thought the plump and good-natured woman capable of.

"Yes, please, Benson," Eleanor murmured in defeat. "I find it easier to deal with Mrs. Chambers when Mrs. Kavanaugh is present. She has a wonderful calming influence I have learned to appreciate her when speaking about the viscountess."

"I suppose there is merit to it, your Grace," he said thoughtfully with a slight cock of his head.

Eleanor smirked at his words, knowing they were true, but it was refreshing to see she was right after all about a small crisis brewing. "Glad you agree, Benson."

"I . . . I am sorry, I didn't mean to—"

"No need and you weren't. Just ask them to come as soon as their duties allow them."

"Certainly." He inclined his head obediently and left to pass on the orders.

When a soft knock sounded on the door to the library, Eleanor put aside her book and reading glasses. She straightened her back and folded her hands in her lap.

"Come in!"

The opening of the door revealed a flushed-looking cook accompanied by a calm and collected housekeeper. Mrs. Kavanaugh closed the door behind them; they curtsied and waited patiently for the duchess to address them. They knew their place and Eleanor knew hers. Asking them to come to the library was the right thing to do, but she saw Mrs. Chambers felt completely out of place. She doubted the cook had ever been in the library before. Although there was a lot about their household that was most unusual, the staff did know what was proper and what wasn't.

The balance between upstairs and downstairs had to be held up for the larger scheme to work out smoothly. The trivial things were what had to be obeyed; the larger ones weren't so much an issue, and the household would continue to function without any annoying interruptions. Eleanor watched the two women, contemplating them silently for a couple of moments before she addressed the cook.

"Mrs. Chambers, I'm sorry for completely ruining your schedule for dinner, but my visit to Contessa Silvestri took far longer than I had anticipated."

"You are too generous, your Grace." Mrs. Chambers blushed to the roots of her hair.

"Not at all, quite on the contrary, I'm afraid." Eleanor felt her own face heat up so that she probably appeared as embarrassed as her cook. "I am certain you have already heard about the rather unfortunate comment his Lordship made regarding dinner before we went to the opera last week."

"Well . . ." The cook hemmed and hawed, clearly reluctant to admit it.

"Of course, you have, but let me assure you it was spoken out of haste, and there was *nothing* wrong with my husband after dinner. He merely was a gentleman and in protecting me, he took the blame for displeasure the Viscountess had imparted. So please, accept my apology for this most unpleasant incident."

"Most gracious of you, your Grace."

Mrs. Chambers appeared bewildered, though by now Eleanor thought the cook should know better. The duchess and his lordship had the tendency to astonish the servants frequently by their actions, often in unusual ways that were unheard of by other members of the aristocracy. Neither she nor Henry talked to peers about how they ran their household, though their servants at times were not so tight-lipped. She thought they probably had the reputation around town of being too soft on the staff.

She said, "Mrs. Chambers, you deserve our utmost respect and gratitude for the fine meals you provide, and you run the kitchen so expertly. And you," she shifted her gaze to Mrs. Kavanaugh, "you, too, are doing a wonderful job. Sometimes it's yeoman's labour keeping this household in line, and you are each marvellous at it."

"Thank you, your Grace," both women said at the same time and bobbed curtseys.

"One more thing, Mrs. Chambers," she said as she thoughtfully tipped her finger against her bottom lip.

"Yes, ma'am?"

"I very much appreciate the effort you put in today's tea. The Viscountess' visit was a surprise for all of us. Very well done, Mrs. Chambers, very well indeed."

The cook stood at least five inches taller at the sincere praise, her chest swelled in pride. Eleanor hoped Mrs. Chambers had long forgotten

Henry's unfortunate comment about dinner. All she could do was smile at the two women.

"You are very understanding, ma'am. Thank you."

"Yes," Mrs. Kavanaugh said. "Thank you."

"You are welcome. Mrs. Chambers, can you serve dinner in half an hour? Would that be all right?"

"Very much so, your Grace."

"Good." Eleanor looked away, indicating that the conversation was over. The servants took the cue and moved to depart. Mrs. Kavanaugh had her hand already on the door handle when Eleanor spoke.

"Mrs. Kavanaugh?"

"Your Grace?" The housekeeper gave her full attention to her mistress, awaiting her orders.

"I meant to ask if you and Mister Benson could confer about spending the summer on the continent. I would say for about five months. You know, think about the necessary preparations, who to take with us, et cetera."

"Certainly, ma'am. Anything else?"

"Not at the moment." Eleanor smiled and swept past them out of the room, leaving a befuddled cook and housekeeper behind.

Eyebrows raised, they swivelled to look at one another, then broke out in giant grins. So, they were going to Vienna after all.

They scampered out to the hall and then in opposite directions, both suppressing excitement as best they could.

Chapter Four

Countess Helen von Hagendorf entered the breakfast room with a distinctive spring in her step and a letter in her hand. Her family and her stepdaughter were gathered at the table enjoying the first meal of the day.

"Why so chipper this morning, my dear?" asked Ludwig von Hagendorf, her husband, with a humorous gleam in his eyes. He smiled at the other four occupants at the table, only to lose his smile when his eyes landed on his daughter's sullen expression. He turned his gaze to his wife again, waiting for her to explain what had caused her exceptional good mood.

"I've just received a letter from my cousin Henry," Helen announced happily. "He confirms that he and his family are delighted to accept the invitation to Emma's wedding."

Surprised, Emma asked, "Is this the same cousin you haven't seen in over twenty years, Mother?"

"What does that have to do with anything, dear?" her mother asked sharply.

"Nothing. Sorry."

"Anyway," Helen waved her off, "he confirmed that he and his family are looking forward to their time in Vienna. They are going to reside at the Palais Schelling over the summer."

"That sounds wonderful, my dear," Ludwig said, wiping his mouth with his napkin before he got up from the table. He kissed his wife's cheek and left to get ready to leave for his office.

The count was already putting on his gloves when his oldest daughter Sophie caught up with him in the hall.

"Father, I would like to have a word with you. Sophie von Hagendorf stood in front of her father, making it impossible for him to leave without being rude. Ludwig groaned at his daughter's insistent manner; he knew what this was regarding, but there was nothing he could do about the whole matter.

"Can't this wait until after dinner? I really need to get to the office."

"Very well." Sophie relented upon seeing her father's resigned expression.

She watched him leave before turning on her heel to climb the stairs to her rooms, grateful that she had plenty of space to herself on the floor where she spent most of her time. From her sitting room or bedroom or her comfortable parlour or any number of other rooms, she could cry or rage or stamp her feet and no one would even notice.

Sophie knew there was no point in arguing about her sister Emma's impending wedding to Count Siegfried von Bernthal, but she couldn't help herself. She felt compelled to talk about her misgivings about the transaction. Because that is what it was, at least in her eyes.

Her sister was a mere pawn in a men's game, fully supported by her stepmother who saw her own ambitions finally fulfilled. Sophie was afraid that no matter what she said, her father would not change his mind about the wedding. She decided to leave her work behind and take a ride to clear her head. To get some distance between herself and the house she hadn't called a home for years.

Limping her way out of the house using her favourite cane, she made her way to the stables. Before she was halfway there, Sophie's stepbrother caught up with her.

"Sophie, wait! Please!"

Anton was hot on her heels, his shock of dark hair in wild disarray from the breeze. Sophie couldn't help but smirk at him. Her stepmother hadn't been able to cause a rift between her and Anton although she had tried her best. Their bond couldn't have been stronger if they had had the same parents. She considered him her brother.

"I am sorry, Anton," Sophie said. "Tonight, I will speak to father, I promise."

"But it will not change a thing, will it?" Anton said angrily, his hands balled into tight fists at his side. Sophie opened her mouth to disagree with her brother's assessment, but she found no words because everything she could say would be a lie and they knew it. She hung her head in shame and frustration. This was 1903, a new century, for goodness' sake; things such as this should not happen anymore. But Sophie knew the sense of progress to be an illusion. Despite all the political activism, women were still treated like property.

She was stirred from her thoughts by a hand grasping one of her own.

"I didn't mean to hurt you, Sophie." Anton tried to comfort her by saying, "It's not your fault."

"Still, I . . ." Sophie felt tears of anger and frustration prick her eyes. She feared her quest to free her sister from an abominable future was a lost cause after all. Her father had made a decision a long time ago; Emma's engagement to the count had been a grand affair last year. Nothing could prevent it. So why did she think she could stop the wedding now?

And it wasn't as if her sister was happy that she was trying to prevent her wedding, on the contrary. Emma was miffed that Sophie kept on agitating against her fiancé, who was only a year younger than their father.

Anton let go of her hand. She knew he had to get ready for university and must return to the house, but as he left, he cast a last glance at her. He was hoping as much as she was that she would find a way to call off Emma's farce.

Sophie felt even worse now that her brother obviously trusted her to find a way out of this, but she was failing. Pleading with her father was the only resource she could come up with as a possible solution.

The stable hand brought Sophie's horse, and though she was capable of managing her way onto Capri's back by herself, she allowed the lad to help her mount. Capri's dark brown coat shone in the sun. Her black mane and tail were just as perfectly groomed as her coat. Her gentle nature and sometimes naughty streak were her most endearing traits. But right now, neither Capri nor Sophie could wait to stretch their legs.

Sophie took the reins and left the yard at a leisurely pace. They continued their slow pace until she spotted the first trees of the Prater, the largest park in Vienna, and she finally let go, racing over the meadows, enjoying the fast and reckless ride.

She knew she should be more careful but what was the worst that could happen? Nothing much after all. Since she had already experienced a quite horrible riding accident when she was fourteen years old, there was nothing she was afraid of anymore when on the back of a horse. If anything, ever since that time, she felt free and strong astride Capri, quite the opposite of how she felt when standing on her own two feet.

After her forceful ride, Sophie let her horse amble at a more sombre pace to cool down. When she reached her favourite spot, she climbed down to let Capri graze. Sophie took hold of her silver-handled cane to walk to the fallen tree where she sat down and took out a silver cigarette holder from her vest pocket. She put one of her favourite cigarettes between her lips and lit it with a match. Sophie took a deep breath from the cigarette before she ruefully shook her head at this bad habit. This very unwomanly behaviour would shock her stepmother into apoplexy if she were to see her smoking. But the truth was, Sophie had never been very decorous, not the way women as her stepmother expected her to be.

She preferred men's attire and reform clothes, and she abhorred those silly novels Helen used to read and all the more those completely useless conversations Helen had with her friends. Sophie shuddered at the thought of these shallow, superficial, uninspired society women whose only care was to marry off their daughters as well as possible and to gossip about those who were the same as Sophie, who were supposedly not that "fortunate."

At the age of thirty-two she was too old to be married off profitably, and she clearly wasn't viewed as desirable with the awful limp and a scar running from the middle of her forehead around her eye, across her cheek and ending near the corner of her mouth. Sophie used to curse her fate for the accident that caused the injuries, but at such times she was glad to have dodged the prison called marriage.

Even if her shortcomings weren't that obvious, the accident had caused her to be infertile which was reason enough for any eligible bachelor to shy away from marrying her. Not that she had ever been attracted to the opposite sex anyway. Sophie had long ago realised that her heart beat exclusively for the fairer sex. Women were so much more intriguing, sensual, beautiful, and desirable.

She took the last drag from her cigarette before stubbing it out in a small travelling ashtray she always carried with her. She whistled and Capri came trotting towards her. Sophie climbed on the mare's back and guided her back the way they had come. A lot of work waited for her at home.

Dinner was comfortable because Sophie knew there was no point in bringing up the marriage topic and aggravating her stepmother. She would speak with her father afterwards.

Later she followed him into his study. He offered her a glass of sherry which Sophie graciously accepted. As he poured, her father gestured at one of the chairs in front of the hearth for her to take a seat, then joined her with glasses of sherry for both of them. After he had handed Sophie her drink, the count took a seat and waited for his daughter to begin their dreaded conversation.

"I suppose you know what this is all about, Father—"

"I might."

"Please, Father, tell me there is a way you might reconsider this whole wedding."

"I am afraid there is nothing to be done. The terms of your sister's marriage to Count von Bernthal have been agreed upon. Your step-mother has already sent out all the invitations."

"But that's the point, Father," Sophie insisted passionately. "No contract has been signed, no vow has been spoken. You could still put a hold to this business."

The count drained his glass in one gulp, his expression became dark. He got up and poured himself another drink, something stronger than the first one which he also swallowed in one swig.

"Emma is a girl of seventeen years who still has so much to see, learn, and experience. Don't do that to her! The Count is fifty years old. He was already married twice and is in dire need of an heir, which I suppose is the only reason for wanting to marry her. And you know as well as I do what happened to Josefine."

Her father rounded his desk and put his glass down with a loud thump. He glared at his daughter with a furious gaze. Never in her life had Sophie seen her father so agitated.

"Listen to me and listen carefully, Sophie! This is the last time we will speak about this matter. Your sister will marry Count von Bernthal as it has been agreed, period. Do I make myself clear?" When there was no answer from his daughter, the count shouted, "Do you understand?"

"Yes, Father. Perfectly." Sophie set her glass on the side-table and without another word, she left her father's study.

Sophie returned to her rooms, where she retreated to her study. With a soft grunt, she sat behind her desk. Since she was the sole occupant of the whole fourth floor of the palais and members of the family seldom came here, she was fairly certain nobody would disturb her for the rest of the evening. For comfort, she had opened the first two buttons of her shirt and put on her reading glasses when a soft knock came at the door to the study.

"Come in!"

Her elderly maid opened the door and curtsied. In a quiet voice, Martha asked "Is there something you need, Countess?"

"No, thank you, Martha. You can go to bed. Good night."

"Don't stay up too late now." She sounded worried.

"I won't, I promise."

When the door closed behind Martha, Sophie thought about the role her faithful servant had played in the family's life. Sophie's mother, the young Karoline von Wilczek, had married Count von Hagendorf, and Martha had been at her side at Sophie's birth and afterwards.

But then a placental abruption while pregnant with Sophie's brother caused Karoline's death at the age of twenty-five. The family doctor had waved off the early signs as a type of common bleeding, and his advice had been to lie down and stop being hysterical. But the bleeding didn't stop, and when he finally returned in haste, it was too late. He could do nothing more than sign the death certificate for mother and son.

Losing her beloved mother had been horrible for seven-year-old Sophie, but under Martha's loving care, she eventually came to terms with it, though nightmares of her mother standing bleeding in the middle of the drawing room troubled Sophie for years. If Sophie woke up crying in the night after such a dream, Martha would spend as much time as was needed to calm her down until she could fall asleep again.

Ever since Sophie's riding accident and her unhappy love affair with Elisabeth von Meiningen, Sophie knew Martha often worried about her and missed the light-heartedness that used to surround them. She thought Martha was probably still worried about her, even though Sophie was a full-grown woman.

She sighed and leaned down to concentrate on the manuscript in front of her. The silence was short-lived because soon after Martha's departure, the door to her study flew open. A seething Emma stomped towards Sophie's desk, demanding her sister's attention with a furious demeanour and commanding tone.

"Who made you my guardian? I can't remember asking you to interfere with my wedding to Count von Bernthal. Who gave you the right to ask Papa to cancel it?"

"I thought—" Sophie wanted to explain her actions to her sister but was cut off.

"You thought what, Sophie? That you were doing me a favour? It might come as a surprise to you, but you weren't. Has it ever occurred to you that I might be fond of my fiancé and not view it as an ordeal to become his wife?"

"What would you know about being married to the man?" Sophie asked.

"Just as much as you, I suppose. Nothing." Emma's voice was full of venom. "I have no intention of spending my life knitting or with embroidery and gossiping about other people's lives. Or do you expect me to become one of those unnatural women like you?"

"What do you mean?" Sophie asked, her voice hoarse with emotion.

"You and Elisabeth, of course."

Sophie stood, grasping her cane like a vise as she went to the table with the cognac tumbler. Sophie carefully leaned the cane against the table and poured herself a healthy glass which she emptied in one gulp.

"I knew all along what was going on between the two of you," Emma said. "I'm not stupid. But Elisabeth preferred the safety of marriage to spending the rest of her life as your companion. She was right. Whatever it was you two did, it wasn't right, and she realised it before it was too late and she, too, was ruined."

Sophie advanced towards her sister, staring at her as if seeing Emma for the first time. Never in her wildest dreams had she thought her sister would despise her. Ever since Emma and Anton were born, Sophie had been the proud older sister, loving both of them.

Coming to a stop in front of her sister, she said, "Do you really hate me that much, Emma?"

"I don't hate you," Emma said with a frown. "I simply don't understand you. You behave and dress against every convention. People let you get away with it because they pity you for your mishap. I don't care if you ruin your life as long as it doesn't interfere with mine. Any scandal you cause could reflect badly on me, so please keep out of my life as much as possible."

"Does it not bother you that your fiancé saw it appropriate to rape and abuse one of our maids while celebrating your engagement?" Sophie played her last trump card only to be laughed in the face by her sister.

"Oh, please," Emma sniffed haughtily. "That little slut. You know full well how these people are."

"No, I don't. Enlighten me, please."

"If anyone should know, Sophie, it's you. After all, *you're* the one who spends two evenings a week in working-class homes teaching them proper German. What such behaviour leads to, you have seen in the last year. They forget their station, have trysts with the footmen or stable hands, and when they are caught in the act, they make up ridiculous stories about the higher classes in hopes of making money."

Sophie couldn't believe her ears. This young woman in front of her looked like her sister, she sounded like her sister, but the words coming out of her mouth transformed her into a complete stranger. Was this the person she had spent half her life with? What had happened to the Emma she knew? When had she become the self-righteous, bigoted, and arrogant woman in front of her?

Sophie said, "The fact that it was me who saw him leave the premises afterwards does not in the least bother you?"

"Why should it? It does not prove anything. Neither do the wild accusations of a mere parlour maid."

"I see." Head spinning, Sophie moved back to her desk and slumped in her chair with her cane nearby. "I will honour your wishes of course. Now would you please leave me alone. I simply must finish this before tomorrow."

Emma merely nodded and turned on her heel, storming out of the room without so much as a good night. After her sister's departure Sophie tried to go back to work but so much was tumbling through her head that she finally took off her glasses and threw them on the papers. She rubbed her tired eyes, still shaking in frustration and anger from Emma's words. Sophie hadn't known her sister held so much disdain for her nor had she known Emma was aware of the real nature of her relationship with Elisabeth.

Despite Elisabeth's promises and spoken words of love in the heat of the moment, she had made it perfectly clear in the end that nothing would ever come of their love. Whereas Sophie had loved Elisabeth deeply and without restraint, Elisabeth had regarded their love affair as nothing but a convenient dalliance before a "real" relationship developed with some future husband.

After Elisabeth broke her heart so carelessly, Sophie vowed to herself that no woman would ever come so near to touching her heart at all. So far, she had kept this promise to herself.

Emma did not have to worry about any repercussions of a possible societal misconduct by her. The matter of their former maid, who had been ravished was, on the other hand, far more serious, and the disregard with which Emma had spoken about the incident worried Sophie more than she was ready to admit to anyone else.

Josefine had been thirteen when she came to work for the count and his family which was not unusual at all. She was from the country, same as most of the servants in Vienna, and like most of the women and girls who were sent to the capital city, she could barely write or read. She was a pretty girl, though, with good manners and a sunny nature.

The previous year, during the celebration of Emma's engagement to Count von Bernthal, Josefine, then fifteen and well-schooled as a maid, was ordered to serve during the festivities. That was when the count's interest in the young girl had peaked.

Sophie remembered the sheer expression of fear and terror in the face of the young girl when she stumbled into her arms in the courtyard. Josefine's uniform was torn, hair in wild disarray, nose bleeding, and her lip split from a vicious slap. Sophie saw the count exiting the stable with a malicious grin on his face.

After much coercing, Josefine told her what had happened, and Sophie still could not forgive herself for urging her to tell everything to her father and stepmother, hoping they would take action on her behalf. Actions they did take, oh yes.

On the very same day Josefine finally found the courage to tell the count and his wife what happened, they threw her out without references and kept her last wages. If Sophie hadn't been to Salzburg for her cousin's birthday, she would have prevented the sacking and Josefine's fate. But as luck would have it, she had only been able to right one wrong for the girl. Like many other female servants, without work in a household Josefine couldn't go back home. Her parents wouldn't have believed her claims, just as the count and his wife did not. So, she did the only thing left to do; she resorted to prostitution to earn her living.

A short time later, Sophie ran into Josefine after one of her lectures at the homes for the factory workers. She had decided to stroll and get a breath of fresh air before she fetched a carriage to take her back home. She was dressed in her usual masculine-looking attire, and a young prostitute approached and offered her services.

Sophie recognised Josefine and bought her a decent meal in one of the coffeehouses nearby. Feeling responsible for what had happened to the former maid, Sophie made arrangements for Josefine to get a ticket for the next train to Salzburg where she found a place in her aunt's household.

She smarted from the unfairness Josefine had encountered and still didn't believe she had done enough for the girl. And she didn't believe she could ever forgive her stepmother.

Chapter Five

The end of April was drawing near as well as the preparations for the journey to Austria, which had been holding the Duchess of Darnsworth's entire household in a frenzy for nearly a month. On one of the more hectic days, the last few before they set off for Austria, the Viscountess of Langdon found it prudent to visit her daughter before she travelled to Scotland. The family was having tea in the drawing room when Benson announced the viscountess.

She entered with her usual air of arrogance and haughtiness. "Good afternoon." She sat down with a ruffle of her skirts.

"Mother, to what circumstances do we owe your unexpected visit?" Eleanor asked stiffly, without being too unfriendly.

"I merely came to bid my goodbyes before I leave." Eleanor's mother sniffed. "I wasn't aware that this would inconvenience you so much."

"It does not." Henry tried to sooth her ruffled feathers. "We're leaving for the continent next Saturday. So, you might forward our letters to Vienna over the summer."

"Vienna?" The viscountess was astonished. "What in God's name are you going to do there?"

"My cousin Helen invited us to her daughter's wedding. We turned down the invitation to her engagement last year, but we're looking forward to attending the wedding."

"How extraordinary common, to get married so soon," the viscountess observed with an indignant tone. "Is there a reason for this haste? She is not by any means, you know—"

"Not that we are aware of, Mother," Eleanor pressed through tight lips. "Neither is it any of our business."

"How can you say that?" Her mother bristled. "It could reflect badly on the family if we were brought into connection with such a thing."

"Do not worry, Mother! You won't even be there. Nobody will think any less of you."

"This cousin of yours, dear Henry, the mother of the bride, she doesn't happen to be the sister of Martin's late mother by any chance?"

"Indeed, she is," Lord Edgewood said, surprised at the careful wording of the question.

"Hmm. That explains a lot. This woman has always been more than suspicious to me. It seems this trait runs in the family."

Eleanor was having enough; she was furious at her mother's implications and derogation of a woman who no longer could defend herself and had never been anything but gracious to the viscountess who never held anything but contempt for her. "Cathleen, her name was Cathleen, mother. All she ever did was treat you with the utmost respect and warmth, even when you were barely civil to her."

"You always had a soft spot for her, Eleanor. You went so far as to let her son call you Mama. It is completely inappropriate, my dear."

Eleanor swallowed her angry retort. To insult her mother and be uncivilized wouldn't be right, but the time had definitely arrived to put a few things straight. The room was eerily quiet. Everybody seemed to have stopped breathing. Eleanor didn't need to glance at her son to know how hurt he was. Martin was as dear to her heart as the children she had given birth to, so yes, she was proud to be called mama by this wonderful young man.

"Dear, would you like us to leave?" Henry asked tentatively.

"No. Please stay, all of you." Eleanor gazed imploringly at each member of her family. "Maybe now is the time to speak a few truths."

"Mama, you don't have to do that." Martin stepped to her side and took one of her hands in his own, giving it a gentle squeeze. Eleanor smiled at the fine young man who was trying to spare her the humiliation of her own mother's scorn and hatred. She cupped his smooth cheek with her other hand and gazed deeply into his green eyes, so very similar to Cathleen's.

"But I do, darling," Eleanor said softly. "It's about time to finally voice the truth."

"This is ridiculous." The viscountess rose from her chair and snatched up the cane she didn't need but believed was a necessary accessory for a woman her age. Slowly, she headed towards the door. "I said what I came here for. It's time for me to leave. I will see you in September."

"Is that what you have come for, mother? To insult my family and to leave before I say out loud what you've always known?"

"I have no idea what you are talking about."

Eleanor let go of Martin and asked him to sit down again.

"You know quite well what I am talking about. Cathleen was my life, and I know full well how relieved you were when she died. She was the love of my life, Mother. That was who and what she was, not 'that woman.' Don't look so shocked! You knew about us. You knew she wasn't a mere companion or friend. We were lovers, in the truest sense of the word."

Disgust in her expression, the viscountess whispered, "Don't say that."

"Why not? Would it be any less real if I didn't?" Eleanor wiped away an errant tear.

"You sound as if you are *proud*. It is an abomination, a vile thing, unnatural and sick."

"I do not expect you to understand. But let me remind you that your own mother, my grandmother, also spent her life with a female lover."

"That Italian scoundrel? It was her fault my mother had such unnatural leanings. I should have known she wouldn't shy away from corrupting you, too. She seduced my mother into this disgusting behaviour and obviously you as well."

"She loves you like a daughter." Eleanor voice was a plea for understanding. "The same way I love Martin like my son."

"No," the viscountess raised her voice, causing everybody to display surprise at the outburst. "She was the reason why my father left us."

"The reason grandfather wasn't there was because he had no self-esteem. Grandmother owned the title and the money. That was why he married her that is why people of our class always marry. His proliferations were cheap whiskey, cards, and women."

"You do not know what you are talking about!"

"On the contrary, Mother. I know *exactly* what I'm talking about." With passion, Eleanor said, "I was there, remember? When he was old and in need of care, he came back to Grandmother asking for help. She gave it without complaint. Grandmother cared for him until he died, and they had somehow reached an understanding, just as he had with Giulia."

The viscountess stood stock still, leaning heavily on her cane. Face flushed, she was clearly furious, outraged at her daughter for saying such things. "It still doesn't make your unnatural behaviour any more moral or rightful, does it?"

"And who are you to judge me?" Eleanor couldn't resist, for her mother always thought she had the right to claim the moral high ground.

"Your mother. It is my right to ascertain that you as my daughter and duchess of the Empire refrain from immoral and scandalous behaviour. It is my duty as your mother that you behave fitting to your social standing as a noble and a woman."

Eleanor rolled her eyes at her attempt at righteous consternation over her daughter's supposed immorality and deviant life when in reality much more could be said about regarding her mother's poor standing as a "noble" and as a "woman.". But certain things were better kept buried for her own, as well as her family's, peace of mind.

"All right, Mother. Whatever you say. We both know you never cared about me or my wellbeing as much as you cared about your reputation. Let us leave it at that."

The viscountess stepped towards the door. She paused for a brief moment with her hand on the doorknob but didn't look back

"I wish you well, Mother."

And then she was gone, leaving Eleanor and her family with raised brows. As usual, her mother had swept out leaving nothing but silence and an empty doorway.

In the quiet of her room, Eleanor stood at the window observing the nannies taking a walk with young children. Another group of women were talking and laughing as they climbed out of a carriage and made their way to the entrance for the house next door.

She had finally told her mother the shocking truth about her relationship with Cathleen, and nothing earthshattering had ensued. Her mother's disgust and self-righteous indignation was nothing she hadn't expected. Now what little relationship they'd had was forever destroyed because Eleanor suspected her mother would not grace her home with her presence in the near future. Or the far future.

The viscountess had never set a foot in her mother's house after she left it, not even for her mother's funeral. Her actions had caused quite a stir, if not a scandal. When the daughter of the duchess refused to attend her mother's funeral, everybody thought it was because she had been passed over from inheriting title and wealth. Eleanor knew the real reason, though, was because of the contessa. Her mother hated Giulia with a passion that was quite remarkable, even for the viscountess.

From her window she noticed her mother exit the house and climb into her carriage. A sigh of relief escaped her lips.

She closed her eyes and took the pendant on her necklace between her fingers, caressing it gently. The locket contained a picture of Cathleen, and the chain held the ring her lover had given her so many years ago. She hadn't been able to take it off and had come to rely on it as a source of strength.

Eleanor moved away from the window to lie on the bed for a nap. The whole unpleasant discussion had exhausted her; she wanted to preserve her energy for their journey, which would be tiresome enough. As always, her last thought was of Cathleen . . . before she fell into a dreamless sleep.

In the drawing room, the family was still contemplating what had just taken place. The confrontation was a lot to take in and think about. Each and every one of them knew only a matter of time would pass before something like that would happen. They had been surprised that their wife, mother, and friend was so outspoken.

Up until now, Eleanor had always refrained from confronting her mother. But ever since she decided to accept the invitation to Vienna, something had changed. She was returning to her former formidable self.

That sudden revelation brought a smile to Henry's face. It would indeed be wonderful to see his wife "alive" again, especially when meeting his cousin Helen who had always been so very different from Cathleen.

"Why are you smiling, Papa?" Philip asked, astounded.

"I feel so good to see your mother again becoming the woman she used to be."

"But what about Grandmother?"

"Your grandmother will do nothing to destroy her own reputation; therefore, she will merely punish us with disregard."

"I had no idea she hated Mummy so much." Martin's soft voice was sad and broken.

Henry put his hand on his son's shoulder, forcing him to face him, "It is the other way around, son. She never truly loved anyone."

"Father is right, Martin," Charlotte chimed in. She took her brother's hands and pulled him from the sofa, "Grandmother is the most unsatisfied woman on earth. She could never look past her own needs. She is unhappy and judgemental."

"Right," Henry agreed. "Now let's get back to the tasks ahead. We have to make sure everything is ready before Saturday. Your nonna asked me to help her with the rest of her preparations. So, will you please excuse me? I will be back for dinner. And don't tell your mother! It's still a surprise!"

Chapter Six

After the argument with her sister, Sophie made it a point to avoid family gatherings as much as possible. She had to take her meals with the family, but otherwise kept mostly to herself, which was absolutely fine with her.

Never in her wildest dreams would she have thought her little sister would become so similar to her idiotic mother. Emma's words had hurt Sophie deeply, for she cared and loved her brother and sister very much. Up until now, they had been very close. More than once during her childhood, Sophie took the brunt of her stepmother's mood or her father's anger when Emma or Anton had been guilty of the pranks or misbehaviour.

Sophie could not understand why Emma was no longer mortified to be marrying a man only a year younger than their father. She had thought her sister was repulsed by his supposed charm and smarmy manners. So, what had changed? When had Emma changed her mind so radically? But this wasn't the only inconsistency in her sister's behaviour. Emma had never spoken ill of either the servants or the working classes in general. She had always expressed admiration that Sophie took seriously her responsibility as a member of the upper class.

Sophie was completely lost in thought when a knock on the door stirred her from her musings and her brother's head poked around the door.

"If it is a bad time, I could come back later." Anton grinned boyishly at her frowning face.

"No. It's quite all right. Come in."

Sophie pushed away from her desk and joined Anton on the sofa, rubbing her tired face with both hands and dreading the conversation she knew was about to take place.

"Do me a favour, brother, say what you have to say and then leave because I have to finish my work and hand it in tomorrow."

"All right." Anton looked slightly put off at the tone in Sophie's voice. She knew she'd spoken with a harshness he wasn't accustomed to.

"What happened between you and Emma? And don't try denying it because I'm not completely obtuse."

"I wasn't going to, I assure you."

Sophie hoisted herself to her feet and leaned heavily on her cane.

The damp weather of the last few days was bad for her hip. Constant dull throbbing in her right leg combined with the fallout with her sister was wearing her down. These were the moments when she questioned the decision to stay in her father's house. He *had* granted her the floor of rooms for her own use, but sometimes the arrangement grated upon her. It wasn't as if she had to stay, but she wanted to for Anton's and Emma's sake. Now she wondered if remaining had been the right thing after all.

Inheriting her mother's wealth had provided her with enough money to find her own comfortable home. Maybe she should think about it again. As she hobbled to the hearth to stir the fire and put on more logs, she realised that the time was right to think about the future, her future. Right now, though, she had her brother to deal with. She stood in front of a fire that warmed her aching bones and gazed apologetically at Anton. He hadn't done anything wrong and didn't deserve her bad mood or grumpiness.

"I'm sorry, Anton. It's just that I'm stuck with the manuscript, and the argument with Emma keeps me occupied as well."

"No harm done. What happened between the two of you? Emma wouldn't tell so I thought I might ask you. I know father won't relent, but what did Emma and you fight about?"

Sophie exhaled heavily. Anton meant well. He had always been the mediator who wanted everybody to be happy and content. She was proud of the young man he had become. He was compassionate, caring, sensitive, and intelligent, everything a decent woman could wish for. Sophie really hoped he would find a woman who would appreciate a man such as her brother.

"It seems that Emma had a change of heart regarding the count," Sophie explained as she took her vacated seat again. "She was terribly upset about my interference to spare her from this marriage. Not that father would listen to any argument anyway."

"How amazing," Anton said. "I had no idea."

"Nothing I could say would change her mind. She's very intent on following through and told me in no uncertain terms that she doesn't want to end up as an old maid or worse: a woman like me."

"What?"

"Also, it seems she knew about Elisabeth, and she thinks that sort of relationship is wrong."

"Elisabeth was the wrong woman all right," Anton said thoughtfully without malice. His voice held a sorrow Sophie knew was heartfelt.

"I had no idea she knew what was going on."

"Which wasn't much actually, as you have been very careful."

"Alas, not careful enough to prevent her from coming to the right conclusions."

"Unfortunately, yes."

Sophie shook her head at the memory of the woman who broke her heart a few years earlier. She had believed with great fervour that Elisabeth von Meiningen was the one for her.

She couldn't have been more wrong.

Sophie had always been guarded, carefully keeping her feelings of affection for any other woman close to her heart, but with Elisabeth she had lost all common sense. She was the daughter of one of her father's business associates from Prague. Elisabeth was not only beautiful but sophisticated and funny, well read, and a pleasant conversationalist. She knew a lot about ancient history and was very interested in Sophie's work for libraries and museums as a translator of ancient manuscripts.

Elisabeth was also a forceful woman who took what she wanted when she wanted it, then let it go when she was done. She was a year Sophie's senior, a blonde beauty whose charm wrapped every man—and more than a few women—around her little finger.

Sophie spent a lot of time with her, talking, taking walks or riding. Before she knew it, Sophie was very much in love with Elisabeth, and it seemed mutual. This romantic notion was violently crushed the last time they were together. Thinking about it still brought a stab of pain, though fortunately with only a fraction of its former intensity.

As her brother sat quietly, gazing out the window, Sophie recalled rust-coloured leaves being blown from trees outside a cosy room in the beautiful villa Sophie's father owned on the outskirts of Vienna, near Schönbrunn Palace. The villa was already closed for winter, so it was the perfect retreat for her and Elisabeth to meet unobserved and without fear of being caught.

The fire in the hearth cast the room in dancing shadows and provided comfortable warmth to ward off the autumn chill creeping into the unoccupied house. Elisabeth was naked under the sheets, her body warm where it fit snugly against Sophie's longer lanky frame. Sophie was still dressed in her trousers and shirt, the same way she usually was.

Never once had Elisabeth indicated any interest in reciprocating the pleasure Sophie so abundantly gave. It was all right, though. Sophie was hesitant to show her scars to anybody, even her lover. Making love to Elisabeth was enough for her. She felt no need to embarrass Elisabeth or feel embarrassed herself. Sometimes though she wished Elisabeth would make love to her as well. She longed for the feel of her lover's touch but had accepted that her body was less desirable and she had to be content to give as much pleasure as she could.

Sophie played with a strand of Elisabeth hair while she pondered their future. "Do you think it will always be like this?" she asked Elisabeth who was basking in the bliss of afterglow.

"Why do you ask?"

"I don't know. Just stupid thoughts." Sophie fell silent again. She had so much she wanted to say, so much she wanted to share with her lover. But this could wait; they had all the time in the world.

"I love you." Sophie had meant to say it a long time ago because she had felt it in her heart for a long time. "Come and live with me!"

"What are you talking about?" Elisabeth asked uncomprehendingly. She propped herself up on a mountain of pillows and pulled the sheets over her bare breasts.

Sophie sat up now as well, brushing a lock behind one of her lover's ears. She thought Elisabeth looked more beautiful than ever, her hair mussed and in wild disarray from the lovemaking, her lips swollen from their passionate kisses, her gaze a bit confused from Sophie's proposition.

"I'm talking about us spending our life together, Sophie explained enthusiastically. "Living together, being together, loving each other." She moved to close the distance between them and kiss Elisabeth's lush lips, but she was stopped by a hand on her chest.

"What do you mean? I'm not sure I grasp what you're implying. Like one of those sad women who couldn't find a husband? Or worse, those lesbians?"

"But we *are* lesbians." Sophie drew back in astonishment, while Elisabeth got out of the bed and started to get dressed.

"I'm certainly not a lesbian." Elisabeth's angry voice was unnaturally loud in the quiet house. "Just because I spend so much time with you and have slept with you doesn't make me one of them."

"Then what does it make you? Merely a woman who enjoys sexual intercourse with another woman to ward off her boredom?" Sophie got out of bed, feeling the floor freezing cold against her bare feet.

Leaning forward, Elisabeth pulled on a stocking. "It is quite acceptable to have a romantic friendship such as ours; it doesn't mean I am one of those inverts."

Sophie stumbled back against the bed at the scathing words. So, it was all right to sleep with another woman as long as you ended up married one day, but it was a completely different matter to be true to yourself? Elisabeth had always enjoyed their lovemaking! How could the thought of spending her life with Sophie and being regarded as a lesbian be so unthinkable?

"I thought you loved me," Sophie whispered brokenly, afraid of the answer.

"I do love you. You are my friend, but this is it. Nothing more, nothing less."

"And you let me make love to you because?"

"Because it was safe. I needed it and it was safe."

"I see." Sophie barely held her tears in check as she watched Elisabeth put on the jacket of her riding dress. She was ready to leave. When Sophie gave no sign of joining her, Elisabeth took her hat and gloves and left without a backward glance.

And that was that. All the woman left behind was a terrible pain in Sophie's chest that faded to an ache she could still feel.

"Elisabeth never loved me," Sophie said matter-of-factly. "She took what she could get and left."

Anton turned from the window. "I am sorry."

"Don't be. She was not at all who I thought she was. Strangely enough, I don't really know how I feel about her anymore. It's been so long. Since my argument with Emma, I've thought a lot about what happened between us. I was such a fool back then."

"Why is it foolish to love somebody?"

"Because it only leads to heartache and pain. And my own stupidity." He shook his head. "I don't believe you, but if you say so."

Anton couldn't stand how she criticized herself when the subject of Elisabeth arose. His sister's sarcasm and pessimism reared its ugly head when she spoke of that viper. But there was no point in arguing with her when she was in such a mood.

Ever since Elisabeth von Meiningen had hurt Sophie so deeply, Anton had observed how Sophie felt all the more like an outcast. Self-pity didn't suit her, but the other woman had left a broken shell who thought herself unworthy of love and undesirable. Sophie tended to make more of her scars and bodily limitations than necessary. Elisabeth had done a good job robbing his sister's self-esteem where romance was concerned; and he felt furious at times. After Elisabeth, at least two women he knew of would have gladly become Sophie's constant companion, but she rudely brushed off every attempt anyone made to get close to her.

His sister wasn't the ugly cripple she saw when she examined herself in the mirror. The scar on the right side of her face was large but could easily be concealed, and her limp was only pronounced when she was excessively tired. Yes, she needed her cane, but she could also walk without it if necessary. About the rest of the scars on her abdomen and leg, he couldn't say anything, but he suspected they weren't as bad as she thought them to be.

He saw the determined setting of her jaw and knew it was time to change the subject. "Sophie, have you ever thought of leaving Austria behind and living somewhere else entirely?"

"Where?"

"Oh, I don't know. How about London for instance?" he suggested with a shrug. "You have the means to do so, and you know as well as I do the British Museum would be delighted to have your expertise closer at hand."

"Yes, well," Sophie grumbled as she rubbed her chin thoughtfully. "I have to admit that's an intriguing idea but leaving Vienna for good is easier said than done."

"No, no, no," Anton broke through her musings. He put a hand on her shoulder. "Don't even think of complications and don't stay out of a sense of duty. You have no obligation to stay if you don't want to."

"But—"

"No. It's high time you live your life as you please. You're not responsible for us and you never have been. I'll always be grateful for everything you've done, but now put yourself first for a change."

Sophie peered at her brother in astonishment, and he stifled a laugh. He could tell his passionate speech made him dearer to her than ever before, and he felt their strong connection as well.

"I will consider that, Anton. I promise, but only if you promise that you will speak to father about what you want from *your* life."

"I promise."

They hugged. Sophie sniffed into Anton's neck which only caused him to tighten the embrace.

"I'm glad at least you are on side, brother."

Before it became too embarrassing to either of them, he let go and leaned back into the sofa, grinning as she heaved a sigh at the same time. He asked, "Do you think mother's relatives will be as boring and tiresome as all of her friends and acquaintances?"

"I do hope not." Sophie snorted as she stretched out her feet, linked her hands behind her head, and stared at the ceiling of her study. "I don't think anybody could be more uptight and fuller of themselves than the people she usually invites to dinner or a reception."

Anton laughed ruefully, remembering all those endless social gatherings his mother loved so much. Her social circle consisted of the most uneducated and pompous people one could find in Vienna. They had a title, money, and belonged to the upper class, but the endless inane chatter they loved so much caused him regular headaches.

"I'm looking forward to meeting cousin Martin though," he said. "I wonder what kind of person he is. All of them actually."

"We'll have to wait and see, won't we?"

Chapter Seven

The Duchess of Darnsworth entered Palais Schelling feeling appreciation as she took in her surroundings. Jonathan had chosen well in purchasing it, not that she had expected anything less. The palais was truly befitting her status and the requirements of her family. Not only was the palais in the city, it also had a garden with wonderful old trees providing enough shade to enjoy the afternoon tea or read and seize the day for a change.

"Perfect accommodations, Jonathan. You have outdone yourself."

He smiled at her and headed for the library.

Baron von Schelling had only recently refurbished the whole palais and it had cost him a fortune. Unfortunately, equipping the building with all the amenities one could think of and his love for costly soirees had left the baron nearly broke. He had to let his palais go at great savings to the buyer, much to the duchess' delight.

Now the family would enjoy every comfort they were accustomed to at their home in London. Jonathan had made sure the grand house had everything they needed, from bathrooms with flush toilets, running hot and warm water, a shower, electricity, and central heating.

Henry, behind his wife, said, "This is lovely, absolutely the best. I am well pleased."

The Contessa Silvestri slowly followed on her grandson Philip's arm. Charlotte and Martin had already climbed the stairs to claim their respective rooms. The servants were busy with their luggage, and the flurry of action all around raised Eleanor's spirits. Perhaps coming to stay here would not be so bad after all.

Benson, who had arrived three days earlier to prepare everything for their arrival, greeted them with glasses of champagne.

"Your Grace," the butler nodded gravely, "I hope you'll find everything to your satisfaction."

"Thank you, Benson." Eleanor took a glass from the silver tray. "I am sure you have thought of everything."

With a slight nod at the trust the duchess set in him, the butler continued offering the champagne.

Eleanor whirled around and regarded her grandmother, "What do you think, Nonna?"

The contessa let go of Philip's arm and sauntered over to Eleanor. She patted her arm gently while she answered with a twinkle in her dark eyes. "I think we will have a wonderful time here."

Saturday and Sunday were most hectic for the servants. Although a few of them had taken care of the necessities beforehand, there was still much to do. The grandeur of the palais allowed for Eleanor and Henry to occupy their own wings, which left their children and the contessa to reside in the central part of the building with their rooms on the first and second floor. The library was quite extensive and very comfortable and soon became one of the duchess's favourite places in the palais.

The stables at the rear of the estate housed wonderful riding horses, much to everybody's delight. On Sunday after breakfast, the duchess and her children were the first to go for their first ride in the Prater. As soon as they finished their breakfast, Eleanor and the children took off without warning to the stable hands, who had their hands full getting the horses ready for them.

A very satisfied Henry watched their happy progress from the drawing room.

Giulia entered the room with her needlework in hand. "This journey was a wonderful idea, my dear Henry."

"I really hope so."

"When was the last time Eleanor joined the children for a ride?"

Henry frowned. "I cannot recall. It has been quite a while." He took a newspaper from the table and joined the contessa on the sofa.

"She seems more alive, more content lately, almost as if she's starting to enjoy life again."

"You are probably right."

They beamed at each other.

Giulia said, "She means a great deal to me, so I hope she's beginning to make a comeback."

"Yes. Yes, that is my hope as well.

Charlotte guided her horse so that she was trotting next to her mother, followed by Philip and Martin as they made their way through the streets to the Prater. Every now and then, she cast an unobtrusive glance at her mother, wondering what had brought on her spontaneous decision to accompany them today. She took in her mother's rosy cheeks, the small smile playing around her lips, and the spark in her sky-blue eyes when she returned the gaze.

"What is going on in that pretty head of yours, my darling?" Eleanor asked, startling her daughter from her thoughts.

"Sorry, Mama." Charlotte blushed becomingly. "I didn't mean to be rude. It's so unusual for you to accompany us. You haven't for a long time."

"I know. I have preferred to be on my own lately. But I've always enjoyed sharing this activity with you. For the past few years, I didn't feel like sharing. I am truly sorry if you felt left out. I never meant to hurt you."

"We know, Mama," Charlotte assured her, looking over her shoulder at her mock quarrelling brothers. Philip saw her glance and urged his horse forward to trot alongside his mother's.

"Are you up for a little challenge, Mama?"

"What do you have in mind, young man?"

Charlotte was pleasantly surprised that her mother was indeed in a spirited mood this morning. Clearly, so was Phillip.

"How about a race amongst the four of us?" Philip suggested.

Charlotte was well aware of how competitive Philip was. He would never suggest such a thing to any other woman, but knowing his mother's and his sister's skills, he knew they'd be up to the challenge.

She saw her mother roll her eyes at her son. When would he ever learn? Philip had never beaten their mother in a race, but she presumed it was the youth's prerogative to give it a try whenever possible. Someday he might be the best horseman in the family, or probably not, because unfortunately he had to take his sister into consideration. Philip was a good rider, as was Martin, but none of them would ever best her. She took very much after their mother in that respect, one of the many traits Charlotte had inherited from her.

"Why not," Eleanor agreed, squinting. "What do you propose?"

"We ride down the main avenue to the Lusthaus. Whoever reaches it first is the winner?"

"And what will the winner get, dear brother of mine?" Charlotte chimed in, already calculating her chances.

"A new pair of riding boots from Vienna's finest shoemaker," Philip boldly pronounced. "Bought by whomever comes in last."

Charlotte knew her allowance, corresponding to her siblings' allotment, would cover such expenses, so it wasn't a far-fetched treat for any of them to provide.

"Spoken like a true lord, my son," Eleanor remarked with excitement. "I look forward to the comfort of new riding boots."

As soon as they reached the outskirts of the Prater, they agreed they would need a starter to keep their race fair and square. Martin spotted a couple taking a leisurely stroll along the main avenue and stopped to ask if the lady would do them the favour of being their starter.

Gently encouraged by the gentleman in her presence, the woman agreed, and Martin joined the others in the middle of the avenue.

The spring weather was warm, but due to a storm the day before which had wreaked havoc all over the city, only a few people were around and the usual carriages on the road were missing. Branches of the chestnut trees lining the avenue were strewn all over the street which made it impossible for carriages to pass but made the conditions for their race more exhilarating.

The riders got ready, their horses prancing and flaring their nostrils in anticipation of the excitement their humans were not so subtly communicating. The woman on the side raised her arm clutching a white handkerchief tightly in her hand. She waved it down suddenly and made a slight hop in the air. The four horses rushed off down the avenue leaving behind a cloud of dust.

Philip took over the lead at once, closely followed by his siblings and his mother. He flew over the fallen branches feeling safe in that he had such a good start. The others were hot on his heels, but when he took a peek over his shoulder, he saw Martin already falling behind. Another few jumps, navigating the last finishing lane, and he would be the first at the Lusthaus, which he could already see in the distance.

Just when he thought victory was safe in his hands, out of the corner of his eye, he saw the white coat of his mother's horse as it passed and jumped over the last branch way ahead of him. Somewhere along the race she must have lost her hat because her white hair was flowing as she raced her horse towards the goal.

He was so surprised by her speed he didn't even notice Charlotte streaking by.

Again, he had been beaten by his mother, not unlike so many times before. He had truly believed that finally, this time, he would prevail. But this was a loss he suffered gladly because for the first time in ages, it felt like old times when his mother was a happy, carefree woman.

Eleanor kept her panting horse moving in front of the Lusthaus. As she cantered, waiting for her children to join her, she smelled the wonderful scent of baking. The Lusthaus was heralded as not only a wonderful restaurant, but also as one of the finest patisseries in Austria. She made a mental note to remind Henry and Jonathan to arrange reservations to dine there soon.

As she predicted, Charlotte had bested her brother again in the end, and Philip and Martin were the last ones to join them. Together they took a moderate pace around the building to give their horses time to cool down after the strenuous race.

Philip knew how to be a good loser and a gentleman. He steered his horse next to his mother's and bowed to her from the saddle. "Congratulations on your victory, Mama," Philip said with grace. "It was well deserved."

"Thank you, darling." She made her own half-bow from her seat.

"When do you want me to call for the shoemaker's visit at the Palais?"

"Wednesday would be fine, I suppose," Eleanor said with a wink, "and make sure your brother and your sister are there as well. I think new pairs of riding boots for all of us are in order."

Philip gave her a stunned look. "Thank you, Mama. Do you mean to say you're sparing me from paying my bet and buying boots for all of us?"

"Yes, and you are welcome. Now, why don't the three of you go on your own way while I take a romp around the Prater. And when your ride is over, you may ride home and ask Mrs. Chambers for a cool glass of lemonade."

"Are you sure?"

Philip sounded so anxious that she laughed. "I know you don't want to leave your mother unguarded, but trust me, I will not be easy to catch."

"This is a foreign city after all, Mama."

"Thank you for your concern., but I'll be fine." Eleanor said goodbye to her children before she took off over a meadow.

The Prater was a wonderful green oasis on the outskirts of a buzzing city, and the whole area was much larger than Eleanor had originally thought. To see something on a map was one thing, but to experience it on your own was completely different. She enjoyed the greenery as much as the solitude when she guided her horse off the trodden paths every now and again.

The sun was very warm on her neck, which was quite a surprise after the thunderstorm the evening before. Eleanor's black riding dress had become overly warm, so she searched for a shady place to rest for a little while. She spotted a clearing ahead where a fallen tree made for a perfect bench and where she could let her horse graze.

Eleanor dismounted and bound the bridle on a branch of the fallen tree before she took off her riding gloves and smoothed her windswept hair. She had lost her hat during the little competition, but it was too late to do anything about it now. Surely it had fallen into one of the many mud puddles on the avenue. She would have to get a new one, a good excuse to visit one of the milliners in the city.

Eleanor was enjoying the quiet and the gentle breeze when she heard the distinct sound of hoofbeats. She shaded her eyes against the sun and spotted a rider on a brown horse coming her way. So much for the quiet and solitude, she thought ruefully.

In the distance she made out a man, who purposefully guided his horse towards her spot. He wore black trousers, a white shirt with sleeves rolled up to his elbows, a brown vest, black gloves, and bowler hat.

Resigned to having company, Eleanor got up and strode out into the sun.

The rider lifted his head and saw Eleanor standing in the sunlight. At the same time, his horse shied and threw him off its back.

Shocked at what just happened, Eleanor's hands flew to her mouth to cover her cry of surprise before she got hold of herself and shifted in to action. The nervous horse was coming her way. With the authority of an experienced horsewoman, she stepped into its way to keep it from racing off.

Raising her arms and using a calming voice made the frightened horse slow down and stop completely right in front of her. Eleanor took the reins and patted the horse's neck to calm it down further before she turned it around to take it back to its fallen rider.

As she strode toward him, she scrutinized the saddle and spotted something strange protruding on the front. She didn't have time to examine it because the fallen figure showed no signs of getting up. Worried that the man was badly hurt, with hasty steps she raced over and when she neared the spot, she heard moans of pain. Eleanor drew a relieved breath, glad that the man wasn't unconscious.

She reached the person on the ground only to stop dead in her tracks. The figure on the ground was no man at all. The rider's hat was lost, and a mass of dark brown hair had fallen around the woman's shoulders. Eleanor could only stand and stare because from the distance she would have sworn a man was coming her way when it really was a woman in men's clothes.

A woman, she now realised, with curves in all the right places, full lips, and a face contorted in pain, but a woman, nonetheless.

After another unpleasant Saturday that Sophie was forced to spend in the company of her stepmother who constantly gushed over the coming wedding and visit of her cousin and his family, Sophie decided to wait until everybody was off to church before she went down for breakfast after which she would leave the house for a solitary ride. She enjoyed the quiet at the breakfast table and when she was finished, she went to her room to dress carefully in her favourite riding clothes before quietly leaving through the back door.

Peter, one of the stable hands, hurried to get Capri ready. Sophie waited patiently until Peter brought the snickering mare outside. She greeted her friend with a special treat, an apple. Capri munched happily on the apple while Sophie stowed away her cane in the leather holding on the front of the saddle before she mounted the mare. Peter helped her put her right foot into the stirrup, while Sophie took the reins and patted Capri's neck affectionately.

"Thank you, Peter." Sophie smiled at the young stable hand, tugging the reins to leave.

"You are welcome." He lifted his cap and watched her ride out away.

Sophie took her usual route to the Prater but chose a different path that wouldn't lead her through the main alley. She was not in the mood for going around all those fallen branches which she was certain would be there after yesterday's thunderstorm. Today it would take her longer to reach her favourite spot, but she didn't care at all. There were not too many people around, so she took it easy which gave her enough time to think about her life and what she should do with it.

She always found it easier to think when she was outdoors, taking a ride on Capri. Away from the constant nagging of her stepmother and the worries for her siblings. Maybe Anton was right, maybe she should leave. Get away from Vienna and the obligations she had heaped upon herself. Her siblings had never asked her to stand up for them and fight what was their fight, but she had felt compelled to do so. She was their older sister, who else would do it?

Her father would never stand up to his second wife, so it was up to her. But her brother had a point; she could take the offer from the British Museum. Her mother's inheritance provided her with enough money to live quite comfortably in a city such as London and pursue her scholarly interests to her heart's content. Maybe she should give it a thought, but right now, she wanted to let Capri graze and to enjoy the tranquillity of her favourite place.

When they reached the vast expanse of meadow, Sophie let her mare race across the damp grass towards their clearing, both of them enjoying the freedom of the moment. Once they reached the top of the slope and neared the trees, Sophie saw another horse at her favourite place. So much for quiet and solitude! She could always ride by without taking a break but why should she give up her private place of contemplation to some stranger?

A woman stepped out of the foliage, into the sun. Capri was as much surprised as Sophie and shied away, then reared back and threw her off.

Sophie landed hard on the ground. Fortunately, she'd managed to roll to her left, and her right side didn't take much of the impact. The ground was still soft from the rain but when she shifted onto her back, she felt a stab of pain in her hip. Contorting her face in pain, she closed her eyes at the sudden agony. When she opened her eyes again, the woman from the clearing stood over her, Capri's reins in hand, staring with shocked eyes.

Sophie groaned at her luck.

The woman had halted Capri's escape, which was indeed lucky, because Sophie had no idea how she would get home. But at the same time, she felt absolutely humiliated in front of this complete stranger. Just what she needed, and what felt even worse was the woman was studying her with eyes full of concern and compassion but also a good amount of surprise. She must have mistaken her for a man, Sophie mused. No wonder. From the distance, and in her men's clothes with her long hair confined under her hat, she surely must have appeared to be a man.

While the woman was still staring, Sophie had the chance to get a closer look at her. Her hair was snow-white, short, with a stubborn lock falling over her right eye. Although the colour of her hair would indicate a certain age, she wasn't very old. Her skin was pale and smooth; she had a long patrician nose, small lips, and eyes the colour of a warm summer sky.

Eleanor realised she'd been frozen in place and took a deep breath.

"When you're done gawking at me," the woman snapped, "could you hand me my cane from the saddle so I can get up?"

The harsh tone combined with the feminine voice jerked the duchess from her reverie. Without thinking she took a step towards the fallen woman and was about to grab her arm to help her up, but had her hand swatted away.

Seething, the woman on the ground said, "Don't touch me, just hand me my cane!"

Eleanor swallowed a retort and removed the item which had puzzled her when she'd first seen it. So it was a cane. She gave it to the rude woman who used it to struggle to her feet. The duchess knew better than to offer an unappreciated hand again. Instead, she retrieved a bowler hat from the ground and held it out.

The woman snatched it out from her hand without so much as a thank you.

"You are welcome," Eleanor said sarcastically.

"I don't need your pity."

"I do not pity you! I merely wanted to be helpful."

"Stop being helpful!" she shot back. She stepped around the woman, took hold of Capri's reins, and put her foot into the stirrup to manoeuvre herself into the saddle. "Just what I need," she muttered. "Must be my bad luck day. Foreigners who think nothing of imposing."

"I did no such thing!" Eleanor's anger sparked. She put her hands to her hips and glared at the woman on the horse.

"Then why are you here?" she asked as she gestured at the clearing.

"This place belongs to the emperor, as far as I know, and he graciously allows it for public use. It is not *your* private property, so there is no need to be rude and impolite."

"If you say so." The rider swung her horse around and sped off, splashing Eleanor from head to toe in mud.

Eleanor stood fuming, covered in mud and dirty water. She stared daggers at the stranger's retreating back. Her hand shook with fury when she brushed a wet lock from her face. She turned on her heel and stomped back to her own horse. With an exhale of indignation, she climbed into the saddle and steered for home.

When Capri pounded off through every single slushy spot, splattering mud every which way, Sophie cringed but rode on instead of going back to apologise. How could she, after she had been so rude to this woman who had been nothing but nice and helpful? She doubted, though, that the elegant woman would believe her if she told her she hadn't spattered her on purpose. Only when Capri stepped into the mud did she realise what would happen, but by then it was too late.

If this was how her day would proceed, Sophie decided, she would stay indoors for the rest of it.

Eleanor returned to the palais on her white horse. She didn't wait for the stable hand to take hold of the reins when she dismounted and stormed inside. The duchess slammed the door shut angrily and called out for Benson, her blood boiling.

"Benson!" she shouted again.

The man came running from the library followed by his lordship and the contessa, all of them wondering what had caused such an outburst. Eleanor ripped off her gloves, threw them to the floor, and glared.

Benson gulped visibly at the furious expression in his mistress' eyes. "Your Grace?" Benson mumbled awkwardly. Never in his entire time as her servant had he seen the duchess so enraged.

"Tell Rose to run me a bath!" Eleanor demanded through clenched teeth. She was ordinarily very much inclined to keep her anger in check, but today was an exception. "Burn these soiled gloves and do the same with this dress and everything else as soon as Rose has helped me take it off."

"Yes, your Grace." Benson rushed off to do as he was told, all the while wondering what in God's name had happened to the duchess. A riding accident, obviously that much was clear, but by the fury she displayed, there had to be more to it.

"Eleanor, for goodness' sake, what is going on?" Henry asked from behind his wife.

The contessa, at Henry's side, frowned at her granddaughter's rigid back then gasped audibly when Eleanor swivelled around to face them.

"Good Lord!" Giulia covered her mouth with a delicate hand. "What happened to you?"

Eleanor pursed her lips and cocked her head before taking a deep breath and explaining what had caused the complete ruin of her dress, hair, and overall appearance. Again, she put her hands to her hips when she answered, feeling with every word how the anger and righteous fury returned. "I happened to run into the most obnoxious, rude, arrogant, unfriendly and awful woman I have ever had the misfortune to encounter."

"But what on earth did you do to her?" Henry asked, shocked.

"All I did was stop her stupid horse which had thrown her off. I was at the wrong time and the wrong place. In short, my only crime was being polite to this absolutely thick-headed, bratty, foul-mouthed wench."

Her grandmother was hard pressed to suppress her smirk at the long string of insults coming from Eleanor's mouth. "Why don't you go back to your newspaper, Henry? We have everything here in hand," the contessa said to the flabbergasted lord.

With her own clean hand, she led her filthy granddaughter upstairs to her rooms, all the while soothing the still-fuming woman.

With a shake of his head, Henry watched the women ascend the stairs, glad that Giulia was there to take care of this catastrophe.

Rose waited anxiously in the bathroom for her mistress. She was wondering about the state and the mood the duchess was in. Benson had been shaking when he came to the kitchen to tell her to get to her grace's rooms and fill the tub immediately.

When she heard the soothing voice of the Contessa Silvestri talking softly to her mistress, Rose exhaled in relief.

The maid's mouth fell open when the two women entered the bathroom. The duchess was dirty and wet, her riding dress was ruined, and her usually shining white hair was caked with brown mud. Rose rushed to her side to help take off the soiled clothes while the contessa sat on a chair next to the washbasin.

"Rose, make sure Benson burns them for good," the duchess said much more calmly than mere moments before.

The maid curtsied dutifully while she helped to peel off the under-garments and put them on the pile. Before she left, Rose put a bar of shampoo in the shower and a scented bar of the duchess' favourite soap on a stool next to the tub. She'd already laid out fresh, fluffy towels on a bench.

Eleanor switched on the shower and stepped under the hot spray. She moaned in appreciation as the water loosened her muscles and washed off the dirt clotting in her hair. She carefully washed her filthy hair down to the scalp, and when she was finished, she turned off the water, slung a towel around her head, and walked over to the steaming tub.

The contessa watched as her granddaughter immersed herself in the soapy foam with a blissful smile. She took her chair nearer to the tub and silently regarded the bathing woman.

Never before had she seen Eleanor like this. When faced with incivility, the duchess never lost her imperious countenance but today she had been furious. This chance meeting had unsettled her in a way Giulia thought most strange. It certainly piqued her curiosity.

"Now, my dear, tell me about this unpleasant encounter," the contessa prodded gently.

Eleanor felt content and lazy, lying in the warm, wonderfully scented water, glad to finally leave that horrible experience behind. "Is that really necessary, Nonna?"

"Not necessary, but it is rather curious, don't you think?"

"Yes and no," Eleanor said with closed eyes. She had been angry about being covered in dirt like a common tramp, but what had irritated her much more was the stranger's way of brushing off her help. Eleanor was neither blind nor stupid. She knew and understood the other woman's embarrassment, but there was no need to treat her in such a way.

"What do you mean by yes and no?"

Eleanor heaved a sigh before she opened her eyes and sat up straighter. She took up a bar of lavender soap and lathered a washcloth with it, ordering her thoughts before she answered. "When this *person*," she said with a touch of contempt in her voice, "came riding my way, I thought it was a man."

"How so?" The contessa leaned in, obviously even more intrigued.

"Because she was wearing men's clothes and her long hair was stuffed under a hat." Eleanor ran the washcloth over her arms and upper body. "She seemed quite a capable rider when suddenly the horse reared up and threw her off its back."

"Goodness!"

"Indeed." She started to wash her legs with the lavender soap. "I stopped the wayward horse and offered my help. This was when I realised the rider was a woman. She seemed to be in pain, but when I tried to offer a hand, she pushed it away and demanded her cane."

Eleanor still fumed at the rudeness. Was it too much to ask for a little bit of politeness?

"From there it got worse. She accused me of imposing myself on her place, which by the way isn't anybody's place at all. No thank you given, just accusations, rudeness, and to top it off, when she rode off, she covered me in mud."

"Maybe she was embarrassed," Giulia offered as an explanation.

"Yes, I have thought that, too. But this is no reason to act so completely obnoxious and awful, is it?"

Eleanor climbed out of the tub, gratefully accepting the large fluffy towel her grandmother handed her.

"I can't say, my dear, why people act the way they do. Often we lash out because we feel vulnerable and don't want to get hurt. Sometimes we do it out of habit, protecting ourselves the only way we know."

"But I didn't know her. I was a complete stranger to her." She headed into her dressing room. She let the towel which she had slung around her body fall to the floor and put on undergarments and a comfortable reform dress Rose had laid out for her. "Most curious, really."

"Besides the way she dressed, was there anything else you noticed about her?" The contessa followed Eleanor into her dressing room and sat in front of the vanity.

"Such as?" Eleanor asked, surprised as she slipped into a pair of flat shoes.

"Well," the contessa chuckled lightly, "was she middle-aged or young? What colour was her hair and her eyes? Was she pretty or plain?"

Eleanor opened her mouth to answer, but when nothing came out, she closed it again. Now that she thought about it, the woman was indeed rather pretty. If she was completely honest with herself, she had to admit that was the second most important thing she had become aware of after the realization that the rider was a woman.

"Yes," Eleanor slowly answered with a frown. She sat on the bench next to her grandmother. "Yes, she was quite pretty actually."

She was still lost in her thoughts as she removed the towel from her head, gave her hair another rub and brushed it out.

"And?" Giulia prodded patiently.

"Well—" Eleanor wrinkled her forehead as another detail sprang to mind.

"What?"

Eleanor looked at her grandmother with wide, sorrowful eyes. She touched the tips of her fingers against her forehead, only half an inch above the middle of her right brow. She let them glide across her temple, cheekbone and across her right cheek to the corner of her mouth. Stopping there she whispered in surprise, "A scar. An angry red scar on the right side of her face. I remember it now. It ran from the middle of her brow to the right corner of her mouth. Strange. It was quite prominent, but I only remembered it just now. Why do you think that is?"

"Who knows? You were probably so angry about her behaviour that you forgot about it until now."

She patted Eleanor's hand reassuringly as she got up to leave her to her thoughts. She had her own ideas why her granddaughter wouldn't have remembered such a thing but kept them to herself. She smiled to herself on her way to her own rooms where she planned to write some letters to friends in London. The contessa was quite certain that Eleanor was slowly reawakening again to the beauty around her. If the encounter this morning was any indication, then she wasn't immune to female beauty any longer either.

Sophie was still fighting against angry tears of humiliation mixed with tears of pain from her fall as she dismounted Capri and limped through the backdoor up to her room. When she closed the door firmly behind her, she leaned heavily against it, taking the weight from her bad leg. She was catching her breath but could no longer stop her tears from falling and neither did she try. The morning couldn't have been more horrible. All she had wanted was time alone to think, and it had instead become a nightmare.

First Capri threw her, and then she had acted like a complete and utter moron. Still weeping, Sophie pushed away from the door to march into her bedroom. She took off her boots and her clothes, leaving them in a heap on the ground for her maid to clean before she stood naked in front of her body-length mirror to examine the bruises that were already forming on her back and left side of her body. Before evening, she would need to take an opium pill against the pain, hoping it wouldn't be too bad. Sophie hated the pills. They made her feel strange, and she was afraid to rely too much on them.

She padded into the bathroom, turned on the shower, and waited for the spray to heat up before she stepped under it. Ever since she had heard of this new bathing invention, she'd pushed to have it installed in her bathroom and today she was grateful for it.

She no longer needed anybody's help in the morning or at any other time when she wanted to get cleaned up. Taking a shower was refreshing and invigorating. Sophie sometimes missed taking a bath but to get in and out of it on her own was too much of a plight.

Sophie resolved not to think of the events of the day. She could not change what had happened, and she would weep no more.

The scent of her citrus soap filled the room and after washing her hair, she stepped out and wrapped herself in a large, soft towel. She dried her hair with another cloth before returning to her bedroom to put on clothes again. Her hair was still slightly damp, but the air was warm enough to let dry on its own.

The last paragraph of the text she had to translate for her mentor, Professor Maierhofer, was waiting in her study, and Sophie found it prudent to finish it so she could hand in her translation by the end of the week. She put on her reading glasses and set to work with determination, but the events of this morning came back, distracting her, and making it impossible for her to concentrate.

Sophie took off her glasses and flung them on her desk with a moan. She was truly disgusted at herself for lashing out at somebody who had tried to help and be friendly. All she had done was be rude, awful and pathetic. The English woman not only stopped Capri from running off, she had also offered a helping hand and she brushed her off so brusquely that she was ashamed. Sophie's only excuse was her feelings of humiliation and embarrassment, but that didn't excuse her harsh words and rude behaviour. What she had been thinking, she couldn't fathom.

What had she become that she couldn't accept an act of kindness? The woman had been a very beautiful stranger, Sophie mused. She had been captivating, even alluring, and that realisation had made Sophie lash out because she didn't want the woman's pity. Her feelings of inadequacy and ugliness had been overwhelming in the presence of such a beautiful woman. Sophie wished she could apologise for what she had said or done. But there was no point in crying over spilt milk. All she could do was go on and improve.

What she would give for another chance to explain, but she knew she should not waste her time on the impossible. So, she picked up her glasses again and continued with her work.

Chapter Eight

The week after the unfortunate incident was filled with a lot of activity and Eleanor had successfully pushed the event to the farthest corner of her mind. Being fit for new riding boots for herself and her children, visits to Vienna's milliners, and the impending visit to Henry's cousin on Thursday let the week pass in a whirlwind.

On Thursday, Eleanor dressed very carefully for the first meeting she and Henry were to have with Cathleen's sister. On the one hand, she was looking forward to this, but at the same time, she felt apprehensive, afraid to be disappointed if Helen was the opposite of Cathleen.

In the carriage on their way to the palais, Eleanor worried for the umpteenth time if Helen would be anything like her sister. She knew Helen and Cathleen had never been close, and Helen wasn't keen to visit nor did Cathleen care to travel abroad, preferring instead to spend time on the continent with Eleanor. How could they be much alike at all?

Their ride was a short one, and when their carriage arrived, the count and the countess welcomed them at the door. Henry and Helen kissed awkwardly on the cheek.

Time had not been kind to Helen von Hagendorf, Eleanor thought sorrowfully. Helen had to be close in age to Eleanor, yet her pinched face and already grey hair didn't flatter her appearance either. The expression she wore reminded Eleanor very much of someone who was constantly sucking on a lemon drop. It was not very becoming and lacked warmth. In contrast, the count was distinguished-looking and seemed to be of a much jollier disposition.

After many pleasantries and introductions to Emma and Anton, they all retired to the drawing room for tea, sandwiches, and the finest cakes from Demel, a superior pastry boulangerie known for creating cakes and confections for the court.

Helen obviously took her role as hostess quite seriously. Eleanor was sometimes wearied by the extent to which people went so they did not show any sign of weakness in the presence of a duchess. Eleanor received her cup of tea from a woman trying hard to please, knowing full well that Eleanor was far ahead of them on the social ladder. Eleanor chose to ignore Helen's nervous agitation.

"I can't wait to meet my nephew," Helen said as she handed Henry his cup.

"He is a remarkable and wonderful young man," Lord Edgewood said proudly. "I assure you he is quite excited to meet his mother's sister."

Helen smiled brilliantly, transforming her face into a far more pleasant expression than before. Eleanor observed her keenly, not quite certain what to make of her late lover's sister. She seemed to be a good hostess and passionate mother, but she reserved her judgement until she knew more about her.

"Did you attend your sister's wedding?" Eleanor asked.

"Unfortunately, no. Cathleen married Lord Northcott while I was away for a lengthy stay in Madeira after a serious case of influenza. When I returned, she was already married and had followed her husband to his estate. We only exchanged letters from then on.""

"Oh, how come?"

"It pains me to admit it, but when we grew older, we also grew apart. We had different interests and quite a different circle of friends. And when we both got married and I moved to Vienna it didn't help overcome our personal distance either."

"I am sorry."

The conversation flowed pleasantly until the butler entered to ask the count after someone named Sophie. He obviously caught his master by surprise, "I don't know where she is, Guttmann. Why?"

"Professor Maierhofer is on the telephone, asking for her, sir."

Anton chimed in. "Tell him she is already on her way, Guttmann."

"Very well." The butler closed the door behind him, leaving a confused couple of visitors behind.

Count von Hagendorf must have seen questions in his guests' eyes and hastened to explain. "Sophie is my daughter from my first marriage. Her mother died when Sophie was seven."

"I am sorry," Lord Edgewood said with honest regret. "I hope your daughter is well?"

"Oh, you mean because of the professor?" Helen waved off his worry. "He is from the university and fancies himself to be Sophie's mentor, encouraging her silly notions of being a scholar."

Eleanor saw Anton bristling at his mother's condescending words. She raised an eyebrow at him, wondering if he dared to contradict the countess.

"It is neither silly nor a fancy, Mother," Anton informed her with fervour. "Sophie is good at what she does."

"And what is it she does," Eleanor asked the passionate young man, "if you don't mind my asking?"

"Not at all, your Grace. My sister translates ancient texts. She knows Greek, Latin, Hebrew, and Coptic."

"That is quite remarkable," Eleanor exclaimed, truly impressed by the countess's knowledge. "Your sister seems to be a very accomplished and fascinating young woman."

"She is." No mistake, Anton was proud of his older sister. "One time she received an inquiry from the British Museum for her expertise."

"I'm truly impressed. I'm looking forward to meeting Sophie."

"Regrettably," the count said, "I am afraid my daughter will not attend the reception on Saturday."

"That's a shame." Eleanor's spirit fell. "Is she otherwise engaged?"

"No, she is somewhat of a recluse where such events are concerned."

"She has always been a bit strange," Helen said dismissively. "Ever since she's kept company with this professor, she has become even stranger. Not to speak of her ludicrous ideas about the place of women in society. Thankfully, she decided not to cause us any embarrassment and will not attend the reception in your honour."

Eleanor cast a glance at the bride to be and her mother and noted similar cat-like smiles on their faces. They appeared rather satisfied with these facts, though the duchess wondered about the phrasing. Why would Helen's stepdaughter cause them embarrassment?

The count gazed towards Eleanor. Did he notice her disapproving glance at his wife? Eleanor hastened to assume a poker face. He steered the conversation into safer waters, likely eager not to cause a misunderstanding about somebody his guests wouldn't meet. Eleanor couldn't help
but think it a shame that this Sophie had been sent away. She very much would have liked to meet her.

Sophie took the tram to the library and had just entered the professor's office when he put the telephone receiver on the cradle.

"Gracious, here you are. I was worried you were late due to the accident on the Ringstrasse with the motorcar and carriage."

"Oh, no, sir. I came by tram and didn't even know an accident had occurred."

"Yes, yes, this is good. I knew you were on your way as I rang up your house. I'm relieved to see you all in one piece."

Sophie refrained from rolling her eyes. She hoped the telephone call had not upset her father in any way. Her stepmother had been all a-dither about their guests arriving, so she had hastened to get away, at least for a while.

The professor offered her a seat and a freshly brewed cup of coffee, but Sophie declined. She handed her mentor the package containing her work and had to laugh at how eagerly he opened it to give it a once-over. To say he was pleased with the result was an understatement.

"Why, this is truly marvellous. I'm quite simply over the moon, Sophie.

"I'm glad to hear it, Professor."

Sophie received another assignment and bid him a goodbye, much to her mentor's dismay. She knew he loved to talk to her and gossip a bit because she wasn't involved in the day-to-day proceedings of the library and thus would keep his confidences. But staying was out of the question today.

Despite her protestations to the contrary, Sophie was curious about Helen's relatives, and though she felt unwelcome, she had a right to be in her own home. She hoped she wasn't too late to catch at least a glimpse of the duchess and Lord Edgewood.

The tram was delayed on her way home. As she rounded the corner of her street, she saw a carriage in front of the palais and her father and stepmother accompanying a distinguished couple outside. Sophie stopped dead in her tracks.

One of the persons exiting the palais was one she least expected.

Even from the distance, and only seeing her profile, she knew exactly who was bidding goodbye to her father and stepmother—the woman she had treated so poorly on Sunday after her fall.

The woman had looked somewhat regal, certainly composed and opinionated, but how was Sophie supposed to have known she was treating a *duchess* like a commoner, or worse?

But on the bright side, she realised, this was her chance to apologise for her awful manners. Maybe the duchess would be generous enough to forgive her atrocious behaviour.

On their way home, Henry and Eleanor were both lost in their own thoughts for some time before the duchess suddenly penetrated the quiet.

"Did you know that the count had a daughter from his first wife?"

"No, dear. I didn't have the slightest idea. Helen never mentioned her once in her letters. Which is quite astonishing, don't you think?"

"It is strange, yes." Eleanor returned to her quiet contemplation of the visit. Helen was nothing comparable to her sister, nothing at all. Where Cathleen had been warm, Helen was cool. Where her lover had been open and welcoming, her sister was distant, even snooty. Helen lacked Cathleen's charm, her easy laughter, and her gentle and loving nature. She also lacked her late sister's beauty and liveliness. Cathleen had been vibrant, beautiful, and full of life. Her flaming red hair and sparkling green eyes, her pale freckled skin and captivating smile were still very much alive in Eleanor's memory.

Helen was the complete opposite. This was a relief but also a disappointment. Perhaps it was too much to have hoped Helen would evoke a touch of her sister to assuage Eleanor's loss.

She was struck by Helen's demeanour. Her attitudes and views, especially regarding her stepdaughter, didn't sit well with Eleanor. She supposed she had to accept the woman's small-mindedness and not make a scene. Saturday was likely to prove quite interesting. She was more than intrigued now to find out what sort of people Helen and her husband would call their friends and who they had chosen as their daughter's husband.

It was plain as day that Anton did not agree with his parents' choice of his sister's husband nor did he support their characterization of the count's daughter. Maybe Anton's half-sister felt the same way he did, and that was the reason nearly everybody in the family was grateful she wouldn't attend Saturday's festivities.

Eleanor thought it was truly a shame. She hoped there would be another time when she could meet this woman who sounded so intelligent and intriguing.

Chapter Nine

For the whole of Saturday, Eleanor carefully prepared herself for the evening's event. Rose had been ordered to make sure the undergarments, stockings, dress, gloves, and shoes were inspected and laid out for her to put on after her bath. She sat in front of her vanity, still clad in her dressing gown, and applied light make up.

Rose entered the room with her gloves.

"Have you taken care of the seam?" Eleanor asked Rose's mirror image.

"Yes, your Grace."

The maid placed the gloves on the bed next to the gown, stepped behind the duchess, and took up a hairbrush to gently smooth and dress Eleanor's short hair.

Afterwards, Rose held out each piece of undergarment for the duchess to arrange herself.

When it came to tying the lighter version of a corset, she made sure Rose didn't apply too much pressure. Eleanor seldom wore any corsets these days, and when she did, she preferred the looser ones. Eleanor took a deep breath after Rose finished with the hooks and was satisfied when she didn't feel too obstructed by it.

Rose held up silk stockings, and Eleanor took seat on the bed to carefully pull each up over her legs and fasten them on her garter. Then Eleanor donned her dark blue gown with its shimmering silk body and ankle-length skirt. It showed a decent amount of cleavage, and the straps circled her upper arms leaving her shoulders bare.

"Help me with my necklace, Rose?"

The maid took the necklace with the locket and closed the clasp behind her neck. The cool locket with Cathleen's ring in it rested prominently over Eleanor's chest while a pair of pearl earrings completed her jewellery.

Finally, she slipped into elbow-length gloves, the same colour and material as her dress. Rose wrapped a light shawl around her shoulders, handed her a wrist bag, and held the door open for Eleanor.

After arriving at the villa in Hietzing, Eleanor accepted Henry's offered arm, and they ascended the steps with Philip and the contessa behind them, followed by Martin and Charlotte.

The butler announced their arrival to the gathering, causing more than one head to turn their way. Henry and Eleanor made quite an impressive couple. Not only were they all dressed according to the most recent fashion, Henry and his sons were as handsome as the women were beautiful. The duchess and her grandmother exuded an air of nobility, which you had to be born into. They radiated wealth and power.

Eleanor contemplated her daughter, the heiress of her title, and was quite satisfied to see that Charlotte had come into her own. She was as regal as her mother and always charming without being too familiar. The future Duchess of Darnsworth was every bit as awe-inspiring as the current one. Eleanor beamed proudly at her daughter, only to see a light blush steal its way to Charlotte's cheek at her mother's gaze.

Giulia joined them and patted Eleanor's hand reassuringly. "Isn't it lovely to have no worries about her, my dear? Charlotte will be fine. You have taught her well. She resembles her mother, every inch the future Duchess of the Empire."

"So long as she is not *too much* the same as her mother," Eleanor said ruefully.

"Nonsense. Look at her! Charlotte can handle herself. You can be proud of her. She is sophisticated, strong-willed, compassionate, and she knows perfectly well that with wealth comes responsibility. Charlotte is not fickle and self-absorbed like so many of her generation."

Eleanor knew her nonna was right, but there was more to a happy life than that, and they both knew it. Now was neither the time nor the place to discuss it, though.

Helen came bustling their way to introduce them to her friends and acquaintances. The "happily" betrothed couple were presented first, of course, although Eleanor wasn't quite convinced about the level of happiness by Emma's behaviour. Emma's smile seemed forced, whereas her fiancé showed every sign of being very satisfied with himself.

Count Friedrich von Bernthal was a man with greying dark blond hair, a well-trimmed beard, and a lined face showing his age. His eyes were a dark blue under bushy brows, and Eleanor didn't appreciate in the least how he leered at Charlotte when he greeted her. By the expression on her daughter's face, Charlotte was equally repulsed by the man, but tried her best not to let it show.

Eleanor wondered what had caused Count von Hagendorf to choose that man as his daughter's husband. If his behaviour was any indication of his true character, Emma was to be pitied.

Before they could exchange another word, though, the duchess was swept away by Helen to meet another important guest.

On Saturday afternoon, Sophie returned late from another meeting with Professor Maierhofer. Her attendance at the reception wasn't necessary at all, which had been made clear by her father. She could understand how he feared she would cause a scene in front of his peers, something he was very keen to avoid at all costs. So, she decided to freshen up and change into comfortable clothes before she went out to the stables to have Capri saddled for a ride to the villa in Hietzing.

When she arrived, she made sure Capri couldn't run off on her own before she entered the property through a hidden door at the back of the garden. Sidling through the bushes, Sophie heard the music swelling inside, a cheerful happy sound. A small labyrinth led to the fringe of the garden right behind the villa where a fountain in the middle of a gravel path was the last barrier that separated the garden from the terrace.

The light from the many lamps illuminated part of the terrace. She went to a stone bench and sat in the shadows, merely observing as her family, their relatives, and the guests enjoyed the music. She caught sight of her sister on the arm of her fiancé, smiling and appearing nauseatingly happy. Sophie also searched for the duchess but after a while, she concluded that she hadn't arrived yet.

With a critical eye she watched Emma's future husband as he undressed every beautiful woman in the room with his eyes. He was worse than a pig. She could not fathom why her sister would have him.

The butler announced the arrival of the Duchess of Darnsworth and her husband, Lord Henry Edgewood. She glanced at the entrance and there she was. The woman she had treated so badly swept into the room on her husband's arm, and Sophie was captivated. The duchess was breath-taking. The colour of the gown accentuated her eyes, and the white of her hair made her complexion appear ethereal in the light.

Sophie shook her head to break the spell, cursing herself for being so easily impressed. But the woman *was* beautiful; there was no other way to describe her.

She watched the whole family, and she had to admit that the duchess and her husband made quite a dashing couple. The children had inherited their parents' good looks as well as their bearing. They didn't seem insecure. On the contrary, they knew exactly who and what they were, and it showed in the way they carried themselves.

Sophie knew the duchess was not only regal but also amiable and at heart a kind person, and she hoped there would be a chance to apologise.

Eleanor felt as if she were suffocating. The hall was unnaturally hot, and the air was thick. The endless stream of mindless chatter was painfully dull. Her conversation with Count von Bernthal had been exhausting. He was the worst example of the male sex she could think of. At first glance he seemed charming, but the more Eleanor had to listen to him, the more his prejudices were confirmed. Could this get any worse? She hoped not.

When it was no longer discourteous for her to excuse herself from his company, she made sure one of Charlotte's brothers stayed at her daughter's side through the evening because she wouldn't put it past the man to try something impertinent. Now she needed to get away. Some fresh air would do her good after such an unpleasant conversation.

Without anybody noticing, she slipped through the French windows at the back of the room. Carefully, she closed the doors behind her before proceeding slowly towards the edge of the terrace and inhaling the cool air of the cloudless early summer night.

With her eyes closed and hands resting on top of a railing around the terrace, she enjoyed the light breeze that carried the scent of the cherry tree blossoms from the garden. She felt the breeze cooling her flushed face and was more than glad to have escaped the inane conversations. She descended the stairs and strolled towards the fountain, away from the chatter and the music to relaxed in the tranquillity of the garden.

A feminine voice startled her from her reverie.

"You should step out of the light if you don't want to be bothered."

With a hand over her racing heart, Eleanor pivoted towards the voice but could only make out a shadow at the end of the path, sitting on a bench in front of what seemed like a hedgerow.

"That would be pointless now, wouldn't it," she replied curtly.

"You are absolutely right, of course. I shall leave." The owner of the voice struggled to her feet and stepped into the light

"You! Of all the people in the world . . ." Eleanor felt her face flush hot with anger before she turned on her heel to storm off.

"Wait, please! Please!"

Eleanor paused. The limping miscreant who'd recently been so rude to her covered the distance between them as fast as she could. She lightly placed her hand on Eleanor's upper arm to stop her from leaving.

The warm hand upon her cool skin caused a shiver to run down her spine. Eleanor inhaled sharply at such audaciousness. She whirled around and glared silently at this presumptuous lout.

The other woman appeared to cringe under her scrutiny, but she didn't release her.

"Sophie von Hagendorf, your Grace." She let go of Eleanor's arm and stood leaning on her cane.

"Usually I would say the pleasure is all mine, but I'm not so sure about that."

"And why is that, if I may ask?"

"Oh, I don't know, perhaps because the last time we met, I was merely trying to be helpful, and you showed your gratitude by covering me in mud."

"Really? Nobody asked you to help. And by the way, was it mere politeness when you were all cosy and nice with that detestable Bernthal? If that is your understanding of nice, I can do without it, thank you very much."

Eleanor couldn't believe her ears. This was outrageous. She felt her hackles rise at these ridiculous accusations. Who did this woman think she was, speaking in such a manner? How dared she?

"Not that it is any of your business, but the count at least has a concept of the rules which apply to a gathering such as this, contrary to your behaviour. How dare you talk to me in such a manner? I am not an ordinary commoner. Good evening!"

Fuming, she gathered the skirts of her dress and stormed off in the opposite direction.

Sophie watched her leave, her eyes glued to the duchess' retreating figure, until she closed the doors behind her. She staggered back to the bench and sank down. Her intentions had started out to be honourable. All she wanted to do was apologise for her awful behaviour the other day, but somehow all she had accomplished was to aggravate the woman further.

What a brilliant outcome, she thought sarcastically.

The contessa caught a glimpse of her granddaughter as she slipped through the doors that led into the garden and frowned when she saw the thunderous look in Eleanor's eyes. She silently wondered what could have caused such a change in her mood. Excusing herself, Giulia stepped to her side and put a calming hand on her granddaughter's arm. She could feel Eleanor shake with anger, her eyes blazing and her nostrils flaring.

"Why don't we find a quiet place," Giulia suggested gently, "and you can tell me what has you so agitated?"

"I have already tried that," Eleanor stated as calmly as possible, now keeping her anger in check. "There is no such thing anywhere here."

"We'll see." Giulia put her arm under Eleanor's and guided her unobtrusively through the crowd in search of an unoccupied room in the villa. They finally found a small library at the end of the corridor. The contessa closed the door behind them and gestured at two chairs. Both took a seat, relieved at the quiet and solitude.

"Well?"

Eleanor closed her eyes in defeat, knowing her grandmother wouldn't let go before she told her about the confrontation in the garden.

"I just had a most unpleasant argument with Sophie von Hagendorf."

"How so?"

"She is the rider who covered me in dirt."

"Oh."

"Yes, indeed," Eleanor huffed in indignation. "I went outside for fresh air and more or less stumbled upon her. She accused me of the most ridiculous thing, and before I knew it, we argued, and I left her in the garden."

Giulia found that most peculiar. "Do you know why she was there?"

"I do not know, and I don't care. The woman behaved horribly! Again."

"You were not in a good mood either when you sneaked out. After your conversation with the count that was understandable."

"Which is completely beside the point."

"Then what is the point?"

"I don't know, and frankly, I don't care. She was rude and confrontational. What she said was utter nonsense, and I would prefer not to have the misfortune of ever meeting her again." Eleanor slumped back in her seat.

"All right. But can you at least tell me what has you so riled up every time the two of you meet? This is so unlike you, Eleanor."

Although she did have a suspicion, the contessa wisely kept it to herself. She was well aware her granddaughter would disagree strongly with any such opinion and discard it as foolishness.

Eleanor sighed at her nonna's question. She had wondered herself why that horrid woman was able to get a rise out of her so easily.

She had thought she could understand and forgive the Sophie von Hagendorf for her awful behaviour, but something else was causing her temper to flare.

"I don't quite understand it myself. It is just that . . . oh, I don't know. Why don't we join the others and make the best of the rest of the evening?"

"Very well, my dear."

Sophie sat on the bench berating herself for being such a complete moron, again. She had come here planning to remain anonymous, and when the duchess exited the villa, she had the best of intentions. Somehow everything turned into a disaster the moment she opened her mouth. It wasn't that she hadn't tried, but when the duchess hadn't accepted her attempt to behave decently, her own temper had flared. She could talk to scum such as Bernthal in the most pleasant manner, but she couldn't give that beautiful woman a chance?

If she was honest, though, Sophie had to admit the duchess hadn't seemed as taken with the count as she accused her to be. She could tell her smile had been fake, not that the man would have noticed.

Sophie realised that her stupid insinuations were completely unfounded, and she should never have voiced them. The duchess had wanted to get away from him and the crowd. She had been hoping for quiet and instead, Sophie had ruined it.

Well done, once again. Could she ever get it right?

Maybe she should simply swallow her pride and give it another try. What was the worst that could happen after all? Being put in her place by the woman again? Thrown out on the scruff of her neck by a footman? It was not as if she didn't deserve it.

Sophie decided it was worth the risk. Tomorrow was as good a day as any, and maybe she would be lucky and the duchess wouldn't be so angry anymore.

One could only hope.

Chapter Ten

Much to everyone's delight, the agreed-upon late breakfast the day after the reception was a pleasant occasion. The conversation was lively and made Eleanor forget her anger over her encounter with the count's oldest daughter. Her children seemed to have enjoyed themselves quite thoroughly, and so had Henry and Giulia. She had to admit that Helen had really tried, although sometimes a bit too much, but the hostess couldn't be held responsible for the inane chatter at such events. No matter what country or city, those occasions were usually filled with frivolous and often ridiculous drivel.

"What do you think of the count, Mama?"

Charlotte's question interrupted her thoughts. "Excuse me, darling. I wasn't paying attention. Which one do you mean?"

"Emma's fiancé."

"Oh. That one." She realized something in her tone made Charlotte raise her eyebrow. It sounded slightly disgusted, as if her mother spoke about an ugly toad, although her expression remained neutral.

"The man makes me feel distinctly uncomfortable. There is something about him I do not care for in the least."

"Is that why you asked Philip and Martin to stay by my side the whole time?" Charlotte asked with amusement.

"I'm sure I don't know what you're talking about." Eleanor feigned ignorance as she took another sip of her morning tea.

"Please, Mama," Charlotte said, "they told me."

Eleanor cast a disapproving glance at her sons who had the grace to look caught. She sighed, knowing how her daughter did not appreciate to be mothered.

"Yes, I did. I am your mother, and I have the right to do so, and it cannot be helped if you are not pleased by it."

"Thank you, Mama." Charlotte put her hand over her mother's on the table top.

Eleanor was surprised. This was not the reaction she had anticipated at all. She smiled gently at her daughter.

"I am glad you were so overprotective for once. The man makes my skin crawl." Charlotte shuddered. "The way he leered at me all evening was very unsettling."

"Don't worry, sister," Philip chimed in, "we would have defended your honour." He playfully puffed his chest which resulted in her throwing a napkin in his face.

"Children, please," Henry grumbled good-naturedly. "I'm sure Benson would appreciate it if you didn't cause too much chaos. Shouldn't you be on your way to get ready anyway?"

"Where are you going?" Eleanor asked, surprised. They had cancelled their Sunday ride because of the late night.

"They are accompanying Jonathan and me to the Museum of Natural History." Henry got up to follow his children to get ready for departure. Jonathan stood and proceeded out of the breakfast room.

"You are very welcome to join us, my dear." Henry kissed her cheek and did the same to the contessa.

"No, thank you, that's very thoughtful. But I think I will take a look at the letters from McIntosh. I am afraid mother is giving the poor man a hard time. Voicing her opinion at every possible chance she gets on the keeping of the castle is going to send the man up the walls. I can only hope he won't quit on me."

"I am sorry to hear that. Do not get me wrong, dear, but your mother tends to bring out the worst in everybody." Henry's words resulted in a coughing fit by the contessa who had desperately tried to suppress a laugh at the excellent characterisation of her late lover's daughter. When Henry rushed to her side to help her, she waved him off with the napkin she had used to forestall her coughs.

"Go ahead, I am fine. Don't keep them waiting." Giulia took a sip of her tea and watched him leave.

"Your husband has quite a talent for understatement, doesn't he?"

"What do you mean, Nonna?"

"Mary, I mean Mary, of course," Giulia explained in exasperation. "Your mother often leaves people with the distinct desire to strangle her."

"Yes, well." Eleanor put her napkin on the table and rose. Her grandmother had finished her breakfast, and together they left Benson and James to take care of the dishes.

With her grandmother on her arm, Eleanor slowly led them to the library. "Mother isn't a very happy or content person."

Giulia snorted at the carefully worded explanation for the viscountess' demeanour. "I would call that sugar-coating the truth."

They entered the library and Eleanor helped Giulia into a wing chair by the windows before she sat behind the small desk in the corner.

"She feels betrayed," Eleanor explained. "Ever since grandmother made her renounce her right for the title and the money, she is bitter and full of contempt."

The contessa observed Eleanor intently. "It's not your fault. And by the way, your mother was that way long before my dearest Bridget made her sign the papers of renunciation."

"Are you sure?"

"I'm positive. Trust me, *Cara*, it has nothing whatsoever to do with you, and everything to do with the choices she made."

"Such as?"

"Marrying your father for one," Giulia said without a second thought. "He was good-looking, but his temper was horrible. He loved the ladies and the cards, which in the end led to his demise as we both know quite well. More than once did your grandmother pay his gambling debts, and she was afraid he wouldn't quit before he spent your mother's inheritance. The only chance to put a stop to it and make sure you wouldn't lose everything Bridget had built was to make your mother renounce her rights."

"I know."

She also knew her mother blamed Grandmother Bridget for her husband's suicide when he realised that the last payment towards his debts would indeed be the final pay-out and that his wife had agreed to an allowance which would be given to her first by her mother, and later by her daughter, to make sure the viscountess could live comfortably.

After his death, they realised circumstances were much worse than initially thought. Only due to enormous amounts of her grandmother's money was it possible to make sure her mother didn't lose everything. Though her grandmother forked over a fortune to pay off each and every single debt her father had amassed, this hadn't kept her mother from blaming her husband's death on her own mother.

With another heavy sigh she put on her reading glasses and turned to her letters just as Giulia opened her book. They sat in companionable silence, each engrossed in her task until Benson entered the library with a silver tray in hand and a calling card on it. He gently cleared his throat to gain the duchess' attention.

"Yes?" She asked distractedly without interrupting her writing.

"You have a visitor, your Grace," Benson informed her with a slight touch of disapproval in his voice as if the unannounced intrusion would prove to be particularly odious. He offered the duchess the tray and she peered questioningly over the rim of her reading glasses, took up the calling card, read it, and felt her anger bubble up again.

"What is the matter, dear?" the contessa asked.

"This woman has the *nerve* to call on me! Unannounced and uninvited?" Eleanor fumed as she stood and handed her grandmother the card.

"Why don't you leave it to me, dear?"

When nothing was forthcoming from Eleanor, Giulia addressed Benson. "Take our guest to the drawing room and tell her to wait. I will be with her shortly."

"Your Grace?" Benson asked to make sure his mistress agreed. She was too furious to speak and merely inclined her head, giving wordless permission that he could do as the contessa asked.

"Well then." Giulia groaned as she levered herself up from her comfortable chair. "I'm intrigued to finally meet the mysterious woman who has kept you so on edge. Feel free to join us when you've calmed down considerably, my dear."

"Maybe I will. Thank you, Nonna."

"You are welcome. Let's have a look at your countess."

"She is not *my* countess." The indignant voice followed Giulia through the door. The butler moved toward the guest to escort her to the drawing room. He offered his arm and accompanied her. The whole way, Giulia twinkled mischievously at Eleanor's flustered tone.

Benson opened the drawing room door for the contessa, and she quietly thanked him. Standing just inside the door, Giulia observed the visitor who hadn't heard her enter. The woman was turned away from her, and even from the distance, she detected a visible tension in the way she stood rigidly in front of the window gazing out into the garden. Her long dark hair was flowing freely down her back, and her right hand had a vise-like grip on her cane. She was dressed in slim-fitting men's trousers and a dark frock coat. How peculiar.

"I am Contessa Silvestri. What brings you here, Countess?" Giulia smirked when her guest slightly jumped at the unexpected voice.

Sophie slowly turned around and glanced, unsure and obviously unsettled. "I'm sorry for the intrusion. I hoped I could speak to her Grace."

"And why is that?" the contessa asked, amusement colouring her voice. She stepped farther into the room to get a better look at her guest. "Haven't you already said enough to my granddaughter?"

Sophie hung her head in shame and shifted her feet at the scolding words. "I suppose so."

"You suppose so? Then why are you here?"

"To apologise," Sophie mumbled.

"Speak up, girl. I can't hear you," Giulia demanded forcefully. She was definitely enjoying this far too much.

"To apologise," Sophie repeated again, stronger and with a hint of something else in her eyes.

Defiance? the contessa wondered. She said, "Ah, now we are getting somewhere."

"Are we? I can't see how. Forgive me, but will you tell me why the person I came to apologise to is not here?"

"Good point, yet I assure you the opportunity to do so will come eventually."

At the disbelieving expression, the contessa headed to a sofa and sat. She patted the space next to her and waited for Sophie to follow her invitation before she continued speaking. "I am afraid my granddaughter is not in the right state of mind either to meet you or listen to your apology at the moment."

"I was afraid she might not be," Sophie said contritely. "I do understand." They both sat in silence for a while, each pondering how to make the best of the situation, when suddenly the door to the drawing room flew open to reveal an angry-looking duchess.

"All right," Eleanor snapped, her eyes blazing at their intruder. "Out with it! Why are you here? Let's get this new confrontation over with so I can concentrate on my letters again."

Sophie gulped and stole a glance at the contessa for help, but the older woman merely patted her hand reassuringly. Sophie stood and took a step towards the duchess but stopped dead in her tracks when Eleanor held up a hand.

"Your Grace, I'm truly sorry for my intrusion. I thought it best to come to beg forgiveness for my awful behaviour yesterday and last Sunday."

"Hmm . . ."

Eleanor studied her imperiously, and it was all Sophie could do not to turn and escape, never to show her face on the premises again.

"You actually sound sincere. Can you at least explain your moronic behaviour?"

Sophie flinched at the words and felt her fury rise again but held it in check when she saw the slight lifting of the duchess's lips. She was baiting her. She did deserve it after the way she had treated her.

"On Sunday, I was angry because you were occupying the place I go when I want to be alone. In addition, I was embarrassed after I made a complete idiot out of myself by falling off my horse. Yesterday, I was irritated that you seemed to refuse to grant me what you offered von Bernthal so freely."

"What would that be?"

"The courtesy to listen to what I had to say. I meant to offer my apology yesterday. To be honest, it was the only reason I came to the villa. I was hoping to find a chance to speak to you alone, but we both know how that ended. I am sorry. Please accept my sincerest apology for behaving akin to an utter moron."

The pleading expression in Sophie's dark brown eyes broke Eleanor's resolve to stay firm and refuse the offer. No matter how hard she tried to stay stiff-backed and severe, she couldn't deny her acceptance of such a heartfelt apology. She was becoming soft and pathetic nowadays. The duchess rolled her eyes—just a little—and said, "Oh, all right. Apology accepted."

"Thank you. This is very generous of you." Sophie was relieved and felt the visit had been the right thing to do after all.

"Yes, yes. It sickens me already, my own generosity." Eleanor's sarcasm earned her a stern glare from her grandmother. "Why don't you sit down, please."

"I don't want to impose. I merely came—"

"Sit!"

The order was spoken in a voice leaving no room for argument. Sophie dropped onto the sofa next to the contessa again while attempting to avoid seeing how her seatmate was smirking at her flustered demeanour.

The contessa leaned over and patted Sophie's knee. "Dear, I may have forgotten to mention that Eleanor can be quite commanding when she wants to. She inherited that trait from her late grandmother."

Eleanor ignored her. "I want to explain a few things. Not that it's any of your business but—

"Of course not." Sophie stopped abruptly cringing at the withering gaze she received. "Sorry?"

"As I was trying to say, though of course it's none of your business, I did *not* enjoy my little conversation with the count at all. To be honest, I do not have the slightest idea why your sister Emma is marrying him. I am well aware of what is expected from a young woman of her social position, but it doesn't mean she has to enjoy it as your sister obviously seems to be, which is a complete puzzle."

"Nor do I have the slightest clue why she's marrying him," Sophie said meekly.

The duchess saw a flicker of pain in her guest's eyes and decided that a change of subject was in order. "Enough about that then. Your brother told me you're quite accomplished as a translator of ancient manuscripts."

Sophie blushed at the praise, "I help with them every now and then, yes."

"How do you know so much about languages?"

"My late mother used to read all the ancient Greek tales to me, and she also translated them. I came to appreciate the beauty of the words. She made sure I had the best tutors to learn as much about ancient languages as possible, and it seems I had an aptitude for them."

"Impressive." Eleanor was more intrigued now than before when she'd heard about it the first time. "I understand that the museum and the library you work for upon occasion have large collections of manuscripts."

"Yes," Sophie said enthusiastically. This was a safe topic, her favourite subject. Might the duchess be somebody who could actually appreciate what she did? "Would you be interested in seeing the collections? May I be so bold to offer you a tour through the Museum of the History of Art and eventually the library?"

The duchess gazed at her grandmother for advice, but Giulia merely shrugged, offering no guidance at all.

"Why not? Perhaps we could consider it as penance," she said with a twinkle in her eye. "When would a tour be most convenient for you?"

"Tuesday. I could come by at one o'clock in the afternoon with the carriage."

"Tuesday it is."

Sophie got to her feet and with a warm goodbye she left the palais.

"That wasn't so bad now, was it?" the contessa teased after their guest closed the door to the drawing room behind her.

"I suppose not." Eleanor sniffed haughtily then held back a smile.

"Please. When you steered the conversation to her work, her whole demeanour changed. Her eyes lit up like a Christmas tree, and when you agreed to take her up on her offer to play your guide, her smile was blinding."

"She seems very passionate about her work."

"Makes me wonder if this is the only thing she can be passionate about," Giulia pondered thoughtfully.

"What do you mean?"

"Don't be obtuse. You know full well what I mean, my dear. She is one of us."

"So?"

The contessa shook her head in exasperation. Obtuse was indeed the correct word she realised, quite fitting to describe Eleanor at times.

Flustered, Eleanor asked, "Are you suggesting what I think you're suggesting?"

"No, dear, I merely made an observation." Her grandmother rolled her eyes and returned to her book, leaving a stunned duchess behind.

Chapter Eleven

Until Tuesday, Eleanor had given some thought to her grandmother's observation regarding the countess, not that she would ever admit it. Giulia's suggestion did have merit. Sophie von Hagendorf was unlike anybody else Eleanor had ever met. She was a contradiction. Up front, brash, but at the same time, soft and vulnerable. Her intellect was as intriguing as her occupation was fascinating.

With great anticipation, Eleanor looked forward to their museum visit because she was convinced that Sophie would go out of her way to be the perfect guide. She wondered what lay underneath the many layers of Sophie's personality. She would see and maybe they could at least develop a friendship of some sort. Sophie would be so much more interesting than all the other women she had met since Cathleen's death.

Exactly at one o'clock, Benson announced the arrival of a guest. Giulia had agreed to welcome the countess and keep her company until Eleanor was ready.

"Contessa Silvestri asked me to show you to the drawing room until her Grace is ready," Benson informed her and led her to the indicated room. He opened the door for her with a haughty expression on his face, "Countess von Hagendorf, madam."

Giulia approached and greeted Sophie warmly. "Welcome, my dear."

"Good afternoon."

"Eleanor will be here shortly."

Sophie seemed nervous in the presence of the contessa. Giulia sensed her unease but would have none of it, so she simply took Sophie's arm and led her to the sofa where they sat down.

"Why don't you tell me what you have planned for this tour?" she inquired politely, trying to put her guest at ease.

"Since I know the museum quite well," Sophie said, "I thought I would let her Grace decide what she wishes to see." She frowned. "My expertise lies with the Greek and Roman collections, of course, but there are many interesting pieces of art there."

Giulia would have loved to ask about the countess' past, but the door opened, and Eleanor joined them.

Sophie rose when the duchess entered the drawing room. She was rendered tongue-tied and breathless. In a light summer dress of pale blue with a closed umbrella in gloved hands, Eleanor looked magnificent. She wore a dainty matching bonnet, and her short hair was swept back in waves.

"I'm so sorry you had to wait, but I couldn't find my gloves."

"That's quite all right," Sophie choked out, finding it hard to breath. She wanted to be alone with this woman, to know her, to be close to her. She was mesmerised, with impossible thoughts running through her head. The most prominent one was that she should leave right this instant because try as she might, she could think of no way her feelings could lead anywhere at all.

She could come up with an excuse for why she had to go, and it might spare her a lot of heartache in the long run. The duchess was probably only being polite anyway and possessed no more than a general interest in Sophie's knowledge for the Museum visit. How could there be anything more to it? And what was the point then?

At least that was what Sophie tried to tell herself, but she could not force herself to make an excuse. It was all she could do not to go insane. Yes, the other day they had found common ground. She felt the duchess respected her now, but what more could she hope for? Friendship? Who was she fooling but herself? Friendship was the best she could hope for and be willing to accept because Sophie was convinced Eleanor could never be more than that. The woman was married, with children, and obligations to see to. She had a lot to lose and probably was not so inclined anyway.

Somebody in the position of the duchess would never allow herself to be associated with a woman such as herself in any other capacity than a friend or companion or minor acquaintance of the platonic sort.

What was she thinking? She hadn't been thinking at all, that was the point. The other day, Sophie had blurted out the invitation without a second thought. Now she had to follow through with it.

"Shall we?" The duchess's voice broke through her thoughts.

"Yes, of course."

Eleanor kissed her grandmother goodbye and followed Sophie to the waiting carriage.

Eleanor opened her umbrella to keep the sun from burning her pale skin. Sophie had decided to take the open carriage so they could enjoy the gentle breeze and the warmth of the sun. Although it was frowned upon if a woman of a certain class wore a tan, she had to admit that it suited her companion, and Eleanor highly doubted Sophie would care what others thought of her when she obviously had no regard for their opinion about her attire.

The driver turned onto Ringstrasse, letting the horses trot at a leisurely pace along the grand boulevard.

Eleanor broke the companionable silence. "I know little about this area of the city. What are all these buildings? When we arrived, I didn't pay much attention because I was rather exhausted from our journey, and the few times I've taken this route in a carriage, I have to admit I didn't give it much thought either. This, I'm afraid, must sound very ignorant."

"Not at all," Sophie assured. "These buildings are fairly modern and hold no historical significance at all. After the Emperor demolished the city walls in the 1850s, the Ringstrasse and its most important buildings were planned and built in its place. The bourgeoisie, like my father, also built their homes along both sides of the boulevard. This new class of factory owners, bankers and patrons of the arts own the many palais, and only a few noble families included."

Eleanor nodded thoughtfully.

"We're just passing the new university." Sophie pointed out a building to their right. "Over the last century the city has been steadily growing, and with the ever-increasing population, the capital was still confined within its medieval walls. To maintain this structure was no longer feasible. So, it was decided to get rid of the walls—or the 'Bastien' as they were called in German—to build this boulevard and connect the oldest part of the city with the suburbs."

"What is that building?" Eleanor asked, as they passed a park in front of what seemed like a gothic cathedral with its tower and arches.

"The town hall." Sophie drew her attention to a building on the opposite side of their carriage. "That is the new court theatre. Can you see the three figures on the top of the entrance?"

"Yes, I do."

"The one in the middle is Apollo, and on his left and right are two of the Muses, Thalia and Melpomene."

"And what does the frieze underneath depict?"

"That would be Bacchus and Ariadne."

They left the town hall and court theatre behind and passed another building Eleanor had found most peculiar ever since the first time she had come across it.

"This one resembles a Greek temple; at least the centre part of it reminds one of the Parthenon in Athens."

"Yes, quite so. It is the seat of the Imperial Council or Parliament, the legislature of the Austrian part of the Empire."

"Who does the statue behind the fountain represent?"

"Athena, the Goddess of Wisdom."

"Is there a reason why she has her back to the building?" Eleanor asked with a mischievous glance at her companion.

"I have asked myself that same question ever since the statue was put up."

"I can't imagine why."

Sophie chuckled at the dry comment. "What do you think so far?"

"It is the most unorthodox mixture of architecture."

"True."

They arrived at their destination, and Sophie helped Eleanor out of the carriage. She dismissed the driver to return to the palais. The countess offered her arm, and the duchess took it with a hint of a smile. She should have known Sophie would be the perfect gentlewoman.

In the middle of the square between two identical buildings was the monument of the current Emperor's most famous ancestor.

"Maria Theresia." Sophie explained at the questioning look.

"Ah! Your highly regarded former monarch. I recall that somebody said she actually never was an empress, is that right?"

"Quite right. I'm surprised that you know that. It's one of the greatest misconceptions."

"And why is that?"

"Maybe because it is a little complicated. She was a queen and an archduchess but never an empress. As long as the Holy Roman Empire existed, there was no such thing as an Austrian Empire. Her husband and her son afterward were the elected emperors of the Holy Roman Empire, but she wasn't. Nevertheless, she reigned wisely over Austria—and every other part of her inheritance—with the help of her advisers. Quite a few significant changes were made, much to the great advantage of the Empire."

"So, which is the museum we are visiting?"

"The one on our left."

"Lead on!"

"Before we enter, I meant to ask you which exhibition you would prefer to see. The building is huge, and we could come back any time to walk through any part you want."

Eleanor blushed. "I've read about the salt bowl by Cellini, which I would wish to see and, of course, the Greek and Roman collection if this is all right with you?"

"Good choices." Sophie beamed, and Eleanor thought it changed her demeanour entirely, as if Sophie was a rather different, more agreeable person than Eleanor had thought.

As soon as she stepped into the entrance hall, Eleanor discovered the building itself was a wonderful piece of art. The hall and the staircase they ascended were decorated with paintings indicating the themes of the collections in a perfectly fitting manner. Although they had to climb quite a lot of stairs, it wasn't such a difficulty for Sophie.

Eleanor did not expect that Sophie would be such a wonderful guide. She brought history to life and had a short anecdote for each and every important exhibition piece they encountered. It made for the most enjoyable visit to a museum Eleanor had ever had. Being in Sophie's company was pleasant, and her understated way of gentle guidance and closeness was most agreeable. Eleanor rued that their time would eventually come to an end, but she hoped it wouldn't be any time soon.

Sophie was pointing at a bronze tablet and describing the oldest surviving senatorial decree when two men came their way. One of them was older with unruly white hair, and the younger one was more composed and meticulously dressed.

"Sophie, my dear," the older gentleman exclaimed, his voice echoing in the quiet room, "the guards told me you were here. I need to show you something. The package arrived only this morning."

Sophie smirked at the man's exuberance; he was completely lacking any manners when something had piqued his interest.

"Professor Maierhofer, please let me introduce you to her Grace, the Duchess of Darnsworth," Sophie tried nonchalantly to remind her friend and mentor of his manners.

He goggled uncomprehendingly at her before he coughed in embarrassment to cover his *faux pas*.

"Please, your Grace, forgive my manners, or, rather, the lack of them." The professor bent over the gracefully held out hand.

"It is a pleasure to meet you, professor. I am very impressed by the museum."

"Thank you, your Grace." Maierhofer shuffled his feet as if nervous. "Would you mind if I borrowed Sophie for a minute?"

"Go ahead. I do understand the excitement of a new discovery. So please, go on, take her with you. I only ask you to let her come back before tomorrow."

"Why would I . . . oh, yes, of course. Come, my dear," the Professor was already shuffling away, expecting Sophie to follow right behind him.

"I am sorry. I *will* be back shortly."

Eleanor smiled at her with understanding. "Go!" she said with a soft chuckle. "I'll wait."

She watched the retreating form for a moment before she became aware of a presence behind her. It was the man who had accompanied the professor.

"Yes?" she asked tersely. "Was there something you wanted?"

"It was my understanding I was supposed to keep you company until the countess returns," the young man informed her with a frown.

"Was it? Let me assure you I'm quite capable of finding my way through the exhibition on my own."

"As you wish." He bowed and turned to storm off in the direction he had come from.

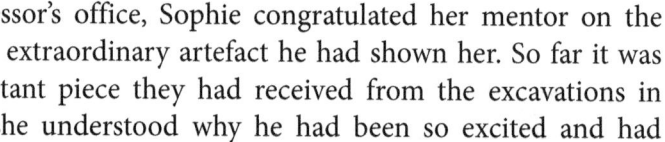

In the professor's office, Sophie congratulated her mentor on the discovery of the extraordinary artefact he had shown her. So far it was the most important piece they had received from the excavations in Ephesus. Now she understood why he had been so excited and had forgotten everything and everyone around him. Sophie agreed to meet him again the next day for a closer examination of all the artefacts from the last shipping.

When she left his office, she bumped into his assistant. He muttered something under his breath and threw her a poisonous glare but didn't dare to say anything. Sophie knew that the man detested her, but it couldn't be helped. With a shrug she continued on her way, searching for the duchess.

She found Eleanor sitting on one of the plush sofas in the portrait gallery contemplating the picture of one of the emperor's ancestors. As

Sophie admired her profile from the doorway, she seemed lost in thought. Her hands were folded on the handle of her umbrella, her head slightly tilted to the side, and her back was ramrod straight as she sat there. A smile stole over her face as Sophie approached, as if she sensed Sophie's presence without even looking.

"Are you going to stand there and stare at me for the rest of the day, or are you going to join me?"

"I'm sorry." Sophie blushed at being caught. She did as she was asked, exhaling with relief when she sat. It felt good to be off her feet. Although it was very soft Eleanor heard it and gazed at her with worry in her eyes.

"Why didn't you tell me you needed a break?"

"Because I didn't know until now," Sophie lied through her teeth. The last thing she wanted was for Eleanor to think her weak.

"Liar." The soft tone of her voice took the sting out of the accusation.

Sophie felt flustered. She opened her mouth to answer but when nothing came out, she closed it again in consternation. Eleanor covered one of Sophie's hands with her own, forcing her to face her as if what she had to say needed to be fully understood.

"I didn't mean to upset you. But I could tell from the way you moved and from the lines around your eyes that you were tired for a while and stubbornly refused to sit down."

"So," Sophie said angrily, "you decided to take pity on me and forced me to sit."

"No! I do not pity you, for heaven's sake. For one, I am tired myself. Strolling slowly through an exhibition is quite exhausting, and it's all right to admit being tired. It is not a sign of weakness to do so, on the contrary."

Sophie saw the honesty in Eleanor's gaze and faltered. Once again, she had acted appallingly. "I am sorry. Again."

"Not everybody has ulterior motives, you know. That is what friends do for each other. They care for the other's well-being."

"Are we friends?" Sophie asked shyly.

"I would care to think so, yes."

"I like that." Sophie smiled with pleasure. "I was wondering if I could tempt you to a wonderful cup of coffee and the most delicious dessert you have ever eaten."

"I won't say no to that."

Eleanor said, glad they had mastered another hurdle in their rocky friendship.

They left the museum sated after indulging thoroughly in the arts and took a carriage to a place where they could indulge in other delicious pursuits. It only took about ten minutes to reach their destination, a side street of Kärntner Strasse. Sophie opened the door of the Frauenhuber, the oldest coffeehouse in Vienna, and Eleanor proceeded inside.

The furniture was a combination of the typical coffeehouse with tables and chairs in the middle and red sofas and tables lining the windows. From the back, the laughter and conversation of gentlemen playing billiards could be heard while in the front of the shop, couples and groups of men and women talked over their coffees and desserts.

Eleanor followed Sophie to a table by the window and both sank gratefully into the soft seats. Before Eleanor could comment on the cosy and comfortable surroundings, a waiter appeared.

Eleanor took off her gloves while she ordered. "A cup of coffee, please."

"Certainly, madam," he nodded dutifully. "Grosser Brauner, Kleiner Brauner, Melange, Einspänner, Kapuziner—"

"Franz!" Sophie interrupted his rattling. "Give us a minute, please."

"As you wish, madam." The man sniffed haughtily, turned on his heels and tended to another table.

Eleanor pursed her lips and in a mock indignant voice said, "You did that on purpose."

"Sorry." Sophie twinkled benignly. "But the look on your face was just too precious. Please, forgive me for the outburst, but I simply couldn't let that pass."

"You are an awful tease. Now I think you should make it up to me and help me with my order.

"Of course. There is one simple rule you must remember when going to a coffeehouse in Vienna."

"Which is?"

Solemnly, she said, "Never ever ask for a mere cup of coffee. You just experienced first-hand what happens when you do. You have to be quite specific about it, otherwise you get swamped with suggestions. Take a gander at the menu and decide before you order."

Eleanor pouted at the suggestion. "But my German isn't that good. Would you order for me, please?"

Sophie rubbed her chin thoughtfully. "I think I know the right kind of coffee and dessert for both of us." She unobtrusively raised her right hand to call Franz back to their table.

"Yes?" he said.

"An Einspänner for my guest, a Melange for me, and for each of us, Kaiserschmarren with Zwetschgenröster."

"Certainly, madam." Franz departed to place their orders.

Eleanor had no idea what her companion had ordered. She simply had to trust her. Her discomfort was written on her face, so Sophie leaned forward and covered one of her hands with her own.

"Don't worry! I promise you will enjoy it. The coffee is good, and the dessert is excellent."

"I feel a bit out of my depth here," Eleanor admitted readily.

The feeling of Sophie's soft hand over hers made up nicely for it. She savoured this feeling of another woman's touch even if it was completely innocent. It had been too long since she had felt the warmth and gentleness of a woman's touch. Eleanor moaned at her train of thought, but she couldn't help it. Ever since Giulia made the observation about Sophie, her thoughts were regularly moving to the woman opposite her.

Her musings were interrupted when Franz put a small tray with her coffee in front of her. Sophie let go of her hand but gave it a squeeze before she did so, causing Eleanor to steal a glance at warm brown eyes that twinkled at her.

"What is this called again?" Eleanor asked as she eyed her order.

"Einspänner is a coffee served in a glass with whipped cream on top. Mine is a simple mix of coffee and hot milk."

Eleanor put a little sugar in her glass and took a tentative sip from her coffee while Sophie watched her with a hint of trepidation.

"It's delicious." Eleanor smiled, feeling delighted wonder as she met Sophie's gaze. "You were right."

"I thought you would like it, especially the whipped cream. Wait until you taste the dessert."

Sophie was telling Eleanor about the new artefacts Professor Maierhofer had shown her when dessert was brought by one of the so-called piccolos. To Eleanor it seemed like a plate full of fluffiness combined with a small bowl of fruit. She peered expectantly at Sophie who chuckled softly at her lost expression.

"Kaiserschmarren with Zwetschgenröster."

"Which means?"

"A combination of sweet and sour. You see, Kaiserschmarren is made of eggs, flour, milk, and sugar or honey, baked in a pan, and cut into chunks. Zwetschgenröster is a sort of compote of plums. Go on, try it."

Eleanor took the spoon and put a piece of fluffy Schmarren and a little bit of the compote on it to taste. Sophie was right; the combination of these different flavours was incredible. She closed her eyes and hummed in appreciation.

"Well?"

"Sinful," she said with a dreamy smile on her lips.

Sophie watched in rapt fascination at the expression on Eleanor's face. It took her breath away how beautiful she was, how sensual, how . . . She shook her head to get rid of the inappropriate thoughts running through her mind and returned to her own dessert.

Conversation flowed easily and lightly between them. There were so many things they could talk and laugh about. Time flew by and before they knew it, it was time to part company and go home. A carriage brought Eleanor to her palais, where she left Sophie with the promise of meeting for a ride through the Prater on Friday.

"There you are," Henry exclaimed as he exited the library at the same moment his wife strode through the hall towards the stairs. She had the most peculiar expression on her face; her eyes were shining brightly like he hadn't seen for a long while.

"You seem to be in an extraordinary good mood today, my dear. Did you have a nice afternoon?"

Eleanor stopped at the bottom of the stairs and turned towards her husband. Apart from the small misunderstanding at the museum, she had to admit that her afternoon had indeed been more than nice. Sophie was a wonderful companion—educated, funny, full of interesting stories, and quite the gentlewoman.

"Yes. Yes, it was quite nice."

With a new spring in her step, she went upstairs to change for dinner and talk to her grandmother.

She found the contessa reading in her sitting room and asked her to join her in her own rooms which Eleanor knew she would gladly do because, try as she might, Giulia could not help but be curious about Eleanor's afternoon, much less her life.

Without the help of her maid Eleanor undressed and refreshed herself in the bathroom before she went to her bedroom to put on her gown for dinner. All the while her grandmother was watching her with hawk eyes, impatiently wringing her hands to find out what had happened.

"Oh, please Eleanor, stop torturing me and tell me!" the contessa complained with a mock stern gaze.

"This is unlike you, Nonna, to be so impatient," Eleanor teased her gently. But she showed mercy to her grandmother and finally told her about her time with Sophie.

"So, the two of you are friends now," Giulia asked knowingly.

"Yes, but you make it sound sinister."

"No, not at all. When will you meet again?"

"Friday. We are going for a ride in the Prater."

"How exciting!"

"It is." Eleanor felt as though she was glowing from inside with excitement. "She also promised me a special surprise for the end of the month."

"Why am I not surprised?" Giulia muttered.

"We have quite a few things in common which makes her wonderful company," she said, her words tumbling out fast. "I enjoyed our time tremendously. She's funny and knowledgeable. You have no idea how pleasant it was. Oh, look at the time! Now I must have my hair done, Nonna. I spent so much time with her that I'm running a bit late. I'll let you know what happens Friday. I'm sure it will be a delight."

"Mm hmm, that's what I thought."

"Quite, yes. Now where is Rose when you need her? Oh, for goodness' sake!" She moved to ring for her maid, already forgetting that her grandmother was still in the room.

Giulia smirked as she turned away. Oh, yes, this was going to be interesting. Maybe Sophie von Hagendorf was indeed the right person to help Eleanor overcome her pain. Their growing affection was there already, she could grasp it from her granddaughter's obvious happiness, but the question was: would either of the two women be brave enough to take it a step farther?

Chapter Twelve

Friday's early morning horseback ride was one of many to follow. Sophie, despite her initial mishap when they first met, was quite an accomplished rider. Due to her injuries, she didn't ride side-saddle, but greatly admired Eleanor's skills riding in that fashion. With each minute they spent in each other's company their friendship grew. It intensified and made them feel more at ease which reflected in the topics they talked about.

Sophie told Eleanor about her late mother and about the accident that had caused her limp and scar on her face. Eleanor spoke about her own childhood and about the friendship with Henry and Cathleen, although leaving out the significance of Cathleen in her life. She knew why she wouldn't tell the whole truth; for one, she wasn't so certain how Sophie would react, and for another, it still wasn't easy to talk about her and her death.

Eleanor's hopes were that their friendship would indeed strengthen to the point where she could talk about her late lover. Eleanor also realised that she was attracted to Sophie, and the more time they spent together, the harder it became to part ways. Eleanor couldn't remember the last time she had felt this free and safe at the same time with somebody who wasn't family.

June and July in Vienna were hot and humid. The best way to avoid the heat was either to flee the city altogether or spend the hottest time of the day in a cool place. That was exactly what Eleanor and Sophie did. There wasn't a church, museum or riding track they didn't visit together.

Sophie knew she didn't have to constantly make up for any of her limitations. She was so brave that one day, when it was unbearably hot, she braided her hair to keep it off her face and neck and help her cool down a bit.

When she met Eleanor with her hair not obscuring her face, she was afraid of the reaction to her disfigurement, but Eleanor merely congratulated her on the decision to be practical in the heat of summer. Eleanor displayed no disgust, not so much as the blinking of an eye, nothing indicating that she was appalled by Sophie's scar.

It was as if it wasn't there but, for the first time in her life, Sophie herself forgot about it in Eleanor's presence. But as soon as they parted ways, she again became aware of the stares and spurred her horse to return home as fast as possible.

Even though they spent so much time talking, there were still topics they weren't courageous enough to bring up just yet. One was their growing feelings for each other and where they would lead them. Another was the fact that Eleanor was, after all, a married woman.

The last Wednesday in July brought the special surprise Sophie had promised. Quite early in the morning she picked up Eleanor at the palais in her regal carriage. When they neared the Imperial Palace, Eleanor thought they were going to visit the Court Library, but when they drew closer, she detected the distinct scent of horses in the air. She looked questioningly at her companion, who smiled mysteriously.

"Do you know where we are going?" Sophie asked with a smirk.

"The emperor's stables?" Eleanor guessed with a frown.

"In a manner of speaking, yes." The carriage stopped in front of an inconspicuous entrance, and Sophie helped her climb down. "We are at the Winter Riding School, home of the Lipizzaner."

"The world's most famous white horses?"

"Yes," Sophie said proudly, "the 'Imperial Whites' as they are also known."

A man stepped through the doors and took off his hat to greet them properly. "Welcome to the Spanish Riding School, your Grace." He bowed over the offered hand before he greeted Sophie like an old friend.

Sophie introduced him. "Your Grace, please meet Chief Rider Moritz Herold."

"How do you do?" Eleanor said. "It is a pleasure."

"On the contrary, your Grace," Herold said, "the pleasure is all mine. Your reputation precedes you. It's an honour to welcome you here and it was decided you will not merely be watching a morning workout session, but we will perform for you the *haute école*, the very Highest School of Classical Horsemanship."

He led them inside to their seats alongside and slightly above the *manège*. The Imperial Box was located at the head of the building, and underneath a chamber orchestra had settled in place. In the middle of the *manège* stood two wooden posts adorned with the yellow and black flags of the Imperial Household.

Seven white stallions and one black one entered through a door from opposite the Imperial box. "A three-hundred-year tradition is the root of this equestrian academy," Herold proudly pointed out. The riders were dressed in white trousers, brown frock coats, black boots, and black hats. They took off their hats in a synchronised motion while the chief rider explained the meaning.

"Every time we ride into the *manège*, we salute the painting of Charles the Sixth, who built the school. What you will see is an equestrian ballet of precision, elegance, and grace."

The orchestra started to play, and Eleanor was mesmerised by the perfect harmony with which the horses and riders performed the movements. She sensed the eagerness of the stallions and the pride of their riders. This was such a special treat and she gazed warmly at Sophie who had made it all possible.

When the horses left the *manège*, another group took over.

"This is the School above the Ground," Herold explained. "Some of these lessons have their origin in military exercises. A rider could clear a path in the turmoil of battle when performing trained jumps."

Two of the riders led the horses by the reins to prepare them for the exercises while others remained in the saddle.

"The capriole, translated as the leap of a goat, is the most difficult of all. The horse jumps into the air and at the same time kicks out its back hooves."

"Every movement appears so natural. How do you do that?" Eleanor wondered.

"It is natural and flowing," the chief rider said, "because we only cultivate movements which the horse is born to perform. Right from the beginning, a rider must inspire trust between himself and his horse. It takes tireless patient work, calmness, and reward."

"I am very impressed." Eleanor eyes never left the horses. "How long does it take until a horse can perform?"

"Six to eight years until it is fully trained. A young stallion learns from an experienced rider, and the young rider learns from an experienced trained stallion." To emphasise the point, they observed the sole performance of a horse whose only connection to his rider was a long rein.

The horses and riders were a pleasure to watch, and when Eleanor saw the man grinning proudly after their splendid performance, she had to smile as well. She felt enamoured by the beautiful and graceful horses. They were the dream of every passionate rider.

After the performances, the chief rider took them to the stables across the street to meet the riders and their horses. The first box was occupied by a dark horse Eleanor had observed with great interest.

"What about this one?" she asked the chief rider. This digression had piqued her curiosity.

"Ah, of course," he nodded knowingly. "One dark horse always takes part in the performance in memory of a time when not all Lipizzaners were white."

"I had no idea."

"They are born with a dark coat and turn white between the age of five and eight."

"When do you start their training?"

"At the age of three they come to Vienna to begin training with us. Until then, they learn the rules of life in the herd at their mother's side."

The chief rider toured at Eleanor's side through the stable, handing her a favourite treat for the last horse. She offered the cube of sugar to the happily snickering animal and was rewarded with a gentle push to her shoulder. When it was time to leave, the chief rider accompanied them to their carriage where Eleanor thanked him again for the wonderful experience.

They entered the carriage to return to the palais for refreshments. Eleanor sat next to Sophie, still overwhelmed by Sophie's wonderful gift. Impulsively Eleanor leaned over and kissed Sophie on the cheek. Sophie's eyes widened in surprise, and Eleanor saw those eyes fill with moisture at the unexpected gentle gesture.

Eleanor realised she had crossed a hurdle, an intimate boundary, and merely took hold of one of Sophie's hands, both of them refusing to let go until they reached their destination.

In retrospect, Eleanor would have kissed her on the lips but didn't dare. There was still so much they hadn't talked about and didn't know about each other. But as fast as their friendship was progressing, she knew they would soon have to.

They met for another ride in the Prater on Sunday. Sophie surprised Eleanor with a picnic at her favourite spot where they had met for the first time. As they neared the place, they saw that everything had been prepared for their arrival. The blanket was spread on the ground in the shadow of a chestnut tree complete with some comfortable-looking cushions. Plates and glasses with a cooling basket for a light white wine were set out next to a basket full of food.

"How did you manage that?"

"I have my ways," Sophie offered secretively. Seeing Eleanor's stern expression though, she gave in, "All right, I asked Guttmann to send one of the footmen to prepare it. I had to give up my secret, but it was worth it."

"It's wonderful. Thank you." Eleanor seemed touched by the gesture.

"You're welcome. Let's dismount and let the horses graze while we enjoy what Cook has put in the basket for us."

The food was delicious as was the wine and the fruit and cheese. A soft breeze on a cloudless day made it the perfect weather for a picnic. After they finished their meal, they put the remains into the basket together with the plates and Sophie lay back on the blanket. She was pondering if she should ask Eleanor all the things she had wanted to know for a long time but if she was honest, she still lacked the courage. She had to admit that while her curiosity was high, she was also afraid of the answers.

Propped up on an elbow, Sophie watched Eleanor lying back against a cushion. She was clearly enjoying the warm day and the light breeze. The questions, though, made for a violent turmoil in Sophie's heart because she didn't want to break the mood. She heaved a sigh, which caused Eleanor to open her eyes and squint questioningly at her. "What is the matter?"

"Nothing, really, I have just been thinking."

Eleanor shifted to her side. With elbow bent and her head against her palm, she said, "You're frowning. You look troubled. Tell me what's wrong."

Instead of an answer, Sophie pulled at the lose fibres on the blanket, avoiding Eleanor's gaze. When a soft hand covered her own, she gazed into mesmerising pools of blue. How could she ask what she wanted to and watch those beautiful eyes cloud over with pain?

"Tell me!" Eleanor encouraged her gently.

"You don't have to answer if you don't want to," Sophie rushed to assure her.

"I know, but there is something troubling you. What is it?"

"This necklace you are wearing . . ." Sophie cursed her curiosity when she felt the hand on hers stiffen and saw the slightly distant look in Eleanor's eyes as soon as she mentioned the piece of jewellery. "Forget it,

I am sorry, I didn't mean to be intrusive. It just intrigues me because you are never without it. You also wore it at the reception."

Eleanor needed to put distance between them, so she got up and went towards the tree line to order her thoughts and calm her emotions. She knew Sophie would eventually ask about her necklace. Sophie was a very perceptive woman. Her habit to reach for it in order to ground herself every time she was troubled drew more attention to it. She also knew that Sophie wanted to know more about her past. They had grown constantly closer over the last few weeks, so it was only natural, this need to learn about the other, past and present.

Feeling bereft of Eleanor's closeness Sophie felt inclined to kick herself for being so insensitive. She struggled to her feet and followed her companion. A step was distancing her from Eleanor and yet it felt like a whole continent. She reached out and gently put her hand on Eleanor's shoulder.

"I am sorry I asked. It wasn't my place. Please forgive me." Her voice was hoarse, and she feared she had caused an unbridgeable rift between them.

Wordlessly Eleanor took off her necklace and handed it to Sophie. She was surprised at her own actions because the question had always caused her heart to constrict painfully, but now she felt no sorrow or pain. Tears had been her constant companion every time Cathleen was mentioned over the last years, but this time none would come. The feeling of loss was there but only as a faint reminder of the woman who had owned her heart for so long.

"Go on!" Eleanor said. "Open it."

"I can't . . . I didn't mean to . . ." Sophie stammered, unsure what to do. On the one hand she desperately wanted to know what the locket contained; on the other hand, she felt she had no right at all to look.

Eleanor gave her hand a reassuring squeeze, "I want you to. Please!"

Carefully Sophie opened the cameo and took stock of the items inside. She found a delicate ring of gold and a small black and white photograph of a beautiful woman inside. Sophie felt her throat constrict at the meaning of these memorabilia.

"She is beautiful." What could she say? Stating the obvious sounded hollow but what else was there to say? So, she had been right about Eleanor, but her anxiety was well-placed. A married woman with a female companion who was probably more than that was unobtainable for Sophie. She felt like a fool. She'd hoped against hope that maybe . . . What?

It was neither the place nor the time for a woman like Eleanor.

With shaking hands, she closed the locket and put it back into Eleanor's hand. "We should go back. I promised Professor Maierhofer I would come by his office in the afternoon to help him with some manuscripts."

Sophie turned on her heels so quickly, Eleanor was left dumbfounded in her wake. While she refastened the necklace, Sophie gathered the horses. She mounted Capri and waited for Eleanor to get up on hers. As soon as Eleanor sat on top of her horse, Sophie stirred Capri back the way they had come.

Back home ensconced in the warm comforting scent of the bubbles in her bathtub, Eleanor thought about what had happened between her and Sophie. She had watched as a myriad of emotions played across Sophie's face when she opened the cameo and looked inside. None of her expressions had made her any wiser because as fast as they had appeared, they were gone. No question was asked, nothing said, except for a statement about Cathleen's beauty.

Every attempt at conversation was blocked on their way home. Sophie hadn't been rude; she was as cordial as ever, but the distance between them had been palpable. There was no time to explain anything for Sophie wouldn't let her.

That was when a sudden thought hit her, and she sat up so fast in the tub that water sloshed over the rim. Hurriedly, Eleanor stepped out, dried off and dressed without summoning the help of her lady's maid. Time was of the essence and the sooner she cleared up this apparent misunderstanding, the sooner Sophie and she could move forward. On her way downstairs she called for Benson to inform him that she needed Parker and a carriage immediately.

Eleanor paced back and forth in the hall waiting for the driver to arrive at the front. When Benson announced the arrival of her carriage, she rushed through the door and urged Parker to go as fast as possible.

With a crack of his whip, he brought the horses into motion but the bustle on the streets was terrible. It seemed as if the whole of Vienna was on its way somewhere. Carriages, motorcars, trams, pedestrians, and people on bicycles clogged the streets. The trip to reach Palais Hagendorf at the other end of the Ringstrasse took longer than she'd anticipated. When they finally did arrive, Parker helped her off the carriage. She hurried up the steps to the palais and rang the bell, waiting impatiently for Guttmann to open the door.

"Your Grace." The butler greeted her with a deep bow as he held the door open to let her pass.

"Good afternoon, Guttmann," Eleanor said huskily. "I wish to speak to Countess Sophie."

"I am sorry, madam, but the countess left half an hour ago."

"Do you know when she will be back?"

"I can't say, your Grace," Guttmann shook his head apologetically, "but from the luggage she took with her, I assume it will be a lengthy stay."

"I see. I better leave you to your duties then. Good day."

She staggered out the door in a stupor. Sophie had left without a word of goodbye. Maybe Eleanor had read more into their friendship than there actually was.

Eleanor was falling for Sophie and that was why she had showed her the necklace, why she wanted to tell her about Cathleen. She had wanted an honest conversation about the past and about them, but she had obviously been completely wrong. Sophie was letting her know she wanted nothing to do with her. Better to know now than later, but she couldn't resist the tear that rolled down her cheek.

Chapter Thirteen

Therese von Hochstetten joined her daughter, Adele, at the door that led to a vast garden with many trees and a pond where ducks brought up their offspring and frogs and fish made up a diverse population. She followed Adele's gaze and frowned at a lonesome figure under a large willow tree in the pavilion. Her niece Sophie was immersed in her papers, furiously writing and completely ignorant of anything else. It has been that way since she arrived nearly two weeks ago and neither of them had been able to reach her, to find out what was so clearly troubling her.

"Has she eaten anything yet?"

"I don't know, Mummy." Adele whispered dejectedly. "I asked Cook to send one of the kitchen maids with breakfast, but I haven't dared to look."

"Well," she squared her shoulders, "I guess it is up to me then. This can't go on any longer. I won't have it." She took her skirt in her hands and with determined steps hustled to the pavilion to find out what was going on with her niece.

Ever since her sister's death, Sophie had become closer to Therese's heart. Karoline's early death was a shock to everybody, and Sophie's father had sent her to stay with Therese soon after. He had no idea how to care for a girl of seven years; neither did he know how to comfort the little girl who had loved her mother so dearly. Therese tried to be there for Sophie, which wasn't always easy, but with cousins her age it became clear that Sophie was opening up.

Therese would never forgive herself for what happened to Sophie during the summer at her estate when her niece was only fourteen. She felt responsible for Sophie's accident, although she knew there was nothing she could have done to prevent it. Sophie had always been a tomboy, but once Karoline no longer had a calming influence on the wild girl, there was nothing to stop her from taking a nearly untamed horse for a ride.

When they found her broken in a pool of blood, Therese thought she wouldn't survive, but the doctors at the hospital worked hard to keep

Sophie alive and to heal as much of the injuries as possible. The recovery took months. Her niece spent the rest of the summer and a good portion of the fall in the hospital, confined in a corset of plaster for her back and hip. Her right leg was put in a cast for it had been broken in three different places.

Fortunately, the doctors saved her right eye, leaving a large scar, but they had to remove her uterus due to an awful injury by a metal rod.

After discharge from hospital, Sophie became more withdrawn than before. It took all of them a lot of patience when she lost her temper over her failed attempts to regain the strength in her limbs. Somehow, with a stubbornness that reminded Therese of her sister, Sophie was able to walk without a cast for her right leg and with only use the support of a simple cane.

All these years later, Sophie had grown up, but she had never recaptured her spontaneous attitude toward life. Therese stood at the edge of the pavilion, reluctant to disturb her niece's concentration and feeling her determination waver when an amused voice startled her.

"Are you going to say what you have come for or not?"

"There is no need to be disrespectful, young lady," Therese shot back.

Sophie slumped in her chair. She took off her glasses and hung her head in shame. "I am sorry, aunt. Forgive me."

Therese went over to her niece and gently caressed her hair before depositing a kiss on top of her head.

"I forgive you, sweetheart."

She sat in the chair to Sophie's right and covered her hand affectionately, forcing her niece to face her.

"I worry about you, Sophie. Something is bothering you, and before you try to deny it, let me remind you who is talking to you. I know you. I can tell that something is very wrong."

Sophie gazed at her aunt's face. Worry lines were marring her otherwise still smooth forehead. The lines in the corner of her eyes were more pronounced than ever, and her green eyes were troubled. All on her behalf. Her aunt resembled her mother so much, not only in her appearance, but also in her demeanour. Her gentle ways made Sophie feel like the lowest creature on earth for treating her so badly.

Aunt Therese had always been there for her. Every time she needed a place to retreat, she would provide it. When she was at odds with her father, which was more often than not after her mother's death, she would go to her aunt for comfort. Maria and Adele were more like sisters than cousins. Sophie looked into her aunt's eyes and slowly felt her resolve crumble.

Therese reached out and gently tucked a strand of hair behind her niece's ear before she cupped her right cheek in her palm.

Sophie didn't flinch. She closed her eyes and let the tears escape silently, no longer able to hold them in, and she didn't have to when she felt her aunt gathering her in a warm embrace.

"I've got you, darling," Therese cooed, all the while stroking Sophie's hair tenderly.

Sophie was a brilliant linguist, but she utterly failed where her feelings were concerned. She could translate any ancient text, but when it came to expressing her emotions she was lost.

When Sophie calmed down, she told her aunt everything about her friendship with the Duchess of Darnsworth. She left out nothing and spoke about the feelings she had developed for Eleanor and thought were mutual. "My feelings are ridiculous because not only is the duchess married, but she also showed me a picture in her cameo of a beautiful woman who must be her special companion."

"Sometimes things are not as they seem, Sophie," Therese suggested gently. "What has she told you about her marriage or the picture?"

"Nothing, because I didn't give her the chance to," Sophie said ruefully. "Besides, what would have been the point? She is a married woman with three children. What is supposed to become of this?"

Therese sighed. She had always known about her niece's preference for the female sex, much the same as her daughter Adele's. Unfortunately, society wouldn't acknowledge it or support such relationships, at least not if a woman openly lived her love for another woman.

Women had always found ways to evade convention and live their lives in accordance with their own rules, and society looked the other way as long as it was done discreetly and according to the boundaries society had set for them. Her niece was brave enough to defy these conventions in her manner of dress and occupation, and Therese admired her for that. But to be regarded as an eccentric for wearing men's clothes was one thing. To live openly with another woman as a couple was something completely different. Society was hypocritical, but not even Sophie's money would protect her if somebody were to call the law on her. Her niece's uncompromising nature had caused her unnecessary heartache, and Therese wished she would take a step back and listen to reason as well as to Eleanor's side of the story.

"You are in love with her," Therese told her, not beating around the bush. Sophie opened her mouth to object, but her aunt put a finger over her lips to prevent her from talking, so she closed it again.

"Don't try to deny it. I know you are. That's why you are here. You ran as fast and far as you could think to go. But let me tell you, it won't simply go away. This is different, I can tell. It is nothing like with Elisabeth. Somehow, I believe this is real, and you know it. That is why you so stubbornly refused to talk about it."

"It doesn't matter, though, one way or the other," Sophie insisted. "Even if we admit our feelings, which I am not convinced are completely mutual, it would be pointless. They return to England at the end of the summer. So better to stop—or rather, not begin anything at all—which is bound to end anyway."

"You could always accompany her." Therese was getting exasperated at Sophie's stubbornness.

"I can't."

"Why the hell not?"

"Because I can't leave them alone."

"What are you talking about? Who?" her aunt asked, utterly puzzled.

Suddenly comprehension dawned, and Therese understood what she referred to. Sophie felt responsible for her stepbrother and stepsister whom she loved dearly.

"You are not their mother. They are not your responsibility."

"But they are, don't you see." Sophie argued passionately. "Emma is going to marry this bloody bastard, and who will be there for her when it turns out to be a mistake?"

"Her parents."

"Hardly." Sophie scoffed at the mere idea. "Father wouldn't listen to any argument, and Helen is looking forward to an invitation to the next Emperor's ball due to Count von Bernthal's connections."

"Still—"

"No."

Her niece would have none of it. There was no point in discussing the matter any longer.

Two weeks had passed since Eleanor asked to forward a letter to Sophie, but when there was no reply, she realised that there was no point in waiting any longer. Their friendship was over, and her hope for something more had been destroyed as well. She hoped Sophie was well and that she herself would be able to put this whole affair behind her. The feelings Eleanor had for Sophie ran deeper than she wanted to admit. For the sake of her family, she put on a brave face, all the while mourning the loss of an unrequited love. The occasional visit of Helen and her family didn't help much either.

One evening after the Hagendorfs had been their dinner guests, Emma handed her the much-longed-for letter from Sophie. Eleanor excused herself and went to the library to read it undisturbed. She ripped open the seal and through the first three lines realised Sophie was gently but determinedly ending their friendship, telling her in no uncertain terms that nothing would ever come of her attraction.

Eleanor sank into a chair, her left hand covering her mouth to stifle the sob threatening to escape. She felt like an old foolish woman who was making a laughingstock of herself for chasing a vibrant young woman. Who was she fooling but herself?

This whole affair had been a mistake right from the beginning. She had already experienced the love others never knew, which had to be enough. Eleanor had been very lucky; she knew that, because ever since she was a girl in her teens, she had known who and what she was. Her grandmother's relationship with Giulia helped a lot to allow her to realise her own nature. Henry's love for her and his own need for protection had afforded her with possibilities she had grasped without second thought.

The moment she had met Cathleen she knew she would do what she could to keep her in her life. Eleanor had been over the moon when Cathleen told her the feelings were reciprocated. Theirs had been a wonderful relationship, full of love and caring. Never once had Eleanor looked at any other woman the way she had at her lover. After Cathleen's death, her desolation was complete for she had lost the love of her life, her mate, her best friend, the second mother of her children. She hadn't thought it possible to feel romantic love again, but here she was, mourning the loss of another lover and they hadn't even kissed yet.

"Stupid woman," Eleanor chastised herself as she threw the letter in the top drawer and slammed it shut. She took off her reading glasses and pinched the bridge of her nose, trying in vain to ward off the headache she had felt coming for the better part of the day. She would live but she wouldn't put her heart at risk again. Time to move on. Another love match was just not in her cards. Such things only happened once in a lifetime, and the sooner she accepted that, the better. Her heart had hoped, to no avail. Better to let bygones be bygones.

"Please, tell me you are not going for a ride now," Adele's voice stopped Sophie dead in her tracks. She slowly turned to her cousin who had her arms crossed over her chest.

"Why not?"

Adele rolled her eyes at Sophie's tone. "Because it is going to rain. There will probably be a thunderstorm and on your usual route there is no shelter."

Sophie laughed at her cousin's forecast. "Don't be ridiculous. It is a perfectly fine day. The sun is shining, not a single cloud is in the sky."

"Sophie, I'm not joking." Adele put her hand on her cousin's arm, her eyes as serious as she had ever seen them. "You must listen to me! It happens very fast here. One minute there is sunshine, and the next, rain is falling heavily, and the temperature drops about ten degrees."

"Nonsense." Sophie shrugged off the hand and stalked out of the house. She shook her head at her cousin, wondering how a rational woman like Adele could tell such superstitious nonsense. Sophie mounted her horse and galloped from the stables. It could rain heavily in Salzburg, she was aware of that, mostly for days on end, but this was ridiculous. So far, this had been the driest summer in years in this part of the country.

The sudden changes Adele had predicted seemed completely out of the question, but when Sophie had been gone for about an hour, the light breeze became a harsh wind followed by rolling thunder. She stopped her horse and studied the sky. The wind was whipping dark clouds westward. A thunderstorm, just as Adele had foretold, was fast coming her way. Sophie spurred her horse into action, hoping to outrun the rain. But it soon became clear there was no point. The first heavy drops were falling, and she could see no place to seek shelter to wait until the storm passed.

With the rain intensifying, the wind turned cooler as well. Sophie wore only a light shirt which was already soaked through, and she was shivering as she forced her horse to go on. By the time she recognised the outlines of her aunt's estate through the rain, she and her mount were both exhausted. She guided the horse towards the stables where a stable hand came rushing out, helped her from the horse, and she staggered to the house where she nearly fell into her aunt's arms.

"Goodness!" Therese caught her and guided her to a chair. "Elsie! Get a hot bath ready for my niece and tell Cook we need a big pot of hot tea and chicken soup as soon as possible. Also, a hot bottle for the bed."

The maid rushed off and did as she was asked as Adele joined her mother to help get Sophie to her room, out of her wet clothes, and into the bathtub.

"Didn't you tell her there would be a thunderstorm?"

"Of course, I did," Adele replied indignantly, "but she wouldn't listen."

Her mother sighed. "Would she ever?"

Together they manoeuvred Sophie into the tub. Although the water was hot, she couldn't stop shivering from the cold that had chilled her to the bones. Her teeth were chattering so badly she could hardly speak.

"I . . . I am . . . s-so sorry," Sophie apologised to her cousin.

"It's all right," Adele said. "Just don't get sick, you bonehead."

"H-How?"

"How did I know? I've lived here my whole life," Adele said in explanation, "we just know such things. Sometimes, like today, you can smell the rain in the air." Adele shrugged.

Sophie acknowledged her comments with a nod. She was desperate to get warmer and could kick herself for her own stupidity. This wasn't good, not good at all.

Aunt Therese had hoped the bath would prevent her niece from falling ill, but when Sophie developed a fever followed by an awful cough, those hopes were dashed. Over a number of days, they tried every treatment they could think of, but when nothing helped, Therese called Doctor Wagner, an accomplished physician and old family friend.

"It's pneumonia," Doctor Wagner announced as he took off his stethoscope after listening to Sophie's laboured breathing. "I will write down a few remedies she'll have to take religiously, and we can only hope she is strong enough to recover."

"Thank you, doctor," Therese said.

"Does she eat? She's very thin. She also needs to drink enough," the doctor advised while writing down a prescription for the chemist.

"I will take care of it," Therese assured him, when they heard a delirious mumble from the bed. The words were not quite intelligible.

The doctor glanced questioningly at the countess. "Do you know what she is saying?"

"A name. Eleanor."

"Where is this Eleanor? Perhaps her presence could help with your niece's recovery."

"Unfortunately, the woman in question doesn't agree," Therese said bitterly. She was already regretting that she had told Sophie to give Eleanor a chance. By the time Sophie was out of her head in feverish agony, Therese sent a letter to Vienna to ask Anton to inform the duchess about Sophie's condition. When there was no answer from the woman in question, she thought maybe Sophie had been right after all and this Eleanor wasn't worth the effort.

"Try again," Doctor Wagner insisted. "It might be too late if you wait too long. Maybe if you sketch the seriousness of the situation, she will change her mind."

"I will think about your advice, Doctor," she said thoughtfully.

The second post had just been delivered when Emma bounced down the stairs. She was hoping for another of her fiancé's letters. Despite his air of superiority, Count von Bernthal seemed genuinely taken with her, proving Emma's sister Sophie wrong. He was charming and not at all the brute her sister believed him to be. Emma was sifting through the post, which mainly contained letters to her parents, when somebody rang the bell impatiently. She didn't wait for the butler to show up but opened the door herself. A messenger was standing on the other side of the door, nervously stepping from one foot to the other.

"A telegram, Miss." He held out the envelope.

Emma accepted it and ripped open the envelope. The short message was from Sophie's aunt, urging Anton to tell the Duchess of Darnsworth that Sophie's condition was serious, and if she held any love at all for her niece she should come at once. Emma crumpled the piece of paper in her fist and closed the door with a bang.

"Who was that?" her brother asked from the back of the hall.

Emma jumped at the sudden presence of her brother.

Anton took off his riding gloves as he bolted towards the table to survey the mail himself.

"Nobody," she said.

Anton thought she was acting strange, and his suspicion was confirmed when his eyes fell on the envelope in his sister's hand. As soon as she realised where he was looking, she tried to hide it behind her back, but it was too late.

"What are you hiding from me, Emma?" he asked as he stepped closer.

"Nothing."

Emma tried to escape, but Anton was faster and caught her arm. He pried open her clenched fist and smoothed out the telegram. Reading through it not once but three times finally made Anton realise what had been going on and what his sister was trying to hide.

"How long have you known about this?" Anton hissed angrily, forcing Emma to take a step back. She had never seen him that angry. "Never mind!"

He swung around and left the way he had entered. Outside, he stopped the stable hand from leading his horse inside, climbed into the saddle, and hurried off to deliver this urgent message.

"I am telling you, I have to speak to her Grace. It is urgent," Anton argued, his voice booming into the hall.

Benson blocked the doorway, annoyed at the young count's insistence. "And I have told you more than twice that her Grace isn't available." The butler stood his ground. If her Grace wasn't inclined to receive visitors, he would be damned if he'd let the count pass because he thought himself more important than the wishes of a duchess.

"What is this commotion, Benson?"

The butler turned towards the voice and found the duchess on the first landing, demanding an explanation.

"I am sorry for the disturbance, your Grace," Benson apologised.

Anton stepped from behind the butler, whose body in the doorway had been shielding him effectively from the duchess' view

"My apology, your Grace. I didn't mean to cause you any inconvenience, but this is rather urgent."

Eleanor descended the last flight of steps. "Thank you, Benson."

The butler bowed humbly and closed the door behind Anton before he silently left the hall.

"What is so urgent, Count, to intrude in such a manner?" Eleanor was slightly miffed at the young man's forwardness.

"It is about Sophie. She has fallen ill." Anton cut to the chase, before the duchess lost her patience and threw him out.

"Come!" Eleanor didn't wait for him to follow but headed briskly to the library where she poured herself a stiff whiskey and took a healthy gulp before she faced Anton again. He stood only a few feet away and had the presence of mind to close the door behind him.

"Tell me!"

Instead of telling her, he held out the telegram from Sophie's aunt. Eleanor read through the message and sank into a chair next to the liquor table.

"What does she mean? What letter? I had no idea Sophie was ill."

"I know," Anton said with regret. "Neither did I." He looked pleadingly at her. "Please, go to her. She needs you. You will never forgive yourself if she doesn't recover and you haven't seen her one last time."

The duchess gazed strangely at him with an expression of anger mixed with desperation and sorrow.

"What is it to you?" she asked.

"She is my sister. I love her, and though it hurts that she isn't asking for me, I do know why she is asking for you. Please, I beg of you, go to her. For both your sakes." Anton implored, seeing a flicker of pain in her eyes but it was too short to be sure.

"I know about loss, young man," Eleanor said sadly.

"I don't doubt that. The more important it is to see Sophie, don't you agree?"

Eleanor closed her eyes and let her heart speak to her. She knew what she wanted, but whether she should was another question. She took a deep breath before she felt her decision.

"In the drawer of the desk you'll find paper and a pencil. Write down the Hochstetten's address and then leave me alone."

Without uttering another word Anton got to his feet and did as he was told. He wrote down all the information she needed to know and retreated to the door. Eleanor's voice stopped him mid-motion as he reached for the handle.

"Thank you. No matter what happens, I consider myself forever indebted to you."

Anton was stunned and didn't know what to say so he merely inclined his head and left the library.

Eleanor didn't know how long she sat there after Sophie's brother left. She reread the message in her hand over and over again. With a heavy heart, she finally went to the hearth to ring for Benson. The trusted butler arrived in the library as quietly as ever, awaiting his mistress' commands.

"Please tell my husband and Mister Carstairs I want to speak to them, Benson."

"Yes, your Grace."

"Thank you. And ask Charlotte to join us as well."

"Certainly, madam."

He left without a sound and Eleanor was already planning her next steps while she waited for the others to arrive. Thankfully enough, the three of them entered together and she didn't have to repeat herself.

"Jonathan, would you please book a first-class compartment on the next train to Salzburg?"

"Yes, of course. Anything else?"

"Make sure a carriage is waiting when the train arrives. A suite in one of the hotels in the city needs to be arranged and another carriage put at my disposal."

"Certainly. Anything else?"

"No." Jonathan left with his assignments. She knew he need not ask why. She rarely asked him to do anything for her and he was always happy to be of assistance to her.

"Charlotte, would you please accompany me to Salzburg?" Eleanor asked.

Her daughter was surprised but agreed readily, "Of course, Mama."

"Hold your horses," Henry interrupted. "I am so unused to you spouting orders injudiciously and travelling on a whim. What is this all about? Why do you have to go to Salzburg all of a sudden?"

"Because the woman I have foolishly fallen in love with over the past few months is in Salzburg," Eleanor explained very calmly, although she didn't feel like it at all, "and she has fallen terribly ill. There is a chance she may not recover, and should that happen without me seeing her one last time, I would never forgive myself."

"So, it is true, then," Henry whispered.

He was watching her carefully, as though she seemed strange to him. She couldn't stop pacing. Her left hand was stemmed into her side while she kept brushing her hair from her forehead nervously. She felt sick to her stomach and didn't have time to deal with Henry's concerns. She only felt gratitude that Charlotte didn't seem to have any questions.

"How and when did this happen?" he asked. "I thought you didn't care for her?"

"Oh, don't be daft, Henry!" Eleanor exclaimed, her eyes burning into her husband's. "Why would I spend so much time with somebody I do not care for?"

"Politeness?" He scratched his bald head awkwardly. "But why her? I mean, I don't know. Isn't she too young? She certainly isn't the type of woman you are usually attracted to."

"Pray tell, Henry, what is the type of woman I am attracted to?" Sarcasm dripped from Eleanor's mouth, thick as honey. "And as far as too young is concerned, she is not. Sophie is thirty-two years old, which is hardly too young. Most would think her too old, and they would call her an old maid, wouldn't they?"

"I just meant that she is nothing like Cathleen."

"Nobody is, was, or ever will be. Cathleen is dead, and I have come to accept that fact. It was very difficult, and you know better than anybody else how much I loved her and thought there would never be anyone else I could love as much, but I think I've found the one person I could feel that kind of love for again."

Wiping tears from her eyes, she turned away from her husband and daughter. They had always hoped she would finally overcome her grief and be happy again, and now that she was trying, they were disappointed. Maybe there was no need to go, Eleanor thought sadly. The telegram from Sophie's aunt sounded quite serious. She could be too late already.

"What Papa meant was," Charlotte gently put her hand on her mother's shoulder, "we don't want you to get hurt. You have been through so much already, and we want you to be happy."

"Oh, darling, don't you think I don't know that?"

Eleanor saw Charlotte's all-too-serious face and cupped her daughter's cheek in her palm and pressed a tender kiss on her forehead.

"I am aware of that, and I love you for it, all of you. We simply can't help who we fall in love with. Sophie is a very loving woman. She is chivalrous, caring, and scared to death. She left Vienna because she was afraid and hurt. I have so much to explain, and I need to do so before it's too late."

"All right, Mama. I will gladly come with you then."

"And I shall go help Jonathan," Henry said as he hastened toward the door.

Chapter Fourteen

The earliest train to Salzburg left Vienna at seven o'clock next morning. Henry brought Eleanor, Charlotte, and Rose, the lady's maid, to the station where they boarded the train after Parker made sure their luggage was safely stowed away. The whistle indicated the departure, and Henry closed the door of their compartment and exited before the train rolled slowly out of the station.

First class was most comfortable. Their compartment featured plush white seats, and the restaurant car they would use for a late breakfast and luncheon was roomy and well-appointed. The nine-hour ride to Salzburg across Lower and Upper Austria was a beautiful experience if one could concentrate on the landscape. Unfortunately, though, Eleanor was too preoccupied to focus on anything else but Sophie's health and her hope that they would be there right on time.

While Rose spent time with her needlework, Charlotte enjoyed the book she purchased before they boarded the train. Eleanor truly envied them. If it was possible, she would have paced the corridor just to calm her nerves, but that was out of the question, so she sighed heavily and settled on viewing the landscape. Her eyes swept over the hills, forests, and lakes. She saw people on the fields bringing in the harvest in Lower Austria. When the scenery changed to mountains and lakes in Upper Austria, she felt herself growing tired. After their luncheon at midday Eleanor finally closed her eyes for a short nap and only opened them again when Charlotte gently shook her awake.

"Mama, Mama, we are in Salzburg."

She slowly opened her eyes and blinked uncomprehendingly at first until she remembered where she was.

"Sorry, I must have fallen asleep."

"It's fine, Mama." Charlotte said, amused at her mother's embarrassment. "Rose is taking care of our luggage and is looking for the carriage to the hotel."

"Good, good." Eleanor put on her hat and gloves and followed her daughter off the train and out onto the platform. They spotted Rose at the back of the train asking a street-porter to take their trunks to the carriage. The man lifted his cap and saluted before he loaded everything on to a cart to wheel it to their carriage.

They joined Rose who followed them to the waiting carriage where she paid the porter and asked the driver to take them to the hotel. They arrived at the hotel at four in the afternoon and were shown to the suite Jonathan had booked for them. Eleanor was exhausted from the travel, but she couldn't wait until tomorrow before she went to see Sophie, so she left everything in Rose's capable hands.

With Charlotte, she went downstairs to drive to Therese von Hochstetten's estate on the outskirts of the city of Salzburg.

"Are you expecting visitors, Mummy?" Adele asked from the window in her mother's study.

"No. Not that I'm aware of. Why?" The countess abandoned the papers she had been studying.

"A carriage is coming up our driveway."

"Most curious."

Together they left the study to greet their unexpected guests. At the front door they waited for the driver of the carriage to open the door before they stepped out for proper introductions and a warm welcome.

First to climb out of the carriage was a young woman dressed in a red travelling dress, her hair the colour of the sun, with eyes equalling the sky. Adele couldn't suppress a gasp as she laid eyes on the woman. To say she was beautiful was an understatement. She was tall, slender, her skin was fair and flawless, and her smile made Adele feel weak in the knees. Adele felt herself blush at the scrutiny from those brilliant blue eyes.

The visitor was dressed according to the latest fashion and her hairstyle was done as meticulously as the light make-up she wore. When the young woman stepped aside to let the other occupant of the carriage exit, both Adele and her mother could only stare at the sheer regal air the woman exuded. They were uncannily mother and daughter. Their elegant features, blue eyes, and fine bone structure gave them away. But whereas the younger woman's eyes were open and sparkling, the older woman's were guarded, distant and cool. She was just as tall as her daughter, but her hair was short and snow white. A lock fell daringly over her forehead into her eyes.

The woman was not as old as the colour of her hair would have suggested for her skin was smooth and pale. Her dress was light blue and brought out the colour of her eyes perfectly. To the Countess von Hochstetten, it was clear as day that their visitors were of high rank, so she smoothed down her skirt and stepped forward to greet them properly.

"Welcome to Hochstetten. I am Therese von Hochstetten, and this is my daughter Adele."

"Good afternoon." Charlotte stepped forward with an outstretched hand to greet them, which Therese found slightly unusual. The young woman's mother looked nervous and closed off, so the daughter jumped in to make introductions in her place.

"Please, accept our humblest apology to intrude in such a way. There was no time to announce our visit beforehand. My mother was anxious to get here as soon as we arrived from Vienna."

"Not at all." Therese waved her off, her interest perked by the mention of the capital. "You've come from Vienna?"

"Sorry, how silly of me," Charlotte offered apologetically. "I am Lady Charlotte Edgewood, and this is my mother, Eleanor Edgewood, the Duchess of Darnsworth."

"Indeed," Therese stated curtly.

After their visitors made introductions, and Rose had emerged from the carriage, everybody was shivering, feeling the sudden chill that surrounded them.

Therese thought of her niece and all she had been through: the heart-ache, the pain, the delirium, the unhappiness. Though she wanted to maintain proper etiquette, harsh words slipped out anyway. "What makes you think you are welcome here?"

The bitterness of the words must have gotten through the befuddle-ment the Duchess of Darnsworth was displaying. She jerked up her head, her face whiter than before. She appeared in pain, as if her breath had been taken away, and she put her hand over her chest as if in fright.

"Please, just tell me if she is still alive or not! Am I too late? We shall leave this instant, but please tell me! That is all I am asking."

Therese doubted she had ever seen somebody's demeanour change as fast as she had witnessed in this woman. There was a myriad of emotions now clearly visible in the woman's eyes which hadn't been there only moments before. She had seen her guard drop, rather involuntarily at her words because Therese was sure they had cut deep. Now she observed pain, regret, longing, and fear on the duchess's face, which made her seem more approachable and human. So, she *was* capable of those deep all-consuming feelings her niece had spoken of every time she had mentioned this woman.

Therese felt for her but was determined not to make it easy for her. She had a lot to answer for, after all.

"You have no right to ask this," Therese said.

"I know, but please, let me assure you that I only wish to know if I am too late."

"You are not." Therese stood silent for several moments, then finally relented and admitted, "She is better actually. Soon after I sent the telegram her fever broke, and she was on her way to recovery. She is up again, still weak and coughing, but better."

Covering her mouth with a trembling hand to suppress a sob, Eleanor felt her eyes water at the good news, but refused to let tears fall.

"Thank you. Come on Charlotte, we do not want to make a nuisance of ourselves."

As she turned on her heels to climb into the carriage, Therese rushed forward to halt Eleanor's departure, stopping her short with a hand on her arm.

Therese couldn't believe what was happening. "Oh no, certainly not," she said, full of indignation. "You came here to demand an answer to your question, which you could have easily gotten by writing a letter. But you are here for whatever reason, and I want to know what the hell took you so long? I sent a letter when Sophie first fell ill which was never answered. Why now?"

Charlotte saw her mother's nostrils flare at the accusation and the unpermitted touch. She stepped between the two women and took her mother's arm to calm her down and was grateful when she saw Adele do the same with her mother.

Charlotte said, "I believe there were quite a few misunderstandings which caused this whole unfortunate situation. With your permission, Countess, let us go inside, and we will explain how and when we came upon the knowledge of Sophie's illness."

"That sounds sensible, mother," Adele agreed with a grateful glance at Charlotte.

"Well, ah," Therese stammered, "I may have spoken too quickly—and more forcibly than I should have. I suppose it is a good idea to sit down and discuss this with reason."

Adele led them into the sitting room and ordered tea to help everybody calm their nerves. Their guests were seated on a sofa while she and her mother took opposite chairs. The battle lines had been drawn, but Adele knew her mother's bark was worse than her bite and that she was determined to spare Sophie further heartbreak.

"Here we are," Therese said. "I'm all ears. Now what happened!"

When she heard the impatient tone in her mother's voice, Adele rolled her eyes, all the while wondering when they would inform Sophie of her guests' arrival.

"Beforehand," Eleanor said, "let me tell you how glad I am that Sophie is well again. Now, I assure you that I didn't know anything about her illness until yesterday when Anton von Hagendorf came to our residence to show me your telegram."

"But how can that be?" Therese said, flustered. "What about my letter?"

"I don't know and neither does he, I'm afraid. The only correspondence I received since Sophie's departure was a letter from her telling me in no uncertain terms she did not wish to continue our friendship."

"Are you sure?" Adele asked, unconvinced. This didn't sound like her cousin, especially after she'd heard her call out for this woman in her fever delirium.

"Quite so. I have the letter with me."

"To sum this up," Therese insisted, "you had no idea of my niece's fight for her life until yesterday? No idea whatsoever?"

"None. You have my word." Eleanor solemnly swore

The door to the library suddenly opened, revealing the source of her distress. Sophie appeared paler than usual, but she was alive and angry. "And when did you think to tell me about our guests, Aunt Therese?"

"I had to make sure—"

"What? Make sure what? She would have honourable intentions? Don't be ridiculous! This isn't a drama novel. I'm quite capable of speaking for myself." Sophie was beyond angry at her aunt. Never in her wildest dreams had she thought to find Eleanor in her aunt's sitting room looking as beautiful as she did when she herself felt weaker and more inadequate than ever before.

"As for you, your Grace," Sophie said, "thank you for your concern. I am well again, and you can go back to Vienna with a relieved mind."

Sophie turned on her heel and slammed the door behind her, making them jump at the sudden noise and her bitter words.

Sophie rushed out of the house and down to the pond where she collapsed on a wooden bench. Her breathing was shallow, and her chest hurt from the strain. Doctor Wagner had made it clear she had to take it slow otherwise there was the possibility of a relapse. Up until now, she had done as she was told, but she had to get away from the only person who occupied every moment of her waking hour and her dreams as well.

Eleanor was not only here in Salzburg; she was in her aunt's house. This was unbelievable. Slowly her breathing returned to normal, her racing heart slowed down, and she found said woman standing right in front of her looking worried.

"May I sit or are you going to run again?" Eleanor asked tenderly.

Sophie exhaled audibly, "I'm less of a runner these days than I usually am. So, suit yourself."

"Thank you." Eleanor gingerly sat next to Sophie, keeping her distance though. She was careful not to put any pressure on her. They sat in silence for a while watching a family of ducks gliding over the pond.

"Why are you here?" Sophie asked.

"I needed to see you. Your aunt's telegram was very blunt expressing your state of health."

"It was close for a while," Sophie said softly. "But I'm better now."

"I'm glad."

"You don't need to stay, now that you have confirmed I'm still alive."

"No, there isn't," Eleanor agreed sorrowfully. She had hoped that Sophie would change her mind. "I suppose what you wrote in your letter still holds then?"

"What letter?"

"Your letter. The one you wrote after receiving mine in which I explained everything about my necklace."

"I never received a letter nor did I write a reply." Sophie was confused. "Do you still have my supposed letter?"

"Yes."

"May I see it?"

Wordlessly Eleanor reached into her bag to retrieve the letter. Sophie pulled her reading glasses from inside her jacket and read through the two pages, shaking her head all the while in sheer disbelief. When she was finished Sophie took off her glasses and gazed uncomprehendingly at Eleanor. She had an idea whose handwriting it was, but she hoped her suspicion could be confirmed.

"Who gave you this letter?"

"Your sister, Emma. Why?"

"I didn't write this, and you have just verified what I feared," Sophie explained sadly. "I can't believe she did this. What I don't understand is why."

"Don't worry yourself. It doesn't matter." Eleanor covered Sophie's hands with one of her own, giving it a reassuring squeeze.

"It matters to me!"

"You do agree with the content, then? I had hoped our friendship was worth something more."

"I can't be your friend, Eleanor," Sophie's voice was tinged with sadness.

"Why ever not?" Eleanor asked huskily. She had thought that a friendship between the two of them was the least she could hope for, but now she felt distraught if that was also out of reach.

"Because what I feel for you goes way beyond friendship," Sophie explained hoarsely. "I am in love with you. I desire you. I long to be near you, to touch you and kiss you."

There it was, out in the open. She had unveiled her heart for Eleanor to turn away in disgust and revulsion. Once Sophie had thought their attraction was mutual, but how could she be sure now, especially when she didn't have much experience. She couldn't look at Eleanor, couldn't bear to see anything but gentle amusement in those sky-blue eyes that kept haunting her sleeping and waking hours.

When she felt the soft touch of a warm hand on her right cheek she gasped in surprise. Eleanor turned her head and found the truth of her words written in those brown depths. With her thumb she gently brushed away the silent tear that had escaped its prison.

"I love you, too, you silly woman." Eleanor smiled radiantly. "I desire you and would love to share everything with you. We still have so much to talk about. So much you don't know that I want to tell you."

"Stay then," Sophie urged with newfound courage. "I am sure Aunt Therese would be delighted if you were to stay."

"I don't want to impose."

"You wouldn't. I still have to recuperate, and it would give us more time to spend together, and you could tell me everything you think I need to know."

"I would like that very much."

"It's settled then." Sophie was elated by the prospect of spending uninterrupted time with Eleanor. She felt bold enough to seal the promise with a light brush of her lips over Eleanor's who welcomed the touch and prolonged it by holding Sophie's head more firmly in place.

"Your mother certainly knows what she wants," Adele said appreciatively to her companion. From the back of the house, they had been watching the two women at the pond. Charlotte had worried about her mother, and Adele had offered to take her to a spot where they could keep an eye on them. A peek at Charlotte told her she was a bit embarrassed by her mother's and Sophie's unexpected display of affection, if the pink hue of her cheeks was any indication.

It wasn't as if Charlotte had never seen her mother kiss somebody because she had. Her mother and Cathleen had always been affectionate, which had led to their children catching them kissing or holding hands every now and then. She just felt like an intruder and if she was honest, it also felt slightly awkward to see her mother kiss somebody else but Cathleen.

"Yes, I suppose we wouldn't be here in Salzburg if she didn't," Charlotte said softly.

"It doesn't bother you?"

"No, not really," Charlotte shrugged. "I mean, it will take some time to get used to it, but our family isn't what one might call conventional, although my parents have a special relationship built on trust, respect and shared goals."

"It certainly sounds unlike the marriages of the nobility I am exposed to," Adele said thoughtfully.

"What is even more out of the ordinary is that they didn't withhold from expressing their love for us children. My brothers and I always felt loved and cared for. They never treated us as if we were an obligation or nuisance. We were truly fortunate to have parents such as them, and the best thing of all was to have two sets of parents."

At the last piece of information, Adele appeared startled, wondering what Charlotte meant by that. Charlotte saw the surprise in Adele's face and couldn't help but laugh aloud at the flummoxed expression, so she took her by the elbow and led her on the path at the other side of the pond and explained the unusual constellations of her family. She didn't mind in the least. Spending more time near Adele von Hoch-stetten was something she enjoyed immensely.

Chapter Fifteen

With Therese's permission, Sophie organised for Eleanor's and Charlotte's luggage to be brought to the house under the watchful eye of Rose who was assigned to share a spacious room with Adele's maid Josefine.

Countess von Hochstetten remained reserved towards her guests, especially the duchess, but soon enough she warmed to Eleanor when she realised that her intentions towards her niece were honourable.

What she couldn't make sense of was Charlotte, who was just as charming as her mother but less self-conscious than the duchess. Therese knew her daughter, and it seemed that Adele was quite smitten with Charlotte. They spent so much time together that one could rightfully say they seemed to be joined at the hip. The countess only hoped that her daughter wouldn't have to suffer much heartbreak when Charlotte returned to Vienna.

Sophie was getting better faster than anticipated under the constant and stern care of Eleanor. It was quite charming to watch them court each other. She hoped Sophie had finally found the love she so desperately longed for and deserved. Her niece wouldn't be happy if she interfered, but she had to know for herself that the duchess was indeed as willing to be an active part in this relationship as Sophie.

"Your Grace," Therese asked nervously as she entered the drawing room where she was certain to find Eleanor after luncheon when Sophie would take a short rest. "Do you mind if I keep you company?"

"Not at all."

The duchess closed the book she had been reading and took off her glasses to put both on the small table next to her chair. She waited for the lady of the house to take a seat on the opposite wing chair and get what was bothering her off her chest.

"At the risk of sounding close to an overprotective mother hen or, worse, a terrible busybody, I want you to know I care very much for my niece. Ever since my sister's death, Sophie has spent a lot of time with us, and I came to love her as my own daughter."

"I am well aware of that," Eleanor acknowledged with a slight dip of understanding. From the moment they had met, it was clear to Eleanor that the countess acted more as a parent than a mere relative, and it warmed Eleanor's heart that her beloved was surrounded by such loving care.

"Well, yes, I appreciate that," Therese mumbled, unsure how to proceed without hurting anyone's feelings or inviting her niece's wrath for being intrusive. She just had to be sure this was the right person for Sophie, not another Elisabeth von Meiningen.

"I simply want my niece to be happy and have the relationship she always wished for since she became aware that she loved women."

"That is very thoughtful and enlightened of you. There are very few people who would share your sentiment."

"I know. I know. It wasn't always like that, I am afraid, but after a lot of reading and talking to both my niece and my daughter, I realised the notion of female companionship as a preparation for the marriage to a man is a misguided one. Being with a woman in every sense of the word is not less true or real than it would be with a man."

Eleanor thought about Therese's strange sort of blessing because that was what it was. She went to the window to view the garden where her daughter and Adele reclined on a blanket, laughing, and talking, under a huge protruding weeping willow. This conversation was not only about Sophie and herself she suddenly realised, but about Charlotte's and Adele's blossoming relationship as well. Because there was no doubt in her mind that her daughter was falling in love with the beautiful and sophisticated young woman with whom she was spending every waking hour. If the way Adele kept looking at Charlotte was any indication, Eleanor was convinced the feelings were reciprocated to the fullest.

"What do you want to know?" Eleanor asked, her back to Therese.

"You are married."

It wasn't a question. Eleanor knew this would be an issue, and how could it not be. "I am. Few people have the courage, position, or disregard for convention to live their lives in the way they want to. Henry is a remote cousin of mine. We have known each other since we were children, and strange as it may sound, I love my husband. I was never *in love* with him, mind you, but he has always been my best friend and confidante throughout my childhood years and beyond."

"So, what does he think of this?"

Unbeknownst to them, Sophie entered the room and caught Eleanor's last words.

"This is none of your business, Aunt."

Sophie's voice startled both women and they gazed towards the door to find an infuriated Sophie staring at her aunt.

Eleanor moved from the window to Sophie the moment she realised her love had joined them. She put a calming hand on Sophie's arm. "It is quite all right, my darling."

"It is not," Sophie contradicted passionately. "She has no right to ask you such questions."

"On the contrary. Your aunt loves you very much and cares for you. She has the right to know what sort of person her beloved niece has chosen."

The door on the other side of the sitting room suddenly burst open, revealing two giggling young women who abruptly came to a halt when they realised. They looked at the tableau before them, from one face to the other, and must have immediately felt the tension in the room.

"I am sorry. We didn't know anybody was in here." Adele blushed furiously, her hand clutching Charlotte's in silent support.

"Never mind," Eleanor said in a soothing voice. "I suggest you two come in. Because I somehow suspect what I have to tell Sophie and your mother might interest you as well." She glanced towards Sophie with a knowing smile.

Adele's blush deepened further. She swallowed hard as if unsettled, but she held her head straight, her eyes never wavering.

Eleanor approved of what she saw, and she nodded appreciatively before she turned to Sophie again. "Why don't we all take a seat and calm down before we continue our conversation?" She moved back to her chair and waited for everybody else to do so before she opened her mouth to start her tale only to be interrupted by Sophie.

"You don't have to do this."

"Yes, I do, and it's time you know everything. I am not ashamed about the past, and this is something we haven't talked about up 'til now. You not knowing caused the original misunderstanding between us, and I don't want that anymore."

"Very well then. Go on, please."

Eleanor first gazed lovingly at her, then she let her eyes glide over to her daughter and her new friend who sat so close together you couldn't really tell where one ended and the other began.

She took a deep breath and launched into her tale starting with her grandmother and her companion. She told about the first time she and Cathleen had met, their life together. How her marriage was one of friendship, safety, and freedom to live and love the one she desired. She left nothing out. The birth of her children, their upbringing with her lover's help. Eleanor told them about the saddest time of her life when Cathleen fell terminally ill and died and the grief she couldn't seem to overcome. And how very much more alive she felt since she met Sophie and fell in love again.

After this tour de force through her life, Eleanor fell back against her chair, exhausted from the emotional upheaval the memories had brought. There were tears in everybody's eyes and a good amount of respect for the woman who had just exposed her heart to virtual strangers. Her own daughter hadn't been aware of some of the aspects of her mother's past.

Charlotte was the first to break the silence that fell over the room when her mother finished. She went to her mother's chair and bent to whisper in her ear. "Thank you, Mama, for sharing this with us. I'm very proud of you."

Eleanor laughed tremulously at Charlotte, her eyes watery as she looked at her daughter. "Thank you, darling."

Charlotte gave her mother's hand a reassuring squeeze before she held out her hand to Adele. You probably need some time alone, so Adele and I will be off."

Therese said, "I have some household matters to attend to, so I shall also leave you." She rose and followed the girls.

When the door closed behind them, Eleanor left her chair and sat next to Sophie who was completely silent and seemed deep in thought.

"Say something," Eleanor urged her gently as she wrung her hands nervously in her lap. She was relieved when she felt Sophie's hand softly covering her own. Lifting her gaze, she found those soulful brown eyes glancing at her with such tenderness and love, it nearly took her breath away.

"I love you, Eleanor, more than words could express."

Sophie leaned in and gently brushed her full lips over Eleanor's. She did so twice before Eleanor put both of her hands against her cheeks to hold her in place and deepen the kiss. They only pulled apart when breathing became an issue. Eleanor wouldn't let go, though. She nuzzled into Sophie's long dark hair which smelled of roses, summer, and something that was uniquely her beloved's own scent.

"Stay with me tonight, darling," Eleanor asked huskily, not wanting to rush Sophie, but she felt the need to be close to her, to hold her in her arms and be held. It had been so long since she had shared her bed with another woman, had felt the softness of the female body, the gentle touch and loving embrace.

"I would love to."

Neither of them was quite ready for the next step in their relationship, but she couldn't think of a place she would rather be tonight especially after these emotional revelations.

In the garden, back on the blanket under the willow tree, Charlotte and Adele were lost in their own thoughts. They had refused to give up their closeness, and Charlotte rested with her head in Adele's lap while Adele softly stroked her hair. The motion nearly put Charlotte to sleep, and she closed her eyes in contentment.

Adele gently cleared her throat in order not to startle her. Charlotte lazily opened her eyes to gaze expectantly at her companion and wondered what was on her mind. Nothing was forthcoming, and Adele chewed uncertainly on her lower lip, avoiding Charlotte's gaze.

"Tell me!" Charlotte urged.

Adele shook her head. Charlotte would leave all too soon and they probably would never see each other again. Nothing would come of this; Adele was no fool. Charlotte was the daughter of a duchess, sophisticated and used to moving in social circles way above her own. How could she entertain the idea of a meaningful relationship with her?

"I think I'm falling in love with you." It burst out of her before she could stop herself. She closed her eyes, feeling the urge to run. When Charlotte sat up, Adele scrambled to her feet and took off toward the tree line.

She heard Charlotte calling, "Adele, wait!" But she didn't wait; she kept on going, stumbling through the small forest until she suddenly felt a hand on her elbow.

"Would you please stop running?" Charlotte halted her escape, her hand firmly on Adele's elbow, never losing her grip. "You gave me no chance to answer."

"It is pointless anyway, isn't it?"

"What is?"

"Me, falling in love with you."

Charlotte cupped Adele's cheeks in her hands and kissed her. Once, twice, running her tongue over Adele's lower lip and seeking entrance, which was granted with a moan. They kissed until both ran out of breath and Charlotte, panting, leaned her forehead against Adele's.

Charlotte whispered, "I think I am falling in love with you, too."

"Love isn't always enough." Adele shook her head and freed herself from Charlotte's arms. She kissed her cheek and returned to the house, leaving a confused Charlotte behind.

Eleanor had joined Sophie in the pavilion. They needed their emotions to settle down, and the best way to do that was by means of distraction, so she had asked Sophie to show her the most recent project. Just as Sophie was pointing out a very difficult passage in the manuscript she was currently translating, Eleanor saw Adele returning to the house. Her steps were determined; her chin set defiantly, but there was a storm raging in the young woman's eyes. Eleanor had kept an eye on her daughter and Adele, and she had wondered what was going on when she saw them running into the forest. By the expression on Adele's face, and the way they had grown fond of each other, Eleanor had a very good idea what the heart of the matter was. She watched Adele march into the house before she decided to follow her.

"Where are you going?" Sophie frowned. The confusion on her face made Eleanor smile as she kissed the top of her head affectionately.

"I think I need to speak to your cousin." She was stopped when Sophie grabbed her wrist.

"Come back, will you?"

"Of course." She put her finger under Sophie's chin and raised her head before gently kissing her on the lips. She smirked when Sophie kept her eyes closed with a dreamy expression on her face.

Adele had already gone to her room when Eleanor entered the house. She met a worried Therese at the bottom of the stairs. The countess clutched the banister in a vice-like grip, torn between motherly worry and her daughter's need for solace.

Eleanor put a reassuring hand on her shoulder. "Allow me. I believe I know what is going on, and without trying to sound too presumptuous, I think I might understand better why she is so upset."

"By all means," Therese gestured up the stairs, indicating for Eleanor to do as she suggested.

Eleanor gathered her skirt to ascend the stairs to Adele's room. After smoothing out her skirt fabric at the top of the stairs, she approached the closed door and rapped her knuckles gently against it.

"Who is it?" a muffled voice asked.

"Charlotte's mother. May I come in?"

"If you must," Adele answered sounding slightly annoyed.

Eleanor stepped through the door and found Adele at a desk by the window. Papers were strewn all over it. Books lay scattered on various chairs. The only place untouched by this creative chaos was the bed. She navigated to the bed and sat, waiting for Adele to start.

"What can I do for you, your Grace?" Adele swivelled in her chair and glared expectantly and a little defiantly at her guest.

"May I ask what you are working on?" Eleanor thought it best to take another route to conquer the problem at hand.

Adele was visibly surprised by the question and appeared completely stunned. "Just some silly essays nobody will ever read." Adele waved her hand over her desk indicating the mound of papers gathering there.

"About what?"

Adele tipped the end of her pencil against her lips, contemplating the question. "I don't know whether to be truthful or not. Not a lot of women agreed with my viewpoints."

"Try me. Perhaps I am more open to unconventional thoughts than you think. So, what are the essays about?"

"Women's rights, the right to vote, and social issues."

"Interesting. Would you mind discussing those issues with me?"

"You don't have to be nice."

Eleanor chuckled at the assessment. "I am not nice, let me assure you. If I wasn't interested, I wouldn't ask. I am not known to waste my time on things I do not care for."

"All right. And why are you really here?" Adele finally asked, although she was certain she knew the answer already.

"What happened between you and my daughter?"

"We kissed," Adele said bluntly. "I am falling for her, but I know it won't ever be enough."

"Why not?"

"Because it wouldn't lead to anything. You're going to leave rather sooner than later now, and I possess nothing I could offer to Charlotte. I have no means, unlike my cousin, no independent career whatsoever and let's be honest, I'm merely the daughter of a country noble. Nothing grand. Charlotte is completely unobtainable to me."

"Don't sell yourself short, my dear." Eleanor tried to admonish her gently.

"I am not. These are the simple facts. What could she possibly want with me? I am sure there are enough women in London who would gladly become Charlotte's companion."

"I suppose so. But if I know my daughter and I think I do, they hold no interest for her. You have a mind of your own, just as your cousin does, and I think that is what drew Charlotte to you in the first place. You are right of course. She does not lack female suitors, but none of them ever captured her quite the way you have."

Adele stared into space, silently.

"The question is: are you willing to risk it and give your relationship a chance? I for one would be delighted to see my daughter happy with the woman she loves."

Eleanor didn't wait for a reply but simply stood and quietly left Adele to her thoughts. She hoped Adele would again find the courage she had shown over the last few days when pursuing Charlotte.

When she returned to the garden, Eleanor found Charlotte in deep conversation with Sophie, but she stopped speaking as soon as she saw her mother striding towards them.

"Well?" Charlotte asked anxiously.

"Give her time, darling. I believe she was a bit overwhelmed by her own courage. But my guess is that she's going to surprise you again."

"I hope you're right, Mama." Charlotte looked crestfallenly at her mother. Eleanor put her arm around her daughter's shoulder. Charlotte let her head sink on her mother's comforting shoulder. She giggled tremulously when she felt her mother deposit a kiss on her head.

"I am quite certain. You'll see."

True to her mother's instincts, Adele asked Charlotte after dinner to take a walk with her in the garden so they could talk. Catching Eleanor's encouraging gaze, they left the table eager to find themselves alone to speak.

The others retired to the drawing room for coffee. Therese handed Sophie and Eleanor theirs before she poured herself a cup. She observed her niece and her paramour carefully. They made quite a striking couple. The only drop of bitterness was that they couldn't outwardly live the love they so obviously held for each other in the way they wanted. She sighed at this sad thought, causing her guests to peer at her questioningly.

"Are you all right, Aunt Therese?" Sophie asked, her voice full of worry.

"I'm fine, dear."

"I meant to tell you I think it's time to go back to Vienna next week."

"Already?" Therese was disappointed. She loved having her niece around. But she knew Vienna was the place she needed to be right now. The same place her daughter would be for the time being until it was time for them to pack their things and leave Austria all together. She was no fool; she knew full well that Adele would follow Charlotte. It filled her with happiness that they both had finally found what they had so long searching for, but at the same time, she felt deeply saddened that she had to watch her daughter leave. London wasn't that far away, and she could always visit, knowing she would be welcome. This somewhat eased her heavy heart.

Therese was stirred from her reverie when the door to the drawing room suddenly burst open followed by two giggling young women. Adele and Charlotte looked slightly flushed, and their hair was in distinct disarray. At least they had the grace to blush at their appearance.

"I am sorry." Adele mumbled at the raised eyebrow she received from her mother and the knowing smile from her cousin.

"I hope not." Eleanor smirked at their flustered faces.

"Mama!"

Eleanor rolled her eyes at her daughter's indignant outburst. "Anyway, if you please, excuse me. I think I will go to bed. Good night."

Sophie stood with her and followed her to the door. They stopped when they heard Charlotte sputter behind them.

"Are you two . . . you know . . . I mean . . . you can't possibly . . ."

Eleanor said, "This, my darling daughter, is not any of your business. Good night!"

Eleanor's voice brooked no argument. There was also a hint of hurt in it. Charlotte cursed herself for her stupidity. She hurried after her mother to apologise. Wasn't that the purpose of the whole journey? For her mother to be with Sophie in every way? Charlotte embraced her mother tightly.

"I'm sorry, Mama. That was uncalled for." She felt a weight being lifted from her shoulders when Eleanor returned the embrace.

"Good night, darling."

Eleanor took Sophie's left hand in her own, and together they left the room. At a moderate pace they climbed the stairs to their rooms, stopping in front of Sophie's door to kiss slowly before Eleanor went to her own room. Both changed into their sleepwear, and when Eleanor heard a soft knock on her door, she permitted entrance without a second thought. She sat in front of the vanity brushing her hair as Sophie entered the room looking a bit insecure. Feeling her heart go out to her beloved, she put her brush down and held out her hand. Sophie stepped forward to take it and was enveloped in strong arms. She let go of her cane and wrapped her arms around Eleanor's body.

Through their thin sleepwear she felt the heat of her skin and the curves of her womanly body pressing so deliciously against her own. Sophie put her head in the crook of Eleanor's neck to inhale the scent of her hair and skin. It was intoxicating; she traced her lips along Eleanor's throat to her chin until she found her lips in a passionate kiss that was broken far too soon for her liking.

Eleanor took a deep breath as she pulled away. Neither was ready for more; it was still too soon. She bent to pick up the cane and hand it to Sophie and caught the flicker of pain in Sophie's eyes at the gesture. So she simply took Sophie's hand to lead her to the bed where they sat on the edge.

"None of that embarrassment, please." Eleanor took Sophie's chin in her hand and turned her face towards her. "I will have none of that. I know who you are and this," she pointed at the cane in Sophie's hand, "doesn't change what I feel for you."

"But—"

"No. I won't get tired of retrieving it for you. Nothing about you distracts from the beautiful woman you are." Eleanor put her palm against Sophie's scarred cheek to strengthen her point. "When we are ready to make love, I want to see all of you. I want you to feel comfortable to show me your body. Until then, I will make sure you believe me that I do desire you very much."

"I do believe you," Sophie objected softly.

"You might not yet entirely, but you will, my darling." Eleanor kissed her again, putting everything she felt for her into that kiss. When they ended their kiss, they got comfortable in the large bed, wrapped into each other's arms. With contentment on their faces, they fell asleep dreaming of the day they would finally become lovers in the truest sense of the word.

Chapter Sixteen

The day of Charlotte and Adele's departure was approaching faster than Therese von Hochstetten cared to admit. A lengthy conversation with her daughter and Charlotte had eased some of the pain she felt when she thought of her little girl leaving for good. Charlotte's sincere words as well as the tangible love she felt for Adele had soothed her motherly worries considerably but didn't make it easier to see them leave.

Sophie, on the other hand, felt her anger bubbling up again as she thought about the coming confrontation she would have with her sister. It was unavoidable; for Emma's cruel actions had caused her and Eleanor so much heartache, adding to the stupid misunderstanding that kept them apart, nearly losing them every chance to be together forever.

She wasn't sure she could ever forgive Emma. What she wanted to know was why she had done it.

Sophie looked up from her papers and through the window saw Eleanor returning from a lengthy ride with her daughter and Adele. She couldn't help but admire the woman as she sat so regally on the horse, her white hair wind-blown and her cheeks becomingly tinted pink.

Eleanor's eyes sought the place she knew she would find Sophie and wasn't at all surprised to find her intently watching. She smiled and mouthed a silent "I love you" to the woman who had so unexpectedly and completely stolen her heart. Never in her wildest dreams would she have thought that after the love she shared with Cathleen, she would find something just as intense and wonderful again.

Sophie abandoned her papers to visit with the three women outside. The damp weather of the last few days had put a strain on her leg, and she leaned heavily on her cane as she crossed the lawn to join them before they led the horses back in to the stable.

"Your Grace," Sophie greeted playfully as she drew near to Eleanor.

"Countess," Eleanor responded in an equally good mood.

"Hey, cousin," Adele spurred her horse forward, "why didn't you ride with us? It was wonderful after nearly four days of rain on end."

"I'm sure it was, but I have to finish the translations before we return."

Eleanor didn't object for she knew it was a little white lie. She was aware that Sophie's leg was troubling her, and that was the real reason she declined the invitation to accompany them. Not that Sophie would ever admit it to anyone, but by the way she moved, from the lines of strain around her eyes, and how she leaned more heavily on her cane were all clear signs to Eleanor. There was nothing she could do, though.

It hurt that Sophie wouldn't admit her physical pain to her, but after so many years of putting up a front, the habit must be hard to break. All Eleanor could do was wait until Sophie was ready to trust her completely and let her help ease the pain. From the constant frown on Sophie's forehead, she thought something else was on Sophie's mind.

"What is troubling you so?" Eleanor asked quietly as she dismounted to walk with Sophie towards the stable.

"Am I that obvious?"

"Not really, but you have been brooding for days now. You have this line on your forehead when you are worried about something."

"So, I'm transparent now," Sophie murmured in mock exasperation. She took hold of Eleanor's free hand as they sauntered next to each other. "It's my sister and the role she played in this whole unfortunate affair."

"I am sorry."

"Don't be! It isn't *your* fault. I had no idea she could do something so awful or hurtful. It's as if I don't know her anymore." Sophie gave a sad shake of her head. "Right now, I'm so angry when I think of the things she has done. I'm afraid when we meet again, I will let my emotions get the better of me and I'll lash out at her."

"It would be understandable." Eleanor squeezed her hand gently.

"But that would accomplish nothing."

Sophie could only hope she would keep her temper in check when talking to her sister, but she feared Emma would aggravate her again. She would have to wait and see.

Therese von Hochstetten accompanied her guests and daughter to the station when it was time to for them to leave Salzburg and return to Vienna. After a tearful goodbye, they boarded the train and waved until she was out of sight, then heaved sighs as they sank down in their seats. Eleanor observed her travelling companions with contentment, but when her eyes fell on Adele's maid she frowned at the girl's bleak demeanour.

Eleanor knew better than to ask her what was wrong because the girl was already too frightened by her mere presence. They belonged to completely different social classes, but Eleanor always had a good rapport with servants. Mutual respect was the foundation for an effective relationship with servants and respect had served her well. Rose was the best example. Although she was quite young, she was still working as her lady's maid after a year, and Eleanor was more than satisfied with her service. Rose seemed quite comfortable with her position as did all of their servants.

Eleanor caught her own maid's eyes of her maid and gestured for her to follow her outside the compartment. "Excuse us for a moment," she said as she preceded Rose through the door.

Rose followed her mistress out of their compartment. A few feet from their compartment, Eleanor stopped and turned to face her. From the look on Rose's face, clearly she was wondering what was on her mind

"I need you to do me a favour, Rose."

"Of course, your Grace." The maid agreed without hesitation.

"You have money?"

"Yes, ma'am."

Slightly annoyed, Eleanor said, "Please take that shivering girl to the dining car for a coffee and a piece of cake before she suffers a stroke or heart attack."

"Do you want me to find out what is going on?" Rose asked. "Is that why you want me to take Josefine for something to drink?"

"I knew there was a reason why I decided to make you my lady's maid."

Eleanor smiled and sent Rose back ahead of her before she joined the others again. The questioning looks cast her way were waved off nonchalantly as she settled in her seat. Charlotte and Adele continued their soft conversation while Sophie put her head on Eleanor's shoulder and gazed out the window.

Rose whispered something to Josefine and the two crept out of the compartment like quiet mice.

"Are you angry with Josefine?" Sophie asked after a while.

"Not at all. I merely thought she'd be more comfortable with just Rose for company for a while." She took hold of one of Sophie's hands.

"Life hasn't been kind to her."

"I thought as much, but it wouldn't do for her to act like a frightened deer all the time. She'll be a part of our household and can't be afraid of her own shadow when working there."

"I see. So, you asked Rose to calm her fears and find out what was the matter?" Sophie guessed.

"Yes."

"I could tell you a bit about her past if you wish."

"Oh?" Eleanor raised an eyebrow in question. "Please, by all means do."

Sophie sat up straight and told her Josefine's story from the time she became a part of her father's household at the age of thirteen—including a rape by Count von Bernthal—and up to the moment Sophie met her while Josefine was trying to survive as a prostitute. She explained how she had rescued the young woman, assisting her in becoming her cousin's maid, and now how Josefine was a good servant but perpetually frightened she would lose her position and be back on the streets.

Charlotte and Adele both listened carefully to what Sophie had to tell. Sophie thought they were as outraged as Eleanor was when they learned the whole truth.

"Now I can't understand your sister's engagement to that despicable man at all," Eleanor said.

"Neither can I," Charlotte agreed whole-heartedly.

Josefine sat subdued in her seat, barely answering the questions Rose was asking. She kept her eyes fixed on the tablecloth, but her eyes went wide when Rose produced Eleanor's calling card to stop the waiter from objecting to their presence before he could utter a single word.

"Her Grace will confirm her orders if necessary as it was she who sent us here," Rose informed the man using the same haughty tone she often heard from her mistress. "But I wouldn't recommend it. You wouldn't want to question the orders of a Duchess of the British Empire, would you?"

"If you say so, Miss." The man sniffed, took their requests, and went off to fetch their orders.

"Is it true?" Josefine whispered.

"What?"

"That her Grace sent us here?"

"Of course." Rose grinned like a Cheshire cat. "She was a bit annoyed that you wouldn't relax in her presence. She hates it when servants are all fidgety and act like scaredy-cats."

"But she is a duchess," Josefine said as though scandalised. "Why would she care how I feel?"

"Because you're part of her household now, and she won't have you cowering in a corner every time she enters a room or passes you on the stairs."

"But I thought—"

"What? What did you think?" Rose inquired impatiently. Her answer had to wait though because their coffee and cake were delivered by a still not truly convinced waiter. When he departed, she prodded Josefine again. "Well?"

"I thought Countess von Hochstetten would stay at the Palais Hagendorf."

"Why would she? The person she wants to be with is the daughter of the duchess, and I know for certain that the both of you are going to stay at the home of Charlotte and her parents."

Josefine breathed a sigh of relief. "Thank God."

"Hey, you can relax. I know you are nervous about being in the presence of such a formidable woman like the duchess, but she's actually quite kind. Especially to those of us who work in the household." Rose reached out and covered one of Josefine's hands with her own. "You'll like it, you'll see. It is a decent household, a good place to work. Nice people upstairs and downstairs."

"Sure," Josefine mumbled, clearly not convinced at all.

Rose knew too much had happened since Josefine became a maid, not to mention beforehand. Rose had heard rumours that Josefine had seen, heard, and experienced too much to believe her luck would hold any longer. The girl was weary, and why wouldn't she be?

"Listen, the duchess is stern but fair. She expects a meticulous work ethic, but she and her family treat us well. Better than most employers would, and believe me, the same can be said about his Lordship as well as their children. Downstairs is quite a colourful collection of people from all paths of life. Whatever it is that has you wound up so tight, it won't happen there."

"As if. Those people take what they need, and then they throw you away like a piece of rubbish. They take your pride, your dignity, and leave you with nothing but the clothes on your back."

Rose heard Josefine's bitterness. She knew her place but being treated like a mere piece of meat had left its marks.

"Some of them do," Rose said. I would be the last to deny that, but this family is different."

Rose felt the need to defend her mistress because when nobody else would have given a damn about any of the servants, the duchess and his lordship had. They took them in, gave them a purpose and with it the dignity Josefine spoke about. When she saw that the other maid was still reluctant to believe her, Rose thought she could tell a few truths about the servants. She wouldn't betray any confidences since none of them was making a secret of their past, and if Josefine were to hear their stories, she might feel better about her new assignment. Rose's fellow workers had survived what life and malevolent human beings had thrown their way and would tell the tale to anyone who was willing to listen.

Upon hearing Josefine's story, Charlotte and Eleanor were convinced she would fit in perfectly with their other servants. They were committed to going out of their way to make her welcome and help her find her way within the household.

"They might need a little bit getting used to." Eleanor said, "but otherwise they're good people." Given their own past experiences, no one in my employ will think any less of Josefine."

Adele was intrigued. "What are their stories, if you don't mind my asking?" She knew Sophie would want to know but was far too polite to ask. Adele and Sophie were both heavily involved in organisations that helped the lower classes better their chances. So of course she wondered what kind of person her beloved's mother was, how she treated her servants. So far, Adele had to admit that the duchess treated her maid far better than many of the lower nobilities treated theirs, as Adele had observed from the behaviour of some of her mother's acquaintances.

"Benson, our butler, has been with my husband's family since he was a mere footman," Eleanor explained proudly. "You might find him a bit intimidating at first for he wears an eye patch. It gives him a roughish air."

Charlotte snorted at that description. "Grandmother certainly thinks so."

"What happened to his eye?" Sophie asked.

"Let's just say my late father-in-law always had a volatile temper, and Henry had to take the brunt of it. He never could do anything to satisfy his father's expectations, and one day it got so bad that his father nearly beat him to death. If it hadn't been for Benson stopping him, Henry may have lost his life. But in his rage, my father-in-law directed his anger instead at the footman, Benson, who then lost his eye."

"Goodness," Adele exclaimed in shock.

"Benson left service, but after my late father-in-law's death, Henry made sure to rehire Benson, which is a benefit to our household each and every day." Eleanor would always be fond of the man who saved Henry's life and become such an integral part of their household.

"I agree with you, Mother," Charlotte said. "He's a very sweet man. Our cook, Mrs. Chambers, on the other hand, is rather more frightening."

Eleanor raised an eyebrow. "She knows her worth, my dear. And rightfully so. I have only admiration for such a feisty woman. I know I can always rely upon her." She turned toward Adele. "Mrs. Chambers was also with my husband's family for a long time before she became our cook. I don't know what I would do without her. The magic she works in the kitchen is unrivalled."

Charlotte asked, "Is that why you felt the need to apologise for Papa's *faux pas* when grandmother visited us last time?"

"My darling, there are times when even a duchess must step down and make amends with those who happen to serve her. Mrs. Chambers had saved me from an otherwise most embarrassing ordeal, and such an effort had to be acknowledged."

"Papa said you asked Mrs. Kavanaugh to accompany Mrs. Chambers?" Charlotte inquired curiously.

"Ever since Mrs. Kavanaugh became our housekeeper, we questioned whether they were going to one day murder or kiss each other, as you well know. I can honestly say I am deliriously happy it was the latter."

This caused everybody to laugh heartily. But the assessment was true. Eleanor remembered how often she or Cathleen had to listen to either woman complain about the other overstepping her boundaries. When Eleanor reached the end of her patience, she ordered them plainly to stop annoying her and to work out their differences between them or she would have to look for new servants.

How she had hoped at the time it would be an empty threat. Everybody held their breath for days . . . and nearly all were more than surprised they hadn't strangled each other.

At long last, the two women finally admitted their mutual attraction and quietly went about rearranging their lives in such a way that most of the other servants weren't aware of how deep their bond became.

What followed then was blissful peace downstairs and people upstairs grateful that everything was running smoothly again.

Eleanor said, "As for our footmen, James and Cedric, I have to admit with great trepidation, they were both involved in the Cleveland Street scandal in 1889."

"Please elaborate, my love." Sophie gazed over at Adele and Charlotte. "By the expression on your face, Adele, I would wager that you're not aware of this scandal either."

"It was a very sordid affair, really," Eleanor said. "There happened to be a male brothel where men of prominent position sought the service of young men."

"It caused quite an uproar, as you can imagine," Charlotte added. "James and Cedric were two of the young men involved, but we only found out about it later, after one of Papa's business associates dined at our house and recognised them."

"What happened?" Adele asked with keen interest.

"Initially the man visiting was very distressed because he thought Henry had arranged this in order to blackmail him." Eleanor snorted out a guffaw at the ridiculousness of the thought. "When we assured him that nothing could be further from the truth, he was relieved but never again accepted an invitation. Not that we were overly sorry about that, mind you."

Adele said, "I suppose you know more about your servants than most other people do."

"We try to, dear, but ours is a large household. We do not know each and every detail about all our kitchen maids, stable hands or many others who keep the place running so smoothly."

"I wouldn't expect you to," Adele said. I appreciate your concerns. It is still quite remarkable how kind you are."

"Thank you, I guess." Eleanor said, flustered. Being praised for what wasn't her doing at all seemed inappropriate. When she felt Sophie entwine one of her hands with one of hers, she leaned back and instantly felt better.

Rose came back with Josefine a quarter hour later, and the new maid seemed decidedly more at ease. Eleanor raised a questioning eyebrow at her maid and after she received a confident nod, she closed her eyes. Trust Rose to make sure the new addition to the servant's quarters would feel more welcome and at ease around the family.

When the train from Salzburg rolled into the station, Lord Edgewood was already waiting patiently for the party. Eleanor's telegram had been nothing short of a surprise to him. He had never thought that not only his wife but also his daughter would return with a significant other at their sides.

The first to exit the train were Rose and Josefine who greeted his lordship respectfully before they hurried off to take care of the luggage and call a second carriage. When Charlotte jumped from the compartment into his waiting arms, Henry joyfully embraced her. He laughed at the exuberant behaviour of his firstborn, holding her tight in a fatherly embrace.

"Papa!" Charlotte inhaled her father's familiar cologne.

"Hello, darling!" He peeked over her shoulder and found his wife waiting for him to help her step down from the compartment. Henry let go of Charlotte and held out his hand to guide Eleanor down onto the platform.

"Welcome home, dear." He kissed her rosy cheek gallantly.

"Hello, Henry," she said warmly.

Both waited for the other two women to exit, and Eleanor made formal introductions. "Henry, dear, please meet Sophie von Hagendorf and her cousin Adele von Hochstetten."

"Lord Edgewood." Sophie and Adele greeted him respectfully. Henry shook Sophie's hand somehow sensing that anything else would not be welcome, but he kissed Adele's hand with a flourish that made her blush.

"Please, ladies, call me Henry when we are amongst family," he asked with a twinkle in his eyes. "Will the both of you come to the palais with us?"

"I should go home." Sophie locked her gaze with Eleanor who understood the need but wasn't ready to say her goodbye right now.

Although Eleanor had told Sophie about the status of her marriage, she thought Sophie might feel insecure when confronted with her beloved's husband. "Darling, why don't you come to the palais with us, and Parker can drive you home later?" Eleanor put a hand imploringly on Sophie's arm. She knew there was no way Sophie could ever deny Eleanor anything. One glance in those sky-blue eyes and Sophie was lost.

Sophie agreed and held out her arm for her love to take which she did with pleasure. Henry led them outside where Parker was waiting with a carriage. Behind it stood another to carry their luggage and their maids.

His lordship and Parker helped the ladies climb inside before the driver took the reins and spurred the horses towards their destination.

Charlotte chattered away happily about their time in Salzburg giving Henry the opportunity to observe Eleanor and Sophie unobtrusively. He noticed the closeness between them and the way they held hands the whole time. It seemed as if Eleanor's presence put Sophie more at ease than anything else. When he'd shook hands with his wife's lover, he noticed the tensing of her body, but her whole demeanour changed when Eleanor touched her arm. Even her features seemed more relaxed with Eleanor so close.

Henry couldn't help but grin from ear to ear when he looked at them. His wife had her beloved already wrapped around her little finger. The willingness with which Sophie had given in to Eleanor's request to accompany them was proof enough, at least to him. No longer did he possess a single doubt in his mind that they loved each other.

Henry let his gaze wander to his daughter and her love interest, finding her equally smitten and very much in love with Adele. Adele felt the same way for his daughter—that much was as plain as day. Henry leaned back with satisfaction, happy that the most important females in his life had found the love they deserved.

The welcome of the new members of the family at the palais was warm and sincere. Eleanor was greeted just as cheerfully by her sons as Henry had been by Charlotte.

Giulia embraced her granddaughter tenderly and said, "Love does suit you, my dear."

"Thank you, Nonna." She drew apart and presented Sophie to her grandmother.

"Contessa." Sophie's greeting was stiff as she held the contessa's hand in her own.

"Call me Giulia, dear."

"Thank you, Giulia."

"See that wasn't so hard, was it?"

Sophie shook her head mournfully, eliciting a laugh from the contessa. She had wanted to fold Sophie in a grandmotherly embrace as she had Eleanor, but she knew it wouldn't be welcome, yet. Giulia had registered how Sophie's body language changed when Philip and Martin embraced their mother and then shook Sophie's hand in welcome. Sophie reminded her of a trapped animal only soothed by the presence of the woman her heart desired.

The young men welcomed Adele warmly, but Philip was clearly more intrigued by the woman who had captured his mother's heart. Martin remained in the background so far which didn't go completely unnoticed by his mother or grandmother.

Giulia barely suppressed a chuckle when Philip bombarded poor Sophie with questions about her work, asking how she had learned all those languages and what she found most difficult when translating manuscripts.

Eleanor finally had to put a stop to it, glad that Sophie was so easily welcomed but sensing her lover's discomfort, so she asked Philip to slow down. "Please, safe some of your questions for later. I am sure Sophie will be happy to answer each and every one of them. Just give her time to breathe and settle down."

"Sorry, Mama," Philip apologised with a healthy blush on his cheeks.

"Why don't you accompany your sister and Adele?" Eleanor suggested. "I'm sure Adele would love to get to know you better."

When the young ones left, she shot a meaningful glance at her husband and her grandmother, making it clear that she needed time alone with her love to say goodbye.

"Henry, my dear," Giulia said, "why don't we fetch Jonathan and have a nice cup of tea." Giulia hooked Lord Edgewood's arm and stirred him towards the drawing room.

Henry caught on instantly. "Yes, splendid idea."

"We'll see you soon, Sophie," Giulia said as Henry swept her toward the door.

"Of course."

Silently the two women watched them trudge off, breathing a sigh of relief when they were finally alone. Eleanor stepped closer to wrap her arms around her lover's neck. She rested her head on Sophie's shoulder. Slender arms pulled her closer against a warm body.

"I am sorry," Eleanor murmured. "They can be a bit overwhelming. But they mean well, and I think they like you."

"It is quite all right, love. I'm not used to such openly displayed affection."

Eleanor pulled back to study Sophie's deep brown eyes. She gently cupped her cheek in her palm and stroked her thumb over plush lips before she leaned in and brushed her own lips over Sophie's fuller ones.

"I am afraid you will have to get used to it, my darling. They care for you, and it is their way of making you welcome."

"They will have to be patient, though."

"Don't worry," Eleanor assured her. "They will be. But even after all these years, Jonathan is still not used to this open and readily displayed affection. He wasn't there to greet me which means he will do so later, in a quiet moment."

"You don't mind?" Sophie asked, surprised.

"Not at all. He is a vital part of the family, and I cherish him very much. It was long ago that I learned to accept his way of conduct. Jonathan is a rock in a stormy sea. Solid, reliable but also warm and loving in his own way."

"I'm looking forward to meeting him."

Sophie kissed her again, lingering with more passion than before. They parted when air became an issue but refused to let go completely just yet.

"I should go."

"I know."

"When will I see you again?"

"Why don't you have dinner with me tomorrow?" Eleanor asked.

She didn't want to be needy or cling too much because she would have preferred if Sophie stayed with her. Going to sleep with her and waking up with her was what she wanted, but she didn't want to push her. Patience was a virtue she had to master right now.

"I would love to."

They kissed for the last time and Eleanor brought Sophie to the door where she stole another kiss before she left for home.

Oh, yes, Eleanor would love to have Sophie with her all the time to kiss and touch to her heart's desire. With a blissful smile on her lips, she decided to change out of her traveling clothes before she joined the family for tea.

Chapter Seventeen

Sophie dreaded the unavoidable confrontation with her sister. She was so angry at her sister for nearly destroying her chance of happiness, and she only hoped there would be time to prepare herself. Right now she was too tired from the journey and emotionally exhausted. Sophie still couldn't believe Emma was capable of such a thing. She had nearly lost this precious love. Emma didn't understand, but why couldn't she simply let her be? She didn't expect her sister to support her but at least accept her. Maybe it was too much to ask. Sophie groaned when she thought of the last conversation with Emma and the hurtful words exchanged between them.

Parker stopped at the front entrance and helped Guttmann carry her luggage inside. Sophie thanked him and listlessly climbed the stairs to her rooms. She was looking forward to a hot shower, change of clothes and a nap before dinner. Her maid welcomed her warmly and mentioned how relieved she was to find Sophie well again after the fright over her illness.

Ever since Sophie's mother's death, Martha tended to be over-protective. Something Sophie had learned to accept and appreciate over the years. After her shower she dressed in her most comfortable clothes and decided to lay down on the sofa in the living room. Her nap was cut short, though, when her brother stormed inside. Anton rushed towards his sister and roused her from her sleep smothering her in his arms.

"Anton," Sophie wheezed, "I need to breathe."

"Sorry." He blushed and let go in an instant. "I'm just so happy you are back and well again."

"Thank you." She patted his arm affectionately. "I owe you, brother."

"No, you don't," Anton said as he sat next to her. "After everything you have gone through, it was the right thing to do."

"Still, I am glad you informed Eleanor about what happened."

"So, does that mean you are . . . you know?"

"Yes, we are." Sophie blushed under her brother's inquisitive gaze.

"Then why are you here and not with her?"

"I need to speak to Emma."

"She isn't here, Sophie," Anton said her with an apologetic shrug. "Count von Bernthal invited her and Mother to his estate. They'll return tomorrow at the earliest."

"It doesn't matter. I'm not up for a lengthy argument at the moment anyway. I just wish I knew what happened to cause Emma to behave in that way. The last time we spoke she was a complete stranger to me." Sophie sighed when she thought about her sister's words and the anger directed at her.

"She certainly wouldn't tell me," Anton said helplessly.

"She always talked to you."

"But that's the point. She didn't this time."

"Why hasn't she?"

"I really don't know." He got up. "Go back to sleep!"

Sophie watched her brother leave before she reclined again on the sofa, her thoughts running wild. Soon though she was fast asleep again, her exhaustion catching up with her.

Eleanor was soaking in her tub when a soft knock on the door stirred her from the memories of Sophie's delicious lips against her own. She could get lost in those kisses, wanting them to go on forever. Before she could respond to the knock, Charlotte peeked around the door.

"Mama?"

"Yes, darling, do come in." Eleanor pointed at a chair across from the tub. "Has Adele found the room to her liking?"

"Yes. Thank you for convincing her mother that it would be all right if she came to stay with us."

"Of course. Although there was not much convincing to do. I have to say though, I was quite surprised by this instant attraction between the two of you."

"I know, Mama." Charlotte was wringing her hands. "I can't exactly explain it myself." In a shy voice, she said, "Adele captivated me from the moment we met. Her beauty, her smile, her passion for women's rights, her love for horses—and she's so charming. Everything about her makes my heart beat faster every time I think about her."

"And when you touch her hand you feel like you never want to let go?"

"Yes."

"When you kiss her, you want it to last forever?"

"Yes."

"Merely being near her is enough to make your heart swell with love and joy?"

"Yes. How do you know?" Charlotte asked flustered.

Eleanor laughed at the love-struck expression on her daughter's face, hoping against hope she wouldn't resemble it when she thought about Sophie. It wouldn't be fitting for a woman her age. But somehow, she feared that was exactly the way she appeared every time she let her mind wander to the beautiful woman who had captured her own heart.

"Darling, you're in love. Completely and irrevocably in love."

"I am," Charlotte agreed with wonder in her voice as if she had just realised what was going on between herself and Adele.

"Hand me the towel, please."

Eleanor stood and held out her hand to accept the fluffy towel. She wrapped it around her trim body and stepped out of the tub gracefully. She went into her bedroom closely followed by her daughter who took a seat on the bed. Eleanor dried off and donned a bath robe, then sat in front of the vanity, combing her short white hair. She could tell from the look on Charlotte's face something else was on her mind, but she hadn't mastered the courage to ask.

"What is it? What is causing those lines on your forehead?"

"May I ask you something, Mama?"

"Of course! You can ask me anything, you know that."

Eleanor left her seat in front of the mirror and sat on the bed next to her daughter. When Charlotte refused eye contact, she raised her head with a gentle finger under chin. Her own confident blue eyes met insecure ones.

"What is the matter? Tell me!"

Eleanor saw Charlotte swallow a lump in her throat, not quite sure how to phrase her question. She could guess what was coming, to ask her mother's advice on the more physical aspect of her relationship with Adele.

"Mama, I—I have never, never been with a woman before, Charlotte whispered with embarrassment. "I'm afraid I don't know what to do when we are finally going to be intimate."

"Sweetheart, there is nothing to be embarrassed about." Eleanor took her daughter into her arms.

"But when will I know the right time? I don't want to rush things, and I certainly don't want to hurt her."

"You'll both know when it is right, trust me." Eleanor pulled back from the embrace to regard Charlotte's serious face. "Do what feels good. Think about what gives you pleasure and be patient and gentle. Everything will be fine."

"Will there be pain?" Charlotte asked anxiously.

"There might be some, yes, but the pleasure you will receive when making love to the woman you love will let you forget about it soon, I promise."

"Thank you, Mama." Charlotte hugged her mother tightly before she flew off the bed to collect Adele and join the family in the drawing room.

"I see you have returned after all before your sister's wedding," Count von Hagendorf said haughtily as he entered the dining room where Sophie sat at the table talking animatedly to her brother.

"Good evening to you as well, Father." Sophie tried not to let her anger show in her voice, but she knew she failed miserably.

"Good evening," the count said stiffly as he took his place at the head of the table. "All is well with your aunt, I take it?"

"Yes. Aunt Therese sends her regards."

"Thank you. What about your cousin? Has she finally found a man who is willing to put up with her silliness?" Count von Hagendorf put a napkin on his lap and started with his soup, not waiting for Sophie's answer.

"Why don't you ask her that herself? She is a guest of the Duchess of Darnsworth for the time being."

"Now that doesn't surprise me," he snorted with disregard. "That pompous woman would be interested in Adele's stupid ideas, all right."

"Why Father?" Sophie said sarcastically.

"I distinctly remember you were most proud to flaunt her name and Helen's relationship to your guests at the reception."

She knew he had felt threatened by Eleanor's position and by the way she carried herself. Her beloved wasn't a woman to be intimidated by someone such as her father or Count von Bernthal.

He said, "It could never hurt to be associated to someone of her social position, but that woman and her whole clan are so damn arrogant. They treated your sister's fiancé like a bloody commoner."

"As he deserves."

"Enough of that." The count slammed his fist on the table, his face beet red from fury. "Your sister is going to marry the man whether you're pleased by it or not. And this is still my house which entitles me to respect from my children. If you can't accept this, you are free to leave. Your mother made sure that you are a woman of independent means. A mistake, but since nobody would ever marry you as you are, I would say you should think about your future in this house."

Sophie was dumbfounded by her father's words. Never before had he spoken to her like this. She had known of course that he resented that her mother had left her wealth to her daughter. He tried everything possible to fight the will, but her mother had made sure legally that he could do nothing about it. Her father couldn't marry her off because she was an independent woman for one, and there had never been a suitor anyway. Sophie had been most grateful for that. She wasn't sure if he knew she was lesbian. She thought he did but had decided to ignore it as long as it wouldn't cause a scandal.

With forced calmness she pushed back her chair, put the napkin next to her plate and stood. Gripping her cane firmly, Sophie marched out of the dining room without another word or glance at the man she called father.

Her decision had been made for her sooner than she had anticipated.

Sophie retreated to her rooms with a new-found determination. She would write to the British Museum and finally accept their offer. It saddened her that she had to end her working relationship with Professor Maierhofer, but there was nothing here for her any longer.

Dinner at Palais Schelling was relaxed and enjoyable. Adele felt welcome and accepted as Charlotte's companion in a way she hadn't thought possible. Lord Edgewood was a charming, witty man whereas his significant other, Jonathan, was far more reserved but still warm. The contessa was a truly remarkable woman—blunt, direct, and funny. Adele adored her already and believed the feeling was mutual.

Charlotte's brothers were harder to decipher. They had been polite and welcoming, but it was abundantly clear they still reserved judgement. Philip had inherited their mother's pale complexion, blond hair, and blue eyes. Martin, on the other hand, resembled Eleanor's late lover, or so Charlotte had said. He wasn't as tall as his siblings and possessed a shock of red hair and startling green eyes. Freckles covered his face quite nicely, which Adele thought made him look cute.

When they retired to the drawing room for coffee the men stepped through the French windows for a smoke, leaving the four women behind to chat.

"Do you find your rooms to your satisfaction, my dear?" Eleanor asked Adele as she handed her a cup of coffee.

"Yes. Thank you."

"And you wouldn't even have to step outside to get to Charlotte's room," Giulia added with a wink.

"Nonna!" Charlotte was scandalised at her great-grandmother's suggestion.

"What, my dear? I am old but still very much alive and in possession of my mind to know what two women do behind closed doors. And must I really point out to you that I used to enjoy a very healthy sex life with your late great-grandmother?"

Charlotte stared open-mouthed at her nonna while Adele was coughing violently after nearly choking on her coffee.

Eleanor patted her back sympathetically and rolled her eyes at her grandmother. She should have known Giulia's frank words would happen sooner or later. Giulia had done the same thing with her and Cathleen. Only Cathleen had taken it in stride whereas she had been as flustered as her daughter was now.

"How long?" Adele asked when she had gathered her wits again.

"How long what, my dear?"

"How long did you enjoy it, I mean? If you don't mind my asking."

"Adele!?" Charlotte gawked at her as if she was completely out of her mind.

"Oh hush, Charlotte," her nonna admonished her with a gentle slap on her arm. "Your mother certainly didn't raise you as a prude. Contrary to many others of your age, I might add."

"But . . .but—"

"But what? As I recall from spending time with you and your family, you and your brothers used to barge in on your mothers when they weren't at all decently attired."

"We were *children*." Charlotte's defence was weak. She was aware such behaviour would have given her mother's mother a stroke if she knew about it. Her family was not conventional in the least, but talking about her great-grandmother's sex life was something different all together.

"Whatever." Giulia waved her off to continue to answer Adele's question. "I am happy to say that we used to make love to each other until the day she suffered her stroke."

The longing in her voice and eyes didn't go unnoticed by either of them.

At that moment, the men returned from the garden. Upon glancing around to take the measure of the room, the young men appeared slightly abashed and distinctly uncomfortable.

"Why do I feel we are not welcome?" Philip asked, as he was the first to find his voice. The others were still shifting uncomfortable at the tension in the room.

"Come on, son." Henry patted his back jovially. "It is plain as day that we're intruding on a private conversation among ladies." He raised a hand to stop his son's question before he could ask it. "And no, we do not want to know what it was." Turning away from Philip, he said, "If you'll excuse us, ladies, we'll be playing a game of bridge in the sitting room. Feel free to join us any time you please."

They shuffled out of the door, looking like kicked puppies. When the door closed behind them, the women laughed out loud.

"Poor Philip." Eleanor wiped away her tears of laughter. "Did you see the look on his face? I could firmly grasp his discomfort. And Martin— he seemed a bit green as well, didn't he?"

With a mischievous grin, Giulia said, "They are such sweet men but simply can't stomach women talk. And neither can you, Charlotte."

"Well, I . . . I . . ." her great-granddaughter stuttered.

Eleanor said, "Nonna, you have never been this open before with Charlotte."

"She has never had a lover before either," the contessa shot back with a raised eyebrow. "I am not ashamed of what I am because I loved Bridget with all my heart. She was a beautiful woman as well as a very attentive and gentle lover. And I still miss her greatly."

"I know, Nonna."

"I have never before had a lover either," Adele suddenly said. Her face flushed with embarrassment when all eyes swung to her.

Giulia covered Adele's hands with her own, giving them a reassuring squeeze. "You are lucky to have this wonderful opportunity that many women like us would have loved to be given to explore each other's feelings and bodies with only another woman. It is a lovely gift. Cherish it."

Charlotte asked, "Do you regret that you weren't granny's first lover?"

"In a way," the contessa answered wistfully. "But I can honestly say that the first orgasm Bridget ever had was with me."

Charlotte and Adele looked wide-eyed at each other, then the floor, a silence ruled the room for a moment before Charlotte, in a sudden bout of courage, asked "What about you, Mama?"

"Yes, Eleanor," Giulia said playfully. "What about you?"

"I beg your pardon?"

Eleanor's cheeks heated up and turned an interesting shade of red.

"Your sex life with Cathleen wasn't dull either, was it?" Giulia offered knowingly.

"No."

Charlotte thought her mother's reply was mysterious and woefully unhelpful. She cried out, "Please, Mama! Nonna was more than forthcoming with her experiences. You know neither Adele nor I have ever made love before. So, it is only natural that we want to know more about you and Mummy."

"Is that so?" Eleanor gulped out.

"We are all in the same boat, my dear, Giulia said. "Nobody is going to think less of you if you share this part of you with us. I encourage you to be forthcoming."

"All right, all right." She was flustered and exasperated, but Eleanor managed to say, "Cathleen was the first person who made love to me. I gave her my virginity and am happy to say it was a wonderful experience. She was everything every woman hopes for and could possibly dream of. Patient, gentle, passionate, but tender at the same time. She was a playful and, at times, adventurous lover. In my experience, being with a woman isn't about reaching a goal. Touching and caressing, the feel of a warm, soft hand on your skin, is everything you need sometimes. At different times you need different things, but whatever you need or want at the time, I have always found emotionally rewarding."

Giulia smirked. "I couldn't have put it better, *Cara.*"

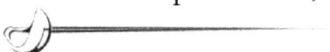

"Do you really think they are talking about, you know, sex?" Philip asked as he sorted the cards Jonathan had just dealt.

Martin rolled his eyes at his brother. Sometimes he could be so daft. "What about it?"

"Are you joking? This isn't a topic Mama would talk about. And Nonna, well, she's *old.*"

Henry put down the cards and glared at his son, wondering how it was possible that this otherwise bright young man could be so obtuse at times.

"Why wouldn't they?"

"They are women."

"So?"

"What do you mean? So?" Philip asked incredulously.

"All right," Jonathan said with authority. "Listen, son, no matter what you or any of your friends think or what those psychologists and doctors believe or say, women do have needs and wants as much as men do. Your mother is a beautiful woman, in the prime of her life, and personally I'm happy she's found love again. This means sharing everything with Sophie, including the physical aspect of such a relationship. The same holds true for your sister and her newly beloved."

"And Nonna?" Philip whispered insecurely. "Surely you don't think she would be interested in that any longer?"

"Why not? Because your great-grandmother is dead doesn't mean she isn't keen on talking or thinking about it."

Martin patted his brother's back, shaking his head at his ceaseless and puerile curiosity. "When you fall in love with the woman you intend to marry, I highly recommend you talk to Mama before your wedding night, brother."

"Why would I do such a thing?" Philip squeaked.

"Take it from me, son," Henry added with a grin, "if you don't want to behave like an obnoxious prick, you do as your brother suggested. Who do you think would know most about making love to a woman in this house?"

"I'll keep that in mind." Philip blushed to the roots of his hair by the sheer thought of having this conversation with his mother.

At the expression on Philips' face, Jonathan said, "Don't let them tease you too much. You will be fine on your wedding night."

"Yes," Henry said, "you will find your way. Just remember that being intimate with somebody is not just about you, but also about the other person."

"I will," Philip said as he tossed the first card on the table, but he didn't look very self-assured.

Chapter Eighteen

Sophie made it a point to avoid her father at breakfast. She went out for a ride very early to clear her head and prepare for the upcoming conversation with her sister. When she returned, she was glad to learn her father had already left. She asked her trustworthy maid to organise the packing of her belongings. To say Martha was surprised would be an understatement.

"Just my clothes and everything else from the bathroom," Sophie ordered with a wave of her hand. "I will take care of the books as well as the other things connected to my work."

"Where will we go?" Martha asked a bit anxiously.

"London," she said, but seeing the expression on her maid's face, she sighed. "Martha you don't have to come if you don't feel up to it. I would understand perfectly if you didn't."

"What would become of me? I have served your grandmother, your mother, and now you. I'm sure neither your father nor your stepmother has any use for me."

She was right; they would toss Martha out without a second thought. Unbeknownst to her maid, Sophie had taken care of this problem more than a year earlier should Martha ever wish to retire from service.

Sophie put a comforting hand on the distraught woman's arm. "That's been taken care of, Martha. Don't worry."

"What do you mean?"

She asked Martha into the living room in her private quarters and motioned for her to take a seat before she went to her study to retrieve a large white envelope. She handed it to Martha and sat next to her. At the questioning gaze Sophie told her to open it.

Martha fumbled with a small black book and a title-deed. Both items had her name on them, and she frowned in puzzlement.

Before she could speak, Sophie explained. "This one," she said, tapping her finger on the small black book, "is a savings book. It is in your name, and the sum will provide you with a comfortable retirement. The title-deed is for a nice, fairly new apartment in the third district, already furnished with all the amenities you could wish for."

"But . . . how? When? Why?"

Sophie smirked at the complete and utter bewilderment on her maid's wrinkled face. Her eyes were already misty from unshed tears.

"Because you served my mother and me so faithfully all those years, and I wanted to make sure you were taken care of. I couldn't bear the thought of you spending the rest of your life in poverty and despair. I can easily afford it, and my mother would have done the same thing."

"I don't know how to thank you." Martha wiped at tears on her cheek.

"You don't need to."

"Thank you, nonetheless."

"Would you prefer to settle in your new apartment while I go off on my new adventures?"

Martha hesitated. "I would miss you very much."

"Don't be silly. I'd miss you as well." Sophie laughed. "I would come visit you and make sure you were faring well."

Martha took a deep breath, held it a moment, then let it out slowly. "All right then. I am ready to settle these old bones. But first, m'lady, I shall do everything I can to prepare you for the next steps you take."

Though seeming a little overwhelmed, she squeezed Sophie's hand before rising to continue with her tasks. She was nearly out the door when she stopped to ask, "When will you leave?"

"As soon as possible. When everything is packed, I'll send the things I don't need now to London. I'll remain in Vienna for a while, but not in this house."

"Where will you stay?"

"Oh, I'm sure the Hotel Imperial will have a suite for me."

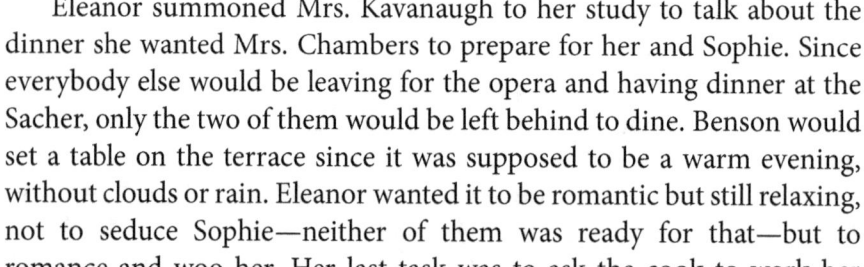

Eleanor summoned Mrs. Kavanaugh to her study to talk about the dinner she wanted Mrs. Chambers to prepare for her and Sophie. Since everybody else would be leaving for the opera and having dinner at the Sacher, only the two of them would be left behind to dine. Benson would set a table on the terrace since it was supposed to be a warm evening, without clouds or rain. Eleanor wanted it to be romantic but still relaxing, not to seduce Sophie—neither of them was ready for that—but to romance and woo her. Her last task was to ask the cook to work her magic. Or, rather, ask her housekeeper to pass on the request to the cook.

"I know everybody downstairs was hoping for a night off, Mrs. Kavanaugh," Eleanor said from behind her desk in her study. "But I'm afraid I have to ask Mrs. Chambers to cook dinner for a guest and me."

If her housekeeper was annoyed at the unexpected request, she certainly didn't show it. Mrs. Kavanaugh was as calm, collected, and zealous as ever.

"Certainly, your Grace. Do you have something particular in mind?"

"As it will be a rather hot day and warm evening, I thought something light would be appreciated."

"Of course, madam."

Eleanor felt her cheeks heat up. She was dismayed when Mrs. Kavanaugh noticed her unease and leaned forward slightly with an inquiring expression.

Unable to choke out a reply, Eleanor nodded and tried to smile.

Mrs. Kavanaugh took the hint. "If there is nothing else, your Grace, I will pass your wishes on to Mrs. Chambers?"

"Yes, that is all, thank you."

The housekeeper inclined her head and left Eleanor to return to her letters. After closing the door behind her, Mrs. Kavanaugh's face transformed from strict, stern, and proper into a huge happy grin. This was too good to be true, but with what Rose had imparted about their employer's time in Salzburg and judging from the light blush she had just witnessed, the duchess was in love.

Mrs. Kavanaugh rushed back to kitchen and briskly ordered the kitchen maids to leave. Annoyance was written clearly on her beloved's face for being so presumptuous in her domain, but Mrs. Kavanaugh effectively stopped any protest by saying with a twinkle in her eyes, "Do not aggravate yourself my dear."

"What?" Mrs. Chambers put her hands on her hips, waiting for the blow.

"Her Grace asked you to prepare dinner tonight for her and a guest."

"What?" Cook's voice exploded into the room. "I thought they're all going out to eat at a hotel, and we could have this evening to ourselves."

Mrs. Kavanaugh groaned. This response was exactly what she'd feared. She took work-roughened hands in her own to gently stroke the backs with her thumbs. "Calm yourself, dear. I think this will be a romantic dinner. Mister Benson more or less already indicated as much."

"Oh?"

"Yes, remember what Rose said about Salzburg?" After an affirmative nod she continued, "I think it's the Countess von Hagendorf who will be the guest. It seems as if the house will be a happy one once again."

"You think so?" Mrs. Chambers asked wearily.

"I certainly hope so. This walking on eggshells and the constant tension was nearly unbearable for all of us, wasn't it?"

"About bloody time," Mrs. Chambers said. She spotted Rose outside her kitchen and called impatiently for the maid to come in. "Rose, a word please."

"Yes, Mrs. Chambers?" Rose smoothed her uniform, looking expectantly from housekeeper to cook.

"You've met the Countess von Hagendorf. What do you make of her?"

"I think she is an honourable woman. I mean after what she did for Josefine. That was jolly decent."

"What about the duchess?" the cook inquired with a stern expression. "Is she good for her as well?"

Rose smirked at the question. Ever since they had returned from Salzburg, the gossip downstairs had run wild. They had bombarded Rose with questions about what was going on, and she had tried to answer them as well as she could without being too forward. Servants knew everything about their mistresses and masters. The only difference in this household was that the people upstairs also paid attention, and they knew more about those who worked for them than any other employer usually did.

At the beginning, Rose hadn't known what to make of the household. The dynamics were most unusual in some ways, but absolutely the same in others. The duchess was an unconventional person in every sense of the word, but so was his lordship. Rose had come to appreciate their ways. When she had lost her work in a big house after being impregnated by the son of her former mistress, she didn't know what to do. Nobody would employ her, but the duchess gave her work and trained her as her lady's maid. She could regularly visit her sister and her little girl. They were both under her Grace's protection, and Rose hadn't once regretted working for her.

The people downstairs were fond of their employer. But most of all, they wanted to work again in a house full of joy and laughter. The gloom that had lingered for the past few years had taken a toll on all of them. With the countess at her mistress's side, Rose believed things would indeed change for the better.

"Yes. I think the countess is very good for her." She moved closer and whispered, "They're in love with each other. Her Grace is really smitten, and I suppose the same can be said for the countess. She treats her with courtesy, respect, and loving care."

"Good. Well, all right then." Mrs. Chambers narrowed her eyes at the maid to search for any fallacies. When she couldn't detect any, she turned briskly to take care of dinner.

Rose raised an eyebrow at the housekeeper who merely rolled her eyes and waved her hand at the door. As they left the kitchen, they heard Mrs. Chambers calling for the kitchen maids to get their lazy bums back inside. They chuckled at the cook's colourful language and her mock exasperation.

The arrival of her sister and stepmother caused such an upheaval that even Sophie was aware of it in her study. She would give her sister time to recuperate from the journey before she went to speak to her. Sophie wanted this confrontation over and done with as soon as possible so she could enjoy the anticipation of seeing Eleanor again. She was looking forward to their time together, berating herself for the intense need to be in her beloved's presence again, to hopefully hold her hand, touch her, and kiss her. She could only hope she wasn't too forward in her advances, but she was certain Eleanor would tell her if she was.

After an hour of silent contemplation, Sophie grabbed her cane and Emma's forged letter and headed for her sister's door. She took a deep breath to steel herself for the ordeal and knocked. Emma's voice drifted through the closed door, asking her to come in. Her sister had her back to the door when she entered, and when she swung around to see who it was, Sophie saw the sudden change of demeanour.

Emma's face fell and her smile disappeared. "Oh, it's you."

"Yes, sorry to disappoint you," Sophie said sarcastically, "but rest assured you will not have to suffer my presence for long."

"What do you want?"

Sophie wordlessly held out the letter, waiting for Emma to take it. Her sister did so with an annoyed sigh. Her eyes flew over the lines, and Sophie perceived that Emma hadn't expected to be confronted with her betrayal. Her face turned white as a sheet, and she swallowed hard. She peeked up at Sophie, clearly expecting an angry outburst. But all Sophie could manage was a whispered, "Why?"

Too strong was the onslaught of hurt now that Sophie stood face to face with her sister again.

"Because it's wrong!" Emma's voice was shrill. "It is disgusting and deviant behaviour."

"I have never asked for your approval. You could have looked the other way just the same way you do with your fiancé." Sophie fast became angry. "You had no right to do this. Nothing warranted such a hurtful action. You are my sister and I love you, but right now I can barely stand to be in the same room with you."

"That makes two of us then. To think that you are one of *those* women is unbelievable. The scandal it would cause should anybody know about it! Father would die of shame if he knew."

"Don't worry, dear sister." Sophie snatched the letter back. "I will remove my vile self from this house and soon enough from this country. You will never have to lay eyes on me again."

"What?"

"Father has made it perfectly clear he no longer wants to be bothered with my presence. Very much the same as you. So, I will honour his and your wishes and move into the Hotel Imperial for the time being. I will come back tomorrow to finish packing, and when I'm done, my things will be sent to London."

"Are you going with *her?*" Emma's expression showed disbelief, as if she were surprised by this revelation.

"What's it to you?"

Sophie waited for an explanation but when none was forthcoming, she turned to leave. With her back to her sister, she offered a last olive branch in parting. "In case you were wondering, I do not hate you. I can't forgive you for what you did, not yet, but I could never hate you. If you should ever need me, you know where to find me."

"I won't!"

"Be happy, Emma."

Sophie stepped through the door without a backward look. In a stiff gait, she went to her rooms to collect a suitcase and her coat. Guttmann had summoned a carriage to take her to the hotel.

Before she left, she handed the butler a letter for her father in which she explained her departure, gave a forwarding address, and indicated she would return a last time for her belongings.

Her departure happened so fast, Sophie barely had time to catch her breath. She was sure the tears would come eventually, but right now she was too wound up.

Eleanor was putting on a light touch of perfume when her grand-mother entered her bedroom. She reached for Cathleen's necklace, the one with Cathleen's picture and the ring in it, but stopped over it and let her hand fall into her lap. Her eyes found Giulia's in the mirror, begging for something she couldn't name.

Her nonna watched the emotions flit over Eleanor's face and stepped up behind her. She put a hand on Eleanor's shoulder and pressed a soft kiss on her head. "Let it go."

Eleanor covered the hand on her shoulder with one of her own. She took the necklace and put it reverently into the top drawer of her vanity, closing the drawer with a feeling of grief in her heart.

With admiration, Giulia said, "That light blue gown brings out the colour of your eyes wonderfully. You look lovely, my dear."

Eleanor blushed "Thank you, Nonna."

"Safe that blush for your special guest, *Cara*." Giulia chuckled. "I'm sure she will be rendered speechless."

"We'll see." Eleanor indeed had high hopes that her choice of dress would be appreciated.

"You do not plan to seduce the poor woman already, do you?" Giulia meant it as a light-hearted joke, but by the frown that appeared on an otherwise smooth forehead, it seemed as if wasn't received as one. "I apologise, dear. I didn't mean it like that."

"No, I . . ." Eleanor put her hand against her forehead in an insecure gesture. "I don't think . . . I—"

"Forgive this silly old woman. Both of you will need more time, and you'll know when it's right. With that, I say good night and ready myself for departure. Enjoy your guest, and don't put too much pressure on yourself."

"Don't worry, I won't," she said in a light tone. "What are you going to see?"

"*Don Giovanni.*" Giulia waved goodbye and left with a rustle of her gown.

Eleanor regarded her reflection and decided to give her hair another brush before it was time to go downstairs and welcome her guest.

Sophie wiped her sweaty palms on a handkerchief before she rang the bell. Benson opened the door with his usual air of haughtiness and stepped aside to let her enter.

"Her Grace is in the garden. If you would follow me, please."

They went into the drawing room and stepped through the French windows into a wonderfully illuminated garden. At the edge of the terrace, Eleanor was waiting for her guest. She had her back to them, and the low line of her dress revealed the pale smooth skin of her back. Her white hair glowed in the fading light of dusk, and when Eleanor turned at the sound of footsteps, Sophie swallowed the lump in her throat.

"Good evening, darling."

With those words, Benson hastened back through the French windows.

"You are absolutely breathtakingly gorgeous," Sophie said in awe as she moved toward her.

True to her nonna's word, Eleanor blushed, although she hadn't rendered Sophie completely speechless but her serious compliments and the look on her face made up for it.

"Thank you." She brushed her lips over Sophie's cheek in greeting. Her hand rested lightly over the thumping heart on her lover's chest. "You are very handsome yourself." Before Eleanor could take a step back, Sophie covered her hand, keeping her close. They locked eyes and found nothing but honest admiration in the other.

"You're beautiful. I mean it," Sophie whispered.

"I know you do." Eleanor's voice was equally soft. They kissed, lingering with their eyes closed, savouring the feeling of the other's lips before Eleanor pulled back. "So did I."

Sophie refused to let go of the hand on her chest, absorbing the warmth where it seeped through the crisp white shirt she wore under her vest and frock coat. Fitted trousers, black boots, and a black cane with a silver handle completed her attire. She had also decided to wear her long dark brown hair in a braid.

With fingertips, Eleanor gently traced the scar on the right side of Sophie's face, feeling privileged that Sophie allowed it. She knew how self-conscious Sophie was about this. Her fingertips caressed a soft cheek and finally stopped at the corner of Sophie's mouth only to be replaced by her lips. A single tear escaped from closed eyes and stole its way down the scarred cheek but was gently brushed away by Eleanor's thumb.

"None of this, my darling, please," Eleanor pleaded softly. "You're beautiful and wonderful the way you are."

The gentle clearing of a throat broke the emotional moment. Eleanor stepped around her love to address the butler, giving Sophie time to compose herself.

"Yes, Benson?"

"I am sorry to interrupt, your Grace." He sounded contrite at his intrusion. He had been waiting in the drawing room for the best moment to step outside. "Mrs. Chambers asks if it would be convenient to serve dinner."

"Yes, please."

Sophie waited for her to hold out her arm and take her to the table in the corner. Sophie held a chair for her before she took a seat herself.

Though she'd been startled, she was glad Benson had interrupted the moment he did. Both needed to take a breath to calm their emotions as well as their desire. Sophie knew it was exactly that—a strong feeling of want she felt when Eleanor's hands touched and caressed her. The feelings were undeniable. Overwhelming. A mutual desire.

She had never experienced anything like this before, and her heart swelled with love.

Benson stirred her from her thoughts when he appeared at her side with the first course of their dinner, trying to be as unobtrusive as possible, which wasn't such a difficult task since both women only had eyes for each other.

The cook and the housekeeper were tidying up the kitchen when Benson came down the stairs.

"Well?" Mrs. Chambers snapped at Benson as he entered the kitchen with empty plates and glasses and the remains from the dinner table. "Did they appreciate my meal?"

"They ate everything."

"That's not what I meant. Was her Grace satisfied?"

Benson smirked at the cook; it was just too good an opportunity to let it go. "I am afraid, Mrs. Chambers, they wouldn't have noticed the difference if we had served a lump of hard bread, potato soup, and a glass of water."

"What?" The cook was fuming. She had let go of her free evening, and now it wasn't even appreciated? Before she could get more upset though, Mrs. Kavanaugh took pity on her.

"I believe what Mister Benson is trying to tell us, dear, is that they were too wrapped up in each other to take notice of anything else. But they ate everything, so they probably found the food divine. Isn't that true, Mister Benson?"

"Yes," he admitted sheepishly.

"You awful tease," Mrs. Chambers grumbled good-naturedly. "They are quite serious, huh?"

"Just as we all hoped, Mrs. Kavanaugh said."

"Amen to that."

In a secluded spot in the garden, next to a fountain, Eleanor and Sophie took a seat on a bench. The onset of evening had brought a chilly breeze. Sophie felt Eleanor shiver next to her she, so took off her frock coat and wrapped it carefully around her shoulders.

"Better?"

"Yes, thank you."

Eleanor put her head on Sophie's shoulder and sighed contently. She felt the lingering warmth and scent of her love in the fabric of the coat.

"With the chill, would you prefer to go inside?" Sophie asked.

Sophie attempted to get up but was stopped by a gentle hand on her thigh.

"No, please, let us stay here a little while longer."

"As you wish."

"Tell me, did you talk to your sister?" Eleanor asked and felt the instant tension in Sophie's body.

"I did, and she wasn't in the least bit apologetic. Not that I expected her to be. Father also told me he would prefer if I moved into my own property."

Eleanor sat up straighter at this news. "How awful, darling."

Sophie shrugged. "We were not that close. After mother's death he didn't know what to do with me. He lost his heir and was left with a girl he never knew or understood. His marriage with Helen provided him with what he desired. I suppose he was always miffed that my mother made sure I would inherit her wealth. So, for the time being, I reside at the Hotel Imperial and am sending my belongings to London."

"Oh?"

"Yes. I accepted an offer by the British Museum to serve as an expert of ancient texts."

"That is wonderful," Eleanor gushed, throwing her arms around Sophie's neck.

"Will you come and stay with me in London?"

"Definitely."

"Are you sure? I'm not being too forward, am I?"

Eleanor shook her head vigorously. "Not at all."

"The house is huge, and nothing would make me happier. What about your family?" Sophie asked.

"They would be happy because I am happy."

"All right then." Sophie still felt a bit hesitant, but hoped Eleanor was certain. Only time would tell.

Their evening was drew to an end when they realised the time. Sophie told her more packing was waiting for her next morning and that she wanted to get everything in order at her father's house as fast as possible.

Their good night kisses were as wonderful as the ones they had shared at the beginning of the evening. The more time they spent in each other's company the more difficult it became to part.

Eleanor hoped the day would come when they wouldn't have to say goodbye at all but would spend the night wrapped in each other's arms.

Sophie promised to have luncheon with Eleanor and the family the next day, and she would have the opportunity to talk to Jonathan about moving her belongings to their Mayfair home.

One last kiss was bestowed on full lips before the door closed behind the retreating form of the Countess von Hagendorf, and Eleanor climbed the stairs to her bedroom with a dreamy smile on her lips.

Eleanor was on her second cup of tea when her family made an appearance in the breakfast room. Her sons appeared a bit frazzled, and Charlotte wore a mocking grin on her face that could only be described as *schadenfreude*. They simply shouldn't drink so much champagne if they felt and looked the way they did the morning after. Henry and Jonathan followed more solemnly while Giulia and Adele were chatting animatedly. Eleanor looked from one to the other before settling on Philip and Martin, neither of whom met her gaze.

"Good morning, Mama," Charlotte chirped happily as she took a seat next to her mother.

"Good morning."

"Did you and Sophie have a nice evening?"

Eleanor shot a questioning look at her husband who only shook his head, indicating to ignore whatever was going on with their sons.

Eleanor turned back to Charlotte. "Yes, thank you, darling. It was wonderful."

"When will you see her again?" Henry asked curiously. She knew Henry wanted to get to know the woman better since she had so completely captured her heart in such a short amount of time.

"She will join us for luncheon today. I want you to get to know each other better since she is coming to London with us."

Charlotte's grin widened as if she knew what was coming next.

"It's as simple as that?" Martin asked with an edge to his voice that took everybody aback. "You met this woman two months ago, and already she's going to live with us?"

"Martin, you are forgetting yourself!" Eleanor warned him with steel in her voice.

"That's rich, coming from you," her son said as he pushed back his chair so violently that it crashed into the wall behind him. "For the last three years you were mourning my mother, and now you've met this perfect stranger, and everything is forgotten. Forgive me if I'm not over the moon about this development."

He stormed out of the breakfast room, leaving a shocked family behind.

When Eleanor rose to follow him, Henry stopped her.

"Let him go! He needs to blow off steam and calm down. Right now, everything you could possibly say would not be met with a clear head."

"What is the matter?" She felt shaky as she dropped back into her chair. "I truly thought he would be happy for me."

"He will come to you later when he is ready to talk. Just give him the chance to explain."

"I will, rest assured."

Eleanor pushed her plate aside, suddenly no longer hungry. In a desperate attempt to lighten the mood, she said, "Tell me, how was the opera?"

Her question encountered a good amount of hesitation before Adele spoke up. "Quite delightful actually."

The others merely nodded in agreement. Even Giulia was uncharacteristically silent, and Charlotte was too busy lathering marmalade on her toast to respond.

"Which reminds me," Henry said, "we met Count Nikolaus von Radványi at the Hotel Sacher. He's going to call later this morning."

With trepidation., Eleanor said, "Oh, my. Was he awfully upset that we came to Vienna after I declined his invitation?"

"No. He was quite gracious. He's going to give a soiree next Saturday and has invited us but I'm sure he'll tell you all about it."

"Splendid," she said.

The sarcastic remark was answered by Henry's raised eyebrow, but she didn't respond, instead gazing into her teacup.

Eleanor could only hope Martin would talk to her about what was bothering him, and she wondered how long that would take. If Henry was correct that the count was as pleasant as he sounded, at least that would be a relief. She would hate for an unpleasant visit on top of all the other turmoil going on in the family.

Chapter Nineteen

Eleanor tried very hard to concentrate on the novel she was reading, but her thoughts constantly circled back to Martin's hurtful words at the breakfast table. Was he right? Was she, after those hard-to-endure years of mourning, moving too fast into a new relationship? She closed her book.

Her impression had been that Martin agreed with everybody else that she should find another love. Obviously, she had been wrong, but before today he'd never said a thing. She did understand his feelings, but what she felt for Sophie was too strong to ignore. Every time they met, she realised she was falling deeper and deeper, and nothing she could do or want to do would stop or change that. Eleanor hoped Martin would eventually understand.

Filled with misgivings, she intended to go back to her book, but was interrupted by a knock before she could open it again.

"Come in!"

Martin stood in the open door, too embarrassed to say anything. Eleanor watched him with a critical eye. The self-confident young man he had grown into had been replaced by the insecure young boy he had once been. He reminded her of the three-year-old boy who, upon shattering the window of the drawing room at Darnsworth Castle with a ball, waited to be admonished and punished for his misdeed.

Her heart went out to the boy she'd held in her arms and comforted when he was sick as well as to the young man who had cried like a child after his mother's death.

When he didn't move, she said, "Sit with me, darling."

She patted the spot on the sofa next to her. Martin wordlessly closed the door and shuffled over, refusing to look at her. He apparently found the fabric of his trousers most intriguing, smoothing his hands over his thighs in an attempt to overcome his nervousness. His hands only stilled when she put one of her smaller ones over them.

Martin finally raised his head and gazed into the comforting and familiar eyes of the woman he'd called mama for as long as he could think.

"Tell me!" she said.

The softly spoken encouragement caused a tear to slip down his cheek but it was brushed away by a tender thumb. Martin closed his eyes at the touch of his mother's warm palm against his cheek. Never had she spoken in anger to him despite the numerous times she must have been furious at him. Mummy would be the one to rant at him, berate him for being reckless and irresponsible, but Mama always waited until she was calm and collected. She would take him by the hand, drag him to the stables, put a brush in his hand, and keep him company while they tended to the horses. When he talked, she listened, offered her advice, and told him to do better next time.

"I'm sorry for what I said to you," he finally pressed out. "I had no right to say those things,."

"You are entitled to your feelings, darling. They just took me by surprise. You've never before indicated those feelings, though. Can you at least tell me what brought this on?"

Before he could answer Benson entered, bowed, and looked apologetically at the duchess.

"I am sorry, your Grace."

"What is it, Benson?"

"Count von Radványi is here and wishes to speak to you."

"Already?" She heaved a heavy sigh.

"I am afraid so."

"Ask him to wait in the drawing room and tell his lordship I would be most grateful if he kept him company for the time being."

"Certainly, your Grace." He closed the door softly behind him.

Martin said, "Maybe I should leave you to your guest."

"Most certainly not," Eleanor said emphatically. "He can wait since he thought it prudent to invite himself. Being a duchess does have its merits, you know."

"Yes, ma'am." He grinned at her haughty sniff.

"Go on, tell me, sweetheart."

"I don't really know," he said with a shake of his head. "When Nonna said you wouldn't wear your necklace yesterday, I felt as if you were trying to get rid of every memento of Mummy. As if you no longer felt anything for her. It made it all the more real. I mean she has been dead for three years, but until yesterday she was still a part of you, of us."

"Martin, she will always be a part of me. Right here." Eleanor put her hand over her heart to emphasise her words. "A part of me will always love her, never doubt that. But she's gone, and I promised her I would move on with my life. I was lost when your mother died, but I'm not anymore. It was hard enough to honour her wish, but I think I've found the person who makes me feel alive again. Someone I can love and who loves me."

"I know, it's just . . ." Martin trailed off. He wasn't sure if he could say what was bothering him without hurting her. But when he felt an encouraging squeeze to his hand he continued. "Seeing you with somebody else than Mummy—I'll will need some time to get used to that."

After his heartfelt words, Eleanor folded him in a warm embrace. "I know, darling and I do understand that. All I'm asking is that you give us a chance. Sophie is a wonderful person, but I don't expect you to fall over yourself in excitement. Try to get to know her on your own terms, as an independent person, not because she is my beloved but because I believe you will find her to be a person worth knowing."

"I will try," he promised sincerely.

"Thank you."

Eleanor smiled, feeling relieved as she patted Martin's hand. "Now I will join your father, greet our guest, and try not to be annoyed at him for barging in like this."

"You could always give him a good tongue lashing." Martin snickered at his mother's raised eyebrow.

"Maybe I should. What is being a duchess worth if you can't at least show your displeasure at uninvited guests, right?"

"Right. But you won't, will you?"

"No, quite unlikely." She stood and smoothed down her dove grey skirt. "That is something my mother would do, and therefore I will refrain from such behaviour."

Martin offered his arm, and Eleanor took it proudly.

"I never thought you would really do it," Anton said, clearly pleased at his sister's decision to leave Vienna and move to London. He groaned as Sophie put three more books on the pile in his arms.

"Neither did I," she said, "but a lot has changed and there isn't so much keeping me here, whereas the most important things will be in London."

"Such as?" He prompted, knowing full well what they were but he wanted to hear it from her.

"Eleanor, of course."

Anton grinned broadly and congratulated himself that he interfered just this one time. "Do you love her?"

"Yes," Sophie whispered with a blush. "I do."

Suddenly the door burst opened, and they glanced at the unexpected intruder. Their father stood stock still in the doorway looking flustered and slightly out of breath.

"Is it true?" Count von Hagendorf asked through clenched teeth.

"Is what true, father?"

"That you are one of those unnatural women? That you're a . . . a—"

"A lesbian?" Sophie provided helpfully with sarcasm dripping from her mouth.

"Are you?" he thundered.

"And what if I am a lesbian?" she asked calmly, feeling anything but. "As you can see, I'm already following your suggestions. I'm leaving your house and this country."

"You are a disgrace," her father hissed, his face red from anger and fury. "An abomination. I can't believe this. My own daughter. If this ever gets out, the scandal!"

"Do not worry, father! I'm currently residing under my mother's maiden name which nobody is going to connect with you. And what's more important, I will leave Vienna at the end of September."

"And until then?"

"Simply do what you have always done," Sophie offered with a shrug. "Pretend I don't exist. It worked well for the last few years. Anyway, I'm sure you will have all the sympathy you require, like you always have. The poor man lost his wife, and he has a disfigured daughter, an oddity. People have probably guessed all along, Father, but as long as nobody is putting a name to it, it doesn't exist."

"What if somebody does?"

"They won't because people only see what they want to see," Sophie snorted ruefully. "If anyone should know that, it's you."

"What do you mean?" he asked with a slight shake in his voice.

"I mean the affair you have been carrying on for years now with the Baroness von Lichtenberg."

"Wha—what—" He could hardly speak, but managed to gasp out, "How do you know?"

"It doesn't matter, Father, and frankly, I don't care. But given your own hypocrisy I'd say you are the last person to be the judge of me."

"My circumstances are completely different," Count von Hagendorf bristled. "You are pretending to be a man, and having sexual intercourse with a married woman is against the natural order."

"What?" Sophie was taken aback by the accusation. When her father mentioned a married woman, she knew for certain Emma had given everything away.

"You heard me." Her father shook his head with disgust. "I can't even think about what sort of woman this would be."

"Then don't," she said with a coldness neither he nor Anton had ever heard before. But Sophie exhaled with relief. Emma obviously hadn't told him everything after all, which left her wondering why. "I will pack my things and be gone forever tomorrow."

"Father, please." Anton had found his voice but was ignored by both of them.

"See that you do!" The count stormed out, forcefully slamming the door behind him.

"Sophie—" Anton started but was stopped by a raised hand.

"Don't! Let's get on with this, please. The sooner we finish the better."

Sophie refused to think about what had just happened. Maybe later in the solitude of her hotel room she would do so and break down crying, but right now she had to continue to put this house and what was in it behind her.

Eleanor greeted her guest with a jovial but fake smile as she entered the drawing room on her son's arm.

"Count von Radványi! What a pleasure."

"I'm most delighted, your Grace. You are most generous." The count bowed deeply. "My humblest apologies for the short notice." He took her outstretched hand in both of his own and breathed a kiss on its back.

"Please, Count, take a seat." Eleanor gestured at a chair and sat in the opposite one. The count thanked her with a bow.

Henry and Martin sat next to each other on a sofa to watch in rapt fascination as Eleanor charmed the man despite the irritation for his complete disregard of etiquette.

"I must ask you to forgive my impertinence, your Grace, but when I met his lordship at the opera and he told me you were in Vienna now, I felt I had to meet you."

"Indeed," Eleanor sniffed haughtily, "and why is that?"

"As I wrote in my letter, I want to speak with you about a business partnership. My late father had a very high opinion of your achievements as a horse breeder and so did our late Empress. Her judgement has always been of great value to my family."

"I see. I must say it does sound interesting. Although, the honour of the achievements you mention belongs to my late grandmother. I merely try to continue what she started."

"And very successfully, if I may say so."

"Thank you." Eleanor inclined her head. "What do you have in mind?"

"I will give a little soiree next week at Radványi Palace in Eisenstadt where my stud farm is situated, and I wish to invite you and your family to spend a few days with me there. I might also have a little surprise for you, your Grace."

"That is very generous of you, Count. I will speak to my family and let you know of our decision."

"Wonderful." Radványi beamed broadly. "Now I will leave you. Thank you again, your Grace, for receiving me." He kissed her hand again with flourish and all the necessary charm of a man of an old noble house.

"Lord Edgewood." The count nodded at Henry and Martin before sweeping out of the drawing room, leaving a frowning duchess behind.

"Well?" Henry prodded.

"I hate surprises," Eleanor grumbled.

"But you *are* considering his invitation, Mama, aren't you? I think I see that old familiar gleam in your eye."

Martin was right. She would consider his offer. She had always shared her grandmother's passion for horses. Over the last few years, she hadn't felt much passion, but ever since coming to Vienna, she felt it returning. So yes, she was considering going and inspecting his famous racehorses. She would ask Sophie to accompany her.

"Yes, I'll go, despite his blasted surprise." Eleanor smirked. "Whoever of you is interested would be very welcome to accompany me. I will ask Sophie as well. If you don't mind? Henry?"

"Do you think it wise, dear? I'm playing devil's advocate because somebody has to. Are you sure it's a good idea?"

"Probably not," Eleanor said thoughtfully, "but I want to share this with Sophie. Horses are an integral part of who I am. I want to spend more time with her in my element. Martin, will you come?"

"I think I will, Mama."

"Henry?"

"Whatever you think is best, dear."

Punctuality was a highly appreciated trait in Henry and Eleanor's household, and when Benson answered the door to welcome Countess Sophie von Hagendorf, he was more than glad that she honoured his mistress and master's wishes in such minor details. She was actually fifteen minutes early.

After finishing with packing at her father's house, Sophie's emotional breakdown at the hotel had taken its toll on her. She hadn't expected her departure to be nearly as difficult as it was. Though she did not see her father or Emma, her last minutes with Anton were excruciating. Despite urging him to come see her often, he was inconsolable. Not only were they siblings, but they had always been each other's best friends. His unconditional love and support had always meant a lot to her. She was also very proud of her little brother. He was already a fine young man, nothing like their father at all.

Now she was dressed, and though she knew she'd be too early, she could no longer stand being alone in her hotel room. She wanted, no, she *needed*, to see Eleanor. Talk to her and feel her comforting arms around her. Despite her best efforts to appear calm and collected, her father's words had cut her deeply.

Now, as she followed Benson into the garden, she felt everything coming back with a forcefulness that nearly took her breath away.

Most of Eleanor's family was gathered in the shade of a tall walnut tree. Their humorous banter was heart-wrenching when compared to the gloom and hurt she felt inside. She spotted her cousin holding hands with Charlotte, his Lordship was sitting comfortably on a small bench next to his lover, while Eleanor and Giulia sat on the opposite bench, smiling indulgently at the men.

Sophie avoided meeting Eleanor's gaze as long as possible because she knew if she looked into her beloved's eyes, she could no longer keep the reins on her emotions. She greeted everybody else with false cheerfulness, but as soon as her gaze locked with Eleanor's, her words died on her lips and her eyes began to water. Not able to stop them, her tears were fell freely until she felt Eleanor gathering her in her arms.

She heard the sounds of the others rising and shuffling off but was too upset to pay any attention.

Eleanor knew the moment Sophie joined them that something was horribly wrong. Her whole demeanour indicated as much. Her eyes were red from crying, her body was tense, and she avoided eye contact. Before the first tear was falling, Eleanor rushed to her side and enveloped Sophie in an embrace, holding her tight. At first, she felt her stiffen, but when silent sobs started to wrack her body, Sophie relaxed. She let her cane slip from her hand to wrap both her arms around Eleanor and hold on for dear life. Eleanor was grateful her family had left when Sophie broke down, giving them the privacy they needed.

She manoeuvred Sophie to the bench Henry and Jonathan had vacated. Without letting go, they sat down. It took quite a while before Sophie could tell her what had happened. Eleanor listened attentively, wishing with all her heart she could undo the hurt. All she could do was hold the distraught woman in her arms and offer as much comfort as possible.

"Your family must think I've completely lost it." Sophie wiped the tears from her eyes with the back of her coat sleeve.

Eleanor smiled at the gesture and handed Sophie a clean handkerchief.

"Thank you."

"You are welcome, my darling." She gently kissed her temple. "They will not think any less of you. I'm sorry about your estrangement with your sister, and I'm sad and angry at the same time at your father."

"It can't be helped." Sophie replied heavily. "His suggestion that I leave the house was quite a blow the other day, and what he said today didn't come completely unexpected. It still hurts, though."

"What I don't understand is why your sister didn't tell him about us."

"Neither do I. Maybe she lost her bravery or keeps it as a trump card. I don't know."

Eleanor put her arm around Sophie's shoulders and drew her snugly against her side. "Since you have managed to pack all your belongings, I would say we have to make sure they are transported safely to London, so they'll be awaiting you when we are back home. Darling, I know this is a huge step leaving behind everything you've known since you were a child."

"Yes, but my future doesn't lie here any longer."

"Why don't we go inside and join the others for luncheon?" Eleanor suggested, to lighten the mood. She got up to retrieve Sophie's cane, which still lay where it had fallen earlier. Sophie opened her mouth to object to Eleanor's action but was effectively silenced by a lingering kiss. When they parted for air, Eleanor held her hand out to pull Sophie to her feet. Arm in arm, they strolled back to the house.

"I had a visitor this morning," Eleanor reported offhandedly.

"Oh? Who? If you don't mind my asking."

"I wouldn't have told you if I did. Count Nikolaus von Radványi showed up with a business proposal."

"He breeds racehorses, doesn't he?"

"Yes. He invited me to visit his stables in Eisenstadt."

"Will you accept?" Sophie attempted to ask as nonchalantly as possible, already hating the idea of Eleanor being gone so that she would not have the chance to see her and talk to her every day.

"I think so, yes. And I was hoping you would accompany me." Eleanor stopped and waited expectantly.

"Are you sure this is a good idea? I mean, I'm not part of your family. I am merely—"

A gentle finger over her lips stopped her from finishing the sentence.

"You, my love, are as much a part of my family as is your cousin. So, there is nothing wrong with you accompanying us. I want to share this experience with you. Please, say you will come."

"I will."

"Splendid."

℘
Chapter Twenty

Martin and Sophie were the only ones who travelled to Eisenstadt with Eleanor. Everybody else preferred to stay in Vienna, which didn't disappoint Eleanor too much. Martin's company truly warmed her heart. His initial reluctance and resistance towards Sophie had been replaced by honest curiosity.

Eleanor was pleased as she half-listened to their conversation while she read through the papers Jonathan provided shortly before their departure. What she read was very enlightening and would make it easier to answer the count's proposal of a partnership.

They would stay at the count's estate from Saturday until Monday and not only talk business but also meet some of the count's friends and acquaintances. Eleanor still couldn't fathom what he had in store as a surprise and dearly hoped it wasn't too atrocious.

Eleanor finished reading and put the files back into the folder. She slid her reading glasses into their case and closed her eyes. The quiet voices of her son and her beloved, combined with the regular motion of the train, lulled her into a dreamless sleep. She only woke when the whistling noise of the train rolling into the station startled her.

"Did you sleep well, Mama?" Martin smirked at his mother's confused expression.

"Where are we?"

"Eisenstadt, love," Sophie answered with a squeeze of her hand.

Martin cast a glance at them, witnessing this gesture. Although Eleanor surmised that any affection from Sophie would still cause him a slight stab, she could also tell he was slowly coming to terms with seeing someone other than his mother at Eleanor's side. He exited the compartment and graciously offered them his help to climb down.

At the end of the platform, Count von Radványi was waiting for them. Martin looked around, searching for Cedric, who accompanied Martin as his valet, and instructed Cedric to take care of their luggage before Eleanor and Sophie each took an arm so he could lead them toward the exit.

"Your Grace, welcome to Eisenstadt," Count von Radványi said exuberantly as he grasped her outstretched hand to kiss it.

"Thank you, Count," Eleanor said with a haughtiness that made Sophie raise her eyebrow. "This is my companion, Countess von Wilczek and my son Martin."

"I am honoured." The count bowed with the same enthusiasm as he'd shown the duchess. "The carriages are waiting. Please, follow me."

While Cedric helped the driver load their luggage onto the carriage, the maids climbed in and waited for him to do the same so they could follow their mistress to the count's estate at the outskirts of Eisenstadt.

Inside the count's ornate carriage, Eleanor settled herself on a well-padded bench across from their host with Martin and Sophie on either side of her.

"If it is agreeable with you, your Grace," the count offered sweetly, "I thought you'd wish to refresh yourself, and then we could visit the stables?"

"Very considerate, thank you!"

Eleanor was short with her answers, leaving it to Martin and Sophie to make conversation with the count while she closely observed him. For a man of leisure, he clearly showed his age. But if Jonathan's information was accurate regarding the count and women, liquor, and gambling—and Eleanor had no reason whatsoever to doubt—then it was to be expected.

As the carriage drove up the pathway to the entrance of the count's estate, Eleanor was surprised to see a large, unattractive building. The dirty yellow front was peeling in various places, and the shutters of the windows could certainly use a new layer of paint. Eleanor let her gaze wander across the yard where a gardener was bravely fighting a lost cause against weeds. This estate had seen better days, that much was plainly visible. She suspected that for the occasion it had been necessary to hire additional servants, and most parts of the house would be locked up with their furniture covered in dust sheets.

It wouldn't be the first time a new generation had to face the humiliation of either selling a large part of their property to keep the rest due to unwise investments or because the heirs had been careless and spent most of the family wealth on costly pleasures. From observing the shabbiness of his estate, she was interested to find out how the count would approach the subject of a partnership between them.

Eleanor was distinctly curious, although her decision had already been made, a decision which hadn't so much to do with the count's obvious unreliability as a business partner, but rather because there was no point of a partnership. She could buy his horses and continue breeding them, but she couldn't merge these two different kinds of breeds. The idea of another, second branch wasn't appealing at all. She rather preferred her own branch to blossom and keep her steeds up to their usual standards. This didn't mean, though, that she wasn't interested in examining the count's famous racehorses.

Since all their rooms were on the same floor, it would be easy to visit either her son or Sophie after everybody had retired for bed. Once the stable visit and meals were over, she wanted to speak to them and get their impressions of their host.

Dressed in their riding attire, Eleanor, Martin, and Sophie followed Count von Radványi to the stables where they could examine some of his finest horses. Afterwards he would take them on a tour of the estate to observe the mares and foals on the meadows. The stable hands were busy cleaning boxes, brushing horses and keeping the equipment in order.

"I have a training ground right behind the stables," the count said proudly as he pointed at his most successful stallion. The black horse snickered when he offered him his favourite treat.

"My jockeys are the best and they know what they are doing. Catalano here is not only the best runner, but he is very high in demand for breeding."

"You have to be congratulated then," Eleanor said sincerely.

"Thank you, your Grace." He puffed his chest out at the words. "One or two of the others give me high hopes for breeding more champions as well. Our new generation of promising horses is right outside on the meadow."

"Lead the way, Count," Martin encouraged.

Eleanor waited for Sophie, who was still scratching the nose of a very friendly brown stallion, to join her on the way to the yard where riding horses were waiting for them. Sophie offered her arm to Eleanor who took it instantly, content to be close to her.

"What do you think?" Eleanor asked as they followed their host.

"Impressive, but I'm afraid he's exaggerating to get your attention. His father was the one who was the real horseman. The count merely profits from his reputation and from his father's wise decision provided him with continuing success for the last few years. Others have long since beaten him on the racetrack. His potential as a successful provider for breeding a new generation of racehorses is still there, though."

"I have my doubts that he will be able to make use of it."

"How so?"

"I will tell you later," Eleanor patted her arm as she broke off their conversation to join Martin and Count von Radványi by the waiting horses. The August day over the Hungarian lowland was invigorating. As far as they could see, the land was scattered with a hut every now and again and an endless plain with wells and cattle. The landscape was very different from anything Eleanor had seen so far. It seemed as if it went on forever, unlike her beloved Highlands with its green hills, lochs, and ever-changing colours. The only contrast that could be found around here was in the far distance, on the horizon, where brown grass touched the light blue of the sky. No lush greens or reds nor did she see the deep blue sky and fluffy white clouds she grew up with around Darnsworth Castle.

One had to love the sparse scenery to stand it, and the count readily agreed that the Hungarian lowland wasn't for everyone. When they reached the place where the mares and foals were kept over the summer, Eleanor had to admit it was a beautiful sight. The young foals were running and jumping around with exuberance, enjoying their freedom under the watchful eyes of their mothers. They spent quite a while watching the horses before it was time to return and change for luncheon.

The count was an attentive host and knew how to keep his guests entertained at the table. He offered the duchess the use of his library while Sophie and Martin went for a walk.

For quite a while Sophie wandered silently next to Martin. He easily matched his long strides and fast pace to her slower gait. Martin seemed less open than his brother or sister. His attitude towards Sophie was more distant, something to which she could very well relate. Fortunately, their silence was not an awkward one. They were both collecting their thoughts before Martin finally broke the silence.

"I meant to apologise for my recent behaviour and might add that I'm grateful for this opportunity to spend more time with you."

"You have nothing to apologise for." Sophie stopped, taking in his humble posture. "I do understand your concerns or misgivings."

"It is not so much that." Martin shook his head with a sigh. "I feel torn. Although I want Mama to be happy again, I never thought I would see somebody else at her side but my mother. When you returned from Salzburg everything became more real."

"I know what you mean. After my mother died, it was very strange to see Helen at my father's side."

Martin linked his hands behind his back, and they continued on the trail towards a small clearing at the edge of the garden where trees provided a calm and shady place. A bench overlooking the vast expanse of land looked inviting. They sat and Sophie leaned forward to cover the handle of her cane with both her hands and rest her chin on top of them.

"Eleanor is a very special and beautiful woman," Sophie said softly. "I'm fully aware that she could do better than me." When she heard Martin's sharp intake of breath to contradict the last sentiment she sat straight and stopped him with a raised hand. "No, let me finish, please."

He closed his mouth without uttering a single word and bowed his head, indicating for Sophie to continue.

"What I said before is true and we both know it. I will no longer question it, though. I feel honoured and privileged that a woman like Eleanor could find me attractive and love me. The feeling is mutual, and I promise I'll never do anything to hurt her."

"I have observed you, both of you, actually," he said sheepishly without looking at Sophie.

"And?"

Martin raised his head and gazed into her eyes. "I can say without a doubt that you treat her with only the utmost respect and courtesy, always underlined with a subtle loving care. I think I appreciate that the most."

With a hint of amusement, she said "Why, thank you," and blushed becomingly.

"No, thank *you*." Martin flashed a brilliant smile before he got up. He motioned for Sophie to stay seated.

From the corner of her eye, she detected a figure coming their way—definitely his mother who probably had no longer been able to rein in her curiosity. Sophie's gaze followed Martin as he strode down the trail to meet her halfway. They spoke for a few moments but were too far away for Sophie to hear their conversation. Martin leaned in to kiss his mother's cheek before he continued on his way back to the house, and Eleanor strolled towards her and took the place her son had vacated.

"You should be very proud of your children," Sophie said as she covered one of Eleanor's hands with her own.

"Oh, I am. I can't tell you how glad I am that Martin seems to have come to terms with me finally finding the courage to move on."

"So am I."

In the shabby-looking guest suite at the count's ramshackle estate, Rose put the last touches to Eleanor's hair. As she stepped back, a soft knock sounded at the door.

"Come in!" Eleanor called out.

Sophie entered tentatively but with more courage when she saw Eleanor's happiness at her presence. For tonight's festive gathering she had abandoned her trousers. She wore a rather simple but stylish long dark skirt with a high-necked white silk blouse under a tartan shawl.

"I'm sorry to disturb you."

"Nonsense." Eleanor waved it off. "Rose was just going to help me put on my jewellery."

"Ah, yes, about that." Sophie shuffled her feet nervously.

Eleanor swivelled around but didn't get up from her seat in front of the vanity. She gave Rose a glance, and the maid scurried off to the dress-dressing room. "You've definitely got something on your mind. What is it?

Sophie gulped in some air.

"Darling, whatever is the matter?"

Sophie lifted her head, afraid this was a bad idea, but it couldn't be helped now. "Well, ahem." She coughed, feeling embarrassed, and stepped farther into the room. "I want to give you something."

From behind her back she brought a black velvet case and opened it for Eleanor. Inside, on a bed of white satin, sparkled the most delicate golden necklace adorned with sapphires. A pair of matching earrings completed the set.

"How beautiful," Eleanor exclaimed and put her fingertips to her lips. She looked up into Sophie's eyes. "I'm—I'm—what a lovely surprise."

Sophie knew she was blushing as if she had a fever, but said, "You were so captivated when you saw them in of the portraits in the museum, so—"

Eleanor gasped. "You had them made for me? But when?"

"Shortly after our visit. I felt bold enough to do so at the time. They were finished when we came back from Salzburg, and I've been waiting for the right moment to give them to you."

Sophie took the necklace from the case and tucked the case under one arm. Eleanor shifted to the side of the vanity chair. Sophie stepped behind her, draped the necklace around Eleanor's neck, and carefully closed the clasp. Eleanor turned the rest of the way so that she faced the mirror.

"That is marvellous on you." Sophie leaned down to press a gentle kiss on her lover's bare shoulder. Letting her lips linger for a moment, Sophie inhaled the subtle sent of Eleanor's perfume with closed eyes before she straightened again.

Their eyes met in the reflection of the mirror, and Sophie saw the love she felt for this wonderful woman fully reciprocated. She reopened the velvet case and removed the earrings that completed the ensemble.

"Beautiful," Sophie said throatily.

"Thank you, my love," Eleanor whispered as she let her fingertips delicately brush over the necklace where it rested over her chest.

"You are most welcome. I hoped you would like it."

"Like it? I love it."

She stood and kissed Sophie tenderly on the lips before calling for Rose.

Rose handed over one glove after the other while Sophie patiently waited for Eleanor to get ready and for heart to stop racing at three hundred beats per minute.

Another knock announced Martin's arrival to accompany his mother and Sophie downstairs, and Sophie opened the door to admit him.

"Your Grace." He bowed at the waist toward his mother who smiled indulgently at his antics.

Eleanor said, "I see you are as perfectly dressed as ever. Not that I would expect anything less from you, my son."

"Cedric was most helpful, indeed. We're lucky to have such skilled people making us look presentable." Martin winked at Rose who blushed.

Eleanor raised an inquiring eyebrow at her maid as Rose looked at the floor and fidgeted.

Sophie knew just how Rose felt. That look from Eleanor was enough to stop anyone—friend, lover, or servant—in her tracks. And Martin could be such a tease. Even Rose wasn't immune to his good looks and fine manners. No wonder she was blushing.

Martin preceded the women into the hall then offered an arm to each of them to guide them down the stairs.

"I'm still curious about the surprise he spoke of," Martin mused as they descended the stairs.

Sotto voce, Eleanor said, "Do not worry yourself unduly. I'm afraid we will learn about it soon enough."

At the foot of the stairs, the count greeted them warmly before he whisked the duchess away to introduce her to some of his other guests.

Eleanor saw that the count had managed to assemble a distinguished gathering. Quite a few members of the noblest families were present from both parts of the Empire. People from political and economic circles mingled with esteemed artists and patrons of the arts.

Unlike the reception at Count von Hagendorf's villa where she had been bored out of her mind, much to her surprise Eleanor found most of the conversation quite stimulating. The count stayed by her side for only a short while, then was called away when a new party of guests arrived.

After she had been "kidnapped "by the count, Eleanor glanced over her shoulder to see that Sophie was doggedly following. Eleanor wanted her by her side but navigating through the crowd and occasionally being stopped by someone she knew slowed Sophie down.

Eleanor was talking to a well-known author when she heard the count's voice behind her.

"Your Grace, I promised you a surprise and here it is."

Eleanor was grateful for the iron control over her emotions at such events when she realised what—or rather *who*—was presented as her special surprise. Next to her host stood, in all her malicious glory, the last person Eleanor wanted to meet, Lady Margaret Harrington.

"Hello, my dear," Lady Margaret cooed as she leaned forward to kiss the duchess' cheek like an old friend. "When I wrote Niki that you were in Vienna, he was so good to invite you to Eisenstadt. He was so excited to meet you."

"Indeed. Tell me, Margaret, how did you learn about our visit to Vienna?"

"Lady Burlington, of course. Your mother told her, and when we met for tea, she mentioned it."

"Of course she did."

"I take it you are enjoying this special surprise, your Grace," the count asked with pride as he bobbed obsequiously as though expecting to be congratulated for his cleverness.

"Splendid, Count," she said in a haughty voice. Eleanor could hardly contain her desire to flee and would have loved to smack the self-satisfied grin off his face. Had she known Margaret and the count were friends, she would have never accepted his invitation.

"Mama, excuse me. Would you do me the honour of this dance?" Martin smiled at her, graciously taking her hand.

"Yes, of course, darling. Excuse me," Eleanor said to the count and Lady Harrington, and Martin led her to the dance floor.

"Thank you, son. Bless you. Your beautiful manners are highly appreciated. How did you know I was in need of a rescue?"

"I didn't," Martin smirked. "Sophie said your body language was becoming more tense by the moment, and she suggested sweeping you away before you did something not befitting your position."

"Did she now?"

"Most definitely. Am I correct to assume that your patience was indeed wearing thin?"

Eleanor chuckled at this description of her feelings regarding her host and Margaret. "Very accurate. And very perceptive of you and Sophie."

As Martin whirled her around the dance floor, Eleanor felt relief from her escape from the two toadies. She was elated that Sophie could read her so well after such a short time. If she hadn't been in love with Sophie already, she would surely fall in love with her now. As it was, the feelings for her beloved grew deeper every day, and this knowledge brought a warm glow to her chest.

Sophie stood in the shadow of a pillar and observed Eleanor waltzing across the floor in Martin's capable arms. When she realised the conversation between Eleanor, the count, and the woman on his arm was anything but pleasant, she had desperately tried to think of a way to pry her away. Martin's appearance by her side had been the solution for this delicate problem. She more or less ordered him to go to his mother and ask for a dance. First, he had seemed flabbergasted at a suggestion made out of the blue, but when she explained the reason, he straightened his back and marched off, a man on a mission.

Watching the relief wash over Eleanor's elegant features when Martin arrived at her side was all the confirmation she needed. Mother and son made quite a dashing pair. They were good dancers; it was delightful to observe them move with grace and elegance. Sophie's only regret, as she watched them fly over the parquet, was that she was not the one who held

Eleanor in her arms and danced with her. It wouldn't be appropriate even if she wasn't handicapped by her leg.

Only so much intimacy would be tolerated in public, though women had greater leave to be physically close to one another than men did. But dancing with Eleanor like any other couple wouldn't be an acceptable level of closeness. She had to content herself with watching and drinking in Eleanor's beauty as she drew her head back to laugh about something Martin had said.

Sophie smiled at the heart-warming image of happiness presented by the woman she loved so dearly.

She was suddenly startled from her contemplation when she sensed a presence behind her. Before she could move, a woman's voice shared an observation with undisguised awe in her voice.

"Eleanor is without a doubt the most beautiful woman in this room, wouldn't you agree, Countess?"

"Yes," Sophie said. She turned to find standing behind her the woman who had spoken to Eleanor only moments ago.

With a strange smirk on her lips, she said, "Lady Margaret Harrington." The woman held out her hand but withdrew it with a slight shrug when she realised Sophie had no intention of taking it. "Niki is an old friend, and he told me who you are."

"I see. And what else did our dear host tell you?"

"Only the truth," Margaret answered cockily, "as far as he knows it, I assure you."

"What is that supposed to mean?" Sophie stared at her.

"It means we both know you are more than a mere companion to our dear Eleanor," Margaret elaborated with a predatory grin. "But do not delude yourself. A summer fling should be nothing to trouble yourself with."

"Meaning?"

"You do not honestly believe somebody like you could be more than a fling to somebody like the duchess, do you? I have known Eleanor for years and I knew Cathleen, the whole family, actually. You cannot honestly think you would fit into that family?"

"What." Sophie was unable to from any more words than that.

"I've heard tales about you before. You may be gussied up tonight, but you don't usually present yourself as a lady of distinction. If you dress in such a manner and look singularly disreputable, Eleanor will never dare show herself with you by her side, and why should she? London is full of gorgeous women. Feminine women. Think about it, my dear. I am merely trying to spare you unnecessary heartache."

Lady Margaret took hold of her skirts and glided away, leaving behind a completely bewildered Sophie. How dare she? Who did this woman think she was to bring up such topics with someone she had never been formally introduced to?

But she couldn't help but wonder if there was merit to her words. As much as it hurt to admit, she knew there was some truth in them. She was already standing on the side-line, wasn't she? She couldn't even dance with the woman who possessed her heart.

Sophie never wanted to be a burden to anyone, least of all her lover, which was one reason she had been so hard pressed after her accident to get back on her feet. She was who she was, and she wasn't ashamed of it. Not even as a young girl had she fancied dresses, and her injury had provided a suitable excuse everybody accepted for her wearing men's clothing in her day-to-day life.

But she saw she'd cause a stir if she were to present herself to Eleanor's peers. She could never be to Eleanor what Henry was—or even what that despicable Lady Margaret could be in all her finery and elegance. Once her beloved discovered how out of place Sophie was, she would drop her like a hot rock, wouldn't she?

Sophie felt faint for a moment. A feeling of loneliness, of utter desolation, coursed through her, and she had to tighten her grip on the cane to steady herself. Who would she be—how could she endure—if Eleanor was not in her life?

Was this merely a fling to Eleanor? Sophie shook her head at the mere thought, thinking how ridiculous the Harrington woman was to insinuate something like that.

Sophie had felt Eleanor's touch and seen the way she looked at her, with love and openness and vulnerability. This was so much more than a short affair, she was certain. She took a deep breath and reminded herself of all the ways she and Eleanor were already solid, despite their short acquaintance.

Sophie was so deep in thought that she didn't notice when Martin and Eleanor joined her. Only when she felt soft lips on her scarred cheek did she surface from the depths of her own mind. She felt ashamed for doubting Eleanor and rushed to apologise to her beloved.

"I am sorry," she blurted out. "Please, forgive me for being a complete and utter idiot."

Eleanor looked surprised, and Sophie was suddenly aware of the frantic tone of her emotional outburst when Eleanor didn't even know what had transpired between Margaret and Sophie.

"Nothing needs to be forgiven, my darling. If anything, I should be thanking you for sending Martin to my rescue."

Sophie felt relieved at her beloved's words, basking in the knowledge that her actions were appreciated.

Eleanor came and went a few more times to speak with various of the count's guests while Sophie and Martin chatted, drank weak champagne, and ate *hors d'oeuvres*.

Over an hour passed, and the next time Eleanor joined them, Sophie said, "Do you mind if I retire for the evening? I feel somewhat tired after today's events."

"Not at all, darling." Eleanor covered her mouth with her hand as she could no longer suppress a yawn. "I think I will do the same."

$\textcircled{\heartsuit}$

Chapter Twenty-One

Sleep was elusive. As much as she wished for it, Sophie had been tossing and turning restlessly for what seemed like hours. She threw off the blanket with a disgusted snort and got up. She pulled her dressing gown from the hook on the door, put on her slippers and left her room. She slowly navigated down the floor towards Eleanor's room, debating if she should knock. When she drew nearer, Sophie heard strange noises coming from that direction. It sounded like a woman's voice but one she couldn't place. Sophie stood in front of Eleanor's door and heard the distinct sound of a woman in ecstasy.

Rooted to the spot and unable to force her legs to take her back to her room, she listened to a woman praising Eleanor's skill as a lover. When she heard her reaching the peak, Sophie pushed away from the door and went back to her room as fast as she could. She shut the door behind her and collapsed against it, silent tears running down her cheeks. Her cane slipped from her grip, and she slid down to the floor. With her head on her knees, she sobbed hard, barely able to suppress the sounds that threatened to spill over her lips. Her body shook violently as the sound of lovemaking played over and over in her head.

What a fool she was, apologising for doubting Eleanor's feelings when it seemed as if everything had been an awful joke. All those heartfelt words about waiting to make love were pure rubbish. Sophie was angry, mad, hurt beyond words, hoping against hope that what she had heard wasn't true, that everything had been a misunderstanding. She didn't know how long she had been sitting on the floor, propped against the door when the sound of a knock drifted through the fog of her brain. Sophie raised her head from her knees and wiped her eyes.

"Who is it?"

"It's me, darling, may I come in?" Eleanor's voice sounded muffled through the door.

"Leave me alone." Sophie sniffed. "And don't call me darling, you lying cheat."

"What? Sophie, what is wrong?" Eleanor's voice sounded shocked. "Please, talk to me! What happened?"

"Did you have a good fuck?" Sophie snarled through her tears. "I hope she was worth it."

"What are you talking about?"

Sophie struggled to her feet, anger boiling in her veins. If Eleanor was with somebody else, she could at least be honest enough to admit it. She threw open the door and hissed at the startled woman.

"I'm talking about the tryst you just had in your room, Eleanor. Is that why you insisted that we should wait because you already had somebody on the side you were fucking?"

Eleanor stepped back at the accusation and crude words. "I have no idea what you're talking about. "I have no—"

"Don't lie to me! I heard you. There's no defence you can use for that."

Eleanor's face was red. Through gritted teeth she asked, "What did you hear?"

"You know exactly what."

"No, I don't. So please tell me!"

Eleanor's hands were on her hips, her nostrils flared, and her eyes flashed with fury.

"I came to your room because I couldn't sleep. I thought you might be still awake so we could talk. Before I could knock, I heard the voice of a woman praising your abilities to satisfy a woman before she climaxed. It seems the good Lady Harrington was right after all."

At the mention of this name Eleanor took a step back, as if somebody had punched her in the chest. "Lady Harrington? Oh, I see. Will you at least give me the chance to explain what really happened?"

Sophie wiped furiously at the tears continuing to run down her cheeks. This was it? Eleanor would explain why she did what she did, and their relationship would be over before it had started? It was probably better that way. She opened her mouth to answer when she heard Martin's voice.

"Thank goodness you're not back in bed, Mama." He approached them, looking from his mother to Sophie. "You forgot the folder in my room." When he reached them, he said, "Is everything all right? Sophie, are you hurt?"

"Everything is fine," Eleanor said as Sophie attempted to compose herself.

"I'm so sorry, Mama. I didn't mean to keep you so long."

"What do you mean?" Sophie whispered uncomprehendingly. "What are you doing in the middle of the night?"

"Neither one of us could sleep," Martin said with a shrug. "Mama came to my room to decide what to do about the Count so we can return to Vienna sooner than planned."

Sophie felt lightheaded at Martin's words. She felt like the biggest moron in the entire world. Not worthy of a woman like Eleanor at all. Her insecurities had been exploited and used against her. She was so ashamed she wished the ground would open and swallow her. The hurtful words could never be taken back. If their relationship ended now, it would be completely her fault, nobody else's.

Eleanor thanked her son for the folder and with a reassuring pat on his back sent him back to his room.

"Come on, love. Let's talk in your room." Eleanor gently took Sophie's arm and closed the door behind them. She picked up the cane from the floor and guided Sophie towards the bed where they sat down.

Sophie had gone completely quiet after Martin had told her where Eleanor had been when she was supposed to be having sexual intercourse with another woman. She stared at her hands in her lap.

Eleanor moved close, so close she could feel how chilled Sophie was. She could also tell that Sophie felt ashamed and didn't dare look into Eleanor's eyes. "It's all right, love."

Sophie whispered, "How can I still be your love after those horrible things I said to you?"

"Because I love you," Eleanor answered simply, as she covered Sophie's hands with her own. "You were hurting, and what you said was in the heat of the moment."

"How?"

"How what, my darling?"

"How did she know when to come to your room," Sophie asked with a frown, "if it was Lady Harrington?"

Eleanor closed her eyes for a moment. Margaret had spread her poison again, making sure it would do its work in the most hurtful way. Sophie's tear-streaked face tore at her heart and as much as she wanted to take her into her arms and never let go, Eleanor knew it wouldn't be welcome at the moment. Sophie's eyes begged for an explanation, one that would make the pain go away and let the hurt vanish, but it wouldn't be that easy. Anger wouldn't do and Eleanor took a deep breath to calm her racing heart before she answered.

"Oh, it was her, Sophie. I don't doubt it. She's a vile, vicious, selfish woman who doesn't deserve the good things she possesses." Eleanor squeezed her hands. "I don't know exactly what happened, but I suppose she must have crept into my room at the earliest possibility to wait for me. When she heard your footsteps, which are quite distinct, my love, she seized the opportunity. She's always been quite good at improvising to injure others."

"It was an awful thing to do."

"You're right, but this woman would do anything to get what she wants."

"And what she wants is you." Sophie stated it as a fact, not a question.

"Unfortunately, yes, and she's a despicable woman." With a finger under Sophie's chin, she lifted her lover's head and gazed deeply into those dark brown eyes, so full of love every time Sophie looked at her. Eleanor leaned forward and met her lover's full lips in a long passionate kiss that left them both panting, wanting more.

"She will never have me," Eleanor said. "For I am yours and yours alone."

"I am yours as well," Sophie said breathlessly before she captured soft lips in another kiss. They only stopped when both had to yawn, causing them to laugh. Together they climbed underneath the blanket, holding each other. Eleanor rested her head on Sophie's chest while Sophie's arm circled her shoulder to keep her close.

Eleanor told her about Margaret and everything that had happened since they'd met for the first time years earlier and how she had tried to drive a wedge between her and Cathleen.

Sophie listened carefully, realising how cunning the woman really was and to what lengths she would go.

When sleep finally overcame them, they rested blissfully in each other's arms.

"Good morning!" Count von Radványi greeted them heartily when they entered the breakfast room.

"Good morning," Martin answered, while his mother and Sophie merely inclined their heads.

The table was long and wide, and both Martin and Sophie took seats as far away from the count and Lady Harrington as they could get.

Lady Margaret chirped, "You seem awfully well rested, my dear."

"Indeed," Eleanor said curtly. "I had the most perfect pillow." She smirked when she registered the slight colouring of Sophie's cheeks. It was true though, falling asleep and waking up in Sophie's arms was utter bliss. She would never get tired of it and if it were up to her, she would love nothing more than do so every day.

Turning her back on Lady Harrington, Eleanor said, "If you don't mind, Count, I want to speak to you about your business proposition after breakfast."

"Of course. Why so urgent?"

"To get on with it," Eleanor informed him, "so we can leave before midday."

"But . . .but . . ." he sputtered at the unexpected news.

With false worry in her voice, Lady Harrington said, "I hope you aren't cutting your visit short on my behalf, your Grace?"

"Don't flatter yourself! You are a nuisance but hardly of importance where my decision to leave is concerned."

Lady Harrington opened her mouth to reply but closed it again when nothing was forthcoming, giving the impression of a fish out of water. She shut her mouth with an evil glare in Eleanor's direction before she returned to her breakfast.

The rest of the meal was spent in silence as nobody felt the need or necessity for small talk. When they were finished, Martin and Sophie went upstairs to get everything ready for their departure while the duchess accompanied the count to his study.

"Let me make one thing perfectly clear, Count," Eleanor said, before von Radványi could utter a single word. "I merely agreed to your invitation because of my late grandmother's high regard for your late father. As I recall he was a true gentleman. Sadly enough, the same cannot be said about his son."

"Now . . ." He opened his mouth to defend himself but was effectively stopped by a raised hand from the duchess. The expression on her face was enough to make him swallow hard and shrink in his chair.

"I do not take kindly to someone's attempts to play me for a fool because, rest assured, I am not a fool, Count. Although it saddens me to see that your father's legacy has gone to naught by your uncaring ways, I will not save you from the impending bankruptcy. Never again contact me or my family in the future. I also highly recommend you think about your ways of conducting business, for I know nobody who is very keen on being tricked, lured, played, and surprised in the most unpleasant manner. Good day, Count."

With a rustle of her skirt, Eleanor swept from the study, climbed the stairs to her room where Rose had finished packing and was waiting for her return to help her change into a travelling dress.

On Sophie's arm she descended the stairs and found Lady Margaret waiting for them in the hall. Eleanor patted Sophie's arm and told her to wait in the carriage for her because she wanted to have a final word with Lady Harrington.

"I knew you wouldn't leave without saying goodbye to me," Margaret purred as she reached out to touch the duchess' arm.

Eleanor caught the offending hand and tightened her grip, eliciting a pained gasp from Margaret before Eleanor caught herself and reluctantly let go.

"Don't ever do that again." Eleanor ordered with pure ice in her voice.

"What, my dear? Touch you—or rile your little slut?"

"Either," she said, ignoring the insult. "Should you ever dare show your face in my presence again, I'll make sure you will rue the day we met. If you go near the von Hagendorf family, I'll ruin you. You will stay as far away from anyone I'm acquainted with now and forever."

Lady Harrington looked like she was shaking in her boots. "Is that a threat?"

"A promise!" She stepped around the woman and left the hall without a look back.

She had never been so direct with Lady Margaret before and was certain she would heed her warning. Risking social exclusion by ruining her reputation was anathema to Lady Harrington despite her *faux* daring attitude.

Should they ever run into each other again, which very well could occur given that their social circles overlapped, Eleanor believed Margaret would avoid her completely.

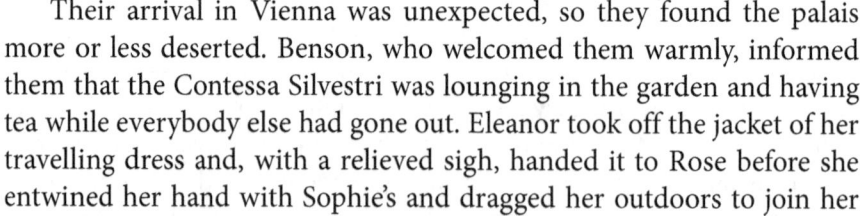

Their arrival in Vienna was unexpected, so they found the palais more or less deserted. Benson, who welcomed them warmly, informed them that the Contessa Silvestri was lounging in the garden and having tea while everybody else had gone out. Eleanor took off the jacket of her travelling dress and, with a relieved sigh, handed it to Rose before she entwined her hand with Sophie's and dragged her outdoors to join her grandmother for tea.

"Eleanor," the contessa exclaimed when she saw her granddaughter coming down the path, with Sophie right by her side. "We didn't expect you before tomorrow."

"It is good to see you too, Nonna." Eleanor laughed as she kissed her grandmother's cheek.

"Hello, my dear," Giulia said warmly to Sophie.

"Good afternoon."

"Does that mean I could have gone with Sophie to her hotel and made passionate love without you bothering me?" Eleanor asked playfully as she sipped her tea.

Without missing a beat, Giulia said, "Why would you go to a hotel? You have a perfectly good bedroom here to do that."

Sophie's tea left her mouth in a spray, and she coughed violently when some of it found the wrong way down her throat.

The contessa patted her back sympathetically. "I am sorry, darling."

Eleanor took Sophie's cup and put it on the table and handed her a napkin to clean herself.

"I didn't mean to startle you, my dear," Giulia said with a gleam in her eyes.

"No, no, not at all," Sophie wheezed. "You took me by surprise, that's all." Never in her wildest dreams had she thought that the contessa or Eleanor would banter this light-heartedly about such intimate matters.

"That is good to know," Giulia continued unfazed, "because I think, my dear Eleanor, Charlotte will have to tell you something when she returns."

"You mean," Eleanor covered her mouth, feeling very emotional at the news, "my little girl is now a woman?"

True to her grandmother's words, when Charlotte and Adele returned from their horseback ride, Charlotte came running out of the palais and flew into her mother's open arms. Adele followed at a more appropriate pace but beamed broadly when she saw her cousin Sophie watching her expectantly. The cousins excused themselves and took a walk in the garden while Charlotte was still in her mother's embrace.

Eleanor pulled back slightly to look at her daughter who was positively glowing. She appeared every bit a happy woman and completely in love.

"Was it everything you had hoped, darling?" Eleanor asked as she put her palm against her daughter's cheek.

"Yes, Mama, and so much more," Charlotte answered dreamily, before she embraced her mother again.

Eleanor returned the hug and felt tears of relief and gratitude well in her eyes. She was happy Charlotte had found such a considerate partner who ensured the first time they made love was a wonderful pleasurable experience.

By the expression on Adele's face when she came back with Sophie, Eleanor was certain Adele had experienced the same love and care during her union with Charlotte, and for that, she was grateful.

Philip, Henry, and Jonathan returned from a visit to the History of Art Museum in time for luncheon. Martin joined in with their laughter and light mood while Charlotte and Adele, both still looking gobsmacked with love, watched in amusement.

With everyone carrying on so gleefully, Eleanor said to Sophie quietly, "Why don't you stay tonight, darling?"

"I don't know," Sophie was reluctant. She didn't want to be presumptuous.

Henry was close enough to overhear and came to his wife's assistance. "Yes, please stay, Sophie, unless of course, the two of you care to accompany us on our evening jaunt."

Sophie cast at glance at her beloved, who raised her eyebrow to leave the decision to her. "Thank you. But I would rather stay behind."

"Very well." Henry sounded oddly cheerful. "The Palais will be all yours then."

"What do you mean, Henry?" Eleanor asked.

"Since we didn't expect you back until tomorrow, we all agreed to visit the opera again for an encore performance of 'Die Zauberflöte,' and I decided to give the servants the evening off. Do you mind?"

"Not at all," Eleanor assured him. She was certain that their need for dinner would be taken care of, so why would she mind?

"Good." Henry smirked. "I have no doubt you are going to enjoy a quiet evening."

When the two of them were left alone in the huge house, they had a light dinner and retired to the drawing room for a game of chess.

Before they even had the pieces set in the proper places, their eyes met over the chess board, and without a word, everything fell into place. Neither felt the need to ask if the other was sure; they both simply knew.

Eleanor stood and held her hand out to Sophie, who took it without hesitation and let herself be led upstairs. Eleanor closed the bedroom door behind them and carefully locked it. She went to the hearth opposite the bed to light a fire, which filled the room with a warm glow.

Sophie stood in the middle of the room looking scared and little bit lost. Her lover sensed her nervousness as she stepped closer. With both hands Eleanor cupped her face, kissing her passionately.

Sophie let go of her cane as she wrapped both arms gently around Eleanor's back to hold her firmly against her body. Eleanor felt the warmth of Sophie's hands seep through her blouse where they caressed her back. Their kisses were a delicious combination of softness, lust, passion, and tenderness.

Slowly and carefully, they undressed each other in front of the fire. As they discarded clothes, each patch of skin revealed was worshipped by gentle fingers. Caresses and touches, followed by lips, kissing, and nibbling the warm tender skin. Naked bodies pressed against each other as they embraced.

Eleanor suddenly felt hot tears on her shoulder. She held on to Sophie, running her hands soothingly over her back, reassuring her through softly spoken words.

Her lover had been hesitant to let her take off her clothes, but gentle persistence had worn down her barriers. Sophie's scars were less prominent than Eleanor had thought they'd be. Though clearly visible, there was nothing ugly or disgusting about them. Their pattern over Sophie's stomach, hip and leg did not distract from her beauty at all.

Eleanor took Sophie's hand and guided her towards the bed, where she pulled back the cover and held up the sheet indicating for Sophie to slip underneath. Eleanor followed suit. Lying on her side, she brushed her fingertips over Sophie's cheeks, and luxuriated in the way Sophie closed her eyes and leaned into the touch.

"Why are you not repulsed?" Sophie whispered with her eyes still closed, too afraid of what she might see in those sky-blue eyes she loved so much.

"Look at me, love," Eleanor pleaded softly. She waited for Sophie to open her eyes again before she continued. "Nothing about you is repulsive. You are beautiful inside and out. I feel very honoured to be with you."

She kissed away a stray tear that rolled down Sophie's cheek before she put her hand against Sophie's chest. With gentle pressure she pushed her on her back. Eleanor rolled over, resting against Sophie's left side. She captured alluring lips in another intense kiss.

Sophie let her hands wander over Eleanor's back, from her shoulder blades, down her spine to the small of her back, applying a subtle pressure when she felt Eleanor trying to slip off of her.

"Stay," she whispered against exceptionally talented lips.

"I don't want to squash you."

"You don't."

Eleanor showered her face with kisses, her lips moving from mouth to chin, over Sophie's jaw to her temple and across her brow. She kissed her eyelids, down her nose and covered her mouth again. Warm lips trailed down Sophie's chin, over her throat to her chest. Eleanor pushed her upper body up and gazed into Sophie's flushed face before she leaned down again to capture one of Sophie's nipples between her lips. She circled it with her tongue, sucking gently. Sophie's moans were all the encouragement she needed to give the other breast the same treatment.

Hands slipped into her short white hair holding her firmly into place as she paid homage to her lover's wonderful breasts. Eleanor revelled at the sounds emanating from Sophie. She enjoyed the way she arched her back and offered those glorious globes to her. Her right hand caressed her lover's stomach, gliding along her waist to her hip and over the top of her upper thigh. Sophie opened her legs invitingly, and Eleanor slipped a hand between them, her mouth never stopping the worship of her breasts. Her body rested between Sophie's legs, and she could feel her lover's arousal against her own lower abdomen. She let her hand slide over the soft skin of Sophie's inner thigh. Reaching short crisp curls, she stopped before she went any further.

Eleanor lifted her head from Sophie's chest, "Darling, look at me." With great effort brown eyes opened and locked with blue ones.

Their hands entwined where they lay next to Sophie's head. Eleanor's fingers slowly brushed through warm wetness. Her lover's hips rose to meet the gentle touch. Soft fingertips drew small circles over Sophie's clitoris, forcing her breath out in pants.

She closed her eyes when wonderful sensations overtook her body, but Eleanor's plea forced them open again. Eleanor kissed her as her fingers slowly slipped lower hovering, "May I?"

"Yes, please." Sophie rasped hoarsely, her eyes never leaving her lover's. She felt their entwined hands tightening their grip as Eleanor tenderly slipped two fingers inside. A short gasp escaped her lips at the intrusion which was soon replaced by moans of pleasure as Eleanor's fingers started a delicious rhythm in sync with her thumb on her clitoris.

Sophie felt her climax building in the pit of her stomach. With a sudden explosion of breath shouting Eleanor's name she came, shaking violently as her body rode out her first orgasm brought on by her lover. She pulled Eleanor's head down and crushed their lips together in another passionate kiss. They only parted when oxygen finally became an issue and gazed breathlessly into each other's eyes.

"I love you," Eleanor whispered reverently, brushing sweaty hair from Sophie's brow.

"I love you, too."

Sophie brought the hand she was holding to her lips to gently kiss its palm before she pressed it against her cheek. Her breath was slowly returning to normal as she fixed her gaze on those blue eyes that shone with so much love.

Before Eleanor knew what was happening, she was lying on her back and Sophie was returning the favour of lovemaking with passion and skill. Sophie made love to her mouth and her breasts before her lips trailed down her stomach over her hip to her thigh, nuzzling the soft skin of her inner thighs close to her core. Eleanor arched her back when she felt Sophie's tongue against her clitoris. Her lover sucked and licked with enthusiasm as if she couldn't get enough of her. The pleasure she felt surged higher when Sophie entered her with two fingers and set a steady pace while her tongue continued to do the most wonderful things.

Eleanor writhed in ecstasy under the gentle but passionate ministrations of her lover, climbing higher and higher until waves of pleasure came crashing down on her. When she surfaced again, she felt soft fingers caressing her cheek and brown eyes gazing down at her.

"Are you all right, my love?" Sophie asked with worry colouring her voice. "Did I hurt you?"

"No, you didn't hurt me," Eleanor let the pad of her thumb brush over Sophie's quivering bottom lip. "You were wonderful."

To emphasize her words, she lifted her head to capture lush lips with her own, tasting herself on them.

They kissed until their passion led to more lovemaking. So lost were they in each other, they didn't know Eleanor's family returned from the opera or hear their lively discussion as they climbed the stairs to their respective rooms.

In the early hours of the morning, they finally fell asleep, exhausted, in each other's arms.

It was lunchtime when Sophie slowly opened her eyes and found a head resting on her chest. She laughed happily at Eleanor, fast asleep in her arms, her body resting half on top of her. The feeling was most pleasurable, especially where Eleanor's knee was pressing against the sweet spot between her legs. She tightened her arms around her lover's body as she felt Eleanor stir and gasped when a warm mouth suddenly closed around an erect nipple. This was all it took to ignite the passion between them anew. Their lovemaking was as passionate as the night before, a delicious combination of unrestrained want and tenderness.

They lay spent between rumpled sheets, panting heavily from their last climax and smiling lazily at each other. Never would Sophie have thought it could be as glorious as this. Eleanor was an amazing lover.

She was basking in the afterglow when a loud rumble from her stomach sent the dignified Duchess of Darnsworth into a fit of giggles. Sophie pouted at being laughed at when Eleanor gently patted her belly.

"Come on," Eleanor said, "let's take a shower together and join the others for tea." She padded naked into the bathroom but stopped at the door when Sophie wasn't following, "Are you coming?"

Sophie sat up and followed the siren's call of Eleanor's gloriously naked body under the shower, which took decidedly longer than they anticipated.

Showered and dressed meticulously, Eleanor descended the stairs on Sophie's arm. They entered the drawing room to find all the eyes of those present upon them. Sophie blushed at the knowing smiles on some of the faces, but Eleanor seemed completely unfazed by the looks they were receiving. As they took a seat on one of the sofa's Henry cleared his throat to break the awkward silence that had descended over the room upon their arrival.

"Eleanor, my dear, may I suggest you wear a high-necked blouse next time after a night of unrestrained passion. A love bite this size simply does not help your air of well-mannered dignity."

As soon as he finished speaking, a pillow hit him square in the face. Eleanor was pleased at her aim. Her husband sputtered at her behaviour which merely earned him a raised eyebrow.

"Serves you right," she said.

The tension was broken, and afternoon tea was the lively and pleasant affair it had always been.

Chapter Twenty-Two

One afternoon in early September, Sophie's head lay comfortably in Eleanor's lap as she dozed on the sofa while Eleanor was reading a book.

"Darling, are you going to attend your sister's wedding next week?" Eleanor asked out of the blue.

Sophie opened her eyes lazily and sat up. Of course, she had thought about it quite a lot recently. The date of the wedding was drawing nearer, and she had fought an internal battle which had brought no solution to the problem.

Eleanor had been well aware of her struggle the whole time, but so far had restrained from bringing up the topic. There had not been much opportunity to do so if she was honest. Since their first night of passion, their focus was not on worldly issues. Sophie had spent every night in Eleanor's bed making love or simply enjoying their closeness. Her belongings had been delivered from the hotel soon after, and she was now living as Eleanor's partner in the palais as she would in London.

"I don't know, Eleanor. One moment I think I should be there, at least as an observer in the background, and in the next, I think it won't matter either way."

She was pacing in front of the sofa now. Torn was the best way to describe how she felt when she thought about her sister. The hurt from Emma's words still lingered, and she highly doubted the pain would vanish any time soon. What would the point be to attend the wedding ceremony when she was fully aware she wasn't wanted?

Feeling guilty for mentioning the unpleasant topic, Eleanor tried to steer her lover's thoughts away by saying, "I have been thinking, maybe we should go out for dinner this evening. Just the two of us."

"Is that prudent, your Grace?" Sophie asked playfully as she sat down again. "What will people think?"

"Why should I care what anybody would think?" She waved it off with an elegant gesture of her hand. "If you're worried about my reputation, we could ask Nonna to be our chaperone."

"Do you believe that would be a good idea?"

"Would what be a good idea?" a woman's raspy voice asked from the doorway. The mischievous twinkle in her eyes made Sophie shake her head. Eleanor's grandmother was certainly one of a kind.

With a dramatic wave of her hand, Eleanor said, "My dearest love thinks it would not be so wise to ask you to be our chaperone this evening."

"She might have a point, my dear. After all, I am known to voice my opinion without restraint. My dear Bridget often suffered a headache because of that."

"I recall that Granny seldom held back with her opinion either. She was quite a sight to behold when she got into something."

Giulia smirked wistfully at the memory of her beloved, her tall stance, flowing hair, eyes blazing, and her Scottish accent more pronounced than ever when she worked up a temper. The late Duchess of Darnsworth had been a formidable woman indeed. Yet at the same time, underneath her bravado lay a gentle soul with a tender heart, a combination that had captured the contessa's heart right from the beginning. She sighed longingly at the cherished memory.

When she gazed at her granddaughter who was looking expectantly at her now, she could see a lot of Bridget in her. It had been the right decision to make Eleanor heiress of the title, never had there been a sliver of doubt in her mind.

"I meant no disrespect," Sophie's voice brought Giulia from her musings.

"Do not worry, my dear. I didn't think you did. Where are we having dinner tonight?"

"Mrs. Kavanaugh, a word, please," Benson softly called from the doorway to the housekeeper's parlour. She was working on the books, and he hated to interrupt her concentration, but it couldn't be helped.

"Of course, Mister Benson. Please, do come in! What is it you want to talk about?"

The butler carefully closed the door behind him. Even though he had known Mrs. Chambers so much longer than the Mrs. Kavanaugh, her temper was something he couldn't handle very well. It was not above him to follow his employer's example and take the easier way out of a dilemma. Benson gently cleared his throat before he elaborated, "It has only been brought to my attention moments ago that her Grace will dine out this evening."

"Oh, dear," Mrs. Kavanaugh said, flustered. "And I take it you are telling me this because you want me to break this unpleasant news to Mrs. Chambers?"

"Would you?"

"Yes, of course. You are aware that tonight's dinner was meant as a surprise for her Grace. Each and every one of her favourite dishes will be served? You could have told us sooner."

Benson felt chastised although it certainly wasn't his fault. "I am aware, but I am afraid it was a rather spur-of-the-moment decision. Besides, I never thought this special meal was a good idea. We all know how much she hates surprises."

"Yes, well," Mrs. Kavanaugh said, "it was well intentioned. Hetty, Mrs. Chambers, thought it would be appreciated."

"It can't be helped now, can it?"

"Maybe it can. Where is her Grace at the moment?"

"Why? Surely you don't intend to—" Benson bristled indignantly. "Mrs. Kavanaugh, you can't be serious. This is . . . I strongly recommend you rethink it. This is most—"

"Mister Benson, please, calm yourself." Mrs. Kavanaugh stood and smoothed her skirt. "It is worth a try, I dare say. I have come to appreciate her Grace as a very tolerant person. A woman of great dignity as well as consideration. I always thought her Grace to be quite a formidable woman, if I might say so. Most admirable, indeed."

"Quite."

"Well, then, where will I find her?" The housekeeper insisted, raising her chin defiantly at the butler.

"Drawing room."

Mrs. Kavanaugh nodded curtly and swept out of her parlour. A determined woman. Her bravery was mostly a front but there was no point in telling Benson so. She had meant every word she had said about her employer. After many years of moving from one post to another, she had been happy to find a place in the Duchess of Darnsworth's household. All of the servants were aware that this was one of the best places to be. At first Mrs. Kavanaugh had been weary, not of her employer but of the strained relationship she had with the cook. The thought of the volatile beginnings between Hetty and herself brought a smile to her lips.

Their fights were legendary, getting so far out of hand that her Grace had to threaten them personally with dismissal if they weren't able to settle their differences once and for all. And settle it they did. The mere memory still brought a blush to Mrs. Kavanaugh's cheeks. Hetty's passion certainly didn't end at her profession, much to her own delight.

Mrs. Kavanaugh's cheeks were still burning as she crossed the hall towards the drawing room, earning her a peculiar glance from James, the footman, who was dusting a painting. Mrs. Kavanaugh shrugged it off and with a deep breath she knocked at the door to the drawing room and waited for her Grace's answer before she entered.

"Your Grace," she said respectfully after closing the door behind her. She nodded at the contessa and at the Countess von Hagendorf, wishing that her employer had been alone.

"Mrs. Kavanaugh, is something the matter?" The duchess beckoned her to come closer. "Are you all right? You seem a bit flushed."

"Yes, your Grace, I'm fine. Thank you."

She held her hands folded in front of her and attempt to look at the duchess and the other women with more confidence than she actually felt. "If I may, your Grace, Mister Benson just informed me that you will be dining out tonight."

"Yes, is there a problem?"

"No, I was merely wondering, your Grace, if it would be too much trouble—and please do not think me presumptuous."

"Mrs. Kavanaugh, there has to be a point somewhere otherwise you wouldn't bother with this convoluted speech," Eleanor encouraged patiently but resolutely. "So please, by all means, get to it."

"I meant to ask, your Grace, if you would be so kind to reconsider your plan to dine out and instead have dinner at the palais?"

There, she said it. The expression on her Grace's face didn't show any sign of anger at her atrociously forward request, but the duchess frowned, her head tilted, clearly waiting for an explanation.

"Mrs. Chambers took it upon herself to change the plan for tonight and decided to prepare all your favourite dishes as a special surprise."

"I see." Eleanor's expression brightened. She was touched, slightly irritated, but touched. "Why?"

When Mrs. Kavanaugh slowly shook her head without giving a reason, Eleanor gazed at her lover and grandmother, asking if they had any objection to a change in plans. They did not.

"Mrs. Kavanaugh, I suppose it wouldn't hurt to postpone our evening out until tomorrow."

"Thank you, your Grace." Mrs. Kavanaugh felt as if a mountain had been lifted from her shoulders. "Please, forgive my interference. I did not forget my station." She bowed slightly as she backed up. "If you could be so gracious as to forgive this most unusual behaviour, it would be very much appreciated."

"Mrs. Kavanaugh, it's quite all right." Eleanor shook her head at her housekeeper's humble apologies. She really wished she would stop begging forgiveness now, so she changed the subject. "I meant to ask you, how is Countess von Hochstetten's maid doing?"

"Quite nicely, your Grace. At first Josefine was rather shy, but now she's doing fine."

"Good. I'm glad to hear it. If there's nothing else, Mrs. Kavanaugh?"

"No, your Grace, thank you." The housekeeper curtsied and left with a spring in her step.

When they were finally alone again, Sophie could no longer contain her curiosity.

In an amused tone, Sophie said, "You cancelled your plans because your cook took it upon herself to change the dinner menu?"

"I know, I know." Eleanor exhaled with an air of drama as she leaned back in her seat. "My mother would be outraged if she had witnessed this.

I would be lectured about what is befitting for a duchess, and the housekeeper would be dismissed instantly."

"But since you are nothing like your mother, which we are most grateful for," the contessa interjected, "you are touched by the gesture, although you hate surprises. You are addicted to Mrs. Chambers art of cooking. So, it wasn't much of a hardship, my dear Eleanor, to cancel your plans, now was it?"

"I have no idea what you are talking about, Nonna." Eleanor sniffed with mock haughtiness but couldn't contain her laughter when she saw the mirth on her grandmother's face and the merriment on Sophie's.

The following evening, Sophie's acquaintance with Frau Sacher secured them a quiet table in the dining room of the hotel's restaurant. Their waiter dutifully and discreetly took care of their wishes. The atmosphere was warm and cosy. Nobody was bothering them or spared a second glance at three women without male company. The duchess enjoyed herself tremendously; the conversation was invigorating and the food delicious.

Shortly after dessert was served, boisterous male voices from another table interrupted their tranquillity. Eleanor frowned at the disturbance, but she saw Sophie's ears perking up with interest.

"What is it, darling?" Eleanor asked, intrigued.

"I think I recognise one of the voices," she answered thoughtfully.

"Who—" the contessa started to say but was stopped by Sophie's raised hand. She cocked her head in an attempt to concentrate harder on what was said. She realized how impolite it was to eavesdrop on other people's conversations, but since she'd heard her sister's name mentioned, she simply had to know what these men were talking about.

"*Yes, my dear von Bernthal, tell us about Emma von Hagendorf,*" *a male voice said, a leer in his voice.* "*Knowing you, I can't believe you're going to wait until your wedding night to get a taste of her.*"

"*You are talking about my fiancée,*" *the count answered with mock consternation before he chuckled suggestively.* "*But you're right, my friend. It seems she enjoyed my little love letters I sent her over the summer.*"

"*Oh, do tell!*" *another voice encouraged.*

"*Nothing too forward, of course. Just testing the water, you know.*" *The count paused before he continued more directly.* "*Since I didn't want to buy a pig in a poke, I decided to take it a little further.*"

"*And?*" *three exited men asked impatiently.*

"*Would you believe that after all the correspondence, she was playing hard to get?*" *Bernthal queried indignantly.* "*Told me she was a virgin, which she was. Imagine my surprise. Last Saturday in the stables of her father's palais, I made her a woman. At the beginning, the little tart was trying to put up a fight, but she soon realised it was pointless. When we're married, I'll have to teach her obedience.*"

"*And you're going to enjoy every minute of it, aren't you?*" *the first man suggested gleefully.*

"*It will be most enjoyable indeed. So much to teach, so much to learn. Never spare the whip when educating a girl.*"

As the last piece of conversation led to joyful laughter all around the count's table, Sophie reached her breaking point. She tried to get to her feet but was stopped by a hand on her own. Eleanor's grip broke through her furious haze. Sophie glared at her when she refused to let go.

Eleanor shook her head. "No! Not here, not now. This is neither the time nor the place."

"But—"

"No."

Sophie's attempt to argue was cut short by a gentle squeeze of her hand and the insistence in her lover's voice. "Listen to me, please. I'll tell you what we're going to do now. We'll ask for the receipt, return to the palais, and together we will formulate a course of action."

"Eleanor is right, Sophie," Giulia said. "You have every right to be angry but barging in on them now will accomplish nothing. This whole issue must be tackled with a cool head, not in an emotional uproar."

Sophie slumped in her chair, wiping away a tear of anger and frustration, but finally nodded in silent consent.

"Good girl. That's the spirit." Eleanor asked for the receipt and when the bill was settled, they left immediately. On their way back to the palais, the formerly festive atmosphere was dominated by icy silence. By the thunderous expression on Sophie's face, Eleanor and Giulia thought it better not to engage her in idle chit chat even if it would lighten the mood. What was meant to be a pleasant evening had become a virtual nightmare. Sophie was closing herself off, leaving Eleanor feeling punished for something she wasn't responsible for.

A distance had cleaved open between them that frightened her. Sophie was cold and unyielding and withdrawn into herself. Eleanor had no idea how to react to this.

Eleanor felt hurt when Sophie climbed the stairs to their room without waiting for her or expressing a word of goodnight to her grandmother. She was slowly growing angrier at the complete lack of manners and disregard from her.

"Don't be angry, *Cara*." Giulia stirred her from her reverie. "She isn't herself right now. Sophie feels responsible for what happened to her sister. Just be attentive to her and offer your advice when asked, otherwise just listen. Be her friend, her lover."

"You think that will be enough?" Eleanor asked worriedly.

"It is everything. Now if you excuse me. I think I will also retire to my room, and I suggest you do the same. Good night, Eleanor."

"Good night, Nonna." Eleanor kissed her grandmother's cheek before she ascended the stairs to join Sophie in their room.

In the bedroom she found Sophie sitting on the edge of the bed staring at her hands in her lap. At the lost look on her face, Eleanor felt her heart go out to her. Silently she sat next to Sophie. Relief flooded her body when Sophie put her head on her shoulder. Eleanor dropped a kiss on her hair, wrapped her arms around her, and closed her eyes; waiting for Sophie to tell her what was on her mind. She wasn't disappointed.

"I was so afraid that something like this would happen to Emma. But I had no idea how awful it would be for her."

"We don't know how Emma feels about this."

"I know my sister, and she would not appreciate being forced. She's still young. And stupid for that matter! I told her he was a beast, and she wouldn't believe me. Oh my, oh my . . ."

"Go on, darling! I know there is more you have to get off your chest." Eleanor encouraged her gently.

"I want to kill him."

"I understand completely."

"He needs to be stopped. I need to do something about this, so it doesn't happen again." She let out an anguished sob.

"We cannot do anything now, but we shall figure out something in the morning."

"You have heard it yourself, love," Sophie lifted her head from Eleanor's shoulder and blinked with tearful eyes into compassionate blue ones. "This man doesn't even care where he is or who hears when he's boasting about the way he treated my sister and what else he has in store for her. And those awful friends of his. They were drooling over his story. And the derogatory way he spoke of Emma, as if she were nothing more than a faithful dog to be brought to heel. It's disgusting."

"What do you want to do about it? Because whatever it is, you have my fullest support."

"I don't know," Sophie admitted. She felt trapped in her helplessness. What could she do, indeed? Confront her sister and her father about tonight's conversation? But would they believe her?

At the very least, she had to try. Emma's wedding was taking place next Saturday, and there wasn't much time to try to stop the insanity.

"Tomorrow I will go to my father's palais and make him see reason. Maybe I can convince Emma to come with me."

"Do you want me or anybody else from the family to accompany you?"

"Better not. No. I don't want to aggravate the situation more than necessary."

"All right, darling. But right now, we should go to bed. You will need your rest for the upcoming confrontation."

"May I hold you?" Sophie asked softly.

"I would love that very much." Eleanor cupped her cheek, brushing her lips over Sophie's, conveying the love and affection she felt.

They undressed and took care of their nightly routine before they climbed into bed together. Sophie opened her arms for her lover and wrapped them around Eleanor's shoulder. Eleanor put her head on her chest and sneaked her arm around Sophie's waist before she closed her eyes with a blissful sigh.

Despite the dread she felt when she thought about tomorrow, sleep came easily to Sophie.

"Are you still mad at me?" Martin asked the back of Sophie's head as they travelled to Palais Hagendorf. She had refused to look at him ever since he insisted on climbing into the carriage with her. Instead, she kept her eyes trained on the buildings they passed on their way.

"Why are you doing this?" she asked suddenly, startling him by her forcefulness. Her eyes were blazing with an anger boiling right under the surface. "I'm quite capable of taking care of myself. This has nothing to do with you."

"On the contrary," he dared to object vehemently. Martin saw that took Sophie by surprise. Gone was the mild-mannered young man she had come to know. His green eyes sparkled with righteous indignation as they had at breakfast when Eleanor told her family what they had witnessed the night before. Sophie had not been able to eat or to face the family, so she missed the indignation all of Eleanor's family expressed.

"Emma is as much my cousin as she is your sister. And my parents have raised me better than to stand back and let something so atrocious happen to her. Respect towards women was one of the most valued lessons my parents taught me. I *have* to accompany you. The women in my family expect nothing less from me."

"I wish I had met your late mother," Sophie said softly. "She must have been an admirable woman. No wonder Eleanor mourned her for so long."

"She was," Martin said. "She would have liked you."

"Thank you."

"I have a request," he said.

"Which is?"

"Let me be in charge of the conversation," Martin said earnestly and before Sophie could object, he carried on. "It might be better. You are far too angry. Besides, your father doesn't strike me as a man who would listen to reason when told by a woman. No offence meant!"

"None taken." Sophie grimaced, but she knew what Martin said had merit. Her father's view of women as being inferior would certainly not help the case. Because Martin was not only a man but also his wife's nephew, his presentation of the matter might work in their favour. The most important thing was not that she win the battle with her father, but that Emma win the war with von Bernthal before it started.

"Martin, as much as I hate to admit it, you do have a point."

Smiling, Martin said, "Glad you agree."

Chapter Twenty-Three

The butler showed Sophie and Martin into the sitting room to wait. Sophie did not seat herself but paced nervously. Since she'd moved out of the palais, she hadn't spoken to either her father or sister. Anton was the only one who had visited her at Palais Schelling and had dinner with her and Eleanor's family.

They didn't have to wait long as her father soon strode into the room. Count von Hagendorf greeted Martin jovially, shaking his hand enthusiastically while he barely spared a glance at his daughter.

"My dear boy, what can I do for you?"

Martin said, "Why don't we ask the others to join us? I think it will be of interest to your whole family what we have to talk about."

The count shrugged. He rang for the butler to inform his wife and children to come to the sitting room as soon as they finished their breakfast. While they were waiting for the others to arrive, Sophie's father settled in his favourite chair and asked Martin to take a seat as well. Sophie was too wound up to sit and remained standing.

"Tell me, Count, what do you know about your soon-to-be son-in-law?" Martin asked boldly.

"What do you mean?" von Hagendorf replied defensively. "He is a man of substantial means, one of my business associates, and a widower." He threw an angry glance at his daughter, but Sophie refused to meet his gaze or to feel guilty for this intrusion on the privacy of her father's home.

"Do you know any of his other friends?" Martin asked.

"One or two, yes. Can you tell me what this is all about?" he asked impatiently but had to wait for an answer because his wife, son, and daughter entered the room. Helen and Emma appeared equally astounded to find Sophie there.

Anton was delighted to see his sister again. He rushed to her and hugged her fiercely. "You look good, Sophie," he whispered. "Love certainly suits you."

"Thank you." Sophie twinkled as she let go of him.

Anton remained by her side. "What's this all about," he whispered.

"Shhh. You'll see."

"Well?" the count said. "Why are you asking about von Bernthal?"

"Since you are so keen to know and you think so highly of the man, am I to believe that it doesn't matter to you that he raped my cousin and is boasting about it to his friends in public?"

Martin spoke as emotionally devoid as possible when Sophie knew he was actually seething.

Emma turned paler than she already was. Helen gasped and covered her mouth in shock while the count went red with fury.

"Emma," von Hagendorf said harshly, "is this true? Did Count von Bernthal violate you?"

Emma concentrated on her neatly folded hands in her lap. She would not look her father in the eye. Sophie had seen that stubborn look before on Emma with shame and anger bubbling up uncontrollably.

Emma jumped from her seat and rushed at Sophie, pointing an accusing finger at her. "This is all your fault," Emma spat out. "If you hadn't been so damn selfish and egotistical, none of this would have happened to me or to this family."

"I beg your pardon?" Sophie was completely taken aback. "What are you talking about? Ever since Father decided you should marry this vile beast, I tried to stop it. You insisted I should step back and not meddle in your affairs."

Emma shouted, "Because you refused to give father the money you inherited from your mother so he could save the factory. He would have lost everything if it weren't for the count. We'd lose this palais, the villa, everything. I have to marry him because *you* wouldn't help. Count von Bernthal said father would risk being shunned by his peers if they knew."

Shocked, Sophie asked, "Is *that* why you told me to back off?"

"Of course. Since you were so adamant to keep your precious money to yourself, what was I to do? You could have prevented this entire mess from the beginning, but you were acting like an awful hypocrite." Emma voice was harsh, and she wiped furiously at the tears of frustration running down her cheeks.

"Father?" Sophie took a deep breath. She felt broken inside at the arrogance of the man. He wouldn't even acknowledge her. He refused to look her way. "Father, how could you? Your own damn pride was more important than your daughter's health and welfare? You'd rather sell Emma to such a disgusting piece of work than ask me for money?"

"That is not the point."

"Of course, it *is* the goddamned point," Sophie shouted, outraged, before addressing her sister. "He never asked me for money, Emma. I didn't know about his troubles at the factory. I was *never* approached by him. You must believe me. Because if he had asked, and if I had known what the alternative was, I'd have given the money to him in a heartbeat."

"You never knew?" Emma asked wearily.

"No. I didn't."

"Why are you here now? It's too late." Emma cried dejectedly through her tears. "It's done. Father took the money, and the Count took me."

She sank into a chair, her shoulders slumped. There was no fight left in her, and the spirited sister Sophie knew was completely defeated.

Sophie looked around the room. Emma's fate was now sealed, and everybody in the room knew the price paid, and on top of everything, Emma had alienated her sister and helped turn her out of her rightful home. Emma had done this because she was envious and willing to be hateful to Sophie in order to get her way.

Understanding came to Sophie as though she'd been hit by a wrecking ball. She understood now that she had always been the strongest of them. She had, despite her accident and mishap, a purpose in life, and she was free to love who she desired. She was free, unlike the family sitting in front of her.

"Slut." Her mother's voice broke the silence. Disgust at her daughter was written on her face. "I can't believe it," Helen shouted. "You're nothing but a filthy little whore."

"Mother!" Anton voice was outraged. He looked to his father, but he sat silently in his chair.

"What? Look at her!" Helen said. "Look at them! One is a filthy lesbian and the other a whore." Helen staggered to her feet and before anybody knew what happened or could react, she rushed over to Emma and slapped her across the face.

Sophie stepped between her sister and stepmother, and Martin was at her side in an instant, glaring at his aunt. "Stop that right now," he said, his words sharp. "She's not at fault. Don't you understand? Emma had no choice in the matter. The man raped her."

Helen ignored him. "She has to marry! Now more than ever. Otherwise the scandal will ruin us. Ludwig, say something!"

Sophie observed her father, who sat sunken in his chair as if he had aged over the last few minutes. He met her gaze, and she no longer recognised the man she used to know. She thought she should feel for him but try as she might she simply couldn't. Not after everything he had done. Her father had been lying and scheming, playing one daughter against the other to keep his pathetic pride and reputation.

So, she did what she should have done long ago. Sophie took a stand, certain he would not stop her. For the sake of avoiding too much uproar, she was willing to give up her mother's inheritance. She didn't care about the money, if only her sister could be saved from marriage to a monster.

"I will give you the money you need," Sophie stated, "to pay off the Count and save your factory, but Emma is coming with me. She will leave this house never to return. I don't care what you tell the count or your friends. That is what we will do."

"All right," he rasped, hanging his head in shame.

"If she leaves here, all she'll get are the clothes she's wearing right now," Helen threatened viciously. "And she will no longer be welcome here."

"Rest assured, she won't need anything else from you, not now or ever."

Sophie held out her hand to Emma who reluctantly took it and let herself be pulled to her feet. Martin took her other hand and they walked to the door

Before they left the room, Sophie stopped and spun around to face her father. "I will make sure everything is in order by the middle of next week. You will have control over my money by then and can get rid of the count. Anton, you are always welcome."

"I know, Sophie," he acknowledged gratefully as his sisters and cousin left. "Thank you."

Martin helped them into the carriage before he climbed in himself and ordered Parker to drive to the palais where he knew his mother was waiting anxiously for their return. The ride was a solemn affair. Nobody said a word while Emma merely clung to her sister's hand like a lifeline. Sophie put her arm around Emma's shoulders and rested her chin gently on the top of her head. With her eyes closed, she sat rigidly, providing the strength Emma needed.

Martin looked at the shivering form of his cousin and the pillar of strength Sophie was for her sister. After everything that had happened between the sisters, he doubted he could have forgiven so easily.

He sighed heavily. If he needed any more proof that Sophie was the perfect match for his mother, he had gotten it. Martin would make sure to tell his mother how he felt now. She deserved to know.

Eleanor descended the stairs when they entered the palais. When she spotted Emma next to Sophie, her lips curled into a slight smile.

"Welcome, Emma," she said as she greeted Sophie with a chaste kiss on the cheek.

"Thank you," Emma mumbled, unable to look at the woman she had betrayed so badly.

"Martin," Eleanor suggested mildly, "why don't you show Emma to the room Mrs. Kavanaugh has prepared for her? The one right next to your sister's."

"Of course, Mama." He offered Emma his arm, which she took hesitantly, and led her upstairs.

Sophie and Eleanor watched them leave before Eleanor took her hand and said, "Come, darling."

Hand in hand, they strolled into the library where Sophie stopped right inside the door to engulf Eleanor in a tight embrace. They didn't know how long they stood holding on to each other but when Sophie felt her inner turmoil was settling, she reluctantly let go of Eleanor.

Eleanor brushed a stray hair behind Sophie's ear and let her palm rest against a warm cheek. She saw the storm of emotions in the dark brown eyes. "Tell me!"

It was all the encouragement Sophie needed to get everything off her chest that she had learned at her father's home. While she spoke, a myriad of conflicting emotions ran through her: anger, frustration, pity, fury, regret, loss, pain. She finished the sad tale by saying, "I still can't believe he did all this."

Sophie rose from her seat and moved over to the windows. Staring out into the garden, she saw the weather changing dramatically. Large, dark grey clouds were gathering, and in the distance, she saw a flash of lightning. It perfectly reflected her mood. She heard the rustle of skirts behind her and felt the warmth of Eleanor's body behind her. Eleanor wrapped her arms around Sophie's waist and rested her chin on her shoulder.

"Nothing of this is your fault," Eleanor said softly, realising that this was exactly what Sophie was feeling.

"I know," Sophie said. "To know the truth in my head is something else than knowing it in my heart."

"Why don't you talk to Jonathan about the transactions that will have to take place? He is very adept in these things. He knows what to do to get everything done properly and without problems or chicanery, and you won't have to bother yourself with it."

"I will consult him. Thank you."

Sophie turned in Eleanor's arms to kiss her, conveying the love she felt for her in the most intimate meeting of lips. When they parted, they rested their foreheads together, trying to catch their breaths.

"Will you still love me," Sophie asked, "when I'm poor and devoid of any substantial means?"

"Darling, nothing you do will make you less dear to me. I love you. Please, never doubt that."

"I love you, too."

"I never thought I would be one of the lucky few to find the love of my life twice in a lifetime," Eleanor said gently before she placed another tender kiss on Sophie's enticing lips. A kiss that was meant to soothe and calm became arousing and exciting. Sophie ran her hands through Eleanor's hair, dwelling in its silky texture as she further deepened their kiss.

"Show me," Sophie suddenly mumbled against her lover's lips.

"What?" Eleanor was caught off guard by the request.

"I need you, Eleanor. Show me your love. Right now, please, I'm aching for your touch." Sophie panted as Eleanor pulled back slightly from their embrace and gazed into her flushed face to find her pupils dilated and her lips swollen from their kisses. Eleanor swallowed hard before she took Sophie's hand in her own to drag her out of the room and honour her request.

As they rushed out of the library, they ran into Henry but before he could utter a single word Eleanor brushed him off, "Not now, Henry. There are more pressing matters we need to attend to."

He shot Sophie a questioning look, but she merely shrugged her shoulders before giving him conspiratorial wink.

Comprehension hit Henry right between the eyes, and he called at their retreating backs, "By all means. Take your time, my dear."

"I intend to."

As his wife's voice floated down the stairs, his grin broadened.

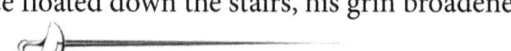

After Martin showed Emma to her new room, she was grateful he soon excused himself to go in search of his sister. Feeling lost and undeserving, she sank onto the large bed that dominated the room.

After what happened, the duchess had shown her more sympathy than she felt worthy of, more understanding than even her own mother.

Before she had too much time to dwell on the past or think of the future, there was knock on her door. "Come in, please!"

"Hello, cousin." Charlotte smiled reassuringly at her. "Do you mind if we come in?"

"Please do."

Emma watched expectantly to see who else was with her. Charlotte stepped into the room followed by Adele, who closed the door behind them. Emma recognised her immediately. Charlotte joined Emma on the bed while Adele chose the chair in front of the vanity.

"Our room is next door," Charlotte informed her warmly. "If you need anything, just pop in."

"Thank you."

"But don't forget to knock." Charlotte giggled, while Adele rolled her eyes at her antics.

"Of course. Why wouldn't I knock?" Emma asked, confused.

"What my love is trying to tell you, Adele said dryly, "is she doesn't want you to walk in on us, which would not happen at all since we make sure to lock our door,".

"So, you mean . . . you two are—"

"Yes, most definitely," Adele said, daring her to utter demeaning words. But Emma merely looked from one woman to the other. She couldn't understand why someone as beautiful as Charlotte would rather be with another woman, even one as fierce as Adele for that. It was much less understandable than Sophie's choice.

Adele, as if sensing her thoughts, continued. "Whatever it is you're thinking either about Sophie, the duchess, or Charlotte, I would highly recommend you keep it to yourself."

"Darling, please," Charlotte chastised her gently. Adele's features softened instantly. This sudden change in attitude didn't go unnoticed by Emma who was surprised by Adele's readiness to back down so easily.

"Sorry, my love. I didn't mean to be harsh." Adele stood and brushed off her skirt. "If you excuse me, Emma, I promised Giulia to show her a couple of my essays on women's rights and suffrage."

Before she left, she kissed Charlotte on the mouth, putting a blissful expression on her face by the sheer gentleness of the gesture.

When the door closed behind her, Charlotte turned to Emma. "Don't worry! Her bark is worse than her bite. She's just very protective."

"Adele was always brash," Emma said. "We never got along that well. Most of the time we merely tolerated each other. I can't hold it against her though. Not after what happened."

"You know, it doesn't matter if you can't understand this, what Adele and I have between us, I mean. Just try not to pass judgement. May I ask you something?"

"Of course."

"Why did you do what you did? Why did you try so hard to drive my mother and Sophie apart?"

"I was angry. I felt betrayed but most of all I think I was jealous. Sophie had her freedom to be who she wanted to be and love who she wanted to. I resented her this freedom, this happiness."

"And now?" Charlotte was genuinely intrigued.

"Now I'm glad my sister is a far better person than I am and has a bigger heart than I deserve."

Sophie's and Eleanor's absence at lunch was noted, but not commented upon. Henry wore a knowing smile, as he inwardly congratulated his wife on her blissful happiness.

He looked around the table at Jonathan, his children, niece, and great grandmother-in-law, seeing content faces all in all. Emma seemed a bit subdued which was only understandable given the circumstances. After everything Martin had told him, she must feel embarrassed and humiliated, but she tried to keep her head high.

Jonathan had already started the business of helping Sophie with her transactions, and he was positive everything could be over and done with sooner than anticipated. He had also assured Henry that Sophie would not be penniless. She would keep some of her financial assets, but the largest portion of her fortune would indeed be gone when she signed the papers he was preparing. Henry had no worries about that since his wife's independent wealth would provide enough for them to live comfortably for many decades.

He gently cleared his throat before he addressed the newest member of his family. "Tell me, my dear Emma, do you think you will enjoy coming to live with us in London?"

"I don't know. I don't want to be a burden."

"Nonsense." He waved her off. "You are no burden. What a ridiculous notion. You're Sophie's sister, Martin's cousin. I'd say that makes you family."

Seeing the distress on Emma's face at the overwhelming kindness, the contessa thought it the right moment to intervene on the poor girl's behalf. "Why don't we give Emma time to adjust before we run her over with our protectiveness and affections. Let's have a nice, relaxed luncheon and give the girl room to breathe. Wouldn't you agree, Henry?"

"Yes, quite, Nonna." Henry saw the blush on Emma's face and had to admit, albeit grudgingly, that Giulia was right.

After missing lunch, Sophie and Eleanor decided to be decadent and spend the rest of the day in bed. Their lovemaking was only interrupted by short naps and a light snack they consumed in bed. Lying blissfully sated in her lover's arms, Eleanor drew lazy circles on Sophie's chest. She was teasing her nipple with a light touch before she captured it between her lips.

"Oh, love," Sophie moaned in appreciation, running her hands through Eleanor's soft white hair. What her lover's mouth did to her felt so good. Never had she thought she'd become this insatiable, but she couldn't get enough of Eleanor's touch. "Please, don't stop."

"Never," Eleanor promised wickedly.

And keep her promise she did, driving Sophie to pleasure over and over until she begged her to stop. Eleanor kissed her way up her body, while Sophie lay on her back, spent, and covered with a fine sheen of sweat, trying to catch her breath.

Eleanor felt incredibly pleased with herself as she propped her head in her hand and gazed into Sophie's smouldering eyes. "You are incredible, darling." Stroking an elegant finger down her brow, over her nose to her lips, she turned Sophie's head and covered her mouth with her own, letting Sophie taste herself on her lips.

"And you are nothing short of amazing," Sophie whispered, her voice full of desire as she pulled Eleanor on top of her.

She loved the feeling of their bodies pressed against each other. Eleanor straddled her waist and slightly lifted her upper body, her lips never losing contact with Sophie's. Sophie's hands caressed her thighs, gliding up her slightly rounded stomach to cup full breasts. Eleanor sat up straight thrusting her breasts into her lover's hands, arching her back when Sophie's thumbs brushed over erect nipples. Sophie was awed by her lover's beauty. Her head was thrown back, her eyes closed and her lips slightly parted. The light of the late afternoon sun bathed her pale skin in a warm golden glow. She looked simply magnificent.

"I need you, darling," Eleanor whispered wantonly.

Sophie let her right-hand slide down her side, to her hip, over her thigh before she found the one place where Eleanor needed her most. She felt her lover's wetness coating her belly and relished it. She let two of her fingers glide inside her lover's core while her thumb was circling her clit. Her left hand tweaked a hard nipple between thumb and forefinger.

"Open your eyes, love," Sophie commanded gently.

Difficult as it was because of the wonderful things happening to her body, Eleanor obliged. Blue eyes locked with brown as she felt the slow but steady building of her orgasm. She moved in perfect rhythm with Sophie's hand, riding higher and higher, until finally, a cry of ecstasy was torn from her lips. Her inner walls clenched around her Sophie's fingers, and Eleanor collapsed forward and felt strong arms around her back holding her tight.

Sophie pulled the sheets over their entwined bodies and pressed a gentle kiss to Eleanor's temple, "I love you."

"I love you, darling."

Giulia leaned back on the sofa she'd been sitting on during afternoon tea with the family. Now that everybody else had left the drawing room, she closed her eyes and thought about the family's unspoken acceptance of her granddaughter's absence. The family had accomplished so much more than any of them had ever hoped for before they departed on this journey. Charlotte found the love she'd sought for so long, and Eleanor had once again fallen in love with a woman her equal in every way, except for her title.

A wistful sigh escaped Giulia's lips when she let the past few months pass by her inner eye. Each addition to the family was welcome and highly appreciated. Adele—she could tell by the way she looked at Charlotte—loved her great granddaughter fiercely. There was no question that Charlotte had her wrapped around her finger, which was quite mutual. Although Adele had a fast temper, Giulia was not at all worried for Charlotte since she had witnessed the way Adele would instantly rein in her temper when talking to her. She treated Charlotte most reverently, with loving care and tenderness.

Watching them together made Giulia's heart ache because it reminded her so much of her own love, Bridget. Yes, those two were a wonderful match. She could sense Adele felt contempt towards Emma, but she hoped that given time, it would change.

The thought of Eleanor and Sophie made her smile wider. Giulia had initially feared their attraction was based more on intellectual grounds than on anything else, but after today she had no more doubt in her mind that their love and attraction was also very physical. It was heart-warming to know that their desire for each other led them to such actions. Good for them.

At the gentle clearing of a throat, Giulia snapped her eyes open to find out who was interrupting her contemplation.

"Sorry, Nonna," Martin said sheepishly from the door. "I didn't mean to startle you. May I join you?"

"Certainly." She invited him to take the seat next to her. "What is it, dear?"

"Nothing, really. I thought you might enjoy some company, but since I saw your content face, I'm not so sure I should have interrupted you."

"I always enjoy company." Giulia patted his arm encouragingly. "What about you? Are you happy?"

"Yes. Seeing Mama with Sophie is still strange though. But it's getting easier. I think Sophie is good for her and vice versa."

"Give it time, my dear."

"I will. I would have never thought that Charlotte of all people would fall in love."

"Your sister had very high expectations," Giulia said, "and your parents are quite extraordinary role models. It is hard for anybody to live up to their standard. I'm glad she has finally found her happiness."

"Do you think so?"

"Yes, I do. They love each other and are already very devoted to each other."

Martin thought about it for a moment before he asked, "Do you think Philip and I will be as lucky one day?"

"I certainly do, darling." Her grandmotherly embrace was returned with care and gratitude. "Now let's go find your father. He still owes me another game of bridge so I can win back my money and reclaim my reputation as the family's shrewdest player."

Epilogue

In the study at the palais, Sophie signed the last paper required to hand over most of her fortune to her father. Enough to save his factory, people's livelihoods, and her sister from an awful nightmare. Jonathan would make sure everything was in order.

While the rest of the family headed home, Jonathan and Henry planned to stay in Vienna for another two weeks to deal with any repercussions Sophie's actions could possibly have. But by the way everything had been handled so far, Sophie highly doubted there would be any issues.

Emma was finding her place within the family, and though Adele was still keeping her distance from Emma, Sophie thought she was slowly warming up to her.

Sophie was deliriously in love with Eleanor, and she looked forward to having a life full of joy and meaning with the love of her life.

Jonathan shuffled all the contracts and paperwork together and placed them in a leather valise. "I'm glad that's done," he said. "I'll take care of the rest on your behalf, and you and Emma will still be well provided for."

Sophie could no longer contain her curiosity. "May I ask why Count von Bernthal has never graced us with his presence even though it was made clear that his wedding to my sister wouldn't take place?"

Jonathan's smile was grim. "Let's just say the good count is less influential than he believed he was. He's also less careful in his questionable and disgusting endeavours than would be prudent., and this is catching up to him."

"Dare I ask what that means? Or is it better for my own peace of mind if I don't know exactly what you're talking about?"

"The latter, I suppose," Jonathan said ruefully. "Emma is a very lucky young woman to have you as her sister. But you can rest assured that the count is heading for a most-deserved fall. Let's leave it at that, shall we?"

"All right," Sophie conceded. "Thank you, Jonathan, for your help and for everything you've done to make this entire process as painless as possible."

"You're welcome. Her Grace seldom asks for anything, and when she does, I'm honoured to provide my help in any way possible."

"She holds you in remarkably high esteem. I hope you know that?" Sophie asked the humble man who preferred to be the quiet but reliable anchor for his Lordship as well as for everybody else.

"I do know. But it's good to hear it anyway."

With a squeeze of his arm Sophie left the study to join Eleanor in the hall where she was patiently waiting for her so they could travel to the train station.

The servants had left for the station already, and so had everybody else. Most of their luggage had been sent on its way two days earlier, and the last remaining trunks, suitcases and bags were also on the way to the station. Henry would say his goodbyes at the station while Jonathan had done so yesterday. Jonathan was a mush ball for a lack of a better word. They would go back to London in a fortnight, but saying goodbye to his family always led to him coming just a little undone, which amused Eleanor to no end.

"Any regrets, my love?" Eleanor asked once their carriage was underway.

"None at all," Sophie said, but after a moment's thought, she retracted that. "Maybe one regret. I won't see my brother as often as I want to."

"Anton promised to visit us for Christmas," Eleanor reminded her gently.

"Yes, I know. But I'll still miss him."

The hustle and bustle at the station was tiresome, and when they finally boarded the train Sophie sighed with relief.

Eleanor said, "Would you prefer to change seats, darling? So, you can take a last view of Vienna?"

"No, I'd rather not look back, but at my future."

"Which is?"

"You."

About The Author

Edith Zeitlberger grew up in Lower Austria, in a spa village that can trace its origins back to Roman times. She now lives on the outskirts of Vienna with her partner and under the iron paw of a certain furry overlord, M. Maurice.

Edith has a degree in history from the University of Vienna. She has always been an avid reader and started writing fanfiction many years ago just for the joy of it.

Fractions and Hinges is her debut novel, which was first self-published in 2012 as *Imperial Whites*. The new version has been updated and significantly expanded.

She is also the host of "Book Lover's Companion," a podcast about books, authors, and their craft which can easily be found by Googling it.